Amanda Hearty lives in Blackrock, Co. Dublin, with her husband Michael and their little daughter Holly. Amanda works in a busy Dublin publishers, and studied Commerce at UCD and has a Masters in Marketing from the Smurfit School of Business, Dublin. Growing up in a house full of books, writing, dreams and ideas, and with her mother, Marita Conlon-McKenna, being a very successful author, it was inevitable that Amanda would one day put pen to paper and begin to write. *Are You Ready?* was her first novel and an Irish bestseller, also published by Transworld Ireland. *Positively Yours* is her second novel.

www.transworldireland.ie
www.rbooks.co.uk

Also by Amanda Hearty

Are You Ready?

and published by Transworld Ireland

POSITIVELY YOURS

Amanda Hearty

TRANSWORLD IRELAND

TRANSWORLD IRELAND
an imprint of The Random House Group Limited
20 Vauxhall Bridge Road, London SW1V 2SA
www.rbooks.co.uk

POSITIVELY YOURS
A TRANSWORLD IRELAND BOOK: 9781848270060

First published in 2009 by Transworld Ireland
Transworld Ireland paperback edition published 2010

Addresses for Random House Group Ltd companies outside the UK
can be found at: www.randomhouse.co.uk
The Random House Group Ltd Reg. No. 954009

The Random House Group Limited supports The Forest Stewardship
Council (FSC), the leading international forest certification organization.
All our titles that are printed on Greenpeace approved FSC certified paper
carry the FSC logo. Our paper procurement policy can be found at
www.rbooks.co.uk/environment

Typeset in 12½/15½pt Bembo by
Kestrel Data, Exeter, Devon.
Printed in the UK by
CPI Cox & Wyman, Reading, RG1 8EX.

2 4 6 8 10 9 7 5 3 1

For my daughter Holly

the most beautiful girl in the world

1

Beth Prendergast sat at her desk overlooking Dublin's leafy St Stephen's Green, its trees ablaze with autumn colours. Out of her window she could see tourists, children and mothers streaming into the city-centre park, with nothing but an afternoon of relaxing, playing and feeding ducks in front of them.

She turned back to work, as her computer screen flickered with numbers and incoming emails. The offices of Burlington Stockbrokers were loud and busy. All around Beth her team were taking phone calls from clients or preparing presentations. As a senior portfolio manager, it was her job to make Burlington's long list of private clients even wealthier. The markets might be jittery now, but investing huge amounts of money around the world still made her heart beat faster.

Each morning as she walked into the office, a

takeout coffee in her hand, the *Financial Times* in the other, her assistant handing her minutes of the previous day's meetings, she had to pinch herself. She still couldn't believe her luck! Beth knew how hard it was for women to scale the ladder in this industry. And she'd had to sacrifice a great deal – nights out, holidays, romances and relationships – to get to where she was now.

As she checked the Dow Jones index, one of the directors, Tom Maloney, walked by, and stopped at her desk.

'Can I talk to you?' he asked.

Beth looked at her boss. Tom Maloney had been one of the founding partners of Burlington Stockbrokers. Twenty years her senior, he was feared in the industry as being one of the toughest you could meet. When she had started working in the company she had heard all the stories about him surviving on two hours' sleep a night, getting through fifteen secretaries, and firing employees for arriving half an hour late for work. But his strength, hard-working attitude and determination to succeed made Beth respect not fear him, and over the years this respect had grown – leading to other feelings too, unfortunately.

She followed him into his large plush office.

'We are pitching to the CEO of O'Brien Construction tomorrow morning,' he said. 'You've shown your expertise with that German property portfolio, and we could really do with you in trying to win this guy over. We want his firm, they're huge,' he said.

Beth listened. Picking the right investments and the perfect moment to buy or sell involved a lot of research and judgement – but she loved it.

'Apparently David O'Brien didn't like the way his last stockbrokers managed his investments, so it's important we impress him,' said Tom. 'The meeting is at 8.30 a.m. I'd like to meet you in the conference room at 7 a.m. to go through possible suggestions for him. I presume that won't be a problem?'

'Seven should be no problem, boss, unless someone keeps me out late tonight!' Beth gazed at Tom in his Armani suit, scarlet silk tie and well-polished shoes. He might be fifty-five, but Beth thought he could hold his own in any group of young men.

He closed his office door, lowered his voice and let his stern face relax.

'Oh, I won't do that! You might be up till the small hours, but we will be indoors all right! I've booked a room at the Shelbourne, their top suite. Why don't we meet there at 9 p.m.? I'll organize the food and wine, you just need to bring your gorgeous self.'

Beth smiled. Suddenly his phone rang, and with that it was back to business for Tom. Beth walked out of his office. She was aware she should know better, and that having a relationship with Tom was wrong. The company disapproved of employees dating each other and doing so could jeopardize her job and the position she had worked long and hard for. But every time she went to finish things with Tom, she just thought about the other guys out there and knew none of them could compete with him, even if he was a divorced man in his fifties.

As she sat back down at her desk, she looked back out the window at the children, grannies and mothers in the park, thinking that kind of life couldn't be further from hers. Then her phone rang and she got back to what she knew and did best – work.

2

Beth found it hard to concentrate on her early morning meeting with David O'Brien, the CEO of O'Brien Construction. She hadn't had far to walk to work that morning, what with the Shelbourne Hotel being only yards from her office, but she had been up late drinking expensive wine with Tom Maloney, and was feeling the effect of it now. As Tom chatted away to David O'Brien, her mind wandered back to the night before, and their dinner in the privacy of the hotel suite. She was falling ever more in love with Tom. He was exactly the kind of man she had always wanted: successful, confident, charming and knowledgeable on everything from stocks to fine art. Beth had never even thought of dating a man from work before, but Tom was no ordinary man or employee.

Until Tom, Beth's love life had been going nowhere

fast. She'd had a few boyfriends and been on plenty of dates, but no one had seemed willing to put up with her long working hours and ambition. And as she had risen through the ranks in Burlington Stockbrokers, she had seen how her success was a threat to men who didn't work in that culture. Initially it would attract them. They'd be pleasantly surprised to see she had brains to go with her tall, blonde good looks, but when they realized her annual work bonus was worth more than their yearly salary, their jealousy and old-fashioned belief that a man should earn more than a woman would get in the way of romance. Even men who worked in the same field felt threatened by her because she knew more about the financial world than they did.

Beth had hated all this, and had dated less and less as her career had taken off. Instead she had used her spare time to search for a wonderful apartment. She'd known her friends had been jealous when, just as everyone else in Ireland was complaining about outrageous house prices, she had been able to buy an apartment outright, no problem. She remembered the excitement of signing the paper for the two-bedroom home in Sandymount. It overlooked the Strand and Dublin Bay, and Beth had been so happy to finally find a place she could call home. Having been at boarding school, then having rented flats with friends for years, she had longed for somewhere that would be all hers, with no more sharing of bathrooms, fridges, sofas or car-park spaces. And even though she had felt a bit lonely the first night, opening a bottle of expensive champagne on her own to celebrate the move, she had hoped that one day she would have a partner to sit with her and enjoy the view of the waves and water.

Unfortunately that day still hadn't come. And as the years went by, even Beth's expensively decorated apartment became less appealing. With no man in her life, she had started spending more time at work, and soon the office felt like her home. It was while working all those long hours that Beth had come to Tom's notice. He was attracted to her brains as well as her looks, and liked the way she had a similar work ethic. And after weeks of working closely on a big deal with a new client, which ended with them having to spend a night together in London, their mutual attraction had become irresistible. Before Beth knew what she was doing she had fallen hook, line and sinker for Burlington Stockbrokers' top man.

Beth watched Tom charm the CEO of O'Brien Construction, and knew how David O'Brien felt. After that night in London, she'd had misgivings, but somehow Tom's charm had made it all OK. He wasn't threatened by her career or salary, and he made her feel proud of her achievements. Of course his six foot four athletic build, dark brown hair and green eyes helped, and every time he looked at her she felt a flush of excitement. And now, one year later, she was still excited each time he booked a night away or a romantic dinner. She knew she should expect more than just the little time he had left over after work. Dating a workaholic wasn't fun, but Beth was in love with Tom and, having no other men in her life, she put up with the problems.

Tom didn't do the obvious, and pretend their relationship would lead to marriage and kids. He often reminded her that he had done the whole rearing babies thing years before, and still had two grown-up children to keep an eye on. Beth tried to convince herself that being thirty-five years old, and with a man who didn't want to settle down, was madness. That she was getting too old to mess about, and that getting a regular boyfriend would be a whole lot more sensible and better for her. But even so, she still found herself melting when she looked into Tom's green eyes. Maybe you can't have the perfect apartment, job and man all at the same time, she thought. But, as she wasn't willing to give up the first two, she had to put up with the fact that even though her love life wasn't perfect, Tom was. Almost!

3

Erin Delany stared at the display of buggies and prams in the Little Tots shop. She was drawn to the denim-coloured Bambino Pramette buggy. It was one of those cool three-in-one travel systems – a buggy, pushchair and car seat. She pulled the buggy on to the shop floor and began opening and closing it.

'Can I help you?' asked an eager-looking assistant.

Erin turned to the girl while balancing the car seat in one hand and buggy in the other.

'I'm just trying to see how this works, and how easy it is to actually open and close the buggy. It is important to be able to open it using only one hand, as the baby will be in the other one, obviously! It seems good, though.'

'Oh, it is,' reassured the shop assistant. With a twist of her fingers she began transforming the buggy into a pram, and reeling off the pramette's selling line that worked on all mums-to-be. 'This is a unique, revolutionary new concept that combines a traditional pram with a practical, lightweight pushchair. Versatile and comfortable, the pramette is suitable from birth and grows with your child into their toddler years.'

'It seems perfect.' Erin smiled, impressed.

'And the handles extend, too,' the young girl explained. 'So, when is your baby due?' the assistant went on.

Erin suddenly felt herself freeze.

'I'm not actually pregnant,' she replied quietly, trying to control her voice. 'Not at the moment. I'm researching baby products for when I am.'

She sounded lame and stupid, and she could tell the assistant was not impressed. She took the car seat from Erin's hands.

'Well, as you can see, we are very busy, and we try to save the staff time for displaying buggy options to people who are actually about to have a baby.'

'I'm sorry,' Erin managed to whisper back to the young girl, who was now returning the buggy to the display.

Erin was about to explain to her that all she wanted was a child – and to spend every weekend in stores like this, discussing cot, buggy and nursery options – but she could see the girl was annoyed. So she turned and walked towards the shop door. As she left she could see the girl pointing her out and talking to another assistant. No doubt they are discussing how crazy I am, shopping for a buggy when there is no baby in sight, Erin thought.

She caught a glimpse of herself reflected in the busy South Dublin baby shop window. Her white face and big sad brown eyes stared back at her. She debated going to the hairdresser to get her long brown hair blow-dried before going out for dinner tonight with her husband and friends, but after the embarrassment in the baby shop, she decided to head home. She looked back at the mums and mums-to-be entering Little Tots, and couldn't help feeling pangs of jealousy. All she wanted was to be pregnant. She placed her hand on her flat stomach.

'When will it be my turn?' she asked out loud.

4

'I have a delivery here for Erin Delany,' said the courier.

'I'm Erin, let me sign for that,' she said. The young man in a helmet handed it to her, got back on his motorbike and sped off.

Erin closed the door behind him, and as she started walking back up the polished oak stairs towards her office she began opening the large wrapped parcel. Out fell two pieces of fabric – one a soft brown cloth embossed with blue flowers, and the other a heavy crimson and gold embroidered piece. Erin had been waiting all week for her supplier to send these swatches of material. They were for one of her clients, who still couldn't find the right fabric for their new curtains.

An interior designer, Erin worked in a small yet bright office in Sandymount alongside her friend

Paula O'Driscoll, an architect. Erin had always been fascinated by colours and materials and had opted to study interior design in college for three years. Her first job had been in the busy design section of Habitat, before she moved on to work in Hudson's – a small, exclusive interior design firm, where she spent most of her time fitting out apartments for investors all over the city as well as supervising two pub fit-outs and working on the concept for a funky new Thai restaurant in Temple Bar. Constantly obsessed with light, colour, texture and design, she went to endless trouble to source new materials from Swedish, French and Irish designers and craftsmen. She got huge satisfaction from the family homes she helped renovate or redesign.

Despite being rushed off her feet, Erin had still found the time to fall in love. She'd met her future husband, John, through her cousin Barry. Barry was mad into sailing, and so was John. Erin and her two older sisters, Alison and Rebecca, were always hanging out with Barry and his gorgeous sailing buddies, and when one night his friend John tagged along, Erin had known from the second they were introduced that she liked him. He had such kind eyes and made her feel so comfortable. She was sick of trying to meet 'nice men' in nightclubs, it just hadn't happened, but then along had come John! Those early days were such fun, with discos in the sailing club and afternoon trips to Howth Harbour! And before she knew it weeks had turned into months, and months into years, and they were married.

The following year her friend Paula returned from working in London, and like many architects wanted to become her own boss. Paula suggested that they go into business together, combining the skills of an interior designer and an architect. She believed they would complement each other, and urged Erin to think about setting up their own company. Erin liked the idea of being her own boss and choosing what projects she got to work on. And so, encouraged by her husband and after much deliberation, the two friends had set up in business together, offering a complete design service.

They had found a run-down office to rent, above an optician in Sandymount village. Despite its neglect, the office's warren of pokey rooms upstairs had two big bay windows that let in great light and overlooked the busy street below. John had been a great help in turning the old and cramped rooms into a brand new office. He was busy working in the bank during the day, but spent every evening helping to get the place right. It had taken a lot of hard work knocking down partition walls to enlarge the work space, but it had been worth it in the end. They had never been so excited as the first day when Paula unlocked the old cream wooden front door and declared the two girls 'in business' at last.

Erin and Paula had gone into partnership when the economy was booming and there was plenty of money to spare. Back then people had been more prepared than ever to spend money on completely refurbishing their newly bought houses, holiday homes and offices. But as the economy changed, business became harder to come by. Months had gone by without Erin working on any new apartments or fancy offices. And with nothing new being built, Paula was finding it harder to get any work also. They were both struggling, but hoping they could ride out the recession. And while the glory years seemed to have gone, Erin had noticed that people were still doing upgrades on their current places. Many weren't buying flash new houses any more, but were staying put and using any spare money to do up what they already had. Attic conversions, remodellings and extensions were what people suddenly wanted and needed help with. And regardless of the economy there was always someone buying an old wreck of a house and needing help not only from an architect but also from someone who could give the place a fresh clean look, too. Erin and Paula were both good with their clients and through word of mouth they gradually got enough jobs to keep them going. They still had to compete with the big firms, but theirs was a smaller, more individual service. They could not only help maximize the space in a house but give advice on furnishing it too, and all within a budget.

Erin enjoyed working with clients and discussing with them what they wanted to do with their property. Each project was individual and different and she could get lost for hours planning and sketching design briefs. To her, each job was as important as the next: she was not only helping someone change their home but putting her own mark on it, too.

She was in a competitive business, and she had to work long and hard, but as the years went by, she didn't mind spending hours measuring rooms, meeting tradesmen, working on budgets or getting quotes on kitchens, because it all kept her mind off the big white elephant in the room, the one thing she wanted more than anything, yet couldn't get no matter how many suppliers she had on speed dial – a child of her own.

5

Grace Miller was searching online for a Hallowe'en costume for her golden retriever Coco when her phone rang.

'Hi, Mum!' Grace said, as she closed the internet down and made her way to the plush oversized cream couch that filled her living room.

'Grace? How did you know it was me?' her mum asked suspiciously.

'We have Caller ID. Everyone in the States has it. I have told you this a million times! So how is every-one in Ireland?' she asked.

'Well, I know I'll see you in America next week, but everyone else is just counting down the days until you are home, pet,' said Patsy Slattery to her only daughter.

Grace smiled as she looked around her large Californian home, imagining how her life was about to change. Grace and her husband Ethan were leaving 'the Golden State' and America to go and live in Dublin. They were only moving there for a year, but it was still a big decision, and even though Ethan was the American and had never spent more than two weeks at a time in Ireland, it was Irish-born-and-raised Grace who was more nervous of the move. She had gotten used to her large house with its own swimming pool, the sun permanently shining in the sky, and the American way of life. And even though she couldn't wait to live closer to her mum and family, she knew she would miss the climate, the twenty-four-hour outlet malls, and the American breakfasts – complete with pancakes, big omelettes, bacon, waffles, grits and coffee refills!

Patsy started to fill Grace in on a welcome-home party that her two brothers wanted to throw for her in November. But before she moved home to Ireland, Patsy was coming over to visit Grace for a week. Not only to help Grace pack, but also to get some sun-shine before the long Irish winter set in.

'Your brothers are so excited to have their big sister home. And I know Ethan's work say it is only for a year, but when you start your family you might decide Ireland really is a better place to raise a child!'

Grace's whole mood changed, and she sat up straighter on the couch and repeated what she had already said to her mother a million times.

'Ethan and I are perfectly happy with our lives. We are a family already; we do not need screaming kids ruining that. How many times do I need to tell you? Please, Mum, no more talk of me having babies, it is not going to happen.'

And with that Grace managed to get her mum off the phone and go back to searching for cute Hallowe'en outfits for Coco.

'Who needs whining children, when I have you, Coco?' she said, as she began ordering a dog's Harry Potter costume.

6

Grace was busy packing up the house in San Diego. They were renting it out for the year they would be in Ireland, so Grace needed to put in storage anything she wasn't bringing home with her. She started with the photo frames, and carefully covered some of her favourites in bubble-wrap. It was while she was parcelling up the three silver wedding gift ones and the fancy glass frame Ethan's sister-in-law Cindy had given them, that she came across an old photo album of the summer she had first come to America. She sat down on her bed and began flicking through the photos and memories.

She smiled, remembering that time when, as gawky students, she and her friend Sharon had spent a summer working in San Diego. It was only supposed to be for a few months, in-between finishing college and starting 'real life and real jobs'. They had arrived over and booked into a motel on Pacific Beach, and immediately Grace had fallen in love with the sunshine, the sea at her front door and the laid-back way of life. She had gotten a job in a restaurant called the Marina Grill, which overlooked the ocean. It had been popular with local residents and tourists alike, due to its stunning location, large fresh fish menu and famous beer-battered onion rings! The staff had all been young, and after their shift ended they had often closed the restaurant but stayed on drinking beer there until the early hours of the morning. Sharon used to join Grace and one of the other waitresses, Rachel, for a drink after her day working as a guide in San Diego's SeaWorld, and the girls had many a fun night with the waiters and any Irish tourist that stopped in. It was while working there that she had met Ethan Miller.

Ethan had been a local, and many a night had had a burger and fries in the Marina Grill. Grace had often served him, and found his confident and chatty manner a change from many of the quiet young Irish boys she'd known back home. Before long, the other waiters started teasing Grace that Ethan only wanted her to serve him. And it had been no surprise when – the evening he'd managed to make eating a basket of fries last two hours – he'd admitted that all he'd really been doing was waiting for Grace's shift to end, so he could buy her a drink.

27

When Grace had finally collapsed into her bed in the motel at 3 a.m. that night, Sharon had known that her friend was smitten. Soon all Grace had talked about was Ethan, but Sharon hadn't complained: it had been great that her friend's new boyfriend was a local, and could show them around California. And they had spent many a weekend piling into Ethan's old jeep and exploring San Francisco, Los Angeles and even Tijuana. As the summer progressed Grace had fallen more and more in love with the Golden State and Ethan. He was everything the Irish men she knew weren't: blond, tanned, athletic and full of life. He said she was different from all the Californian blonde bimbos he knew, what with her long red Irish hair and clear green eyes.

Before Grace knew it, the summer had been over and it had been time to go back to Ireland. Sharon had been eager to get back to Dublin and start a career in finance – after studying business for four years she'd been keen to make her mark on the Celtic Tiger – but Grace hadn't wanted to return to 'rainy old Ireland'. She had studied marketing, and as Ethan had kept reminding her, she could work in marketing in the States, too. The thought of working in America, where Grace was beginning to feel at home, with the man of her dreams beside her, had been too tempting. It had been a huge decision, but one she'd felt was right, so after returning to Ireland to pack her belongings and break the news to her family, Grace had bought a one-way flight to San Diego and begun her new life with Ethan in America.

It had been exciting hanging out with Ethan's friends and spending days on the beach trying to get her Irish skin tanned. Unlike along the East Coast of America, being Irish had still been a novelty in San Diego, and Grace had soaked up the attention, and questions like: 'Do you know Bono?' But the transition had been hard at times, too, and she had often been homesick, missing her family, and in particular her mum, a lot. When she had heard that her friend Sharon had not only gotten the big job in finance that she craved, but also met a man and bought a house with him, Grace had felt a little jealous. And there had been days when all she had craved were Denny Irish sausages and a bottle of Lucozade; but still, having Ethan had made up for all of that.

She had moved into his rented duplex apartment, only a ten-minute drive from the beach. Ethan and his friend Alex had been setting up their own IT company, and even though Grace had found it hard when he worked late hours, he'd kept saying that it was all for her, and that one day his firm would be huge, and then they would be able to afford a house right on the beach.

Once Grace's working visa had come through,

she had begun looking for jobs. Her marketing degree and Irish charm had stood her in good stead, and before long she had got a job in a small yet busy marketing firm in Old Town San Diego. The firm had specialized in helping companies market themselves and San Diego to tourists, and Grace had been the ideal person for the job. Being Irish and a visitor not so long ago herself, she'd known exactly what Europeans wanted from a big trip to the States. From holidaying families to honeymooners, she had enjoyed helping tourists get the inside track on SeaWorld, the San Diego Zoo, and many other local haunts.

Grace had got on well with the other girls who worked there, too, and even though at first she had been disgusted by the way health-conscious Americans would be up hours before work to go to the gym, and seemed to swing constantly between the South Beach or Atkins diets, it hadn't been long before she'd adapted to their Californian lifestyle. Within a few months of living on the West Coast, she had been up jogging on the beach before work, too, drinking smoothies until they came out of her ears, and forgoing relaxing weekends for energetic mountain hikes with Ethan. Of course she still had her Irish appetite and loved it when visitors came over – because then she'd had an excuse to bring them out for pancakes! But the American way of life had suited Grace, and the day Ethan rang her to say his company had landed a huge contract she had known her life would be firmly based in the US. And, as promised, within weeks of his company's success they had been able to afford a house nearer the beach. It had needed some renovation, but Grace had felt content. Being from Dublin and an island, she had never been far from the sea, so it had comforted her to know the ocean was close by. And Ethan had been happy to get the chance to put his own imprint on the run-down property. New projects always excited him.

And then one weekend, while visiting a winery in Napa Valley, Ethan had gotten down on one knee and proposed. Grace had been overwhelmed by the romantic setting and the amazing diamond and emerald ring.

'The emerald is to match your green eyes, and remind you of your home – Ireland,' Ethan had said softly, sliding the engagement ring on to her finger. Grace had never been treated so well, and knew how lucky she was to have found the man of her dreams.

Their new house with ocean views had been a far cry from the small city-centre house in Dublin she had grown up in, but Grace had relished the change, and as she'd agreed to marry Ethan she'd felt she was letting go of that Irish past.

As Ethan's career had soared so had their lifestyle, and Grace had become quite used to nice cars, houses and clothes, along with the sunshine and healthy living. And now, because of Ethan's job, she was going to have to get used to Irish living all over again. Ethan's firm were interested in expanding, and as Ireland was seen by many as the technical hub of Europe, they'd decided to open a new office in Dublin. Ethan's business partner Alex had planned to oversee its start-up, but when his wife had suddenly become pregnant he had decided he wanted to stay in San Diego. And so, with only a few months to go before the new office opened, Ethan had agreed to uproot and move to Ireland. He would spend a year in Dublin employing staff, getting new contracts and making sure the firm was going well before returning to San Diego. Ethan had also thought a year back in Ireland would make Grace happy. And she had initially been delighted, thinking of how great it would be to be surrounded by family and friends and people who understood what *The Late Late Show* was and thought 'Have a nice day!' sounded corny and fake. But now, as the time got closer, she worried she had become too settled in America, and that Ireland might be a let-down. But then, as she looked back down at the old photo album and saw her friend Sharon's face smiling back at her, she realized how lovely it would be to catch up with her and all the girls. She wondered, was Leeson Street still the place to be seen on a Saturday night?

7

Beth Prendergast pulled into a parking spot just near the door of the newly built Blackwood Golf Club. She checked her reflection in the rear-view mirror, and fixed her short blonde hair back with a clip before locking her black Audi A3 and entering the club. Beth spotted her dad sitting in a cosy looking armchair overlooking the eighteenth hole, with the Sunday paper in one hand and glass of white wine in the other. Beth hadn't seen her father in a few weeks, so was a bit surprised to see how much weight he had lost.

'How are you? Busy as ever with work?' he asked, as Beth ordered a Diet Coke for herself.

'Yeah, it's tough at the top, Dad! But are you OK? You have lost weight.'

'Oh, I'm fine. It's just this new golf course. Ever since they relocated the golf club to here I just can't resist playing an extra few holes each day! But it is keeping me young and fit, so don't you worry,' her dad said, as they both looked out over the new fairways.

Beth's father, William Prendergast, had been a member of the golf club for as long as she could remember. He loved the interaction with the other members, and spent many a Sunday afternoon enjoying the roast carvery, the Sunday paper and a glass of white wine. A few years ago the golf club had announced that it was relocating to Wicklow. Most of the members had complained, but for William it had been great news, as it had meant the club would be even closer to home. And when the doors had finally opened a few months ago, all the begrudgers had eaten their words, as the new club house was state-of-the-art, and the course itself fantastic! Nowadays William always seemed to be either on his way to or from the golf club whenever Beth had time to call him. She had felt guilty she hadn't seen him in weeks, and known the best way to catch up would be over a nice Sunday lunch in his new home from home.

As they ordered food Beth was reminded of her dad's popularity. Many members came up to say hello, and ask how she was, and they all seemed to have time for William. He was, indeed, very charming, and a real gentleman, but she could not help feeling that his fellow-golfers knew her father better than she did. Being an only child and a girl, Beth had always found it hard to connect with her father. She knew her parents would have loved more children, and her avid sports-fan father would have loved a boy to teach golf to, but it had never happened. And as the years of trying for another sibling for Beth had progressed it had become obvious that Beth's mum wasn't well.

Beth had only been ten years old when her mother had died after a long battle with breast cancer. She could barely remember the weeks after the death, everything had seemed like a nightmare. One minute she'd been in her mother's bed listening to her reading *The Worst Witch*, the next her dad had been coming home from the hospital and explaining that her mum had gone to live with the angels in heaven. Beth had tried to finish the book on her own, but without her mum's funny reading voices it hadn't been the same, and she hadn't wanted to ask her father, as all he had seemed to do was cry when he thought she couldn't hear him. At night she'd hear sobbing coming from behind his study door. She'd been scared, and had just kept waiting for her mum to come home and explain what was happening, but she never had.

Beth had been so lonely that she'd been glad when, after a few weeks, her father had suggested she spend the summer with her cousins in Cork. She'd missed her dad, but known he was busy with work, and she'd enjoyed the company: her boy cousins had taught her how to play cards, go-kart down steep roads, and keep the score in rugby. When she'd eventually returned to Wicklow at the end of the summer she'd realized her dad was finding it hard to deal with her. William had been old when she'd been born – and her being a girl was always going to be difficult for a man who couldn't tell Barbie and Ariel, the Little Mermaid, apart. When September came around he'd sat her down and asked her if she'd like to go to school in Dublin. Beth had been excited, as she had always loved going to the big city with her parents, especially at Christmas, when she could gaze at the Switzers Christmas window display. But it wasn't until her dad had explained that she would be boarding at this school that she had got scared. But before she knew it, William had had her uniform, books and clothes packed for St Teresa's boarding school. Beth had looked jealously at the girls who had mums dropping them off. While her dad had given her an awkward goodbye hug Beth had watched over his shoulder as mothers ran fingers through their daughters' hair, kissed them all over their faces, and waved at them right up until the last second.

Boarding school had been difficult at first for Beth, but the nuns had been very kind to the new motherless girl, and soon she had not only settled into life as a boarder, but started excelling at her studies, too. It was here that she'd been set apart from the other girls. Of course she'd loved the girly chats and the obsessing over any boys who came near the school, but Beth had been very hard-working, and had soon become a top student. She'd also known how proud it made her dad to receive her school reports, their pages filled with As and encouraging comments from her teachers. There had never been any chance she'd be on the top hockey team, but her brains had made sure that she was not only made a prefect in her final school year but also did brilliantly in her Leaving Certificate. Before long her school days had been over and she'd been heading off to UCD to study business and make her mark on the world.

Beth probably could have commuted from Wicklow to the UCD campus each day, but after eight years of living away from the family house it had no longer felt like home, and so she'd moved in with friends and started living the student life. Of course she'd still seen her dad as often as she could, but they'd both known they would never be that close. Even the summers she had spent home from boarding school had never been relaxed. Beth had tried to be the companion she imagined William would have wanted – she'd read up on golf, rugby and business so she could talk to him – but it had never really worked, and by the end of August each year she'd been looking forward to returning to her small all-girls boarding school.

Looking back, Beth realized how trying to become strong for her distant father had shaped her character, making her more determined to succeed in her studies, and then her career. But as her dad tucked into his vegetable soup and talked about how he and his friends were planning a golf trip to the Algarve, Beth found herself longing for a deeper relationship with him. Even though they were sitting right beside each other they somehow could never be as close as she was sure her dead mother would have liked them to be.

After a pleasant afternoon Beth got up to return to Dublin. She didn't know if it was the wine talking or the fact that they hadn't seen each other in almost two months, but her dad gave her an extended hug.

'I know I don't say it enough,' he said, 'but I want you to know how proud I am of you. You have turned out to be a fine woman, so clever. I just hope one day you will make me even prouder by giving me the pleasure of walking you up the aisle. We could even have the wedding in this new club house! Everyone tries to book their wedding here now, but I have been here long enough to get you a slot.'

Beth sighed. Her dad knew that there'd been someone in the background for the last year, but she hadn't wanted to admit she was seeing a divorced man who could barely commit to dinner, let alone marriage, so she'd avoided all conversations about boyfriends and men, and her dad had been too much of a gentleman to push her for information. But she was sure he was wondering why his only daughter hadn't settled down.

'I'm just not at that stage, yet. But I promise you, you'll be the first to know when I need a wedding venue, and the club house would be a great one!' And with that she gave her dad a hug and picked up her bag.

'I just want you to be happy. That's all your mother would have wanted, too,' William said, as he sat back down and stared out of the window at the now dusky evening.

'I know, Dad, and that's all I want, too, to be happy. Just like you and Mum were.'

But as Beth drove home alone, in her brand-new car, to her perfect yet empty apartment, stopping to buy the *Sunday Business Post* along the way so she could get ahead of any financial news, she wondered if somewhere along the line she had forgotten what real happiness was, and had been striving for something altogether different.

8

The sound of ABBA filled the crisp autumn air as Beth walked through the gates of Lansdowne Rugby Club. Tonight was the office end-of-summer barbecue, and every year Burlington Stockbrokers took over the rugby club and invited all the staff and their partners. As usual, Beth had no partner, and arrived on her own. She fixed the straps of her cream Karen Millen dress and walked into the club house. Beth always felt slightly self-conscious on nights like tonight. Years of working in a very male-orientated office had made her want to project a very strong image of herself in front of her work colleagues. She hated to let her guard down and allow anyone to see behind the work facade, and yet, at dos like this, after a few drinks, people expected to see the true Beth.

She headed for the food, and, as she helped her-self to a burger and salad, heard her work colleague,

Graham O'Reilly, call her name. He waved for her to come over to where a big gang of men were sitting, stuffing themselves. Beth made her way over, and it wasn't until she sat down that she saw Tom was in the group. He was holding a beer in one hand and a mobile phone in the other. His phone was pressed to his ear, and he seemed to be deep in conversation.

'Doesn't he ever take the night off?' Graham whispered to Beth. 'No wonder his marriage broke up years ago! His poor ex-wife! He's totally obsessed with work. But then I suppose I would be, too, if I was that wealthy and successful!'

Beth just shrugged, her face a little flushed. She knew what everyone thought of Tom, and that they'd consider her mad to put up with a workaholic like him, but as she watched him run his fingers through his thick dark hair she felt no one knew him the way she did. No one knew about his passion for the Arts, or about the amount of unpublicized charity work he did. No one else saw his softer side, but she did and that was why she loved him. Tom finished his phone conversation, smiled at Beth, and then turned to one of the head partners, who was telling everyone about his new house in Portugal, and how the golf course beside it was the best in Europe. Beth excused herself from the group and went to refill her glass of wine.

★   ★   ★

Three hours later, as the sound of Madonna blared through the room, the dance floor filled. Beth was enjoying watching everyone dance when she felt a tap on her shoulder. It was Tom.

'Hi,' he said, looking deep into her eyes.

Beth forgot all about the music as she smiled back at the tall gorgeous man in front of her.

'You look great,' he said, staring at her new dress. 'You always do.'

Beth felt butterflies in her stomach. No one could make her feel the things Tom did.

'Let's get out of here,' he suggested.

She didn't need to be asked twice. She waited until he'd found his coat and gone outside before heading there herself. As much as she couldn't wait to feel his arms around her, she didn't want anyone to see her leave with the boss. He wasn't married any more, but their relationship was complicated, and the last thing she needed was an office rumour. After checking that no one she knew was out on Angelsea Road, she stepped into Tom's blue Jaguar and nodded at his driver. Being CEO of a very successful company had many benefits, and Larry the driver was one.

Tom took Beth's hand and kissed it. 'Let's go to my place,' he said, as he placed his hand on her leg.

Beth agreed, and as the car whizzed through Donnybrook and headed for Dalkey and Tom's house, she finally felt herself relax, and thanked God the work evening was over and their own special time was only just beginning.

Tom sat on the oversized armchair at the end of his bed. He opened a bottle of vintage red wine as Beth hung up her dress and removed her shoes. Her feet sank into the plush cream wool carpet. Tom only had the best in his large house in Dublin's wealthiest village. Everything about Tom's home – from the flat screen TVs to the small indoor swimming pool – left Beth in awe of it, and well aware why he always suggested they slept there. After his divorce, his wife had moved to Wicklow to be nearer her family, leaving Tom with the family home. And while his two children were both in college and mainly lived with their mum, they still had their own bedrooms here. Because of that, Beth was always careful not to leave any of her own belongings around in case they found them. Tom had redone the whole house after his wife moved out, and while it looked like a bachelor pad it still oozed class; Beth loved the art that hung on the walls in every room.

Tom had clearly drunk more than usual, and Beth was momentarily surprised as he whisked her off the bed and swung her around the room dancing to David Gray. He held her tight, and she seized the moment and hugged him back. As she clung close to his tall frame and listened to him hum the words

44

of the songs she imagined what it would be like to live here permanently. To wake up with Tom every morning, to fall asleep in his arms every night. To have her own wardrobe, to have dinner parties, to be a proper normal couple. Suddenly Tom pulled away from her and opened the drawer beside his bed. From it he pulled a small black velvet box.

'This is for you,' he said, as Beth sat down on the bed beside him and gazed in surprise at the gift.

She opened the box. Inside was a white-gold bracelet. It was encrusted with diamonds. Beth was in shock.

'What's this for?' she said, as she immediately placed the bracelet on her wrist.

'No reason,' Tom said, helping her close the clasp. 'Well, it's for being you, I suppose.'

Beth felt herself blush. Her heart raced.

'For being lovely you,' he said. 'Most women wouldn't put up with me and my lifestyle. I know I work too hard and that our relationship can be difficult. But I'm so glad I have you. You're like me, driven and ambitious. It's what I love about you.'

Beth swallowed hard. Her whole life people had praised her for being hard-working and ambitious, and told her it was her biggest asset, but that wasn't what she wanted to be loved for.

'What we have works, Beth. We want the same: a great career, travel, friendship and, of course, fun!

45

We're made for each other,' Tom said softly, as he kissed Beth's neck.

She bit her tongue. Tom was offering her everything except what most women of her age really wanted: marriage, kids, a family. She knew he had already had those and didn't want them again, but sometimes she wondered if she was mad not to demand them. She looked at the bracelet; it felt tainted. She knew Tom was offering her all he could, but was it enough?

Suddenly he flung his arms around her.

'I'll miss you while I'm away,' he said, referring to the trip he was taking the following Monday to America for a week's business. Beth didn't reply.

'You know I love you, don't you?' he said, as he began kissing her neck. Beth didn't know if it was the drink talking or the romantic music in the background softening him up, but with that statement of love, she forgot all about engagements, babies and weddings, flung caution to the winds, sank into the soft Egyptian cotton sheets, and held tight to the man she loved.

9

Erin Delany drove along red-brick Donnybrook Street and parked outside No. 23. She grabbed her appointment book, measuring tape and client folder and headed for the front door. Pretty young Ciara Ryan opened the door and beamed to see her standing there.

'Come in!' she said.

Erin looked around the hallway of her newest client. Ciara and her husband Mark had recently bought an old house that needed a facelift. Erin knew the area, and from the start had been impressed that people so young-looking could afford such a big house. Situated on the south side of the city, Donnybrook was one of the most affluent suburbs of Dublin. Only minutes from the busy city centre, the area was known for its elegant period buildings and leafy tree-lined streets; a fashionable and exclusive place where many wanted to live.

Over the past few months Erin and Paula had been working with Mark and Ciara, helping them plan the refit of their new purchase. At the initial consultation Mark had admitted their first ideas had changed.

'To be honest, when we put a bid in on this house we initially planned to redesign the whole thing, from basement to attic. But now, with the recession, we've had to make cutbacks, and our budget's been slashed. But we still want to alter the important rooms.'

The recession was certainly affecting many clients' plans. But if Ciara and Mark's budget had been cut Erin was still happy to help. She'd learnt over the years that if she did even a small job for a client and they were happy with it, then months, or even years, later they would come back to her. Times were changing and any work was good.

Once the couple had decided on Paula as their architect Erin's work had begun. And after seeing the house a few times she'd felt she knew what needed to be done. The main thing Ciara wanted was a bigger kitchen. The current one was small, dark and unattractive. But there was a tiny dining room connected to it, and Paula felt that knocking these two together – and, if possible, extending out into the south-facing garden – would change the whole house completely. Kitchens were the heart of any home, and like many other clients, Ciara wanted an open-plan room that would be a cooking and dining area – and provide family space, too.

After getting the initial brief, Erin submitted some sketch proposals. At this early concept stage she was used to meeting her new clients many times as they tried to agree on a plan and design. And, to be honest, she felt that the more she met them, the more she'd understand their needs. Ciara and Mark were a pleasure to deal with, and after a few weeks they finally applied for planning permission for the proposed extension to the kitchen and family room. It would take another two months for the permission to be granted, but while they waited Erin started getting kitchen quotes, and putting together ideas about how she thought the place could be finished. She was prepared to help Mark and Ciara with window panels, colour schemes and kitchen designs – whatever they wanted.

Erin had called to the house today to show Ciara some ideas for kitchen flooring. Tiles, timber and stone were all options, and the couple needed to narrow their choices before Erin talked to her suppliers.

'This room is like a blank canvas,' said Erin as she took out her camera and showed Ciara examples of other, similar jobs she had worked on. 'We really are starting afresh. I like to keep things pure and simple.

Of course you will need soft furnishings too, but let's start by choosing the correct kitchen units, windows, floors and colours.'

'I know the room will be completely different from how it looks now, but we do still want to try to retain some of the character of this old house,' Ciara said.

Erin smiled. It was a relief to see someone as young as Ciara with taste. She was often surprised and disappointed by how many people wanted to tear down and destroy older houses, only to turn them into modern, soulless bachelor pads, full of blacks, greys and over-the-top plasma TVs.

'Don't worry, I know exactly what kind of look we should be going for,' said Erin, as she accepted a cup of tea and began showing Ciara her ideas.

As the girls chatted, Erin could see Ciara glancing at her engagement and wedding rings.

'They are beautiful. Did you pick them yourself?' Ciara asked, staring at Erin's sapphire, diamond and white-gold engagement ring, and the matching wedding ring.

Erin was delighted with the compliment, and smiled as she recounted how John had proposed to her.

'We were on holiday in the South of France, and I had dragged John to Monte Carlo for a few days, as I just love Grace Kelly, and wanted to see where she had lived. So we visited the Cathedral of St Nicholas where she is buried, and after laying some fresh flowers, we decided to take a walk. The views from there are just beautiful. They look right out over the sea; it's fantastic! And suddenly, before I knew it, John was on bended knee saying how Grace Kelly might have been Prince Rainier's princess, but I was his and would I marry him? I almost died! I didn't think we would get engaged for years; none of our friends were yet, and it was just such a surprise. And an even bigger one when he pulled out this gorgeous ring.'

'Wow,' exclaimed Ciara, pouring Erin more tea. 'He sounds so romantic. And what good taste in jewellery he has! You were so lucky to find him. I'm sure he has you and your kids spoilt rotten.'

Erin felt her stomach drop, yet forced herself to smile.

'We're not parents yet. We have plenty of time for that.'

'Oh, of course!' Ciara replied. 'I'm sure you are so busy with your job you don't have time to think about children. Anyway, let me show you some interior magazines I bought the other day. I've marked some articles that have great photographs of remodelled kitchens.'

Erin felt so deflated as she followed Ciara into the front room. No matter how successful people thought she was, she felt such a failure. All she wanted was a child of her own. Millions of people got pregnant every day, yet she could not manage it herself. It was humiliating.

As Erin started taking notes about Ciara's ideas, she wondered: how is it that I can make an old house into a beautiful modern home, yet can't make myself into a mother?

10

Erin was getting stressed. She and John had an appointment with her GP, but John was running late and Erin was sitting alone in the small cramped waiting room, full of out-of-date magazines, kids with runny noses and old people complaining. Finally, John walked through the door. His face was weathered from a weekend of sailing, his sandy brown hair stuck out all over the place, and he was sweaty from running to the doctor's surgery.

'Sorry, I got held up at work and then the traffic on Merrion Road was a nightmare. My God, it's roasting in here,' he said as he pulled off his suit jacket and tried to fan himself with a leaflet on chlamydia.

Erin started laughing, her stress fading away.

'This is why I love you. You never fail to make me relax and laugh,' she said, as she handed him a bottle of water. Then she checked her watch to see exactly how late their appointment was running.

Eventually the receptionist stood up, and shouted to be heard over a screaming baby with flushed cheeks.

'Mr and Mrs Delany? The doctor will see you now.'

Erin and John stood up and headed to the doctor's office.

Dr James Flynn greeted Erin warmly; he was her family doctor, and had known her since she was a small child. Erin and John sat down on the metal chairs, and Erin felt John look for and hold her hand.

'So, do you have my blood test results?' Erin asked, excitedly.

James Flynn looked at Erin, and saw the hope in her eyes. He remembered when she had had mumps aged six, and then glandular fever at seventeen, and couldn't believe that Paddy and Mary's little girl had grown up to be such a lovely young woman. But it still didn't make it any easier to say what he had to tell her.

'The test results show nothing out of the ordinary. Your hormone and thyroid levels all came back normal. And, of course, we already know that John's sperm is healthy.'

'But then, what is the problem?' asked Erin, who had been expecting answers.

'I don't know why you and John are having problems conceiving,' Dr Flynn said. 'I know this is tough for you.'

John squeezed Erin's hand. She looked annoyed, and shrugged him off.

'Well, where does this leave us? I mean, we've been trying for months now. I know you said it takes time, but there must be a reason why we can't get pregnant.' Her voice rose. 'All I want, all we want, is a child.'

'I'm sorry,' the doctor said. 'If there was a definite problem we could try and work it out, but some people do take longer than others to conceive. And you're not in your twenties any more, so things will take a little longer. But if the situation stays the same I'll recommend a specialist, someone who will carry out more tests – and maybe provide drug therapy.'

Erin said nothing.

'But for now, maybe we should look at your lifestyle. I know you are both very busy with your careers. Maybe your diet could be better?' Dr Flynn asked.

Erin glared at him, and her face started to get flushed.

'Do you not think I am taking getting pregnant seriously, doctor? Of course I'm eating properly. I haven't eaten a chip, chocolate biscuit or even had a can of Coke for months now. I have reduced my

55

caffeine intake, I barely drink alcohol any more. I joined the local gym and I swim three times a week. What else am I expected to do? I mean, how is it that I see underage schoolgirls walking by with buggies in one hand and cigarettes in the other? I doubt they are avoiding junk food, and yet they seem to be popping out babies left, right and centre.'

John stared at his wife, embarrassed by her outburst. Then he looked apologetically at Dr Flynn.

'Erin, calm down, he was only suggesting we both look at our diets. Maybe it's me. I'll try to eat better from now on, I promise. No more takeaways. But let's all just calm down. Doctor, what else can we do?' John went on, as Erin sat fuming.

James Flynn felt sorry for Erin. She wasn't the only patient he had at present who was desperately trying to get pregnant. But what was he supposed to tell all these women? That they had left it too late to start trying for a child? That while they had been off travelling the world, getting great jobs and meeting men their chances of getting pregnant had rapidly plummeted? He looked at Erin's face and could see the stress and tension there.

'I know that you want a child more than anything, but I also know the pressure you are putting yourself under to make this happen. Sometimes you just have to understand that although there may be no obvious medical reason why you can't get pregnant, you need to de-stress your life. Maybe you could cut back on work? Take a break – a nice holiday? And relax about the healthy eating. If you feel like a takeaway or a glass of wine that's fine. I'm sure John won't mind indulging in a nice bottle of wine with you tonight! But as regards a medical reason for why you are not pregnant, I can see none at present, which is good news. I know that is hard to hear when you came looking for definite answers, but you and John are both healthy – the fear that you're not is all in your head. You just need to be positive and relax.'

Erin looked at Dr Flynn, and felt herself going from angry to sad and numb. Why can't I do this? she asked herself. She felt useless. To be a woman and not be able to get pregnant was humiliating.

As they left the surgery John gave Erin a big hug.

'It's good news!' he said as they walked back out to the car park. 'Even if this takes a while longer, we can wait. This will happen. We can do it. We just need to get more organized: "Fail to prepare and prepare to fail" – and all that! And before you know it we will be parents, and will only be visiting Dr Flynn for chicken pox, measles and mumps! Now, let's swing by Café Mao for dinner and wine. I'm sure I can tempt you with their Penang Pumpkin Curry!'

And with that John started chatting about his day

at work and what food he was in the mood for. Erin just sat there in the car clasping her hands, annoyed with Dr Flynn for once again reminding her that this problem was all just 'in her head'. And at the same time she wondered what she could have done wrong in her life to deserve such disappointment.

11

On Sunday, as they drove to Booterstown Church, Erin tried to put the doctor's visit behind her. Her sister Alison had given birth to a gorgeous little girl called Sophie a few months back, and today was her christening.

'I bet you can't wait to see your little godchild in her christening robes!' John said encouragingly to his wife, as he parked the car outside the church.

Erin couldn't stop herself feeling miserable. She had felt unhappy since the doctor's appointment, and nothing John said could change that. John knew she blamed herself for not getting pregnant, and he tried to coax her out of her mood with light conversation. Erin just nodded as she fixed her make-up in the car mirror. John switched the engine off and turned to her.

'I know how sad you are at the moment, but trust

me, this will pass. We'll have kids, plenty of kids! I know we will, because you are already the best wife in the world, so of course you'll be the best mum, too! Now, today is Sophie's big day, and I know how much you love her, so let's help her celebrate by putting all thoughts of fertility, doctors and due dates out of our heads. OK?' John leant over and gave Erin a big hug.

Erin hugged her husband back and gazed at him. He really was the kindest and best man. He always knew what to say to make her feel better, and she would be lost without his constant love and friendship. As he gave her leg an encouraging squeeze, Erin was reminded of the night when she'd realized she had fallen madly in love with him. They'd been on their way home from a dinner dance at the yacht club, and he'd casually rested his hand on her knee while he chatted to her. But Erin hadn't heard what he was saying, because the minute his hand touched her she had felt her heart start to flip, and she had known she was caught hook, line and sinker. And there had been no looking back, that had been it. She'd been John's for ever. And as she looked at him now, fixing his tie, she realized she needed to cheer up and thank God that even though she wasn't pregnant, at least she had John.

'Thanks,' Erin said. She smiled at him. 'You always know what to say. I think you must have two

hearts inside that chest of yours, you are so loving!'
And with that they got out of the car.

As they approached the church and the crowd of mothers and crying babies that stood outside, Erin felt herself tense, but John squeezed her hand.

'Look at it this way,' he said. 'At least you can get drunk today and not have to worry about it affecting your unborn child. Or about having to deal with a hangover and a screaming child in the morning! Let's get this church bit done and then some nice champagne into you. We should enjoy the freedom to do whatever we want while we can!'

Erin laughed, and felt herself lighten up, and as she saw her sister Alison standing in the church doorway with little Sophie she smiled and realized she had plenty to be thankful for.

The church ceremony passed as quickly and smoothly as a christening of four different babies could. The priest obviously knew the quicker the better when it came to trying to hold newborn babies still, and had everyone out the door before Sophie's head and hair were even dry! Erin posed for plenty of photos with her new godchild outside the church, and tried to help her sister feed Sophie before they got to the nearby hotel where Alison and her husband David were holding the christening party for friends and family.

John was propping up the bar with the other men when Erin finally arrived at the hotel, so she sat down and joined her eldest sister Rebecca at a table that was full of Alison's friends and neighbours. As it was a table of women at a christening, they talked mainly about their children; and as two of Alison's friends were pregnant, upcoming motherhood was also a big theme. Erin had the urge to remove herself from this conversation, but she knew she couldn't run from every pregnant woman she met, so she poured herself more wine and got stuck in.

'So when are you due?' she asked Alison's neighbour, Martha.

'Oh not for ages! I am only sixteen weeks, but I already feel like I've been pregnant for ages! And I am craving so much junk food it's awful. I swear I could eat ice cream all day long! I can't walk Dun Laoghaire Pier without one in my hand!'

'Well, once it's not a Teddy's ice cream you are fine, Martha!' Erin said as she helped herself to a sandwich. Teddy's was the most famous ice-cream shop in South Dublin, and come wind, hail or shine people always queued up for a whippy ice cream before walking the famous Dun Laoghaire Pier.

'What do you mean, no Teddy's ice cream?' Martha asked, concerned.

'Oh, Martha, I didn't mean to upset you. I just presumed you knew that pregnant women can't eat those whippy ice creams. It's like soft cheeses, paté, nuts, sushi . . . just one of the foods you need to avoid until after the baby.'

Martha looked a little surprised, but thanked Erin for warning her.

'God, you know so much! I'm surprised you haven't thought of having kids yourself,' she said, as she began checking the sandwiches for other foods she should avoid.

'Oh, my sister is an expert on all things baby-related,' Rebecca said, saving Erin from Martha's prying questions. 'But Erin is only young, she has plenty of years to become an exhausted old mother like us! She is too busy being the best godmother ever! The "fairy godmother" is what my daughter Lucy calls her!' Rebecca looked sympathetically at her sister, knowing that being stuck at a table of mothers and soon-to-be-mothers was hard for her.

'So you are godmother to more than one child?' Martha asked.

'Oh, yes,' Erin replied. 'I have three godchildren. They are all wild but fabulous!'

'Wow, three times, you must be enjoying it! That's great,' Martha said, turning back to the food.

'Yes,' Erin half-mumbled. 'Always the godmother, never the mother.'

Only Rebecca heard. She gave her youngest sister a hug and ordered more wine for her. Suddenly a drunken yet smiling John danced over to the table, grabbed his wife, and before she knew it she was being swung around the dance floor to Take That. As they laughed, danced and kissed, Erin realized that some days you did have to put the baby worry away and just relax, dance and enjoy the moment.

12

Grace Miller stood in arrivals at San Diego International Airport waiting for her mum. Grace had to laugh as she saw Patsy Slattery walk through the door. She looked like Grace, what with her very Irish red hair and green eyes, but their similarities ended there: Grace realized that her mother had somehow managed once again to befriend a family with plenty of children. Patsy was actually holding a young infant in her arms.

'Now, you call me next time you are in Ireland, and you must bring the kids to the amusements in Bray, they would love it,' Patsy was saying to a frazzled-looking mother as she handed the child back to her.

'What are you doing?' Grace asked, as she approached her mum and started wheeling her suitcase out towards the door.

'Oh, this American family sat near me on the plane

and they have the sweetest children! I had the eldest child speaking a coupla focal of Irish by the end of the flight! They were just so adorable!'

'Mum! You can't start speaking to people in planes like that, you will annoy them. And I'm sure those children don't want to speak Irish,' Grace said, as she flung Patsy's luggage into her Lexus 4×4. Patsy's face flushed.

'Just because you want to disown your Irish roots and live the American life over here, doesn't mean other people might not appreciate Irish culture. I love children, and enjoyed the company on that long plane journey. And it's not every day I get to spend twelve hours in the company of children.'

Grace swallowed hard. Another grandchild dig from her mum. She was about to shout at her for bringing up the 'grandkids' issue again, but when she saw how tired her mother looked after the long flight from Ireland, Grace just bit her tongue. She reminded herself how nice it would be to spend time with her and pulled on to the highway, turning the radio up.

By the time Grace and Patsy arrived at Grace's house they had both calmed down, and Patsy was talking about how Grace's two younger brothers were breaking hearts all over Dublin.

'But no sign of any steady girlfriends for either of the boys. I don't know what to make of men any more, they seem to have too much choice, and the girls all seem a little desperate. And I know there are so many single girls in Dublin, but really they should have some respect for themselves and not put up with these guys and their lack of commitment. Maybe Ethan can talk some sense into Colm and Aidan next time he sees them.'

Grace had to hold back a laugh, knowing all too well her younger brothers would have no interest in Ethan telling them about commitment, marriage and settling down. Colm and Aidan had always been a little wild, yet Grace loved and missed them and their antics, and the thought of seeing them again was the one thing that made her really look forward to her move home to Dublin.

'I'm sure you are tired after your flight, would you like to lie down while I prepare you a sandwich for later?' Grace asked as they entered her large, pristine, sunny house.

'Lie down? I'm only here for one week. It is lashing rain in Ireland, and I'm determined to go home not only relaxed but tanned. Let me get my swimming suit on and I'll meet you in the pool. I bought a lovely swimsuit in Dunnes Stores and can't wait to get it wet!'

Grace laughed at how the minute any Irish visitor arrived in San Diego all they wanted was to sunbathe and swim! But after helping her mum with her bags, she changed into a bikini and made her way to the pool, too. Grace had been so excited when Ethan and herself had bought the house and pool. In Ireland, having a swimming pool at home was as rare as finding someone who didn't love U2!

Grace dived into the blue-and-white tiled pool, and surfaced just as her mum arrived down in gold togs, large white sunglasses and an oversized straw sunhat. Grace didn't know what kind of look her mum was going for with her pale Irish skin gleaming white against the gold shiny material, but she was glad it was only the two of them in her back garden, and made a mental note to take Patsy to the shopping mall the next day. Patsy made her way towards one of the large wooden chairs that sat overlooking the pool and lush garden.

'Oh, Mum, don't sit on that chair. That's Coco's. You can sit on the other one, the one with the blue cushion.'

Patsy stared at her only daughter, and laid her handbag and straw hat down on another chair.

'Are you telling me that dog has its own sun chair? That is madness, he is just a dog.'

Grace sighed as she pulled a lilo into the pool. She knew how her mum felt about Coco. The dog was like a child to her and Ethan. He was so gorgeous and good; great company for Ethan on his morning runs on the beach and for Grace when Ethan worked late, which was almost every night. She had never been much of a doggy person when she had lived in Ireland, but here in America everyone seemed to love their dogs, and even though at first she had laughed at all the doggy day spas and costume shops, she now found herself treating Coco more and more like a human being. He was no longer 'just a dog', the way her mum saw him. Grace ignored her mum's remark about Coco's sun chair, and pretended not to notice Patsy's look of shock as the golden retriever came running out of the kitchen, jumped on to the floating lilo, and, after a quick swim, climbed back up on to his padded sun chair.

'Grace Slattery, does that dog have his toes painted?' her mum almost screamed, as the golden retriever stretched out his long legs and dried off in the sun.

Grace tried to justify Coco having his toenails done. He needed it: every other dog on the block had theirs painted too. Patsy sighed as she lowered herself into the pool.

'Well, just promise me you won't be telling the neighbours when you move back home to Ireland that your dog gets manicures! My God, people will think all that American sun has gone to your head, and I would never be able to show my face in the local shops again. Just promise me his nail varnish will be gone by the time you all arrive.'

'I promise, Mum,' Grace said, knowing she was

losing a battle. 'And, anyway, Coco won't be coming over to Ireland for a few months. You actually need to start preparing your pet for immigration a minimum of six months before travelling, and because we only decided to move to Dublin recently, we just haven't got Coco ready to fly. You wouldn't believe all the vaccinations and blood tests he needs to have done. He even needs a microchip!'

Patsy threw her eyes to heaven, but Grace was oblivious to her mother's disapproval.

'Luckily Ethan's brother, Matt, and his wife, Cindy, have agreed to home Coco. They are big animal lovers, and already have four gorgeous dogs. So when they heard about our problem with Coco they kindly said they could squash one more dog into their home. It's just for a few months, until he gets his vaccinations and papers in order, but also, really, we want to wait until we have a proper place of our own in Ireland before bringing him over. Your house will be lovely for us, Mum, but he isn't used to small gardens, it would upset him.'

'Upset him? It doesn't upset me, and I have been living in that house for over thirty years! My God, he is just a dog. He'll be fine! He can run around the local park.'

Grace got out of the pool and sat beside Coco, stroking his long golden hair.

'Oh, it's fine, Mum, he will love Matt and Cindy's

big yard and swimming pool, he'll have plenty of room to play in. And like Ethan, Matt is really good at IT, and has promised he will use his web camera to keep us posted on how Coco is doing. It's great because it means even though we will be in Ireland, Ethan and I can watch him online while he is swimming!'

'For heaven's sake, you should be watching a child of your own swimming, not a flipping dog!'

Grace felt her blood pressure rise. No matter what conversation she had with her mum it all came back to the fact that she and Ethan did not have children. She understood that being the eldest of her family, and the only daughter, the pressure really was on her to produce some grandchildren, but Grace was not the maternal type and had no urge to procreate. This was something her mum did not seem to understand. As a mother of three herself, it seemed Patsy had presumed Grace would want that life, too. But Coco was the closest Grace would ever come to having a child.

There was some tension around the pool, but once Coco went inside to eat Patsy seemed to relax. Grace caught up on what was happening back home, and they both discussed how she ought to pack up for the trip to Ireland.

Before long the sun went in, and it was time to get some dinner.

'Let's go out tonight, Mum. A great new sushi place has opened in Seaport Village.'

'Raw fish? Oh, that doesn't sound safe to me, love. No, I will stick with chips if they have any.'

Grace sighed. Her mother could be so old-fashioned sometimes. But she ignored Patsy's remark, and, after quick showers, they headed to the nearby waterfront shopping, dining and entertainment complex. After some shopping and a few cocktails they headed for the sushi bar, and as Grace got stuck into some sashimi, Patsy ate a 'safe' chicken noodle salad.

After dinner they returned home, and Patsy was delighted to see her son-in-law's Jeep in the drive-way. Ethan was waiting for them in the living room.

'Patsy! It's great to see you! Sorry I missed dinner, but I got held up at work. But you girls sit down, as I have a nice bottle of champagne chilled for us.' And with that Ethan headed for the kitchen. It wasn't long before the three of them were relaxing on the couch, and Ethan was filling Patsy in on his work, and his plans for their 'stint in the Emerald Isle'!

As Ethan chatted away, Patsy noticed that Grace was unusually quiet and seemed to excuse herself to go to the bathroom a few times. But since she didn't indicate anything was wrong, Patsy said nothing, too. As Ethan was showing Patsy the plans for his new Dublin office, Patsy shook off her shoes and curled her pale Irish legs under her new dress. She saw Ethan glance at Grace.

'Oh, Mum, we don't allow feet on seats in this house. The couches were very expensive.'

Ethan nodded his head in agreement. Patsy turned and looked at Coco the dog sprawled out on one of the cream couches, feet and all on board.

'Well, that's funny, Grace, because I don't remember you ever caring about couches before, especially not the ones at home. Remember how you used to drive your father mad by painting your toenails on them? There are still bright pink stains on the three-seater from the time you spilt a whole bottle of my good nail varnish on it.'

Grace looked at her mum and started to cry, and then ran for the bathroom. Patsy immediately felt guilty and ran after her.

'Oh, I'm sorry, pet, I won't mention that blasted nail-varnish accident again, but it's hardly fair that Coco is allowed to put his grubby dog feet on the couch when I, your mother, can't!'

'It's not that,' said Grace, reaching for the toilet. 'I don't feel well all of a sudden. I think it was the sushi, my stomach is upset,' and with that she started to cry.

Patsy resisted the urge to remind her daughter that she had told her raw fish wasn't safe. Instead she did what every mother does best: she rubbed Grace's back, and looked after her all evening. And later, as Ethan and Patsy helped her to bed, Grace thought that, as mad as her mum drove her about not having children, sometimes it was worth all that fighting just to have her around. There was no one like your mum.

13

Patsy Slattery's week in San Diego flew by. Grace had been sick for a few days with food poisoning from the blasted sushi, but Patsy had busied herself sunbathing, reading Hollywood star gossip-magazines and shopping in a nearby mall. She was just coming in the door when Grace greeted her.

'Hi, Mum. I'm so sorry I couldn't get up this morning. My stomach was in bits again, but I do feel much better now. I see you found the shops OK, though!' Grace helped her mum, who was struggling with eight oversized paper shopping bags. When she flung them down on the counter out poured jumpers, jeans, bracelets and toys.

'Who are these toys for?' Grace asked, surprised to see a Disney bag crammed full of dolls, games and T-shirts.

'Well, the dolls are for Tara and Jade. And the games and T-shirts are for Michael, Tommy and little Paul,' Patsy replied, as she took off her shoes and rubbed her tired feet.

'Who the hell are Tara, Jade, Michael, Tommy and what's-his-name?' Grace asked.

'Well, they are the kids I babysit for! I have no grandchildren to mind, so when Brona and Derek across the road asked me to help out and babysit their four kids a couple of afternoons a week I said yes. Brona's studying for her degree in science and needed some help. And then her sister Angie had to go back to work, and her Tommy's such a sweet little boy – well I just couldn't say no. They are all real dotes and I have great fun with them. Wait until you see Jade! She has just learned to walk and is causing havoc!'

Grace looked at her. She felt half-annoyed by the usual grandkids digs and half-sad that her mum was so looking forward to being a granny that she was minding friends' children. Grace decided to take the high road and avoid a fight, so she simply walked to the large fridge and began to pour her mum some organic lemonade.

After Patsy had recuperated from her morning's shopping, she and Grace decided to go for a walk, as Grace needed some fresh air.

'I'm sorry for being sick the last few days, Mum. I hope I haven't ruined your trip,' she said, as they slipped off their sandals and began walking barefoot on the beach.

'Not at all, pet,' Patsy replied, taking in the beautiful surroundings. 'I just love being here with you and Ethan, in such a gorgeous location. You're going to miss all of this.'

Grace looked around at the beach, ocean and bright sun.

'I have to admit, Mum, I will miss San Diego, it's been my home for ten years now. But of course I am looking forward to spending more time with you, and being able to see Colm and Aidan more regularly. Sometimes I feel like I don't know my little brothers at all. When I lived at home they were still in school, playing computer games and trying to persuade me to buy them alcohol! But now when I hear they have jobs and are living with "mates", I feel so distant from them.'

Patsy looked at her daughter and knew it must be hard to have your husband on one continent and your family on another.

'Don't worry about your brothers! Those two lazy lumps haven't changed at all. They're still playing computer games, leaving their washing in my house, and trying to get me to buy the alcohol, so they can "save" their money for important things! Nothing has changed. We all still love you and can't wait for you to be back in Dublin.'

Grace smiled.

'I just wish your dad was here to bring Ethan for a pint in O'Donoghue's. Dad would have loved that, bringing a "real Yank" to his local!'

Grace looked at her mum, and knew she was still grieving for her husband. It had been five years since Teddy Slattery had gone to work one day, to the bakery factory where he had been for over thirty years, and never returned. Patsy's beloved husband had suffered a massive heart attack and died before she could say goodbye. Grace and Ethan had flown to Dublin straight away, and Grace had spent three weeks with her mum, but eventually she'd had to follow Ethan and go back to work. She'd felt so guilty at abandoning her mum, and leaving her to deal with becoming a widow all on her own. Patsy had plenty of close friends, and the neighbours had been great keeping her busy with bingo and long chats, but it had taken a few years for her to accept her new, lonelier, life. And now, with Colm and Aidan living out of home, and Grace being so far away, Patsy did feel at a loss what to do and who to talk to. But since Teddy's death she had accepted Ethan's generous offer to fly her over to visit Grace more, and she admitted she was becoming quite used to her biannual visits to the West Coast.

'I'll miss the sun and shopping myself,' Patsy said as they sat down at a local beach bar and ordered ice creams.

'Well, maybe we should find you a nice American bachelor, Mum! So you can spend more time here with me!' Grace laughed as they watched men of all shapes and sizes jog past.

'Oh, I don't know. They all look a little too "pretty" over here, a bit too "feminine" for me. I mean, how could I date a man who uses more moisturizer than me? Or who works out more than I ever have? Your father never worked out anything, apart from how to save enough money for pints on a Friday!'

Grace laughed at her mum, but saw Patsy still kept her eyes firmly on the joggers as they ran past looking like Abercrombie & Fitch models!

As it was such a hot evening, Ethan decided to cook outside, and they all enjoyed his famous barbecued beefburgers and ranch salad before they began talking about the 'big move', and how Ethan was looking forward to enjoying a big proper family Christmas for once and seemed to expect it would be a 'white one'.

'I hate to disappoint you, but we never have snow at Christmas in Ireland. It's cold, but never that cold,' Patsy explained, as Ethan's face dropped.

'But don't worry, honey, once you try Mum's mince

pies and Auntie Mary's stuffing you will forget all about snow,' Grace said, starting to get excited herself about the move.

And soon Grace and Patsy were telling Ethan about all the places in Dublin he would have to go and see. He had only been twice, and both had been flying visits, and he seemed keen to 'get to know the real Ireland' this time.

'Well, we don't mind you visiting the *Book of Kells*, but watch out we don't see you turn into a complete American tourist and start wearing any of those Guinness T-shirts or taking photos of buskers on Grafton Street!' Patsy laughed.

After reminiscing about how great Ireland really was Grace decided she was tired out and headed for bed. Patsy decided to stay up and watch a Danielle Steel made-for-TV movie.

'You just can't get good films like this in Ireland,' Patsy exclaimed, as Ethan groaned at the corny name and opening credits of the film.

Later, when Patsy was going to bed, she saw Grace's bedroom door was open and the light was on, and so popped her head in to say goodnight. Grace and Ethan were both sitting up in their large four-poster bed, reading the newspapers, while Coco lay in-between them, on top of the expensive-looking Egyptian cotton sheets.

'Please God, one day you'll have a child lying between you there instead of that dog,' Patsy said. She waved goodnight to them, and closed the door quickly, before Grace could come back with a comment.

14

Beth Prendergast was distracted as she sat in on an early department meeting. As team leader she knew she should be more enthusiastic, but she'd slept badly the night before, and spent the night tossing and turning before eventually giving up on any chance of sleep and just started reading the new Harry Potter book. She had gotten lost in the pages of magic, and found herself reminiscing about her own days at boarding school as she read about Harry in the best boarding school of them all: Hogwarts! But now, as she sat in on this very boring meeting she regretted not trying to sleep, as even her third cup of coffee couldn't keep her eyes open. She caught Tom's eye, and could see he wasn't impressed with her lack of energy and spirit at the meeting, but she couldn't muster up enthusiasm – even for him. Beth hadn't seen Tom in almost three weeks, what with his business trip to the States getting extended, and Beth herself being flat-out busy with a new client. But she hadn't had the energy to suggest a night out; she had being feeling unwell all week, and it was getting to her.

After the meeting she walked back to her office, bumping into her only real friend at the company, Susan Morgan. She wasn't as senior as Beth, but, being the only two high-ranking women in the office, they had struck up a friendship. It at least meant Beth had someone at work to talk to about clothes, movies and *Sex and the City*.

'Are you OK? You look a little washed-out,' Susan asked kindly.

'I don't know. I'm sure it's nothing. I'm just tired this week. I think it must be my glands, as they're so sore. I feel wrecked.'

Susan looked at her friend. Beth, in her very expensive Chloé suit and slicked-back hair looked the picture of professionalism, but under her make-up Susan could see she was tired and not herself.

'Well, why don't we go out for lunch today, somewhere nice? And if you feel you need to go to the doctor we can go there, too.'

'Oh, I won't need the doctor,' Beth said suddenly, realizing she must look even worse than she felt. She didn't like to appear weak in the office. 'But lunch at

Milano's would be nice. I never say no to a pepperoni pizza!'

The girls arranged to meet outside the office later, and then Beth got back to her desk and mounting workload.

She struggled with the work that morning. Along with plenty of client meetings, her job involved a lot of paperwork, and she was not in the humour for it today. She managed to pass some of the donkey work on to Declan, the junior portfolio assistant, who was only too happy to take it on and prove himself to Beth. He might only be preparing printouts, taking minutes in meetings, and generally shadowing her, but he knew all of this would one day help towards building up his own client list, and hopefully becoming a portfolio manager soon. Beth thanked him for his help as she checked how her property funds were coming along, and then counted down the hours until lunchtime.

Finally it was 1 p.m., and soon Beth and Susan were sitting in the Italian restaurant discussing Susan's upcoming wedding.

'It's impossible to find a good band. I mean, everyone we rang said they were booked out at least a year ago, some even two years ago! Like, who does that? Who are these girls who are booking their whole wedding one or two years in advance, and taking up all the hotels, churches and bands in the process? It's unfair! We have no chance of getting any good band or DJ!'

'It's the same women who book their children into primary schools before the child is even born!' Beth laughed.

Just then the waiter delivered their pizzas, but as he set the extra pepperoni pizza down in front of Beth the smell of the meat hit her, and she suddenly felt sick.

'Oh, I'm sorry, can you take that away, please?' she asked, as she gulped back a Coke and distanced herself from the pizza.

'Are you OK?' Susan said, looking worried.

'I'm fine,' Beth lied, and then turned to the surprised-looking waiter. 'I'm sorry, but could you bring me some of your garlic dough balls instead? And sorry about the pizza.'

The waiter shrugged, and went off to get Beth her food. Susan looked concernedly at her.

'Before you say anything, I'm fine!' Beth said. 'I'm just not feeling the best, and between that and the lack of sleep it's obviously affected my appetite. But I'll go to the chemist on the way back to the office and get something. Don't worry about me – tell me about your honeymoon plans instead!'

As Susan filled her in on her plans to spend a month travelling around South America, Beth couldn't help feeling a little jealous. Even though Susan wasn't as senior as her, she still had a great job. Susan worked hard, and was well-respected by her peers, and yet had managed to balance her life better than most of their employees. She not only had a successful career, but a great social life, and a gorgeous fiancé, too. Beth wondered if she would ever plan a wedding and honeymoon of her own. The way things were with Tom she knew they would never happen with him. Of course it made her sad, as every girl dreams of one day walking down the aisle. But she did love Tom, and with that love came the understanding that she and Tom had a relationship that was different from others. As Susan questioned her about her love life, Beth did feel guilty lying as usual, and saying there was no one. She knew she could never tell anyone in work about Tom. She would instantly lose respect from colleagues like Susan. She didn't want anyone thinking she had gotten so far up in Burlington because of Tom, so she kept their relationship to herself.

When they had finished eating Susan headed straight back to the office for a meeting, while Beth went to the chemist's to get some painkillers. As she stood in the queue she saw someone familiar.

'Jeananne? How are you?' Beth said to an old school friend who she hadn't seen in years.

'Beth! How lovely to see you. Wow, you look great, so professional. I heard you were some high-flying financial whiz. Congrats!'

Beth looked at her old classmate, who was holding one child in her arms and clearly had another on the way. Jeananne caught her looking at her stomach.

'Yes! I'm pregnant again! Scott is two years old, and now I'm expecting again, and due in four months' time. So it's all go go!' Jeananne said, as she tried to clean little Scott's nose and hand in a prescription to the chemist at the same time.

'Congratulations, that's great. How are you feeling?' Beth asked politely, but thinking at the same time that if that little boy and his snot came anywhere near her very expensive suit she would die.

'Oh, I'm fine now. Tired, but that's pregnancy for you! But I'm glad I'm into the second trimester. I tell you, nothing prepares you for those first twelve weeks. The morning sickness, the tiredness, and I swear my breasts and glands were so sore. My God, I couldn't let my husband touch me! And there were some smells I couldn't stand: like, if anyone even ate onion near me I thought I would puke! It's funny how different pregnancies are; I mean, I was fine with Scott. Anyway, I had better go, we are meeting the hubby for lunch. Take care.'

Beth wished her well and then rejoined the queue, but as she waited to be served, what Jeananne had said about being tired, having sore glands, and feeling an aversion to certain smells played in her head.

No, I couldn't be! Beth suddenly thought, almost falling down with the shock. I couldn't be pregnant, could I? No, I'm just tired, she tried to convince herself, as she walked out of the chemist's and began the walk back to her office.

But even when she got back to her desk, opened her emails and started returning clients' phone calls, all she could think about was being pregnant, labour and babies. And she didn't know if it was due to these thoughts or her glands, but she felt sick for the whole afternoon.

15

Beth stood in a queue in O'Neill's late-night pharmacy. She pulled her baseball cap down over her face as she approached the till and asked for the small box. Her hands shook as she counted out the money. She paid as quickly as possible, and, after stuffing the purchase into her pocket, almost ran to her nearby parked car. As she drove through the quiet Dublin streets she felt sick. She would know within minutes whether her life had changed.

She walked back into her apartment, but it looked different now. She felt like a stranger in her own home as she made her way to the bathroom. She sat down on the toilet as if she had never sat down on one before. As she pulled the box from her pocket she checked the bathroom door was locked. She felt as if someone might burst in and discover her secret.

Beth began unwrapping the plastic from the box

and stared at the stick. The box claimed it contained the most accurate pregnancy test in the world. She read the instructions for the tenth time before finally using it. As she sat and gazed at the red-painted walls of her bathroom Beth felt her head spin. What will I do if this is positive? she thought. I just can't be pregnant! She tried to convince herself, but there was a niggling voice in her head telling her that she could. Beth had spent the past few weeks feeling nauseated, tired and sore. But nothing felt as bad as this new worry in the pit of her stomach. The worry that she could be pregnant. The thought alone made her feel like vomiting.

As she looked down at the diamond-encrusted bracelet that Tom had given her she cursed herself for not being more cautious that night. Beth had always been sensible, but now one night of passion might have changed everything.

She said a quick prayer as she checked her watch to make sure she had allowed the correct amount of time to pass. There was nothing wrong with having children, but, for Beth, getting pregnant now was not part of her plan, and she knew it would definitely not be part of Tom's, either.

Then she took a deep breath and looked at the stick. There was a very distinctive dark pink line.

It was positive. She was positive. She was pregnant.

16

Beth stared at a report from an internal buy-side analyst and tried to sift through the relevant information, but she felt as if everything was happening in slow motion. It was like some out-of-body experience.

Ever since she had done the pregnancy test, Beth had been going through the motions of everyday life but not actually experiencing it. She had driven to work each morning, had turned on her computer and downloaded her emails, but she read them as if they were news from outer space, they meant nothing to her. She sat and watched TV every night, but she couldn't tell you what was happening in her favourite shows, because she couldn't concentrate. To the outside world she looked the same, but inside she felt like an impostor in her own body. This can't be real, she thought every morning when she woke. But she had done other pregnancy tests and they had read positive, too. Beth's bathroom was scattered with every brand and type. They might all look different, but they all said the same thing: Beth was expecting.

Just then she got a call from Tom, asking her to come into his office.

'What's wrong with you?' he asked as Beth sat down and helped herself to a glass of cold water. She gulped it back while Tom watched.

'What do you mean?' she eventually replied, terrified he would work out her big secret.

'You haven't returned my calls all week, and you're quiet as a mouse in meetings. What's wrong?' Tom asked.

For a split second Beth felt like confessing, and telling Tom he was now the father of her unborn child. But as she watched him sitting there, strumming his fingers against his desk, impatient for an answer, she knew now was not the time for honesty.

'I'm sorry. I'm just a little run-down this week. A bit wrecked.'

Tom didn't look very sympathetic.

'I'm sorry you're not feeling well, but we have two big meetings this week. I need you to be on top form. Can I rely on you or not?'

Beth knew how important being professional and strong was to him. She sat up, and put on a big smile.

'I'll be fine, boss. I swear.'

Tom relaxed.

'OK, good to hear. Now, why don't we go somewhere quiet for lunch? I haven't talked to you properly in weeks. And I was thinking it's high time we went away for the weekend – somewhere nice, my treat. We can talk about it over lunch.'

Beth would have loved nothing more than a nice big lunch with the man she loved, but she had something important to do and couldn't delay it any further.

'I'm sorry. I can't today. I've got plans,' she said, feeling awful for lying to Tom.

Tom looked a little put out, but then made Beth promise they would catch up at the weekend instead. As she walked out of his office she felt sick, thinking of the secret she was withholding from him.

Beth had been avoiding her family and friends all week. Ever since she had done her first pregnancy test she just hadn't been able to face talking and lying to those who were closest to her, and so she had switched her phone off, hadn't replied to any personal emails, and had ignored any messages from her dad. It felt as if her life were on hold, and the longer she avoided telling anyone her secret the longer she could avoid facing reality. There were times she did feel excitement at becoming a mum, even if it was unplanned. But then she would think of the reality of it: she was unmarried, in a relationship with a man who didn't want kids, and it was not the ideal situation. And so she had put off telling anyone for another week.

But today she knew she couldn't avoid what had to be done. She had an important phone call to make, and it was to the National Maternity Hospital at Holles Street. Beth had been born there, and after discussion with her own GP it was where she knew she wanted to book herself in. Going to her own doctor to get confirmation of her pregnancy had been an uncomfortable experience. As her GP had congratulated Beth and handed her some leaflets on pregnancy she'd felt like admitting that she didn't really want to be pregnant. But instead she had taken down the names of vitamins and a list of foods to avoid, and promised her doctor she would book into a maternity hospital asap, as apparently they got booked up quite quickly. That had been three days ago now, and Beth knew she finally had to make the call.

As soon as she could leave the office Beth grabbed her woollen coat and headed over to St Stephen's Green. She found a quiet park bench and dialled the number. Her voice shook as she asked to be put through to the first gynaecologist her doctor had recommended.

'Hi. Is that Dr McWilliams's secretary? My name is Beth Prendergast and I would like to book in with the doctor. I'm pregnant.' Beth almost whispered the last two words.

'Oh, congratulations, when are you due?' said the friendly secretary.

'I'm not sure of my dates,' Beth admitted. 'But I think I'm due around the end of July.'

There was a pause on the phone.

'Oh,' Beth said. 'Am I too early to book in? I suppose July is miles away! I can ring back in a few weeks if you want.'

'Too early?' the secretary replied, almost laughing. 'Darling, you are way too late. I'm afraid Dr McWilliams is all booked up. I'm sorry.'

'Booked up already?' Beth said surprised. 'How is that possible? I've only just found out I am pregnant. How could I have rung any earlier? This doesn't make sense.'

'I'm sorry, pet, but you should have rung weeks ago. We are all booked up until the end of August.'

'But if I'm only a few weeks pregnant, and I'm due at the end of July, how could other people possibly know already that they're having a baby at the end of August? This is madness.' Beth's pulse raced, and her blood pressure rose.

'That's just the way it is nowadays,' the secretary said, matter-of-factly. 'Everyone knows they have to book early. I suppose with all those new pregnancy tests you can now find out you are pregnant days after conception. So we're all booked up.'

Beth was shocked. She was only about six weeks pregnant, and yet she was too late to book in with her preferred consultant. She hung up, and looked at the list her GP had written out for her. She was sure one of the other doctors would be free. But the names meant nothing to her. How was she supposed to know which doctor was the best? She had no mum or sister to ask, and it was too early to admit her problem to her friends. Beth looked at the list and randomly dialled one of the doctors' numbers.

Half an hour later she was fuming. She had rung five doctors and all were booked up. How is this possible? she asked herself again and again. Earlier on she had dreaded making a call to the doctor. She had felt booking in with a gynaecologist in a maternity hospital would make the pregnancy all too real, but now all she wanted was for everything to be settled. She dialled another number. This time the secretary, a lady called Karen, at least seemed to sympathize with her.

'It is madness, I know! We're all booked up, too. But we do get girls who book in very early, in the hope they will be pregnant that month. Now some of them do unfortunately have to cancel when they find out they aren't, so I could take your number and ring you back if we get any cancellations. But I should tell you, it's highly unlikely there will be.'

Beth felt gutted.

'To be honest,' Karen added. 'Your best bet is to ring me back later. We'll pretend we've never talked, and you can just lie about your dates. Pretend you are not due until August and I should have some availability for you. OK?'

Beth didn't know what to say. It was her only hope, but she didn't feel comfortable lying.

'No, I can't do that. I had hoped to attend Holles Street, but I guess at this stage I'll have to go elsewhere,' said Beth, deflated.

'I'm sorry,' replied the secretary.

Beth didn't bother replying.

'Listen, just give me your number, and let me see what I can do,' said Karen suddenly.

Beth gave her the number and hung up.

There was not one doctor in Holles Street available. It suddenly occurred to Beth that she might have to have the baby at home. A home birth! She began to laugh, imagining her perfectly tidy apartment suddenly covered in towels and blood. What the hell am I going to do? she wondered. Who were all these lunatic women who booked up all the maternity hospitals months in advance? It was so unfair. And as Karen had admitted, a lot of the time they weren't even pregnant; they were just taking up bookings in the hope that they might be in the future. It was total madness. Beth suddenly remembered her friend Susan telling her how it was impossible to get a band to play at her wedding, as they were all booked up years in advance. So, thought Beth, there must be this one group of highly organized and annoying women who went around ruining everyone's weddings, and then a few months later booked up all the maternity hospitals. What psychos! she thought, getting more and more annoyed.

Suddenly her stomach rumbled and she remembered her lunch. She took a sandwich out from her handbag and began to eat, but as she did she felt sick. Beth felt queasy the whole time and was finding it hard to keep anything down. Being pregnant sucks, she thought, and a home birth is going to make it a whole lot worse.

She managed to stomach a few bites of her sandwich before binning it and heading back to work. Just as she entered the doors of Burlington Stockbrokers her phone rang.

'Is that Beth Prendergast? This is Karen, Dr O'Connor's secretary.'

'Yes, this is Beth.'

'You're in luck. I've managed to squeeze you in. Dr O'Connor will take you on.'

Beth suddenly felt such huge relief. No home birth, thank God.

'Great. Thank you so much,' she replied.

Karen took Beth's details and booked her in for an appointment.

'Good luck, Beth. And I will see you and your partner in seven weeks' time.'

Partner? Even hearing the word made Beth feel ill. She had no idea how she was ever going to tell Tom, and she just could not picture him in Holles Street. Beth and Tom weren't a very public couple, they preferred being alone together, but now she was going to have to ask him to hold her hand as they went for months of hospital visits, scans, classes and of course the labour itself. God, this is all moving so fast! worried Beth, as she got the lift up to her office.

Beth sat down in her chair and was about to sip on the extra large coffee she had bought on her way back from the park when she put it down. She suddenly remembered her GP mentioning something about watching her caffeine intake. She had been avoiding looking up pregnancy websites until now. But suddenly she felt an overwhelming urge to find out if coffee could hurt the baby. Beth worked in a pod of four people, with their desks all facing each other. It was hard to hide what you were looking at from your team, and it was at times like this when Beth wished she had her own office, instead of working in an open-plan space. And so, while pretending to be studying a spreadsheet that had just been emailed to her, she tilted her computer screen so no one could see, and then opened the internet. Two hours later she was hooked: there was website after website full of information on being pregnant, having a baby and how to cope with it all. There was plenty of factual information on being pregnant, like what food to avoid, and Beth was gutted to hear that shellfish was off the menu for the next eight months. But it was the fun things like how to choose a baby name, or old wives' tales on how to tell if you were carrying a girl or a boy that made her smile! Beth wasn't one to avoid work, because she thrived on it, but for once she felt OK pushing aside the growing pile of files on her desk and submerging herself in being pregnant. It was the first time in a week that she had felt happy and excited.

As the office buzzed with the usual humdrum meetings, phone calls and office chat Beth lost herself in the sudden excitement of being pregnant. As she learned how her foetus was growing she became amazed at how quickly babies developed and became human. She immediately signed up to a website that promised to email her regularly with information on her baby's week-by-week development. She checked her inbox a few minutes later and was delighted when the first email came through. She immediately learned that her foetus's ears and eyes were formed, and that the heart had begun to pump blood. But it was its size that shocked her: 'Your baby is now the size of a lower case "o".' She had to reread the sentence. Only the size of a lower case o? She looked at a file on her desk, and saw a word that contained an o. She stared at it in amazement. How could something so minuscule already make her feel so unwell and so different? Her life had been turned upside down by an o. She began to laugh. A little o.

Beth eventually got back to work, but all afternoon long she couldn't stop smiling every time she typed the letter o. It had a whole new meaning for her.

17

Erin walked into the kitchen of her home in Blackrock and turned on the kettle. It was a cold winter morning and she needed a cup of hot water and lemon to get her going before a long day at work. Just then she saw a huge bunch of flowers sitting on the kitchen table. There was a note attached.

'Happy Friday, Erin! Have a good day. See you later tonight. Love, John.'

She sat down, read the note and smiled. Once again she was reminded how lucky she was to be married to John Delany, who really had a heart of gold. He worked hard every day in the bank, yet never complained about work. He always had time for Erin, his friends and sailing. John was full of energy, and while after a week of work she would happily spend a weekend relaxing and pottering around the house, John was always dragging her out for an afternoon of sailing, or for a pint in their local pub.

She sent him a text to thank him for the flowers. She had to restrain herself from asking him to take it easy with the beer when he was out with his friends tonight. She had managed to persuade him to give up smoking, but he still drank at the weekends, despite all the research she had shown him on alcohol and men's fertility. She just wanted them both to be in the best health they could; it would make trying for a baby easier. But since she was due her period, she guessed one more night of alcohol wasn't going to hurt their baby-making potential. Erin was tired, she always was when she was about to get her period. There was a time when she would take a pregnancy test the second she thought they might have conceived, but last month John had put his foot down about that.

'I can't wake up again to find you crying in the bathroom. No more early pre-test test kits. We have to let nature take its course.'

'But, John—' she started to say.

'No buts. From now on we only do tests if you think you are late. OK?'

Erin had to fight every urge in her body to agree, but she knew he was right. Over the last few months she had spent a fortune on buying every possible make and brand of pregnancy test. Unfortunately they all said the same thing – not pregnant – but that hadn't stopped her rushing out to buy more. She knew John was right, she had to try to relax, but he just didn't understand how much she wanted a little baby, a child.

She looked around their home. It was an old red-brick four-bedroomed house, with a reasonable-sized garden, and was within walking distance of Blackrock Village. They had stretched themselves to buy the house in the affluent suburb, but it had been worth it. It was in a great location, not only near their friends and family, but near good schools, too. Of course John was just happy he was only minutes from Dun Laoghaire Harbour, and the yacht club. They both knew it was a beautiful home, and Erin had spent a lot of time, energy and money making it perfect. From top designer curtains to Egyptian cotton sheets, they had made sure their home looked immaculate. But as she ran her hand over the large brown leather couch in the living room, she was reminded how they had picked it because leather was the best option when you had kids. She knew John had agreed when getting their garden decked that it was worth paying extra for splinterless decking, as it would make it safer for children in the future. And she had insisted they kept the old bath in the master bathroom, because you needed to bathe children when they were young. But with no children on the horizon she wondered if she'd been too presumptuous. She'd never even considered that children might never live in the house; that there might never be a baby to bathe, or a toddler to crawl around on the decking. Erin shuddered at the thought. That future was unbearable. She finished her tea, locked up the house and headed into work.

Later that day, Erin sat in her latest client's house, opened her large satchel and started pulling out kitchen catalogues to show Ciara Ryan.

'I know we need to keep an eye on your budget, but you would be surprised how often a bespoke kitchen can cost just the same as a ready-made store-bought one. And at our firm we work with some of the best carpenters in the country. I can even bring you to places I've worked on before to show you examples of kitchens in real houses. Seeing a real kitchen being used in a busy house can often help you decide what works or what doesn't.'

'That would be great. I love all of your ideas. The whole redesign is starting to fall into place,' said Ciara.

Erin smiled. She was always delighted when a new client agreed with her suggestions and was happy with her work. Ciara and Mark owned such a fabulous house that she'd been thrilled to get her hands on it. To them it might only be the redesign of a few rooms, but to Erin it was a large project. Having your own business was tough, you were always worried that work might dry up, but on days like today Erin revelled in the knowledge that she was working at her dream job and was good at it. Setting up her business with Paula had been the right move.

'OK, well we can set up a time to see some of my previous clients' kitchens, but in the meanwhile let's talk about that front room. I know Mark wanted to see ideas on how to maximize the space so he can turn it into a study.'

Erin opened the large folder where she kept ideas on the latest project she was working on. It held light fabric samples, paint colours, sketches and photos. She had everything covered. She was always prepared and organized.

'I know the room is small, but since Mark only wants to use it as a home office, we can save space by taking out that large couch and replacing it with a good-sized desk and some clever shelving.'

Ciara smiled, and then took a deep breath.

'Oh, I wasn't going to tell you yet, but I suppose I need to. You see, I'm pregnant!'

Erin's heart dropped. She couldn't help it, she was instantly jealous.

Ciara didn't notice her dismay.

'We didn't think it would happen this soon, but it has! I'm only eight weeks, but Mark is delighted, he is so excited. I still can't believe it myself!'

Erin looked at Ciara's animated face, and could see how happy she was. She felt guilty for being so jealous, but she couldn't help it. It was as if everyone Erin knew could get pregnant at the drop of a hat except for her. She knew Ciara was waiting for her to say something, so she stood up and gave her client a hug.

'Congratulations! I'm so happy for you both.'

'Oh, thank you so much,' replied a very excited Ciara. 'To be honest we haven't even told most of our friends yet. But I suppose you need to know, because now we will need to change some of the house plans. The study will now need to be a playroom. And we'll have to talk about a nursery for the baby. Do you think you can help?'

'Of course,' Erin replied, even though all she felt like doing was running out the door and leaving the pregnant Ciara behind. 'So when are you due?' she went on.

'In June,' Ciara replied. 'It will be a summer baby!'

'Which doctor are you going to?' enquired Erin as she started to take a new notebook from her bag.

'A guy called Dr Kennedy. He seems nice.'

'Dr Kennedy? Oh Ciara, you're so lucky! Everyone knows he's the best doctor. He has such a good reputation. He's the best in the business, and Holles Street is such a brilliant hospital. I wouldn't go anywhere else.'

Ciara laughed. 'Wow, with all your baby knowledge I'm surprised you haven't thought about having kids yourself.'

Erin winced. 'All in good time,' was all she said before pumping Ciara for more info. 'How have you been feeling? Any idea if it's a boy or a girl?'

'I hope it's a girl! But of course we don't mind! I've been feeling OK, but I'm exhausted. I literally can't get up without having a bottle of Lucozade first. I'm so tired I need the energy!'

Erin frowned. 'I'm sorry you're so tired, Ciara. I remember when my sister Alison was pregnant she was exhausted the whole time too, but you should try not to take too much sugar or caffeine. It's not good for the baby.'

'Oh,' said Ciara. 'Well, don't worry, it's not like I'm drinking hundreds of bottles. The doctor did give me a list of foods and drinks to avoid, so I am trying to stick to that. But it's hard. I already miss prawns!'

'But, for your child, it's worth it,' replied Erin. She knew she was beginning to sound bossy, but some people didn't know how lucky they were to get pregnant so easily, and they just didn't take the whole thing seriously enough.

'Oh, don't worry, sure I have my mum ringing me every day demanding to know what food I've eaten. The baby will be the first grandchild in our house, and Mum is already so worried and concerned for its health. Honestly, if she could she would move in here just so she could force-feed me steak and vegetables every day! But I suppose it's because since my dad died earlier this year she's been so heartbroken. And now she is so excited about her first grandchild. It's really lifted her spirits.'

Erin felt guilty. She realized that Ciara had more important things to worry about than bottles of Lucozade and her caffeine intake. She'd dealt with the death of her father, and was now trying to enjoy bringing some happiness into her family. Erin felt she shouldn't have been so judgemental.

'I'm sorry about your dad,' she said. 'The baby couldn't have come at a better time for you all. What a blessing for your family!'

'It really is. We all can't wait.'

'Anyway, now that you have this baby on the way I will certainly revise the design plans,' said Erin. 'The playroom should be easy: we just need to pick out some nice bright paint and ensure we have plenty of storage units in there for all the toys! But the nursery will be trickier. You and Mark have a good-sized bedroom and en suite, but the remaining three bedrooms are so tiny. What do you think about knocking two of them together? I'm sure Paula could get you some quotes to let you know how much it would cost.'

'Why don't we go upstairs and have a look?' suggested Ciara.

Ciara proudly showed Erin into one of the sunny back bedrooms.

'I'd like the baby to have a nice, light, happy room. I can't wait to pick out cots and baby furnishings!'

Erin swallowed hard. She didn't want to admit that for years she had been collecting ideas for baby rooms of her own: girly pink bedclothes, baby-blue wallpaper, dinosaur curtains, princess beds, wooden cots from Scandinavia, and quilts from America – she had all her ideas and hopes in a special book.

'I think we should paint the room yellow,' said Erin, trying to focus on the work at hand. 'It's a neutral colour, so would suit a girl or a boy, and although the wooden floors might need sanding, I think the biggest problem here will be space. I will work on some ideas, but I think if we could knock this room and the one next to it together it would create a big, bright, and nicely proportioned nursery.'

★   ★   ★

For the rest of the afternoon Erin let herself revel in doing nothing but talking about babies. Yes, she was incredibly jealous of her client, but Ciara was a sweet girl who had survived a tough year, so Erin tried to push aside her envy and instead enjoy talking about baby cots, nursery ideas and how to baby-proof the newly renovated house.

'OK, I've taken enough of your time today,' she said eventually. 'Email me your thoughts on the kitchen floor, and I'll look for a brochure I have somewhere at home on a Norwegian company who make the most beautiful wooden nursery furniture. Children's cots aren't something we supply, but the catalogue might be of some use to you.'

'Thanks, Erin. And thanks for all your tips on vitamins, food and exercise. I've learnt more from you this afternoon than from any baby book!'

Erin said nothing, she just stole a quick glance at Ciara's belly. Of course there was no sign yet she was carrying a child, but still Erin couldn't believe there was a little person right there with them.

'I hope you have a good weekend. I'll talk to you next week.'

'Thanks,' said Ciara again as she began to close the front door. And then she added, because they'd talked about it over coffee: 'Best of luck with that fortune-teller, too! I hope she tells you what you want to hear!'

Erin thanked her before getting back into her car and heading home. After a long day at work, focusing on someone else's good news, she couldn't wait to get ready for her night of predictions. She only hoped the fortune-teller would give her the answers she was looking for.

18

Tonight Erin and her two sisters were going to meet Ula, a very well-known fortune-teller who lived in Wicklow. Earlier, Erin had told Ciara Ryan she was being dragged along by her older sisters to meet Ula, but really it was her who had made the appointment. Erin had read every pregnancy book, could relay word for word the medical advice from all the top getting-pregnant websites – but still, nothing could tell her when or if it was ever going to happen. Her doctor kept saying that medically there was no problem, and her husband kept reminding her she only had to relax, but she wanted something more definite than that. And then she had bumped into an old school friend who swore by Ula.

'I'm telling you, everything that woman told me has come true: from finally finding a man, to getting a new job. She even told me my mum would be in an accident. Luckily Mum's OK now, but honestly, Ula has the gift.'

That was all Erin had needed to hear. She had immediately rung Ula, and booked an appointment – which had been weeks ahead. And then she had persuaded Alison and Rebecca to come with her.

'I'll go, but please don't pin all your hopes on this one person. This lady is just some fortune-teller, not a fertility expert,' Rebecca had said.

'I know, I know,' Erin had said, trying to get her eldest sister off her back. She knew her sisters were dying for her to become a mother, but she also knew they worried about her putting so much pressure on herself and John to become pregnant.

'Getting pregnant will happen in time. Just enjoy being footloose and fancy free. Enjoy your time alone with John. Don't put all this pressure on him, too.'

Erin promised not to, but of course she had. John was the kindest man she knew, but at times she wondered if he was taking getting pregnant as seriously as she did. It was a bone of contention between them, but one she hoped the fortune-teller might shed some light on.

Half an hour after leaving her house, Erin was at the front door of the famous fortune-teller. Ula was younger and prettier than she had imagined. She lived in a small house, and Erin had seen two small children run up the stairs while the three sisters were being shown into the living room. Ula sat down and chatted to them all before beginning the readings.

'There are things I can tell just from looking at a person's aura. Others the cards will tell me,' Ula told the girls, as she offered them all a cup of coffee.

'Do you have green tea?' Erin asked. She had read that green tea was much healthier for you when you were trying to get pregnant. She hadn't had coffee, or proper tea, in weeks.

'I'm sorry, no,' Ula said, staring at her. Erin suddenly felt very self-conscious. She was sure Ula could read her mind, and could tell why she only wanted green tea. Erin pushed back her long dark hair, and asked for water instead.

Rebecca was the most sceptical of the three sisters, but had insisted on going first. Being the eldest she always wanted to go first. So while Erin and Alison waited in the living room, Rebecca was shown to a smaller room just off the kitchen.

'She's very young, isn't she?' said Erin, as she looked at the framed photos of Ula and her children. The room was piled high with books.

'I suppose it doesn't matter what age she is. She seems kind. It's whether she can honestly see into our futures that is important.'

Erin realized she was being too doubtful about Ula. She had been expecting an old, wise woman, not a young mum, to answer the door.

'Anyway, what are you going to ask about?' Erin asked her sister.

'Well, of course I would love to know things about baby Sophie's future! Will she get into any of the flipping schools? I mean, at two weeks old we had her down for every good school in South Dublin, but were still told we had left it very late to book her in! What are you supposed to do, book a baby into primary school the second it's conceived?'

Erin laughed. Alison had only just realized how organized other mums were, and that she and Sophie had to compete against them.

'And to be honest,' Alison went on. 'I'd love to see if Ula says anything about David's new job. If we knew this renewable energy company was going to work out, we could risk buying a bigger home. I can't stand living in our apartment any longer. It's not easy bringing up a baby in a two-bedroomed second-floor apartment. No matter how beautifully you decorated it for me, it is still too small. Poor little Sophie is already running out of places to crawl to.'

Erin knew how hard Alison and David had found living in the apartment since the birth of baby Sophie. Living there had never been a problem until a baby, and her cot, toys, bouncer, highchair, mounds of clothes and never-ending piles of washing, had arrived.

'Let's hope that Ula will tell you she can see Sophie running around a huge house, after a day of being in your preferred school!'

Before long Rebecca arrived back in the room.

'Oh my God, girls, she is amazing!'

'What?' both sisters said, stunned. Rebecca had been so cynical the whole way down in the car. Erin had reminded her she didn't have to go, but although Rebecca had been happy just to have a night away from her two children, Lucy and Peter, she'd also been strangely insistent she had to go to the fortune-teller, even if she didn't believe in psychics, cards or crystal balls.

'Yeah, she just knew everything! She knew all about that job interview I went for this week. She said she could see a blue aura around me, which means I was successful in the interview and that I've got the job! She even told me to look under Peter's little bed for something precious that I've lost. I misplaced my eternity ring two weeks ago, and have been avoiding telling Geoff. Luckily he is the most unobservant husband in the world, and hasn't looked at my hands in a long time. But if it is there, then I can rest easy. Peter is such a scamp, honestly how did I end up with the wildest boy in the world?'

'Because you were the wildest child yourself,' said Alison matter-of-factly.

Rebecca huffed, but was so delighted to be told her ring would turn up, and that she might be offered a new job, that she ignored Alison's dig.

'OK, so who wants to go in next?' asked Rebecca.

Erin pushed forward.

'Me! Oh God, she might have answers for me too,' she said excitedly.

Alison placed her arm around her younger sister.

'Don't expect so much. She isn't a doctor. You can't expect her to know when you will get pregnant. It's just a bit of fun.'

Erin agreed, but already she could feel her stomach flipping. She was nervous and excited at the same time.

Erin walked into the small dark room. Ula was sitting at an old oak table. In front of her was a pack of cards. Erin noticed that on the walls were unusual paintings.

Ula saw what she was looking at, and said: 'Back in Poland my father was a painter. He also had the gift of foresight. He didn't use it to make profit, but instead often painted what he saw would happen. In this one you can see a girl on a boat, she is travelling a long distance from her home. This little girl is me. He painted me this when I ten years old. I told him he was wrong, and that I would never leave home, but then six years ago I followed the man I loved to Ireland. And now I am far from where I began, yet I have my father's paintings to remind me of my loved ones and of my true home.'

Erin looked at the paintings, but it was Ula she was most fascinated by. She had the most piercing blue eyes. Erin felt Ula could see into her soul.

'Can you shuffle these cards, please?' Ula asked her, as she sat down on a large comfortable chair.

'I see a very loving person by your side.'

'Well, that's probably my husband John,' Erin replied, studying Ula.

'He has a very good heart,' Ula said. 'You are lucky to have someone like that.'

Erin agreed, but really she was here to hear about her own future as a mum.

'Many girls come to me asking about love. I look into their futures and I see many different men, but rarely do I see someone with such a clear, good heart. You must treasure him.'

'Oh I do, I do,' Erin said, as she looked down at the cards Ula had spread out on the table. Erin wondered which one, if any, represented new life.

'You are searching for something.'

Erin nodded.

'Your quest is important.'

Erin nodded again.

119

'Sometimes we are looking for things we don't have, but in the meanwhile don't look at all the good things we have already been blessed with.'

Erin started getting a little frustrated. She just wanted to hear about a baby, her baby, not about what things she already had.

'What is meant for you will come your way,' said Ula, gazing into Erin's eyes. 'Remember that.'

Erin said nothing. She didn't understand. Was Ula telling her a baby will come along or not? She had to find out.

'I want to have a baby. Will that happen for me? What do you see?'

Ula looked at Erin and then at the cards. She took a long time to answer.

'You will have a happy life, but soon, very soon, there will be a big change. A decision out of your hands will be made by someone, and that will determine your future, too. But you have the choice to control this situation. You need to let people know how you feel. You need to appreciate what you already have, before anything new can come into your life. And what is meant for you will then come your way.'

For the next fifteen minutes Ula talked about family, friends, work and travel, but she didn't seem to directly answer Erin's baby question. As Erin paid her and went to leave, Ula suddenly placed her hand on Erin's.

'Your wish will come true, but just don't let it hurt your heart.' Ula paused, and added, 'You need to care for what is important.'

Erin suddenly felt her heart race, Ula must see a child in her future! Once again Ula mentioned love and appreciation, but Erin wasn't listening. Ula hadn't come outright and said it, but from what she had implied she must have seen a baby in Erin's future – because that was all Erin wished for. And Erin realized she should care more, yes that was what she needed to do. Ula was right: she couldn't let herself fall behind on everything she had to do to get pregnant, she needed to watch her diet more, and exercise more. If she focused on getting her body into shape then it would only be a matter of time before she was ready. Erin thanked Ula for her advice, and then Alison went in to get her fortune read.

Forty minutes later the three sisters were all in a local restaurant discussing their night.

'I just can't believe how accurate she was,' exclaimed Rebecca, as she poured herself a large glass of white wine. 'I mean, to know about my job interview and the missing ring, she's unreal.'

'I know, sure, I still can't believe how much she knew about me,' said Alison who was enjoying a night off from the baby, and knocking back the wine.

121

'She knew exactly what kind of job David has. She told me to trust his instinct with the company, and go with buying a house. She even described the house to me! Although, when she said she saw two twin boys running around after Sophie I almost died. Imagine me with twins!'

'She said you would have twins?' Erin said, surprised.

'Yeah, she said she saw two blond-haired little boys running around. David will collapse when he hears. He is still in shock about being a father to Sophie. I can't imagine how busy we would be with another two.'

Erin was gutted. Ula had been spot-on with her two sisters. She had told them both exactly what they wanted to hear. Yes, she had told Erin her wish would come true, but she had seemed so obsessed with lecturing Erin on looking closely at what she already had that she hadn't really confirmed that Erin would be expecting soon.

'Why don't you have a glass of wine?' Alison said to Erin. 'Sure, you can leave your car here tonight. John will give you a lift to it in the morning.'

'Oh, no thanks,' Erin said, as she poured herself another glass of water. 'John has some club race tomorrow, and anyway I've got my double yoga class in the morning, so I need to be up and organized early.'

'Well, I can give you a lift tomorrow, then,' offered Alison.

'No, Ali, it's OK. I'm off drink, anyway. I've read article after article on the effect alcohol has on your fertility levels. And as I said, even Ula herself said I need to focus more. No, if I want to get pregnant I need to take this whole thing more seriously.'

Rebecca and Alison looked at their younger sister.

'Erin,' said Rebecca softly. 'You couldn't take trying to get pregnant any more seriously. It's all you talk about. Ula said to care about what is important. You know that could mean lots of things, from family and friends to work and, of course, John.'

'But those things are all fine,' Erin said to Rebecca. 'It's my inability to get pregnant that's the only problem in my life, so she must have meant I need to concentrate more on that.'

Rebecca said nothing. She knew how important becoming a mum was to her sister. It was easy for her to tell Erin not to worry when she herself already had two children, but still, she thought Erin was putting too much pressure on herself.

'Well, regardless of what Ula and those reports say, I think alcohol has no effect. Sure, wasn't Peter a honeymoon baby? And, trust me, I was pretty much drunk for our whole two weeks in the Caribbean! Poor old Peter was a result of an overload of Piña Coladas!'

Erin said nothing. It wasn't fair that both her sisters could get pregnant so easily and she couldn't. And she shuddered to think what effect all those cocktails must have had on Peter.

'Just don't lose focus on all the other great things in your life, Erin. You have a house that I'm insanely jealous of, and a career that most women would kill for,' said Alison, hugging her.

'I know, I know. It's just I want more,' Erin replied.

'You can't have it all,' said Rebecca philosophically.

Erin said nothing but just looked enviously at their glasses of wine. She resisted, though. Regardless of what they both thought, she was sure she needed to work harder at becoming a mum.

Later that night Erin couldn't sleep, partly because of the loud snores that erupted out of John's mouth every two seconds. He had obviously drunk way too much. She also couldn't sleep as she was waiting for her period. It was 3 a.m., and she was late. She knew it was only by a few hours, but technically it was Saturday now, and she was due, yet nothing had happened. Erin was always bang on time, so being a few hours late gave her a glimmer of hope. Technically she could indulge herself now, and go ahead and see if she was pregnant. Erin crept out of bed and headed for the bathroom. She opened the bathroom press, and found the old shoebox that she kept full of fertility and pregnancy tests. She pushed aside the ovulation ones, and searched for a pregnancy test. She hadn't realized her stock was so low. Finally she found a box, but it was empty. Erin couldn't believe it. It was the one time she could be pregnant, and she had no test. She sat in the bathroom wondering what to do. She resisted the urge to go to an all-night chemist and instead climbed back into bed and snuggled up to John.

All night thoughts raced through her head. Ula had said her wish would come true, but surely it couldn't happen so soon? Erin felt her head spin, she was so excited. Was she really pregnant? She thought back to sitting in Ciara Ryan's living room, with her notebook filled with ideas for the baby room. Only hours ago she had been jealous of Ciara, but now she felt different. Maybe in a few months she, too, would be painting her spare room yellow, erecting a crib, filling it with soft toys and waiting for the arrival of a baby. Erin finally fell asleep with thoughts of babies swimming around her head.

19

'Are you coming to my race?' asked John as he passed Erin a plate of French toast and bacon topped with maple syrup.

'Yum!' she said. She had been on a strict low-sugar diet for the past month, but since John had gotten up early to make her favourite breakfast she couldn't resist, and now, if she was pregnant, she wouldn't have to limit herself to the high-fertility diet, and could eat a wider range of food.

'So, are you coming?' asked John again, kissing Erin. She could taste the maple syrup on his lips.

'Oh no, I can't make it today,' she replied as she helped herself to more toast. 'You know I have my yoga class in Ranelagh at noon.'

'Well, come after,' he suggested.

'No, today it's a double class, and then I've got a

few errands to run. No, you go ahead and enjoy the race. Sure, I'll see you later.'

John looked very disappointed, but said nothing. Erin didn't notice, though; she was trying to eat as quickly as she could. She wanted to get to the chemist's before her class began. Erin had only started yoga the month before. She had read somewhere that it made people who were finding it hard to get pregnant more relaxed, and they conceived more easily. The minute she had discovered this she had signed up to the double classes that took place on a Saturday. Yes, it ate into her weekend time with John, but she had felt that since the most important thing to them both was a pregnancy, it was worth the sacrifice. If Erin was honest, up till now she hadn't been sure if yoga had been helping her relax, but now that there was a slight possibility that she might be pregnant she felt she owed it all to the classes. Her teacher, Pippa, had also told her that yoga was great to do when you were pregnant. Erin made a mental note to find out when the pregnancy yoga classes were on.

After a hasty goodbye to John she jumped into her car and headed to Ranelagh. She had briefly debated telling John about her pregnancy suspicion, but she didn't want to get his hopes up, and anyway he seemed preoccupied with his race. No, I'll tell him later when I know for sure, Erin thought, parking her car and walking to the nearest chemist.

As she passed the shops a maternity boutique caught her eye. Erin had often walked by it before, and admired the flattering outfits in the window and the stylish pregnant mums coming in and out of the shop. She hesitated outside the shop door. She was on such good form, and her hopes were so high, that on a complete whim she walked into the shop. Since it was a Saturday morning it was very full. Erin discreetly stared at all the bumps. Some were huge, others barely noticeable. She was fascinated, yet all the women seemed blasé about the miracles they were carrying. Most were just looking at the clothes or chatting to friends. When I've a bump I will be touching it all day long, I will be so proud to show it off, thought Erin. 'I know I won't be able to think about anything else,' she whispered to herself.

'Can I help you?' asked a middle-aged woman.

Erin got a fright, she hadn't planned on staying longer than two minutes in the shop, let alone talking to anyone.

'Oh no, I'm OK, but thank you,' she replied politely.

'You're at the early stages, I see,' smiled the woman. 'I know you are probably thinking you will never need clothes like these, but trust me once that little bump appears it will just grow and grow! Of course it's so exciting, but it's worth having some clothes on hand for the day you suddenly wake up and find your trousers are too tight!'

Erin was about to tell the shop assistant that she didn't even know if she was pregnant, when out of the corner of her eye she noticed a beautiful classic black and white dress.

'Oh, I see you've spotted our new collection. It's only just arrived. Would you like to try that dress on? It's been flying out the door. The amount of women who have bought it for weddings they are attending is unbelievable. I suppose it's a great shape, very classic, and it will last you right up until you have the baby. The waistband expands to accommodate any size baby!'

Erin looked at the dress. It was gorgeous. She could see herself in it.

'Is it for any special occasion?' asked the assistant.

Suddenly Erin remembered her friend Amy's wedding. This dress would be perfect for it.

'Well, I am going to a wedding, but it's not for a while! Sure I can come back closer to the time.'

'No need to,' said the woman as she started ushering Erin into the changing room. 'We have a wide range of prosthetic bumps that you can use when trying on the dress. You wear whatever one will be closest to the trimester you will be in then. It's very handy really, saves you having to run around shopping when you are larger and probably in no mood for shopping!'

Erin knew she should have walked out of the dressing room, out of the front door of the shop and at least done a pregnancy test before she tried on the dress, but she got caught up in the moment, the excitement. Before she knew it she was standing in front of the large mirror, with the dress and a fake bump on her. Erin looked at her reflection and felt amazing. This is it, she thought, this is what I want. She rubbed her hand over the large bump. It felt wonderful.

'Now, to be honest, that dress is a little too big on you. Unfortunately we don't have any smaller sizes in stock right now, but we should have some next week. If you leave me your name and number I can give you a call when the dress gets in,' the assistant said, while helping Erin out of the bump.

Erin would have gladly left the bump on her all day, but she could see there was a small queue of women all wanting to try it on. She smiled at them all. They were her fellow-friends now, fellow-mums-to-be. She knew she shouldn't really have left her name and number with the shop, but seeing the dress on her had made her feel so womanly, so excited, so happy, so pregnant.

It wasn't until Erin left the shop that she'd realized she was running late for her yoga class. She had intended to do the test before the class. I'll just have to do it at the break, she thought as she ran into the chemist and bought the top-of-the-range, most expensive digital pregnancy test she could find.

'OK, ladies, let's begin,' Pippa the yoga instructor said, just as Erin got into place and took off her jacket.

Pippa was as encouraging and calm as she always was, but Erin found it hard to concentrate. Just metres from where she stood was a little piece of plastic, a small test, that could tell her if in a few months' time she would be a mum.

The second the class stopped for a break, Erin grabbed her handbag and looked for the toilet. She had to go up a small narrow old staircase, and down a long dark corridor before she finally found it. She locked the door behind her. But as she went to take the test from her bag she noticed her surroundings. The room was small, cold and, to be honest, pretty dingy. Erin was a planner, and, along with having her wedding mapped out years before she even met John, had always had a clear idea what would happen on a day like today. Erin would go into their gorgeous new marble bathroom, she would watch as the test turned positive, and then she would fling open the door and start crying as John held her and screamed out loud with joy that they were about to become parents. Doing the test now, alone in a dingy old toilet, was not part of her plan. And so she put the test back into her bag, went back down the stairs and joined the class.

After another hour of stretching, Erin was finally free to race back home and do the test. She rang John on the way and asked him to meet her at home.

'We've only just got back into harbour now. I'm going to hang around here for a while, catch up with the lads, but I'll be home later to get changed for tonight.'

'Tonight?' Erin asked.

'I told you weeks ago! Its Rory's fortieth tonight. It's in the yacht club. You promised you would come.'

She had no idea what he was talking about, but just wanted him home.

'Just please come home soon, as quickly as you can. And then we can go to the party later.'

John wasn't pleased, but promised to be home within half an hour.

'By the way, we won our race,' he said.

Erin felt guilty for not asking, but she had more important things to worry about.

'Oh OK, great. We can celebrate that later,' she said, getting excited about seeing John and telling him what she thought would be the best news of his life.

★　　　★　　　★

Twenty-five minutes later Erin heard John's key in the front door. She quickly rushed to the bathroom, she couldn't wait another second.

'Erin? Where are you?' she heard him call.

'I'm in the bathroom. I'll just be two minutes,' she replied.

Erin quickly unwrapped the pregnancy test. She waited as it did its magic. She was almost shaking with excitement. She could hear John enter the bedroom, and hum to himself as he walked around the room. Erin smiled, he was always on such good form. Just then the small screen flashed. She held her breath. Suddenly two words flashed up. *Not pregnant*.

Erin looked at the screen again. *Not pregnant* flashed again. She dropped the test on to the ground, and burst out crying. She heard John bang on the door.

'Are you OK? What's wrong?'

Finally Erin came out. She held the pregnancy test in her hand. John didn't need any more of an explanation. He walked over and gave her a big hug.

'I'm sorry.'

Erin felt numb. She had been so sure.

'That useless fortune-teller,' she said, raising her voice.

'What?' said John, confused.

'That girl, Ula, she said my wish would come true. She said I would get pregnant.'

'You didn't pin all your hopes on some psychic, did you?'

She glared at her husband. How could he say that to her at a time like this?

'Thanks for being so supportive,' she said, as she turned her back on him, and went to fling the test in the bin.

'I'm sorry, but we don't need a fortune-teller to predict our future. I know we will get pregnant soon, and you will be the best mum ever. Don't worry, it will happen.'

Erin felt like flinging the test at his head.

'How can you say the same thing every month? My God, you are like a broken record,' she shouted.

John's whole mood changed.

'I love you, and I'm only trying to be positive.'

'Well, rather than trying to be positive, why don't you try not to drink, or smoke or eat takeaways. I saw that empty McDonald's bag in the bin the other day, you know.'

'Christ! Are you saying that a cheeseburger is the reason you are not pregnant? Give me a break.'

'Give you a break?' she shouted, dumbstruck.

'Yes,' he replied. 'Give me a break. I haven't smoked in three months. I only have a few pints at the weekend, and by the way that McDonald's was actually Rory's. He called in the other night when you were at the gym. Maybe if you spent less time preparing your body for the baby, and more time at home relaxing – or with me – we might get pregnant.'

Erin was enraged. John had never spoken to her like that before.

'You know I want for us to have a child just as much as you do,' John said, sounding tired.

'It doesn't seem like that to me,' she replied smartly.

'I'm sorry you see it that way,' he said, walking out of the bedroom.

Erin was just climbing into bed when John stopped and turned back to her.

'I've adored you from the second I met you. You've made me the happiest man alive. But recently all we seem to talk about is trying to get pregnant. You never ask me how my work is, how the sailing is going. You never wonder what my ideas on pregnancy are, never wonder how I feel. I live here too, you know. I want this baby just as much as you do. I know getting pregnant is the number one priority, but surely our marriage, friendship and lives are important, too?'

Erin didn't reply, she was too annoyed, upset and angry to say anything. She was fuming at John, at the pregnancy test, at the fortune-teller, at the flipping yoga classes, at people like Ciara Ryan who got pregnant so easily. She was annoyed at everyone.

Later, when John tried to persuade her to come to his friend Rory's birthday party, she refused. She couldn't believe John would expect her to go out, to socialize and mix with others after hearing she was once again not pregnant.

'Please just come and have one drink with me. I'm sorry for the way I talked to you earlier. I love you, just come out.'

Erin refused, and so John went alone.

And later that night, when her body confirmed what the test had already told her, Erin crawled back into her queen-sized bed, and pulled the large duvet over her head. She cried and cried until she eventually fell asleep. She was devastated. Today was another day she wanted to forget all about. Another day that had started with hope and excitement, only to end with a negative test and a broken heart.

20

'Have a nice day,' said the airport check-in assistant, as she handed Grace Miller back her passport.

Grace took one look at the friendly lady, and started crying.

'I hope you have a nice day, too,' Grace sniffled.

'What the hell is wrong with you? Why are you crying?' asked her husband, stunned, as he ushered Grace away from the American Airlines check-in desk. 'You hate all that "have-a-nice-day" stuff!'

'I know, but I think she really meant it, Ethan. And it might be the last time someone tells me to have a nice day.'

'I'm sure they'll tell you that in Ireland, too!'

'In Ireland? Are you mad, Ethan? You'd be lucky if a shop assistant handed you back your change, let alone wished you a good day.'

Ethan stopped walking, and stood in the middle

of departures at San Diego International Airport. He studied his wife.

'Grace, you're overreacting. You're Irish, you love Ireland. What's wrong with you?'

Grace suddenly felt guilty. Today was the day they were leaving their home in San Diego for Ireland. Ethan was very excited, and as usual super-organized, but while he had been arranging to hire an automatic car at Dublin Airport, Grace had been having last-minute doubts about her move back home. She knew she was ruining his good mood, but she was nervous. Suddenly Ethan put his arm around her. She melted into his large frame.

'You're just tired from all the packing and saying goodbye to our friends. And I know you already miss Coco, but in a few hours we will be with your mum, brothers and family, and you'll have forgotten all about America. Trust me. I know deep down you must be dying to get home and see them all.'

But Grace wasn't sure. Yes, after years of living thousands of miles from her family and friends, she did love the thought of being able to pop in to visit them whenever she wanted, but at the same time she had left Ireland and made a better life for herself. Herself and Ethan's lifestyle was far better than the one she had left behind. And the move, while at first an exciting venture, now felt like a step backwards.

'OK, I know what will make you feel better.

Let's forget a healthy meal, and go out with a bang, American style! Let's head for the all-you-can-eat buffet counter. It might be the last time you see one for quite a while!'

Grace smiled at her husband; he always wanted to look after her.

'OK,' she said. 'But let's swing by the duty free as well, I want to stock up on Hershey's chocolate, too. I'm going to miss it all.'

Ethan took his wife's hand.

'No, you won't. You'll have one pint of Guinness, or a full Irish breakfast, and I'll have lost you for ever. You'll be the real Irish girl I met all those years ago again!'

Grace didn't know about that, but she hoped he was right, because she didn't want to feel like a stranger in her own country, and as it stood now she was worried she might be.

Grace had never been so happy to have gotten off a flight. While Ethan had fallen asleep shortly after take-off, she hadn't been able to relax, and so, without any books packed, had had to watch the in-flight movies. Unfortunately there had been a problem with the movie selection and so she had been stuck with the kids' choice. And after watching *Finding Nemo* five times she was determined never to see it again as long as she lived. Yes, Nemo was extremely cute, but she didn't know how parents could watch the same movies with their kids over and over. It was torture.

As Ethan collected their matching luggage Grace checked her appearance in her little compact mirror. Her red hair was tied back, and her fair skin looked even paler than usual. She was dying to get into bed, and start sleeping off the jet lag which was sure to hit soon. Once Ethan had all their bags they walked through security and out to Dublin Airport arrivals.

'There she is. Oh my God, boys, there she is!'

Grace looked around, surprised to hear the familiar voice. It was her mother's. Suddenly Grace noticed a small group of people all waving to her. Right bang in the middle was Patsy, waving and crying.

'Oh my God!' said Grace to Ethan. Ethan began laughing.

As soon as Patsy saw her daughter she held up a big card that read: 'Welcome Home Grace and Ethan. We've missed you.'

Grace saw the other flight passengers stare at the luminous yellow sign. She ran over to her mother.

'Mum! I only saw you a few weeks ago. What do you mean you've missed us?'

'It's so good to finally have you home,' said her mother, clasping her tight. Grace was about to remind her that she wasn't home for good, it was only for a year, but as she hugged her mum, she saw her brothers

Colm and Aidan shaking hands with Ethan, and her two aunties smiling at their niece. She realized her mum had made a big effort to get everyone to come to greet her and Ethan.

'Sorry about the sign, Gracie,' said Colm, as he gave his big sister a hug.

'Yeah, Mum made us bring it. You would think you had just arrived in Ellis Island after weeks of travelling on some stinking boat, instead of getting to Dublin after a few hours on a plane! Anyway, how are you? Any gifts for us?' said Aidan cheekily.

Grace smiled at her two younger brothers, they hadn't changed one bit.

'Yes, I've gifts for you all. But they're packed in the suitcases somewhere. I'll give them to you over breakfast.'

It was a huge surprise for Grace to see her family at the airport, especially as she had arranged weeks before with Patsy that after collecting the rented car, herself and Ethan would stop into her mum's for a big fry-up. Ethan might be health-conscious, and Grace certainly didn't eat much fried food any more, but even she had her cravings. And so back in sunny San Diego she'd requested her mum's famous fry as a homecoming treat.

'We just couldn't wait until breakfast to see you, pet. Yes, it was hard to persuade these two lazy brothers of yours to get out of bed and meet us here.

If I could drive I would have collected them myself. Instead I had to just keep on ringing them.'

'Yeah, after the thirtieth phone call I knew it wasn't safe to stay in bed,' said Colm, who looked a little rough, and Grace suspected he hadn't even showered. But she didn't mind. All that worrying about Ireland seemed to fade away as she looked at her family, and realized how much she had missed them.

'Anyway, your Aunt Mary is driving, so we will meet you back in my house. I have Esther from next door keeping an eye on the oven while I'm here.'

Grace was surprised at how much effort her family had gone to for her arrival. She hadn't realized what a big thing it was for them all, especially her mum. Patsy had gotten everyone involved, even her poor neighbours. Grace was suddenly dying for her mum's food. She and Ethan said goodbye to everyone, and then headed to collect their rental car.

Grace and Ethan had a rocky start to their trip to Dublin city centre. Ethan insisted on driving.

'I need to get used to driving on the left, and there is no time like the present to learn,' an enthusiastic and ever-confident Ethan said as they piled into the fancy blue BMW that he had rented. Grace had barely buckled her seat belt when they almost crashed. Ethan had swung out of the rental company showroom and on to the wrong side of the road. A large truck had

142

to swerve to avoid them, and the driver bellowed his horn, almost making Ethan crash again. Twice more Ethan swung on to the wrong side, before finally allowing Grace to drive the rest of the way to her mum's.

Grace felt like a tourist and a stranger pulling up outside her mum's small red-brick house. The fancy rental car stuck out a mile on the small road. Patsy didn't even drive, and a lot of the residents didn't. Being so close to the city meant they didn't need to, and some couldn't afford a car, either. Grace met two of the neighbours on the way in. They had heard about her arrival home, and been told by Patsy all about her great life in America.

'And is it true you've a swimming pool?' asked one.

Grace nodded.

'Good work! It's far from that you were raised. And what a lovely car! Fair play to you,' they said, all the while taking in handsome Ethan.

Grace had enjoyed driving the comfortable car, but now she hurried in to the house. She suddenly felt awkward. She didn't want people thinking she was showing off.

The minute she walked in the door of No. 32 St Joseph's Road, with its porch bursting with plant pots, and its hall full of family photos, she felt like she was a child again. She was home. It was tiny compared to the house she had left in San Diego, but it felt so cosy and warm.

'You made it! We were getting worried,' said Patsy, as she stood in the kitchen with every pot, pan and baking tray full of food. She had on her old red apron. Grace laughed as she looked at it. Some things never changed! Grace had given her mum that apron when she'd been a teenager, and it was very worn and torn, yet Patsy refused to wear any new one she was bought.

'Mum, that old thing has seen better days!' said Grace, as she gave Patsy another hug, all the while taking in the smell of cooked rashers, sausages, eggs and black pudding.

'You bought me this with your own hard-earned cash. I'll never forget the summer you slaved away in that horrible hot shoe shop. But I was so proud of you, earning enough money to help pay for insurance on your dad's car, and buying us some gifts, too. Your dad always wore those lovely cufflinks. I still have them in a drawer upstairs.'

Grace was surprised her mum had remembered the gifts, and that she had kept them. It made her realize how different she and her mum were. Grace had become very cut-throat about keeping old things. In America people didn't hoard stuff like they did in

Ireland. Sure, on Christmas night you could often see Christmas trees being put out for the trash. It was awful, but Grace had gotten used to it. But as she watched her mum fix her apron, she felt a little guilty. She realized that sometimes it wasn't about the age of an item, but the thought behind it.

She also felt uncomfortable because she had worked so hard that summer to get insurance on her dad's car simply so she could get out of the house. She'd wanted some freedom. Patsy had never been able to drive, but she didn't seem to mind. 'Sure, everywhere I need and want to go is nearby!' she often said. But Grace had always had the urge to move, go away, travel. She had adored her home, and had always known she was lucky to have such loving parents, but it hadn't stopped her wanting to be able to get into her dad's old Nissan and go to other parts of the city, to see how others lived. To go visit friends, and just get out of St Joseph's Road. And Grace had felt that urge to be somewhere else until she'd met Ethan and fallen in love with him and sunny San Diego.

'Anyway, Ethan, sit down, get yourself comfortable. It's been a long time since you ate in this house,' said Patsy, pointing at her son-in-law.

Ethan squashed in between Colm and Aidan, and began helping himself to toast.

Grace got the milk from the fridge, and took her favourite old mug from the cupboard. She had been looking forward to a cup of Barry's Irish tea for weeks! Soon Grace, Ethan, Colm, Aidan, Patsy and Grace's two aunts – Mary and Joan – were all sitting around the table helping themselves to fried sausages, rashers, potatoes, tomatoes, black pudding and heaps of toast. Grace noticed Ethan limiting his intake of the meat. He had never quite got used to the amount of oil used in an Irish fry. She knew it was unhealthy, too, but she still dug in.

Hours later, after handing out gifts to the whole family, Grace and Ethan had to go to bed. They were wrecked from the move and long flight. For the next few weeks Ethan's company was going to put them up in a hotel until they could find a nice house to rent. But tonight Patsy had insisted they stay with her, and sleep in Grace's old room. Ethan knew not to go against the wishes of his kind mother-in-law, but Grace sensed he would have liked more space. She had to stand on the bed while Ethan got changed, there was so little room to move. She laughed watching him try to balance his wash bag on top of the big pile of Care Bears that Grace used to collect. She had told her mum to give them away to charity years ago, but Patsy had wanted to keep them for her grandchildren. 'You can't get good quality toys like that any more.'

Ethan fell into a deep sleep the minute his head

hit the pillow, but it took Grace hours to relax. It felt weird to be sleeping in her old room with her husband. As she looked around her room, and took in all the old memories, she felt like she had two different lives. The old Grace, who with her red hair and pale skin and love for her mother's cooking was as Irish as you could get – and the new one, who looked at Ethan and thought of the exciting life they had together. It was completely different from anything she had experienced here in Ireland. Grace wondered how these two very different parts would mix, now that she would be living back at home. She walked over to her chest of drawers and grabbed her old Good Luck Care Bear. She took him into the small bed and hugged him. She could do with some sleep, and some of his comfort and luck.

21

'This house might well be the one for you both,' said the young real-estate agent to Grace and Ethan Miller. 'It's close enough to the city for work, yet right in the heart of the best Southside bars, restaurants, parks and shops. And this group of houses have a twenty-four-hour monitored security gate.'

The girl kept chatting as she showed Grace and Ethan around the empty four-bedroomed house in Donnybrook, South Dublin. They had only been in Dublin for a week, yet had already seen four houses, two penthouse apartments and one lovely, yet very small, townhouse. And they still couldn't decide where to live. Ethan had hit the ground running in his new firm, and had spent all week interviewing for new computer analysts, design engineers and programmers. Grace was still very tired from the journey, yet had also been busy, trying to search for a house for their year's stay, and at the same time catch up with her family. Her mum rang her about twenty times a day.

'Mum, I've been home lots of times before. It's not that unusual to see me in Dublin. You don't need to keep ringing me to see if I'm OK,' Grace had protested, the night before.

'But it's different this time. Before you've only been home for flying visits that have passed too quickly, but now I have you all to myself. I've missed you so much. Those brothers of yours are grand, but they don't care about the neighbourhood gossip, or your aunt's new hairdo. I've no one to talk to about the little things.'

Grace didn't care too much about the little things either, she had more important concerns, like finding a new home and job, and making sure Coco was doing OK without them, but she promised her mother she would call in the next day, after viewing the house in Donnybrook.

'But why would you live there?' Patsy had asked, surprised. 'Sure, that's nowhere near me or the boys. Does Ethan not want to live beside us?'

Grace had to handle the situation delicately. She didn't want to upset her mum, but she was reluctant to admit that both herself and Ethan wanted to live it up while in Dublin, and since their home in San Diego was being rented out, and Ethan's new firm were paying his rent here, they could afford to splash out on somewhere fancy. And unfortunately that did rule out living in a very small house in St Joseph's Road.

'Anyway, I wanted to ask, could Ethan lend you the car tomorrow? I haven't been up to your father's grave in weeks, and I thought we could both visit him. I'm sure you've been meaning to go.'

Patsy left Grace stuck for words. She felt awful admitting she hadn't been up to visit the grave yet. She had no excuse. She had adored her dad. Being the only girl of the family she had always been his pet, but the last week had flown by and she just hadn't given a thought to visiting St Augustine's Cemetery. But the next afternoon, after dropping Ethan back to his new office, which was on Mount Street, she picked up her mum.

Grace laughed when she arrived in St Joseph's Road. Her mum was outside the house chatting to her two neighbours. Patsy could chat for Ireland. As Grace pulled up outside the house she saw children running around the small front garden of her house.

'Get out of the car!' said Patsy excitedly. 'Come and meet some of the children I was telling you all about. Now this is Tara, Jade, Michael. Say hello, children, this is my daughter, Grace.'

'Are you the one with the swimming pool and the

dog who has his toenails painted?' asked the young boy, staring at Grace's big car.

'Do you know Paris Hilton?' asked the elder girl.

Grace answered the questions while Patsy picked up the youngest child, who was wrapped up warm in big pink earmuffs.

'This is Jade. She's only one, but would you look at her, Grace. Isn't she like a young Shirley Temple? Honestly, she's so cute.'

Grace agreed with her mum that the little curly-haired child was very cute, but tried to remind Patsy that it was getting dark, and that if they didn't go soon they wouldn't make it to the cemetery on time.

'OK, sure, you'll be meeting the kids a lot more now that you're home. I mind them every second afternoon, and the odd morning. Sure, you can give me a hand. If little Jade doesn't make you want to have kids, no one will.'

As Patsy's neighbours were there Grace held her tongue. She would have to tell her mum to stop putting pressure on her to have children. Being a mum was just not something she had ever craved after. Although she did feel slightly guilty at depriving Patsy of being a grandmother, Grace had to do what she felt was best for her and Ethan.

Finally Grace managed to say goodbye to Patsy's neighbours, but not before they made Grace promise to call in for a cup of tea soon.

'Patsy never stops talking about the great life you have made for yourself in America. Honestly, she has us all jealous, with the tales of your great job, husband, house and lifestyle. We'll have to get you to talk to our children. Encourage them to be as successful as you!'

Patsy was smiling, and looked as proud as Punch as the neighbours admitted their jealousy of Grace's fortune. Grace glanced at her mum, realizing again that Patsy only meant it for the best. She was always proud of Grace, Aidan and Colm. For Patsy her children were her life. Which is why it was probably hard for her to understand why Grace wasn't interested in having kids herself.

'Are you OK?' said Patsy as they walked to the car. 'You look so pale and washed-out.'

'I'm fine, Mum. Just still a bit jet-lagged, and it's tiring trying to find somewhere to live. It's hard to find somewhere half as nice as our house back in America.'

Patsy didn't say anything, just stared at Grace's pale complexion and the dark circles under her eyes. But once in the car Patsy forgot about Grace and started a running commentary on all of St Joseph's Road. She seemed determined to bring Grace up to speed on everyone in the neighbourhood.

'Slow down, Grace. Have a look left. What do

you think of that awful extension Mrs Maguire has on the house? Honestly, it's an eyesore. But then I suppose she had to, what with those two lazy lumps of children still living at home and sponging off her.'

'Jonathan Maguire still lives at home?' Grace said, surprised. Jonathan had been one of her first boy-friends.

'Oh yes, you had a lucky escape there. He's trouble. Poor Mrs Maguire has been driven demented by his bad debts and string of jobs. Anyway, if you look left now, you can see Suzi Murphy's new man. He's a good bit older, isn't he? She's after his money, no doubt!'

Patsy made Grace drive all around their neigh-bourhood so she could see how well the area was coming on, and catch up on all the gossip.

'That's the new playground and primary school. It's got some great facilities.'

Grace didn't comment on the school, or the throngs of children and their parents entering the park. Finally they got to the cemetery. As Grace put on her long winter parka jacket, Patsy fixed her hair, put on her Sunday best gloves and hat and headed for her beloved Teddy's grave. Grace still couldn't believe it had been five years since her dad had died. Five years since she had talked to him. He had been a quiet man; well, as everyone said, he had had no option but to be quiet, what with a complete chatterbox like

153

Patsy as a wife. But even in his quietness he had been a great person to talk to. He had believed in family and hard work, and his life had been about making sure his family were close, cared for and well. It was while worrying about his wife and children that he had ignored his own ill-health, and the signs of his heart problem. Grace placed a new bunch of flowers on the grave, as her mother silently said a prayer and touched the stone. Patsy was very quiet. Grace knew that even with all of her friends to call on, neighbours to gossip with, local children to mind, and Grace's arrival, it still was her husband Patsy missed and loved the most. Grace put her arm around her mum. The two women stood arm in arm until the chill got to them.

'Why don't you come home for dinner? I have some lovely steaks. You look like you could do with some iron. Ethan can come, too,' said Patsy as they got back into the car.

Grace rang Ethan, but he said he needed to work late, and would just get food back in the hotel. He was enjoying living in the hotel, with its room service, gym and bar. Grace decided she would eat with her mum, and maybe even stay the night at home.

Once in the house, Patsy lit the fire, and Grace was surprised to see her old slippers in the hall. 'I washed them for you. There's nothing like a pair of warm slippers to come home to after a few hours in the cold.'

Grace smiled. Her mum didn't need fancy things to enjoy herself, it was simple pleasures that made her happy.

After a lovely home-cooked meal, they sat down to watch TV. Patsy never missed her soap operas. As the wind howled outside the window, Grace thought back to two weeks ago, when she and Ethan had thrown their going-away party. She had filled the house with candles, flowers and very expensive champagne. They had gotten caterers to serve some wonderful food, and it had been a great party. At the end of the night everyone had ended up down on the beach, slugging wine and promising to stay in touch.

Now, as Grace sat watching the TV, wrapped up warm in a big woollen jumper, with her slippers on and a big mug of tea in her hand, she felt like the party had been a dream. San Diego was only a plane ride away, yet she felt like she had left it years ago. She also really missed Coco. She couldn't wait until he was in Ireland. Grace felt tired, sad and a bit homesick for California, so she decided to go to bed. She stood up, but suddenly felt very faint. She immediately sat back down.

'Grace, pet. Are you OK?' asked a shocked Patsy.

Grace said nothing, she felt awful.

'What's wrong? Let me get you a glass of water. No, forget that, you're as white as a ghost, I'll get you a glass of whiskey. You've been looking awful all day. I should have made you go to the doctor earlier. I'll never forgive myself.'

'Mum, calm down,' said Grace, who was starting to feel a little better. 'I'm fine. I told you earlier, I'm just tired from the move. And I'm so hot. You've the flipping fire and heating on! The place is like a furnace.'

Grace removed the warm jumper she'd had on her all day. Herself and Ethan had both been wrapping up warm all week, they just couldn't adjust to the freezing cold Irish weather.

'God!' said Patsy, looking at Grace, who was now sitting in her T-shirt.

'What?' said Grace, looking at her T-shirt, too, embarrassed that it might be dirty or sweaty.

'Well it's just you've always had a great figure, Grace, but unfortunately like myself you're not very ample-chested. But my God, it's grown! That T-shirt is too tight! No wonder you're all hot and bothered. Do you want me to get you one of your brothers' old T-shirts? I've lots upstairs.'

'Go away, Mum,' said Grace, pulling her jumper back on. 'God, I faint and all you comment on is my breasts. I think I might go back to the hotel instead. I'm sure my husband will look after me there. Thanks for being so mean,' Grace shouted, as she flung off her old pink slippers and went to put her shoes on.

Suddenly Patsy went very quiet and pale. She almost started to shake. Grace immediately felt guilty for shouting at her.

'Oh, Mum. I'm sorry. Don't get upset. I'm just so tired, and emotional about the move and all, and embarrassed now for wearing this stupid T-shirt. Listen, let's forget my big chest, and go back to watching the TV. I'll get you a glass of whiskey, you look like you could do with one. I'm sorry for almost collapsing on your floor! But don't be upset, I'm fine.'

As Grace walked to the sideboard and poured her mum a small glass of Irish whiskey, Patsy kept gazing at Grace, but then she began to smile.

'How could I not have seen it before? You've looked different all week, but I was so caught up in your move home, and seeing Ethan, that I just didn't put two and two together.'

'What are you talking about?' asked Grace.

'You're tired, pale, washed-out, your chest is huge. But more importantly, you just look different from when I last saw you. It can only mean one thing.'

Grace frowned at her mum, she didn't know what she was on about. Patsy was behaving like a lunatic.

'You must be pregnant!'

Grace dropped the tumbler of whiskey all over the

cream carpet. The golden liquid seeped into the thick carpet. Neither moved to clean it up, they had more important things to worry about.

'What the hell are you talking about?' said Grace, who was starting to feel light-headed again.

Patsy pulled Grace on to the couch beside her.

'Were you keeping it a surprise? Is that it?'

Grace said nothing.

'It's just such amazing news! I should have guessed, though. And there was me at your father's grave today praying for you all to be happy, healthy and safe, but mainly praying that He would send us a little grandchild. God, He answered that prayer quickly!'

'Mum, stop right there. I'm not pregnant, OK?'

Patsy said nothing.

'Just because I'm tired, or I've maybe put on a little weight, doesn't mean I'm pregnant. God, you're so obsessed with me having children.'

'Whether I'm looking forward to you having kids or not is irrelevant. I think you're pregnant, pet. You should be happy! OK, I really need a glass of whiskey now to celebrate. I would offer you one, but I suppose alcohol is off the menu for you!'

Grace groaned. Her mum wasn't listening. Grace didn't want to go into every detail with her, but decided to tell her that she was on the pill, and had been for years.

'Oh,' said Patsy as she poured herself a large glass of

whiskey. 'But the pill isn't 100 per cent guaranteed to work. Sure, loads of people get pregnant on it. Didn't Martha across the road get pregnant after forgetting to take it for a few days?'

'Well, I never forget to take it. So end of discussion. I'm not pregnant, just tired. And I'd ask you not to talk about this again. It's hard enough to be going through all this change this week without you harping on about kids, pregnancy and wanting to become a granny.'

Patsy looked unhappy, but decided to bite her lip.

'Thank you,' said Grace, as she picked up her things and headed for bed.

An hour later, as Grace lay staring at the ceiling with the thought of being pregnant playing in her head, she heard her mum at the door.

'Are you warm enough, pet? I could get you an extra blanket? And what about some more pillows?'

'I'm fine, Mum, thanks,' replied Grace curtly.

'OK. Well sleep tight. I love you.'

'Thanks, Mum,' Grace said, softer this time.

'And don't forget it's better for the baby if you sleep lying on your left side. Now good night and sleep well!'

And with that Patsy almost skipped out of the bedroom with joy. Grace went to protest and remind her once again that she wasn't pregnant, but Patsy was long gone.

Grace was fuming. She knew she urgently needed to curb her mum's fantasy about her being pregnant. If she didn't do this it was certain Patsy would tell all the neighbours and be buying baby clothes by tomorrow afternoon. No, tomorrow morning she had to explain again to her mum how she was on the pill and took it every day.

Grace was just nodding off when she sat up with a fright. The sushi. The flipping sashimi!

It had been well over a month since her bout of food poisoning from her sushi bar dinner with her mum, but Grace suddenly had a bad feeling. She had continued to take her pill that week, but it had never occurred to her that she must have thrown it up when spending all those hours sitting beside the toilet bowl. Oh Christ, she thought, maybe her mother wasn't insane and imagining things.

Mum could be right, I could be pregnant, she thought, as she felt her world turn upside down.

22

'Congratulations. You're pregnant,' said Dr Collins.

Grace almost collapsed. She went white, and started shaking. The doctor passed her a small plastic cup of water. Grace sipped the cool liquid.

'Are you sure?' she finally mumbled.

The doctor looked at Grace and nodded. 'The blood test came back positive. And I'm positive, too. You're pregnant.'

'But how is this possible? I took the pill every day, and I still got my period this month. The blood test must be wrong.'

'I know it's a shock, but from what you've told me about that bout of food poisoning, I would imagine it caused the pill not to work effectively. And the bleeding was just a little breakthrough bleeding, it wasn't a proper period.'

'You don't understand,' Grace started to explain. 'This was an accident.'

'Most babies are,' interrupted the doctor, with a smile on her face.

Grace didn't know what to say. There was complete silence.

'Listen, I know this is a shock, but it's good news. I had two patients in with me this morning heartbroken because they just can't get pregnant. You're fortunate: you're over thirty and got pregnant without even meaning to. Consider yourself lucky.'

Grace didn't feel lucky at all. Herself and Ethan didn't want kids right now, or maybe ever. God, she cursed her own stupidity for not taking more caution after being sick. Of course the pregnancy explained her tiredness and even paler than normal skin, but to hear she was over two months' pregnant was a complete shock.

'OK, I'm going to give you a list of gynaecologists' names; you need to book in with one urgently. I'll also give you some leaflets on healthy eating, and foods to avoid while pregnant. There are some great websites nowadays that will answer any questions you have, and trust me, once the news sinks in, you will have lots! But don't worry, you will be fine,' said Dr Collins, as she handed a shell-shocked Grace the leaflets and lists.

'I'll see you again in a few weeks. Keep well, and

remember this is great news. I'm sure your husband and family will be delighted when they hear.'

Oh God, thought Grace, how was she going to tell Ethan? She left the doctor's surgery in a daze.

She didn't know where she was headed, but she just started walking. Before long she found herself going down O'Connell Street. As she passed shop windows she looked at her reflection. Could people guess? Would people know she was pregnant? She felt so different, but looked the same.

As throngs of people passed her by, she watched a little girl and her mother cross the busy road. Grace remembered what a treat it had been when her own mum used to bring her into town for the day. Up at the crack of dawn, they would start off with a big breakfast in Bewley's, followed by hours of clothes shopping, with a pit stop for an iced bun in Anne's Hot Bread Shop. They would then head home exhausted, and laden down with bags. Colm and Aidan had hated being dragged into the city centre, and only went when they had to get new school uniforms or shoes. But Grace had loved the buzz of the shops, and the treat of eating out. But as she watched the little girl clasp her hand tightly around her mother's she realized that really she had loved just spending time alone with her mum. God, Mum is going to burst with excitement when I tell her the news, Grace thought, as she walked through Temple Bar and headed for Starbucks.

Before long she had found a nice quiet table to sit, enjoy a coffee and let the pregnancy news seep in. She ignored her mobile phone as it rang. It was Patsy again. For the last two days she had been ringing Grace non-stop to find out how she felt. Grace thought she had finally convinced her last night that she was not pregnant, and that Patsy was not about to become a granny. But now, as she read the blood test result again, she knew she would have to tell her mother soon, but she couldn't face it now. Patsy's excitement would be too much for her to handle. Normally when people told their family that they were expecting they were so excited and bursting with the news. They weren't supposed to feel appalled, and dread telling their husbands.

Being pregnant was not something Grace had planned, so she couldn't rustle up the joy most mums-to-be would have felt. Grace ran her hand over her belly. Never had she imagined that there would be a little person living and growing inside her. I'm a bad mother already, she thought. I never even knew my child was alive. I never felt it, or dreamt about it; I don't feel anything.

Grace sat alone in the busy coffee shop for an hour, watching the rain hit the window pane. I would do anything to be back in San Diego, she thought – no rain, no problems, no baby. Suddenly Grace looked at her watch; she hadn't noticed the time, she was late. She was meeting Ethan and the estate agent at some fancy apartment down on the quays. Grace quickly hurried out of the coffee shop and hailed a taxi.

'OK, so there is only one bedroom, but it's enormous, and it's got a huge amount of storage. And sure there are only the two of you, so one bedroom is plenty!'

Grace gazed at the young estate agent. Little did she know there were now three of them viewing the penthouse.

'Wow, this place is amazing,' gasped Ethan. As they were shown the super-luxurious living room with its underfloor heating, and a balcony that had a bespoke audio-visual system, Grace felt her stomach flip. She needed to tell him soon.

'This penthouse comes furnished, and as you can see the owner has very expensive taste! It also boasts its own private lift, and access to the complex gym.'

This was music to Ethan's super-healthy ears. 'There's a gym in this place?'

'Yes, for residents only. This complex is very ex- clusive, as you can tell by the rental cost, but it is high-spec and at the cutting edge in design.'

The place had everything Ethan could dream of. He knew he could live very happily here for a year.

'Now, let me show you the bedroom. No shoes

allowed in here, though. The all-cream room has a very expensive carpet.'

'OK, that's it,' said Grace to Ethan.

'What?' he asked as he bent down to take off his loafers.

'This place isn't suitable. It's not for us,' Grace replied.

'What are you talking about, Gracie? It's beautiful! Look at the views, and the furniture.'

'It only has one bedroom. And that bedroom is totally unlivable in, it's all cream. God, who can keep such a place so pristine?' Grace asked.

Ethan looked at his wife, embarrassed that she was talking down the penthouse in front of the eager estate agent.

'Our house back home is pristine. And we never even use the other bedrooms.'

'Well, that was different,' Grace said. 'Things are different.'

Ethan turned to the estate agent. 'Could you give us a few minutes, please?' he asked her.

The girl nodded and walked into the living room. Grace opened the balcony door, she needed fresh air. Ethan followed her outside.

'We can't live here,' she said with her back to him. Her long red hair was blowing in the wind. Grace pushed it back, but it just kept flapping across her eyes.

Ethan lent forward and brushed her hair back. 'Are you OK?' he asked, as she touched his hand.

Grace felt so sick. He was her husband, it was his baby just as much as it was hers. Yet, as she tried to get up the courage to tell him about it, she felt like she was the one responsible for the unplanned pregnancy, that it was her fault. Finally she spoke.

'I'm pregnant.'

Ethan let go of her hand.

Grace watched him. He was looking at her as if she had just spoken Japanese. He didn't seem to understand what she was saying.

'What did you say?' he said, perplexed.

'I'm pregnant.'

Ethan looked at her tummy, then drew his blue eyes upwards to look at her face.

'I don't understand,' he said, running his hands through his blond hair. 'I thought you were on the pill.'

'I was,' she replied. 'I still am!' she laughed.

He didn't laugh with her.

'I still don't understand how all this has happened, myself. But either way it's true. I'm due in seven months.'

Apart from the wind blowing and the rattling of the wooden balcony furniture there wasn't a sound.

Ethan was not one to be stuck for words, but as Grace looked at her husband she could see he didn't know what to say. Grace turned away, she was frightened of what he would tell her. She peered over the edge of the iron rail. As she looked down, all around she could see the city light up. From Ringsend to the docks she watched the city she had grown up in come alive. Watching it all from this height would usually have made her feel on top of the world, but she was numb. The sounds of the city were drowned out by the loud beat of her heart. She waited for Ethan to speak, but he didn't. The estate agent broke the silence.

'I'm sorry,' she said as she walked out on to the balcony, 'but I need to get back to the office. If you would like more time to look around I could show it to you again tomorrow. Maybe sometime in the morning?'

As the girl went to open her diary and check her schedule Grace leant into Ethan. She could smell his Hugo Boss aftershave. She could see the small blond hairs on his neck standing up on end.

'I know this is a huge shock,' she whispered. 'We can talk properly when we get back to our hotel, but for now just tell her we're not interested. I know you like the apartment, but we have different needs now, and a bedroom for the baby is one! And all these expensive cream carpets would be destroyed by a baby. No, please just tell her it's not for us.'

Grace couldn't believe she was already talking

about nurseries and baby mess, but Ethan had to understand this place was a bachelor pad, not a family home. Ethan took a deep breath, turned to the eager estate agent and explained that it wasn't what they needed.

'It might be what we want, but unfortunately it's not what we need now,' he said in a voice that didn't even sound like his.

His words confirmed how Grace knew he would feel: shocked, upset and a little put out. The lift ride down to the car park was a nightmare. The agent seemed oblivious to the fact that both Ethan and Grace were a whole lot paler coming down than they had been going up. As she rattled on about property prices, availability and rent flexibility Grace zoned out and just watched Ethan. He was politely nodding, but she could see sweat rolling down the back of his neck.

Finally they got out of the lift and walked alone to their car. Grace sat in the front, and waited until she saw the estate agent drive off. She then turned to Ethan, who with a heavy sigh switched the car engine on. Grace reached across the car and hugged him.

'It will be OK. And don't worry, we'll find an even nicer place to live,' she said, trying to lighten the mood.

'I just never saw kids in our future,' he finally

said. 'I know nothing is ever set in stone, but, well, I thought we both wanted other things from life? Babies, diapers and saving for college fees wasn't something I was planning for.'

'Same here,' Grace admitted.

'I like our life. I don't want it all to change,' Ethan replied quietly.

'Me neither,' said Grace, although she already knew their life was drastically changing – and she'd only found out she was pregnant three hours before.

'This feels unreal,' he said.

'I know,' she agreed. 'I couldn't even admit to you over the last few days that I thought I might be pregnant. I didn't want it to be true, and I thought saying it out loud might make it so. I feel my body has betrayed me: it got pregnant without my consent.'

Ethan smiled. Grace hadn't meant it to be funny.

'I just can't believe I've been walking around, travelling, drinking, eating God knows what, and all this time I was pregnant. I just can't get my head around it,' admitted Grace.

'Well, I suppose it does explain why you've been so tired and emotional,' said Ethan. 'I mean, when you began crying the last time you used TiVo I should have guessed something was up. It wasn't America you were sad to say goodbye to, it was the baby inside that was making you an emotional wreck.'

Grace felt a little put out at being called a wreck,

but was so glad Ethan was talking, and making light of their unexpected news.

'I'm sorry. If I hadn't eaten that flipping sushi, I would never have got us into this mess.'

'It's not a mess,' he said. 'Most people can't wait to get pregnant. It's just I didn't really see us as parents. Not now, anyway.'

'I know,' agreed Grace.

As Ethan began asking her questions about how she felt, how the baby was, and when the next doctor's appointment would be, Grace knew he was trying to be as interested as he could, but she could see in his eyes he was upset. It was a huge shock for him.

'What time is it?' he asked, after they'd been sitting in the car outside their hotel for over an hour.

'It's almost 7 p.m.,' replied Grace.

'I'm supposed to be taking some new clients for dinner in a place called Chapter One tonight. I'll have to cancel, or ask someone else to take them,' Ethan said as he went to get his new Irish mobile phone.

'No,' Grace said, putting her hand on his arm. 'We've talked about this enough today. And I'm sure you could do with a drink. You go out.'

'Are you sure?' he asked, surprised. 'Do you feel well enough to be on your own?'

'I've survived ten weeks of pregnancy without even knowing it, I'm sure I'll be fine for a few more hours! And to be honest I need to call into mum before she explodes with curiosity. She'll die when she hears the news.'

Ethan leant across the car and kissed Grace. 'I'm sorry for not being more excited myself. It's just a lot to take in. It's going to change everything.'

The last few weeks he had been so enthusiastic about his new job, new surroundings, all the new people. His big blue eyes had been sparkling, but as Grace looked into them now they just seemed lifeless and sad.

'I know,' she said, worried about what lay ahead of them.

'OK. I had better go,' Ethan said, giving her a hug before getting out of the car.

As he walked away Grace jumped into the driver's seat and turned the engine on. Suddenly Ethan knocked at the window. She rolled the glass down. Ethan stretched his hand through the window and placed it on Grace's stomach.

'Our child,' he said seriously.

He wasn't happy or sad, just pragmatic. He then turned around and headed off into town, leaving Grace sitting there.

This is going to take us some time to get used to, thought Grace, as she started the car and headed to St Joseph's Road.

★　　★　　★

'I'm pregnant, Mum. You're finally going to become a granny.'

That was all Patsy Slattery needed to hear. After almost squeezing Grace to death, she pushed her aside, and began to run across the road.

'Dolores!' she shouted as she ran up her neighbour's path. 'I was right. Grace is pregnant! My prayers have been answered!'

Grace stood horrified as her mum literally called door to door on their road telling all the neighbours and friends. Grace tried to stop her, or at least slow her down, but nothing could come between Patsy and the news she had been dying to hear and tell people for years.

It's going to be a long pregnancy, thought Grace as she went back into her home and got herself a cup of tea. Whether she liked it or not she was pregnant, and now the whole world was beginning to find out, too. Grace's stomach was flipping, she was so nervous of what lay ahead. But as Patsy finally came back into the house and began ringing relatives, Grace knew no matter how she or Ethan felt, there was at least one person who was over the moon at the news. Granny Slattery was a very happy woman.

23

'Would you like a drink?' asked the young waiter.

Beth Prendergast studied the drinks list. She would have loved an extra-large glass of white wine, but unfortunately alcohol was off the menu for her.

'Just a glass of sparkling water, please,' she replied.

She sat at the best table in Peploe's, waiting for Tom to arrive. It was Friday night, and after avoiding him all week, Beth had finally suggested they spend time together, and proposed a night in so they could catch up and talk. But he had insisted on a meal out in one of his favourite haunts. It wasn't the ideal venue, and Beth had been debating all day whether tonight would be the right time to tell Tom that she was pregnant. She was so nervous about it. She had no idea how he would react, but even though she had been avoiding this conversation she knew she had to tell him. She was seven weeks pregnant, and he had to know the truth. It was going to be a huge shock for him, but she hoped that, like herself, once the news sunk in he might start to get a little excited about it all.

Suddenly Tom walked into the restaurant. Beth saw women stare in his direction. His looks and confidence were for ever attracting the opposite sex. As she watched him stop to chat to a well-known businessman Beth said a silent prayer that tonight would go OK.

She smoothed back her blonde hair and took a sip of the cold refreshing water. Tom made his way to the table and gave her a quick peck on the cheek. The smell of his aftershave suddenly seemed too power-ful for Beth. Certain smells had been affecting her recently, and his expensive cologne was making her retch. As he sat down she tried to ignore the sick feel-ing in her stomach.

'So how are you? You've been avoiding me,' Tom joked, as he glanced at the wine menu and signalled for the waiter. Tom was a good client of the restaurant, and the staff were at his beck and call. He ordered an expensive bottle of Merlot. Beth noticed he didn't even ask her if Merlot was what she felt like. He always took charge, and normally Beth felt happy to let him do so. She was used to living alone, and having to make most decisions on her own, but for some reason as he ordered the wine and more water she didn't feel the usual relief, but was slightly angry at his assumption that he always knew best. But then, as he complimented her on how she looked and asked how work was, her irritation faded and she got lost in conversation. As they chatted and ordered dinner Beth almost forgot that this was not just a normal night. That tonight was the night she needed to tell him about the baby. Their baby.

'You haven't drunk any of the wine.' Tom finally noticed. 'Do you not like it?' he asked, surprised.

Beth put down her knife and fork and knew this was the time to come clean.

'I can't drink tonight,' she said, looking right into his green eyes.

'Why?' he asked, a little put out. 'Do you need to work tomorrow?'

'No, it's not that. I actually have some news,' she said, almost holding her breath. 'Something big. I've been meaning to tell it to you for a while.'

'Christ,' Tom said, putting down his oversized wine glass. 'Don't say you're quitting your job.'

Beth felt her body tense. Why did he think every-thing was to do with work?

'No, I'm not leaving Burlington, you'll be glad to hear.'

'Well then, if it's not a work problem, what could possibly be this important?' Tom said, getting impa-tient.

'There is more to life than work, you know,' she replied, trying to lighten the mood. But Tom did not look impressed.

'What is it you want to tell me?'

He'd always been a straight-talking man, and now was no different.

Beth put her hand on top of his.

'I'm pregnant.'

There was utter silence. Beth and Tom stared at each other, and time seemed to stand still. In the distance she heard someone open a bottle of champagne, and she caught a man at a nearby table complaining that his potato gratin was overdone. She could hear noises all around the restaurant, but at their table there wasn't even the sound of a pin dropping.

'What did you say?' said Tom eventually. His tanned face suddenly looked a good bit paler.

'I'm pregnant. Seven weeks pregnant.'

Tom broke eye contact with Beth and gazed into the distance. The look on his face was one of utter bewilderment.

'How is this possible?' he whispered.

It wasn't an actual question, more an expression of shock. Suddenly he looked right at Beth.

'Is it definitely mine?'

Beth gasped. She felt her heart thump as she looked at the man she had loved and been faithful to for over a year.

'How dare you?' she managed to reply, fighting back tears. 'How dare you even suggest that? This might be shocking news, but don't insult me with that question. You know what kind of person I am, and you know I would never cheat on you, or anyone.'

Beth couldn't believe how this conversation had gone. She'd known telling Tom the news would be hard, but she'd never imagined the man she was loyal to would suggest she'd slept around. She was crushed, but more than anything she was annoyed.

'I'm sorry. I didn't mean that, it's just that this is a complete shock to me,' said Tom, taking a sip of wine. 'I didn't mean it.'

Beth noticed his hand was shaking. She had never seen the strong and powerful Tom Maloney so unnerved. She took a deep breath and decided to try and forget that he had suggested the baby wasn't his. They were in the middle of a very packed popular restaurant. Now wasn't the time for a big argument. They just had to sit down and talk about the baby.

'OK, I know this is a big shock. I still can't believe it, either. But it's true I'm pregnant, and you are the father.'

Tom suddenly looked around at the nearby tables.

'Keep your voice down,' he said. 'God knows who might hear you.'

Beth looked around, but recognized no one.

'I know it's not what we planned, and most people don't even know we are a couple, let alone soon to be parents! But somehow I'm pregnant, and I'll be showing in another few weeks. This is big news, and I suppose eventually people will find out. We'll just have to get used to it.'

'So you plan to go ahead with all of this?' he asked.

All of this? Beth didn't know what he meant. She looked at him questioningly.

'I mean there are other options, you know. We should seriously think about them before we go ahead with telling people.'

Other options? Suddenly Beth knew exactly what he meant. Abortion. The thought made her freeze. He couldn't be serious. But suddenly Tom's mood changed, and he began enthusiastically telling her about a friend of his who got caught out while having an affair, but had taken care of it after a weekend trip to the UK. Beth felt a stranger was speaking, not the man she loved.

'But we're not having an affair, so why would we need to do that?' Beth asked, her voice unsteady but loud. She was furious.

'It's just, you know, I never wanted this. I've done the whole babies and nappies and late nights before. I don't want to do it again. You've always known that.'

'It's not like I secretly planned this. We got pregnant by accident. It happens.'

Tom said nothing. Beth looked at the two uneaten plates of food.

'Trust me,' said Beth, her voice softening. 'It's been a huge shock for me, too. I haven't been able to think, eat or sleep since I found out. But we just have to deal with it.'

'We don't. This thing can be taken care of.'

'This thing?' she said, once again feeling her blood pressure rise. 'This thing is a tiny little baby, our baby. It may not be planned, but it's not something to be ashamed of, either.'

But as Beth talked she could see Tom straighten his back and clench his fists. It was something she had seen him do a million times in board meetings when he wasn't getting his way.

'If you're not going to get rid of this baby, then what do you want me to say? Are you expecting me to bend down on one knee and propose? For us to announce our love to the world and begin life as a happy family? That was never the plan. You know that. And what about work? Have you told anyone? This news could ruin us.'

Beth looked at Tom as if he was a stranger. This couldn't be the man she was about to have a baby with.

'I'm not expecting a diamond ring. You know

I can buy myself any jewellery I want,' she said angrily. Tom knew money and material items were not something Beth had to worry about. She earned great money, and was self-sufficient. It was support and love she craved for. 'And no, I've haven't told anyone in the flipping office.'

Tom looked at Beth, seeing again the hard-talking self-assured woman he knew and worked with. He seemed to soften.

'I didn't mean it like that. It's just, you know me, I'm at a place in my life where work – and of course a little fun – is what I want. It's what I've worked towards. And spending nights pacing the floor with some screaming infant is not my plan. And I know it's not what you want, either, so let's leave ourselves open to all the options, and try not let this mistake ruin our relationship.'

Beth looked at Tom as he began eating. He hadn't once asked her how she felt, or when exactly the baby was due. Suddenly she felt trapped. She needed to get out of the restaurant.

'I need to go home,' she said, as she reached for her handbag and put her black cardigan on.

'What?' said Tom. 'OK, let's go and discuss this situation more in my place. We've a lot to talk about.'

'No,' she said. 'I want to go to my own apartment.'

Tom said nothing. 'Oh, it would be handier to go to mine. I've got golf with some new clients at 8 a.m. and my clubs and gear are all in Dalkey. So let's just go there.'

'Golf? I've just told you I'm pregnant and all you care about is golf?'

Tom looked impatient. 'Beth, I've told you how I feel about this. I don't want a child. I already have two children, and that's plenty.'

Beth looked at him in disgust, and for once felt huge pity for his ex-wife. How could she have had two children with a man like him?

She knew they needed to talk more, but not tonight. She grabbed her coat and made for the exit, and as she pushed through the doors and walked out on to the street Tom hurried after her.

'There's no need to make a scene. Listen, we're both in shock. Maybe we both need a night alone to think about it all, and we can talk more about this tomorrow. OK?'

Beth knew it was not a suggestion but an order. She put her hand out and hailed a taxi.

Tom gave her a kiss on the cheek as she got into the back of the car, but she didn't kiss him back.

As the taxi drove off Beth saw Tom standing there alone on the street. He seemed relieved Beth and their problem were safely heading off in a different direction from where he was going. She felt she was going to be sick. It had been a horrible night. And as the taxi sped to Sandymount she sat shaking in the back of the car. She had never been so annoyed, disappointed and alone in her life.

Beth walked into her apartment. It felt cold and empty. She put on the heating and turned the TV on, but she still felt so alone. Tom had broken her heart. She had rehearsed everything she had planned to say to him, but nothing had come out right. It had all happened so quickly. She'd known he wouldn't be over the moon with the unexpected news, but she had never expected his cold, clinical and heartless response. And his even suggesting abortion had completely shaken her. It still all felt unreal.

This can't be happening, Beth thought. She wanted to go back to her old life. She had only been pregnant for seven weeks, but already she could divide her life into the old and new version. The carefree years were over. The grown-up part of her life was really beginning. She didn't know what to do. She could accurately tell people which were the best shares to invest in, she could name the heads of every financial institution in Europe, but now she felt helpless. Could she persuade Tom to be happy about having the baby? And if not, could she really have it on her own? How would she manage? And how could she tell people she was having a baby with a man who wanted her to abort it?

She hadn't told most of her friends about Tom, so it was going to be hard now, to confess to them about him and their unexpected baby. Beth was suddenly filled with such regret. I shouldn't have let our relationship be so secretive and under wraps, she thought. So what if he is divorced? I should have made him come out with my friends. Should have brought him to dinner at my dad's, should have told everyone in work. If I had done all of that, then being pregnant wouldn't be such a problem now. How did I let myself get into this situation? she asked herself.

Suddenly her phone rang. It was Tom. She ignored his call. She had nothing to say to him. He had made it clear how he felt, and now no matter what he told her she could never forget what he had already said, and how he had made her feel. Beth had been shocked and upset when she'd first realized she was pregnant, but then the last few days she had started to feel a little excited, and more and more interested in what was happening inside her. She hadn't been quite ready to shout her news from the rooftops, but at least she had begun to see that being pregnant wasn't so bad. As a little girl she had dreamt of becoming a mum, and even though that dream had been on hold for many years, it was coming true. Even though it was not happening in exactly the way she planned, it was still a little bit magical. And she was so annoyed at Tom for spoiling that excitement. For making her feel this baby was a big problem and a mistake.

She caught a glimpse of the diamond bracelet he had given her. She pulled it off her wrist as she sat down and took off her shoes. She had been feeling physically exhausted the last few weeks, and working long hours hadn't helped. But tonight she felt mentally exhausted, too. She made herself a cup of tea, but instantly felt sick from the smell of it. She felt nauseated all day every day. She hadn't actually vomited much, and she knew she was lucky, as some women were really unwell for weeks, but it still made everyday life hard. She poured herself a glass of water instead, and sat down at her round glass kitchen table. It was 10 p.m. on a Friday night, and she was completely alone. She could hear the two lads from the apartment above her having a party. They were always having parties. She sat listening to the music and the sounds of a good night. She didn't mean to, but she started crying. So this is what I have ahead of me, she thought. While everyone else will be out partying, or playing golf, I will be stuck in this apartment trying to raise a baby on my own. She tried to picture where a crib would fit, or how she would lift a buggy up the communal stairs, and suddenly felt claustrophobic. I can't do this. I can't do this on my own.

She felt her heart race and sweat pour down her face. Suddenly she wanted out. And Tom's get-out plan of action came back to her. Maybe with another man and at another time this would work, but it isn't going to now, so maybe I should end it, she thought. Take Tom's advice and book myself a flight to England. No one knows I'm pregnant. She hadn't even had the nerve to tell her father yet, so no one would ever know. She ran through the logistics of it. She had plenty of holiday time to use up, and if she rang some clinics on Monday she was sure she could find someone who could help her.

For a second she considered it. But then she thought of her little baby, the lower case o, and felt horrified. Even if no one else knew, I would, she thought. Even if no one ever found out, I would know for ever. How could I even think about it? I don't agree with abortion. How could I even consider ending a little baby's life? She felt disgusted with herself. She began crying again. She cried and cried, gulping back air and tears. She felt like the worst person in the world. Suddenly she wanted nothing more than to have this baby, her baby. 'I'm so sorry,' she said over and over to her little o.

Eventually she dragged herself to bed, but it took hours for her to go to sleep. She kept reliving the night over and over in her head. From Tom's heartless reaction to her moment of madness in thinking she could do away with her baby. She pulled her duvet up over her head, trying to block out the bad memories. Her mind raced, but as the hours passed and the party above her ended she finally came to a conclusion. Tom might have let her down, but she was going to have this baby with or without him, and even though she knew nothing about being pregnant, labour or raising a child, she would learn. She dreaded so much of it, and knew her life was about to change completely, but something deep inside her was saying she might just be able to do it.

24

'I still love you. We can make us work. But you know how I feel about this baby.'

Beth gazed at Tom Maloney as they sat in his big living room. Tom had a CD of his favourite classical music playing in the background, and a large gas fire glowing. As he sipped on a glass of red wine, she noticed how the scene looked like a perfect romantic night in. But, as she gulped back her glass of water and tried to ignore her constant nausea, she realized how far from idyllic the situation was. They had both avoided being alone for almost two weeks, ever since that fateful night at Peploe's. Beth would never forget what Tom had said. She had ignored his phone calls and text messages. In work neither had wanted to talk about it, but even so Beth had found excuses to be busy whenever Tom came near her. But when he had suggested they sit down and talk properly in his

188

house after work one night, she'd known she had to agree.

'You have your career to think about too, you know,' Tom said, as he tried to hold her hand.

'What does that mean?' she said accusingly, shaking him off and moving further away on the couch.

'You're very good at what you do. You're smart, quick-thinking, precise and reliable. You're one of the best employees we've ever had. You could go all the way.'

Beth acknowledged the compliment.

'But how will six months of maternity leave affect that?' he asked. 'We all know having a baby affects women.'

Beth looked at him, horrified.

'You can't be serious. That kind of thinking went out with the Stone Age. There are thousands of very successful working mothers.'

'OK. Well, how many successful female senior portfolio managers with children do you know?'

Beth was caught off-guard. She knew there must be some, but for the life of her she couldn't think of a single one.

'That's irrelevant. I was the youngest female to become a SPM in Burlington, so I'm sure I can set the bar for working mums, too.'

'That's what I love about you. Your drive, your determination to succeed, and your inner belief,'

Tom said, smiling. 'But I'm trying to tell you how, even with all those, when people have a baby their life changes.'

'There's nothing wrong with change,' said Beth, who over the last few weeks had realized all the changes she should have made years ago. She should have focused less on her career and put more work into her relationships, both with men and women. She had always been too busy to spend much time with her girlfriends. She loved meeting them, but between working hard to build up her career and trying to find time to spend with Tom, she knew she had let some of her friendships slide. And with no siblings to turn to, either, she had felt very alone the last few weeks.

'I'm just trying to make you realize all the sacrifices that come with having a baby, and that your career is inevitably going to suffer.'

'And what about your career? Or is it only my life that the baby will affect?'

'We both have a lot of decisions to make, but you know how I feel about this. I want you, but I don't want another baby. I'm in my fifties. At this stage it's not about babies, I've got my career to focus on. I'm sorry to upset you, but honestly, that's how I feel.'

And that was it, Beth had her answer. And now she just had to make the decision: a life with Tom or raising a child alone? It only took one heartbeat.

She stood up and took a last look around the room that was filled with Markey Robinson paintings and expensive crystal.

'You've worked hard and it's paid off. But sometimes it's not about work. I've planned every inch of my life, been careful and always played it safe, but now it's all been turned upside down. I have no idea how my life will change, and how it will pan out, but I've got to go with my heart and not my head. I'm sorry you don't want this child, but I do.'

It took every ounce of strength for Beth to say it. Every inch of courage to decide to leave the man she had loved and have a baby alone, but it felt right.

Neither of them said anything for a while. Beth watched the fire, while Tom gazed at her.

'Are you sure about this?' he said, obviously shaken. 'Because you know what it means? I don't want to raise this baby. You understand that?'

She nodded.

Tom covered his face with his hands. He was stressed, and for once not in control of the situation.

'But how will this work? What will we tell everyone?' he finally asked.

Beth had no idea what would happen, but having a baby alone would be better than losing one just so she could keep a man.

'I don't know. We can think about it. I won't tell anyone yet, at least not until I'm twelve weeks.'

'And will you tell them I'm the father?'

'Tom! We're not a pair of fifteen-year-olds who just got caught having sex! We're adults, and we're old enough to have kids whether we stick together or not. It's not some big scandal.'

'For me it would be,' he whispered.

Beth knew she had Tom over a barrel now. But as much as he'd hurt her, she knew it would be hard telling everyone she was pregnant by one of the directors. She would need to think this through.

'I don't know what I'll do.'

He looked slightly relieved. Beth had never felt so completely turned off by a man as she did now. She could feel acid in her throat. How could I have loved someone who reacts like this? she asked herself. She was starting to realize that she might have good business acumen and judgement, but her ability to see clearly what kind of man she was with had been off kilter.

'I have to go. We can work out the details another time,' she said. She wanted to get out of his house. She never wanted to see it again.

'Of course I can look after all the financial costs. I can guarantee that.'

Beth said nothing. She knew money was not a problem for him, so offering to pay her doctor and hospital fees was hardly a big gesture. She might take him up on it, but for now she was hardly going to gush over his generosity.

As she reached the hall door she turned to Tom, who was still looking pale.

'I thought I knew what kind of man you were. But I realize I've wasted a lot of time on someone not willing to go the distance. This is your baby, but if you're not man enough to own up to your responsibilities, then at least I know that now, and I'll make sure your child does, too. It seems all the money in the world can't buy you a heart.'

And with that Beth managed to find the strength to run down his long driveway and just about make it into her car before sobbing uncontrollably.

There was no going back now. Herself and Tom were over. She was having this baby on her own.

Beth's hands were shaking as she turned her car engine on. She was still crying, but determined that Tom would not see her upset. She pulled away from his house. As she drove through affluent Dalkey her mind raced. The last few weeks all felt so dreamlike. She didn't look any different, she didn't have any bump, yet there was this little thing inside her that might have been small but was big enough to have changed her life for ever.

Beth pulled her car in on Vico Road, and sat and watched the lights of all the huge family houses that looked out over the Irish Sea. She had come from a family with just one other person, her dad, and as loving as he was she had always felt lonely. No mum, no brothers and sisters. She had vowed that if and when she ever got married and had kids she would have a big house full of children, noise and love. But now she was about to bring a baby into the same environment that she had grown up in, only worse, because at least she'd had her mum for ten years. This little baby would have no dad. How would it cope? Already Beth felt protective towards her little unborn child. She only wanted the best for him or her.

Beth was overwhelmed with emotion. From the break-up with Tom to the fear of how she would cope alone, it was all too much. She needed to tell someone about it, to have them reassure her that it would all be OK, that she could do this. She didn't know who to call. The news of her pregnancy would shock all her friends. But then she looked at her watch and realized it was almost midnight, and too late to call any of them. She sat in her car and looked out of the window, watching the moonlight reflect off the tide. Suddenly she got the urge to drive somewhere she hadn't been for quite a while. She turned the engine on and headed to her real home – where her dad was.

★　　　★　　　★

Beth drove through the old iron gates and parked her car on the gravel next to her dad's spotless old Jaguar. She felt nervous. She hadn't planned to tell him yet, but there was no one else to turn to tonight. Suddenly, it occurred to her that he might be out, or in bed, but then she saw light streaming from his front living room window. She walked up to it and through the curtains saw him sitting in his blue and white pyjamas, watching an old movie and sipping a cup of tea. She saw the empty couches: he looked so small sitting alone in there. She started crying again. All this time she had thought she was the only one who was lonely, but here he was, by himself on a Friday night, with no one even to watch TV with. All at once, she felt so guilty for not spending more time with him.

She went to the front door, let herself in, and walked through the hall, which was filled with her dad's golf clubs, and had all his shoes neatly lined up under the stairs, the way he always stored them. Beth smiled. She heard their old dog, Rusty, bark and fling himself up against the living-room door.

'What's wrong, boy?' she heard her dad ask.

Beth walked in the door just as he came out with Rusty. He jumped as Rusty clambered all over Beth.

'Jesus Christ!' he said, putting his hand over his

heart. 'You gave me such a fright! What time is it? Are you OK? Why are you here?'

Beth managed to calm the dog down and settle her dad back into his chair.

'It's so late, are you all right, darling?' he asked as he switched off the TV. He was still a little shocked to see his daughter. She was usually so organized, and arranged every visit in advance.

Beth looked at her dad, and saw the genuine concern in his eyes. He cared. Tom had sat gazing at her all evening without that expression, but now that she saw it she crumbled. All the weeks of hiding her news and doing the thinking, worrying and planning on her own had taken their toll. She was exhausted and very emotional, which were two things she was unused to feeling. She spluttered out the news.

'Dad, I'm pregnant.'

William Prendergast did a double take. He looked intently at her, and then glanced at her tummy. She started crying again.

'It's still early days, but I'm almost ten weeks pregnant,' she admitted, waiting for him to be upset at the unexpected news. But it was also such a relief for her to say the words out loud to someone other than Tom. It also made it sound real. She was having a baby. It was really happening.

Her dad stayed still for a few minutes, looking very

surprised, but then walked over and sat down beside her.

'It's OK. It's great news, don't cry.'

Beth looked at him as he put his arms around her. She hadn't been hugged by him in a long time.

She could smell his Old Spice aftershave and the distinct smell of Baileys, which he drank every night before bed. These smells brought back childhood memories. She couldn't stop crying. She was filled with different emotions: relief at having told him, happiness at being at home and in the arms of someone who cared for her, and worry about all the things that might go wrong. Finally she stopped weeping and pulled away.

William passed her a tissue. As she wiped her eyes he poured himself a glass of Baileys from the side table.

'On a night like this I need a second helping.' But he didn't have to justify himself to Beth, she would have killed, too, for a drink to help her relax and unwind.

'So, tell me everything,' William said, and with that Beth decided to be honest and start from the beginning.

'You know Tom Maloney?' she asked. 'Well, he's not just my boss . . .'

Half an hour later she stopped talking. She had told her dad everything. How she had loved Tom, even though she knew she should have dated someone younger, simply because he was everything she'd thought she admired in a man. And how he had reacted when she'd told him the news. Beth knew it was a lot for her dad to take in – an hour ago he hadn't even known she had a boyfriend, and now she was explaining how she was pregnant.

'So he wants nothing to do with this baby?' asked William, his face flushed. Beth could see he was annoyed.

'Well, he did say he would pay any bills,' she said, knowing it wasn't the answer her dad was looking for.

'Well, I should hope he will! It's his child after all, and he can well afford it.'

Beth felt embarrassed. Even though she was in her thirties she still suddenly felt like a teenager who'd had sex and got caught out.

'I'm sorry,' she said, feeling ashamed.

Her dad stared at her.

'There's nothing to be sorry for, pet. I know it wasn't planned, but we just have to deal with it now. And, to be honest, I'm happy.'

'Really?' said Beth, unconvinced.

'Well, I'm not happy that Tom has let you down. But I've been looking forward to being a grandad for years. This house is too big for me on my own, it feels empty. But can you imagine what it will be like when there is a little boy or girl running around here, causing havoc? And they will love the garden, it's perfect for playing in. And I still have your old cot. I never threw it out. It might need a lick of paint, but I can fix it up for the baby for when it stays here.'

Beth was surprised, she had never thought her dad wanted to be a grandfather.

'But how will I cope on my own? Being a single parent. It will be impossible.'

William came over and sat beside her on the old couch. The light from the fire carved deep wrinkles in his face as he took Beth's hand and squeezed it.

'I was a single parent too, you know.'

Beth found it surprising for her dad to put it like that. She was starting to realize all the things they had in common. And of course, she'd always known that he had found it very difficult being on his own and raising a daughter. As if he read her mind, William spoke.

'I know I wasn't the best father. I found it so hard. I really regret sending you off to boarding school, but I didn't know what else to do. I know now that it affected our relationship. But grandchildren can be my chance to fix things, a new start. And it will be fun!'

Beth smiled, still feeling upset. Her mind raced, and at the same time she felt so tired. Her dad leaned forward and hugged her tight.

'Congratulations. You will be a great mum. And I'm here to help, too, every step of the way.'

And suddenly Beth was calm. She finally had what she'd been longing for: someone who was happy for her and telling her she could do this. She hugged him back. She never would have imagined her dad would be the first person she'd confide in, or that he would take the news so well, but as he made her a sandwich and they sat up for hours talking about the baby, Beth realized she had made a mistake in not trying to be closer to him earlier. He hadn't sent her to boarding school to put distance between them; he had done it out of desperation. But she was an adult now, and should have made every possible effort to see him and spend time with him. She knew it would take a while for them to get to know each other properly now, but they would. And Beth was lucky to have him: she had no one else.

25

'Ciara Ryan rang again.'

Erin Delany sat down at her desk and looked at Paula. The two women worked well together, because, while Erin was slightly more organized, Paula was the calmer and more relaxed of the pair. They balanced each other well.

Unfortunately for Paula, though, Erin had been on terrible form recently, and over the last two weeks Paula had been lucky even to get a hello from her, let alone any friendly banter or conversation. Of course, Paula didn't know that ever since Erin had found out that once again she wasn't pregnant she'd been taking her frustration out on the world. She'd barely been able to bring herself to care about work, family or friends. She'd been too busy swinging between heartbreak, and outright annoyance and anger. Life was so unfair, she thought. All day long she passed mothers and their babies, children running along the road, pregnant women smiling as they smugly rubbed their swollen bellies. She just couldn't stick it, it was so unjust.

'You need to calm down. This will happen for us,' John had insisted the night before, over dinner. Erin had barely spoken to him all week. Everything he did drove her mad. He just wasn't as committed to it all as she was, she thought.

'Here's a cup of coffee, let's just lie on the couch and watch TV tonight. A quiet relaxing night in is what we need.'

Erin gazed at the cup, then pushed it aside.

'You know I'm off coffee. I'll have a quick cup of green tea, and then I'm off to the gym. I read some-where how weight can affect fertility, so I really need to start going to the gym more than once a week.'

John sighed.

'What does that mean?' she asked, annoyed at his attitude.

'It's just that you've barely talked to me the last two weeks, and then the only times you have it's all been about yoga, or green tea, or ovulation, or my sperm count. It would be nice to discuss the news, or work, or – God forbid – something frivolous, like what new movies are out. I'd love just to talk about something fun.'

Erin stood up, and started to put her coat on.

'I'm sorry you think I'm so boring, but while your head is thinking about films, music and irrelevant stuff, my head is trying to work out my cycle, find out which food will help us conceive, and calculate our fertility levels. It may not be fun, but it's a lot of work and stress.'

'It shouldn't be that hard,' John replied automatically. 'Every day people get pregnant without even trying to.'

Erin felt like she had been slapped in the face. She felt he was mocking all her efforts to help them conceive.

'Well, if I had a partner who cared it might not be so difficult.'

John looked into her eyes for a long time. His expression was so sad. Finally he walked across the kitchen and tried to put his arms around his wife, but she shrugged him off.

'I'm going out. Enjoy your night of TV and relaxing.' And with that Erin was gone, once again leaving John home alone.

And now Erin found herself in work, after a bad night with John and with a whole day stretching ahead of her.

'Is there a problem with Ciara Ryan?' asked Paula.

Erin had been avoiding Ciara as much as she could the last fortnight. She didn't mind working on their new kitchen but she just couldn't face talking about baby nurseries, cots and playrooms with her client. She knew it would break her heart.

'I'll ring her later,' she replied, as she closed the door to her office and rested her head in her hands.

As she looked around her small office, bursting with floor samples, bathroom fittings, curtains and catalogues, Erin knew she was so lucky to have her own business, to be in charge of her own career. But to her, as every day passed, the things in life that she knew she should be grateful for – her kind husband, her beautiful home, her great job – all paled in comparison with what she really wanted: her own child.

Paula knocked on the door and handed Erin that day's post. Erin opened some bills, and then a large envelope postmarked Norway. She peeled it open and out fell a large catalogue. It was from the Norwegian wooden furniture company that Erin had been telling Ciara about. She hadn't been able to find a copy of their brochure to give her, and so had contacted the company and asked them to send out another. Erin flicked through the pages filled with hand-crafted tables, chairs and beds, but it was the nursery furniture section that made her freeze. She couldn't look at it. She closed the book after opening a page that showed a happy couple smiling as one of their children lay in a cot and the other sat on a wooden rocking horse. I can't do this, she thought.

She walked out of her office and went looking for Paula. Her friend was busy on the phone to a builder, but eventually wrapped up the conversation.

'I need to ask you a favour,' said Erin.

'Sure,' said Paula kindly.

'Can you drop this catalogue and some curtain samples in to Ciara and Mark's house? And while you're there, can you also find out if they have made any decision on the couches for their new kitchen?'

'Are you sure you don't want to talk to them yourself?' asked Paula.

Erin was never so sure of anything in her life. She needed to distance herself from Ciara Ryan and her bump. She didn't want to spend weeks talking to Ciara about babies.

'I am,' replied Erin. 'I just don't have time to spend all my day talking to Ciara about nurseries and playrooms.'

'Are you OK?' asked Paula.

'I'm fine,' said Erin, returning to her office.

Erin knew she should offer Paula more of an explanation for her odd behaviour, but she didn't want to. Ciara Ryan would be disappointed too, but Erin didn't have time for her feelings. She had more important things to worry about.

But later, as she watched Paula head to Donnybrook

to meet Ciara and Mark Ryan, Erin did feel a twinge of regret. Her behaviour had not been professional. She knew she wasn't acting like herself, but then her perfectly organized and planned life was not going according to plan, either, and she couldn't cope.

26

'So you're not going to drink at the hen party?' John asked Erin as he buttoned his shirt, put on his tie and got himself ready for another day at the office.

Erin was brushing her long brown hair as she watched him look at her in surprise. Tonight she was going to her friend Amy's hen party. The girls had been at school and college together, and afterwards, while Erin had been happy to get married and lay down her roots at home in Dublin, Amy had got the travel itch and had spent her time living in one continent after another. Erin had thought she would never settle down, but then Ryan Sincock had come along, and after a love affair that began in Byron Bay, Amy had rung home to say she was engaged and would be getting married in six months' time in Dublin. Erin had been so happy for her friend, and so impatient to see her. It had been a long time since they had caught up. But now that Amy's hen was only hours away, Erin didn't want to go any more. She wasn't in a celebratory mood, and she certainly didn't want to give up her healthy eating and drinking diet just so she could attend the hen.

'I will allow myself two glasses of wine, but honestly I need to stick to this new diet, especially since I should be ovulating tomorrow, which means it's the best time for us to conceive.'

John didn't look too happy, but said nothing. Instead he put his coat on and kissed Erin goodbye. Just as he was leaving he turned and said: 'Amy is your best friend. She flew home from Africa that time you were really sick with your appendix, and when we got married she travelled back from New Zealand, even though it took almost two days to get here. She's a good friend, the least you could do is forget about your own troubles tonight, have a few glasses of wine, relax and enjoy being out with the girls.'

Erin said nothing. She knew what John was saying was fair and true, but the stubborn side of her refused to give in. If she wanted to get pregnant she needed to take the whole thing seriously, and that required willpower and focus.

'I can relax without getting drunk,' she replied curtly.

'Really?' he said, his look deadpan. 'You haven't been relaxed in a long time.'

Erin was about to fly off the handle, but John closed the door before she had the chance. She was furious. She was going to start another day annoyed.

Erin was on bad form, and after a quick meeting with some clients in Bray she'd decided she wasn't in the mood to be around other people, and so she'd rung Paula to let her know that she would work from home today. The beauty of her job was that it was possible to open her laptop and work on anything from sketch proposals to ordering materials, all from the comfort of her own home.

After a quiet, but productive morning, Erin was just taking a break when she heard the doorbell ring. She opened her front door to find her dad standing there.

'Hi, pet. I didn't know if you would be around today, but I just wanted to ring the bell in case you were. I plan to spend a few hours in the garden. I can let myself through to the back.'

'No, Dad, come in this way. Do you want a cup of tea before you start?' Erin offered, putting her arms around him. It felt good to be hugged back.

'I never say no to tea!' replied Paddy Walsh, as he set down his gardening gloves and favourite hand trowel.

Paddy loved gardens: from planting flowers to

trimming trees he had a fascination with the out-
doors. Erin's family home had a massive garden that
was immaculately kept, which Paddy prided himself
on. But recently he had taken to offering his gardening expertise to his daughters.

'John doesn't seem to be keeping a close enough
eye on those hedges,' he'd said to Erin recently.
'Does he not care about the layout of your back
garden?'

Erin didn't want to admit that, while she and her
husband thought it imperative to have a house with
a good-sized garden, neither of them knew much
about shrubs, compost or landscaping. And so before
she knew it, her dad had offered to call once a week
to get their garden in order.

'If we start working now, then by the time the
summer comes we will have this place in great condition,' he'd said to the couple. Neither John nor Erin
thought the place looked that bad, but Erin suspected
the project was as much about her dad keeping busy
as anything else.

'Ever since your father retired he's been at a loose
end, but it's great now that he has your place to keep
him focused and energized. And, to be honest, I'm
delighted to get him out of the house for a few hours
each week!' said Mary, Erin's mum.

Her dad's offer of his services to Alison had been
slightly less well received.

'But we only live in an apartment,' her sister had pointed out, at a recent Sunday lunch.

'Ali, no job is too small. I will start with planting some nice hanging baskets, and by summer we will have that small balcony packed with colour and beautiful plants.'

Alison hadn't been entirely convinced, but had said nothing; none of the girls ever wanted to upset or insult their beloved dad.

And now Erin was getting used to coming home from work to find her dad pruning shrubs, or bent over the large border.

'I think I'll work on those roses today,' said Paddy, as himself and Erin sat down to enjoy a cup of tea.

'You're the expert,' replied Erin, making Paddy smile.

'How's Mum?' she asked, as she offered her dad a biscuit.

'She's got her hands full today! Alison asked us to mind baby Sophie while she goes to meet some friends for lunch and gets some shopping done. But your mother is only too delighted to help. Sophie is a pet, and your mum adores showing her grandchild off to all the neighbours. The house was packed when I left!'

Erin felt herself tense up. Her parents adored their three grandchildren, nothing made them prouder. She felt like such a failure for not being able to give them more. They knew she wanted children, but she would never admit to them the huge pressure she and John were under. Erin adored her two nieces and wild nephew, but at times she avoided calling in to see them, as every time one of her sisters hugged or kissed their children it reminded her how bereft she was. She used to spend hours with her sisters discussing how many children she would have, what schools she preferred, what names she liked, but now she avoided those conversations. What use was picking out a good school if you had no child to send to it?

'Are you OK, pet?' asked her dad. 'You've been awfully quiet recently, and we haven't seen yourself and John together in our house for weeks.'

'I'm fine,' replied Erin automatically. 'We're both busy in work, that's all. Someone has to pay the mortgage on this big place!' she added, trying to lighten the mood.

Her dad didn't say much, but just studied his youngest daughter. She looked tired and lonely.

'This house is great, and between your good jobs and hectic lifestyle you two certainly seem to have it all. But you know, pet, sometimes life is like a garden. People want to have an immaculately manicured lawn, full beds and all the flowers in bloom, but what they don't realize is that in order to sustain that perfect garden they need to work really hard. They need to spend months planting, pruning, cutting and weeding. They need to get their hands dirty. Nothing comes easy in life, we all need to put time into something in order to make it work. And a good relationship is so important.'

Erin could see where this conversation was going.

'Don't worry about me, Dad. I'm fine,' she said, standing up. 'Anyway, I've got to get back to work, but why don't you help yourself to another cup of tea before you tackle those rose bushes?'

And before Paddy could express any more concern, Erin had the door of her study closed.

But by the time it was 5 p.m. Erin was dying to shut her laptop and head into town to Amy's hen, anything to get her mind off houses, families and babies. After a quick shower she changed into a new blue cocktail dress, and a pair of her favourite Nine West shoes. She tied back her hair, locked the house, and then hopped into a taxi.

Erin and the girls were all meeting Amy in the Shelbourne Hotel for champagne, before heading to the Unicorn for dinner. After that Amy's younger sister Jenny had reserved four tables in the VIP section of Krystle nightclub so they could dance the night away. Erin didn't think she would last until then, though. She knew she should be cheerful for Amy's hen, but after that last negative pregnancy test something in her had changed, her spirit had broken.

Deep down she knew she was not a pleasure to be around, but no one sympathized with how she was feeling, no one understood how disheartened and worried she was. And all she could do at this stage was up the ante, try harder, even though she just felt like lying in bed and crying.

Erin was jumping out of the taxi when her phone rang.

'Hello. Is that Mrs Delany?'

Erin did not recognize the voice.

'Yes, it is,' Erin replied as she began walking through the revolving door of Dublin's most famous hotel.

'Oh, hello Mrs Delany, this is Margaret here from Yummy Mummy in Ranelagh. I'm ringing to say we finally got that order of new stock in and we have the black and white dress for you here.'

Erin froze. She had completely forgotten about her moment of madness in the popular maternity store.

'So, will you be in over the weekend to collect it? We are open all day tomorrow and again on Sunday afternoon.'

Erin stuttered with her words, she didn't know what to say. Across the hotel lobby she could see Amy looking stunning in a white halter-neck dress, her bronzed skin giving her a healthy glow. She was so happy and carefree. Meanwhile Erin felt panicked and embarrassed. She was mortified, yet had to admit to the shop assistant that she wouldn't be in to collect the dress.

'I'm so sorry,' she said stumbling on her words. 'I don't need the dress any more.'

'Oh,' said Margaret, surprised.

Erin hadn't meant to add anything else, but suddenly the words tumbled out of her mouth.

'You see, I'm not pregnant. Trust me, I wish I was, but I'm not.'

There was utter silence on the phone.

'I'm sorry,' added Erin.

'I'm very sorry, too. You poor thing,' Margaret said sympathetically, before hanging up.

Erin flung her phone back into her handbag. Any small bit of excitement she'd felt at heading out on a Friday night with her best friends to celebrate with the bride-to-be Amy had now been shattered. She took a deep breath and walked into the bar. All the girls were crowded around a large table that was full of drinks. As she walked up to the group she couldn't believe it: there was not just one, but two very large bumps squeezed into party dresses. Erin felt terrible. After Margaret at the maternity store thought she'd had a miscarriage, the last thing she wanted was to have to party all night with two pregnant women.

'Oh my God, Erin! You're here!' Amy shouted as

she raced over and hugged her best friend. Erin held on to Amy a little longer than necessary.

'Are you OK?' asked Amy, a little concerned.

Erin felt like telling her everything, admitting how her seemingly smooth-running life was not all plain sailing, that she and John just couldn't get pregnant, and that she was finding it harder and harder to be around expectant mums, but then she looked at Amy and realized it was her big night. She didn't need to be weighed down with Erin's worries.

'You look like you could use some champagne,' said Amy and she moved Erin over to the reserved seats. 'Would you believe it? My two cousins are pregnant, so it means there's more alcohol for us all!'

As Amy handed her friend a big glass of bubbly Erin was about to explain how she wasn't planning on drinking too much, but then the worries and exhaustion of the day hit her. And as she watched Amy's cousins glow and gush over their bumps, Erin grabbed the glass. This was no time for taking it easy, she needed alcohol and plenty of it.

'I always knew Take That would reform,' slurred Erin to Amy, as the band's hit song 'Never Forget' blared across the nightclub's dance floor.

'No, you didn't. You cried the day Robbie quit the band, and we all knew it meant the end was nigh.'

Amy was trying to dance, but she kept falling over her handbag.

'No, I loved them, and in my heart knew they would return. Maybe the DJ will play the song again.'

'Erin! He's already played it for us twice. No, go and ask him to play some Justin Timberlake.'

Erin stuttered towards the DJ box, but her drunken legs were not the steadiest, and before she knew it she had crashed into a large group of men. She immediately received lots of attention, but it was all unwanted, because her mission was to keep the bride-to-be happy and get JT playing asap. She was really enjoying the night; it was nice to catch up with her friends and enjoy a lovely meal, but mainly it was great to unwind. She hadn't been this drunk in a long time, and had forgotten the way each glass of wine made her whole body relax more and more. It was fun, too! Amy's sisters had gone to lots of trouble to make sure Amy enjoyed her hen night. From buying silly gifts to taking plenty of photos, they had it all covered. Although their insistence at making sure everyone did shot after shot of tequila was responsible for the state Erin was in. She hadn't realized how drunk she was until she tried to read a text John had sent, and found she couldn't even see the screen properly. But still, she soldiered on, and was at the bar, trying to order another bottle of champagne, when she felt a pair of strong sturdy arms wrap themselves around her.

'I thought you were only having two glasses of wine?'

Erin turned around to see John smiling.

'I'm drunk,' she announced.

'I can see that,' he said, noticing her slurred words, messy hair, and the small rip in her tights. It was all very unlike Erin, but John was delighted.

'How did you know I was here?' she asked suspiciously.

'You texted me!' he said, laughing. 'Do you not remember?'

Erin had no memory of that.

'I'm glad to see you've enjoyed your night. Are you OK, though?'

'I'm fine, I'm fine. Let's dance!'

John guided Erin to the packed dance floor, but after Erin's third fall on to the sticky floor he decided she needed some air.

Once out on the nightclub balcony John could see the full state that Erin was in.

'Maybe we should go home?' he suggested.

'What? No! I need to dance with Amy,' Erin slurred.

'Amy was brought home by her sister twenty minutes ago. She's locked.'

Erin knew she was defeated, and so, after finding

her coat, which was in a ball under a chair, she leant into John's body.

'Take me home, please,' she said, as she looked into his brown eyes, and then snuggled into his warm chest.

'Gladly,' said John, as he protectively wrapped his arms around her and helped her into a taxi. He hadn't felt as close to her in weeks.

And when they got home Erin peeled off her party dress and fancy shoes, and willingly got into bed with John, and this time there wasn't any mention of ovulation or timings — it was all about true love.

27

'Do you want me to call the doctor?' John asked, staring at the closed bathroom door.

Erin sat on the cold tiles, her pyjamas covered in sweat, her greasy hair tied back, and as she leaned her face against the rim of the toilet bowl she thought she might die. She had been throwing up all weekend.

'I think I can still taste tequila. God, maybe I have alcohol poisoning,' she said, but deep down she knew that she had just drunk way too much at Amy's hen. At the time it had seemed like a good idea, and even for the first few hours at home, wrapped up in bed with John, the drink had knocked the edge off her, but then had come the vomiting, and it hadn't stopped. Erin hadn't left the bedroom and bathroom all week-end. John had spent the last two days walking up and down the stairs, under orders to get more toast, more water, more painkillers, more towels. It had been a weekend of hell. Erin had been feeling sick, upset and annoyed, and had taken it all out on him.

Suddenly the bathroom door opened and Erin walked out and slipped right into bed. John handed her a glass of cold water. He then placed his hand on top of hers, but Erin shrugged it off.

'You were the one who told me to drink.'

'Excuse me?' asked John, not understanding.

'You stood here on Friday morning and told me I would be a bad friend to Amy if I didn't drink plenty at her hen party.'

'I told you to have a few drinks, not enough to almost put you into a coma.'

'Well, why didn't you bring me home earlier, then?'

'I took you home from Krystle ten minutes after meeting you. You are being unreasonable. Listen, I know you feel sick, but we've all had nights when we've drunk too much, and regretted it.'

'It's not the drink I regret, you know. In case you cared, this weekend was the prime time for us to have sex, I'm at my peak of ovulation. But I was in no state last night, and I can barely move my head let alone have sex tonight, so once again we will have to go another month childless.'

'We had sex on Friday,' John said very matter-of-factly. 'Or does that not count because you were on good form and happy?'

221

'Friday wasn't the right day, and anyway you should hope I didn't get pregnant then. With all that alcohol in my blood the baby would be affected.'

John raised his eyes to heaven. 'Christ, I'm sure half the children in the world have been conceived after a night on the tear.'

'Well, I don't want our child to be,' Erin replied, turning her back to John.

John gazed at Erin. The room was in utter silence.

'I'm glad to see you're back to your usual happy self,' he said sarcastically.

Erin spun around in the bed.

'What does that mean?' she demanded.

'It means you have been in a self-pitying, self-absorbed bad mood for months now. Don't you think that I'm worried we won't be able to have kids? You seem to think you're the only one in this relationship.'

'That's not true,' Erin replied.

'No, I suppose that's not entirely true, but you seem to think I'm only good for collecting you when you're drunk, looking after you when you're vomiting all weekend, and of course I'm the one you come to for sex, but only when it's the right time, day or hour for baby-making. I love you, but you're making it harder for me to care each day. You're pushing me away.'

Erin was stunned, but rather than apologize she was fuming.

'I'm making it hard? God, you're the one who doesn't have to worry about dieting, fertility levels and periods. I'm doing all the work here.'

'It shouldn't be work. I've told you that before.'

'Well, we aren't gonna have this baby the easy way, that's evident from the past year of trying.'

'Maybe we should look at alternative options, then.'

'What?' she spat. 'I've worked out, done yoga, given up junk food, barely drunk in four months, and now you're saying you want me to forget all those sacrifices and what, just adopt? We are not taking the easy route, John.'

'I don't think adopting is the easy route at all,' he said. 'But all those "sacrifices" are driving us apart. When was the last time we just sat in and watched TV for the night, or spent a whole day in bed? Or went out and got drunk together?'

Erin said nothing.

'You don't care about me any more. You might care about my alcohol level, or worry if I have a cigarette, but you don't care about me.'

'That's not true,' Erin replied, but her voice was cold.

'Really?' John asked. 'When was the last time you asked me about work? Or came to one of my races?

You're too busy going to flipping yoga or fortune-tellers, all in the effort to help create a family. Well, I'm your family, and I'm right here, at home.' John felt his pulse and heart race, but neither said anything.

Suddenly John's phone rang.

'Oh Christ, it's Stephen. What will I say about tonight? I suppose we should cancel,' said John.

Erin had forgotten all about their planned night with their friends Stephen and Ruth. They had a fourteen-month-old baby, Jessica, and she kept them busy most of the time, so Erin and John rarely got to see them, but weeks ago Ruth had said they were long overdue a night out and so had booked all four of them to go to dinner in a new restaurant in Dun Laoghaire. Erin had no interest in going outside the house, and spending time with John, especially since she was feeling so sick, but the meal was still hours away and she knew how excited Ruth and Stephen were at the prospect of having a night off from the baby.

'We can't cancel on them, they've been looking forward to it for weeks. We'll have to go,' said Erin. 'We can continue our conversation later,' she added.

'Fine,' said John, walking out of the room as he answered the phone to his friend.

★　　★　　★

Erin and John didn't speak all afternoon, both feeling the other should offer an apology.

After an afternoon in bed Erin finally managed to drag herself into the shower and fling on jeans and a top.

'I'll drive,' said Erin to John as they locked the house. 'My stomach is in no mood to handle any more drink, but I'd appreciate it if you would keep an eye on your drinks, too, we still might have a chance of conceiving tonight.'

'Are you off your head?' John laughed. 'You expect me to sleep with you tonight?'

'Don't talk to me like that,' she said, turning on the engine.

'You can't treat me the way you do and then expect me to have sex, all because you need to at a certain time. God, I thought you had changed on Friday night, but I see that was just the drink talking and acting.'

Erin bit her tongue. She didn't need John to get more annoyed with her than he already was. This baby-making project couldn't work without him.

They drove to the restaurant in silence, but just before they walked through the doors John put his hand on Erin's arm.

'Let's just try to relax and enjoy ourselves tonight. We haven't seen Ruth and Stephen in ages.'

Erin agreed, she knew John was right.

'Jessica almost gave poor Stephen a heart attack the other day. She climbed out of the cot! Stephen found her in the bathroom. She'd climbed into our shower and was eating an old sponge!'

Erin and John laughed as Ruth filled them in on baby Jessica's antics. She was a gorgeous child, but wild, and they had their hands full with her. Erin knew they had been right not to cancel their night with Ruth and Stephen. It was lovely catching up with them. Erin's appetite had finally come back, too, and she was ravenous from a weekend of nothing more than toast.

'Although, I suppose Jessica will have to move out of the cot soon, anyway, and not just because she can pole-vault over it,' said Stephen, grinning.

Erin looked at him, confused. Stephen turned to Ruth.

'Go on, Ruthie, we might as well tell them.'

'Well, you're not going to believe this, but I'm pregnant,' said Ruth.

Erin and John were both surprised, they hadn't thought the couple would have gotten pregnant again so soon.

'I know what you're thinking,' joked Ruth. 'Trust me, this wasn't planned.'

'God, no,' added Stephen, as he ordered another pint of beer.

'No, not planned. The flipping pill didn't work. Again!' said Ruth, shaking her head.

Erin felt her pulse race.

'Yip, once again we got caught out. Honestly I must be the only person in the world who, trying every brand of the pill, has managed to find two that got me pregnant. It's a disaster!'

Erin couldn't keep her mouth shut any longer.

'How can you describe being pregnant, which is a true blessing, as a disaster?'

Ruth looked a bit put out.

'Oh, Erin! It's not that we didn't want children, but just not right now, what with our jobs and all. Of course Jessica was a blessing in disguise, and we love her more than anything, but still she wasn't exactly planned. And we certainly didn't want to have two babies under two. And now, in less than seven months we will be back to night feeds, colic and weaning all over again.'

'God, I'd almost forgotten about night feeds,' whined Stephen.

Erin was enraged.

'You know, there are plenty of women who would kill to be in your position. It's not fair.'

Ruth looked perplexed; she didn't understand her friend's anger.

John intervened.

'Congratulations, Ruth. We are so happy for you

both. I suppose it just reminds us that we need to get going!' John tried to make light of the fact that Erin was embarrassing him in front of his oldest friend.

'I still think you shouldn't go around complaining that the pill didn't work. In my opinion too many of us have taken the pill for too long. It's ruined many women's chances of getting pregnant.'

'Whatever you say,' said Ruth, who was clearly annoyed.

John and Stephen both tried to deflect the conversation away from babies, and soon the food arrived and they all got stuck in.

Erin was very quiet, her mind racing. She knew she was at the age where most people were having babies, but she honestly felt she was being bombarded from every possible angle by pregnant women, taunted by smug mothers.

'Erin, guess who I met the other day? A blast from your past – Judy Kennedy.'

Erin giggled. Ruth had known that would make her smile. Judy had been an old neighbour of hers, who also knew Ruth through college. Erin hadn't seen her in years, but unfortunately Ruth had got stuck with her on many nights out. Like Ruth, Judy had had a daughter – and just recently a son. She was a complete snob and socialite.

'Is she still queen of Dublin's nightlife?' asked John, who found her utterly unbearable.

'Oh yes,' said Ruth. 'We were comparing notes on babies the other day, and I asked her if her newborn Conrad was sleeping through the night, and she had no idea. "Our night nurse tells us he is," she said. "But of course, who knows if it is true? But it's not our problem!"'

'Imagine having a night nurse,' said Stephen wistfully.

'That's awful,' said Erin. 'I knew she had lots of babysitters, but a full-time night nurse! I would never do that.'

'I bet if you had the money you would,' added Stephen, who evidently was sleep-deprived.

'No, I never would,' said Erin adamantly.

'Anyway, isn't she going to the South of France for two weeks next week, with the kids and their nannies? We still haven't brought Jessica abroad, we haven't been brave enough! I just can't imagine how much luggage we would need to bring.'

'I imagine Judy will have lots of things to bring, what with two babies,' said Erin as she finished off her meal.

'Oh no, she has none! She told me she couldn't be bothered to organize and pack for the holiday, so she bought a second of everything that the babies needed. And a few weeks ago she shipped it all to the five-star hotel!'

'I'm surprised she didn't ship the kids over, too,'

added John, joking. 'Just to save her the hassle of bringing them on a flight!'

'Oh, trust me, if she could have I'm sure she would,' laughed Ruth. The guys were now laughing, too. Everyone found the story funny except Erin.

'Why would someone like her have children if she isn't going to act like she cares? If she isn't going to mind them at night-time, isn't going to organize and pack for their holiday? God, it makes me sick. It's all so unfair.'

'Calm down. That's just Judy for you,' said John, trying to nudge her under the table.

'Stop touching me,' yelled Erin at John.

There was silence at the table. Suddenly the waitress came to take away their empty plates.

'Can we get the bill, please?' asked Ruth. 'I didn't realize the time, we'd better get home to relieve my mum.'

John knew Ruth could have stayed out later, but she wanted to get away from Erin.

After paying the bill, the couples said their goodbyes, and Erin and John got into the car.

'Well, I reckon we can say farewell to that friendship,' said John. He was outraged. 'You were totally irrational all night. What is wrong with you?'

'Me? I can't believe you were all joking about Ruth's mishap with the pill, and Judy and her night-nurse addiction. My God, do you even want children?'

John covered his face with his hands.

'I can't do this any more. I can't have the same conversation a thousand times.'

Erin wasn't listening. She drove home as fast as she could, wanting to get away from John. He was clearly not on her wavelength.

John opened the front door to their home. It looked so neat and perfect, yet was so silent and empty. Horribly empty, thought Erin, who knew only the sound of a child could fill that space.

'You are going to have to ring Ruth to apologize,' said John, as they walked into their bedroom.

'Why should I?' she asked, irritated.

'Because she's one of our closest friends, and when she told us she was pregnant, all you did was jump down her throat over her use of the pill. You had no right to do that, Erin.'

'Don't tell me what to do,' replied Erin angrily, as she began taking her make-up off.

'Well, someone needs to tell you, because you are losing it. You acted totally out of line tonight.'

'Me? You were the one drinking, and I know you sneaked out for a cigarette. You aren't taking this seriously. No wonder we're not pregnant.'

John looked at her in shock.

'You blame everyone but yourself for not being

pregnant. It's your life that needs to change, not mine. You're probably too uptight to get pregnant. But either way I don't care any more.'

'What does that mean?' Erin asked snootily.

'It means you have lost track of all the good things in your life. You're too busy focusing on what you haven't got. And it's clear you don't care about me, either. I think you don't care who you have a child with, just as long as you get pregnant. You are so baby-focused that I'm not a part of your life right now. And I can't live like this.'

Erin felt emotionless. John was clearly upset, but she was sure that once she'd got pregnant they'd have plenty of time to worry about their own relationship and their friends. The main thing was the baby.

Suddenly John stood up and pulled down his old gym bag. He started flinging shirts, jumpers and shoes into it.

'What are you doing?' asked Erin, surprised.

John didn't answer, he just continued grabbing clothes from the wardrobe.

'John?' Erin asked again, this time seizing his arm.

He shrugged it off, but as he turned to her she could see there were tears rolling down his face. Erin hadn't seen him cry for years. She was immediately shocked, and more aware of what was happening. This was real.

'I'm sorry. I can't do this. I love you, but you've pushed me too far,' John said.

'Where are you going?' she asked.

'My brother's house, I guess,' he added quietly, his face white.

And with that John picked up the bag and stormed down the stairs.

Erin ran after him, but he got into his car before she made it to the front door. She watched as he reversed. She sat on the porch as he drove off. She started shaking. She grabbed her phone and rang his number, but it rang out. She kept ringing it until eventually his phone was switched off. She sat on the stairs for hours, watching the driveway, waiting for his car to come back, but it never did. The house lay empty and still. She was all alone.

28

'He's got a look of your father,' said Patsy Slattery very seriously.

'Mum, what are you talking about? It looks like an eel, or some kind of jellyfish,' replied Grace, as she took the picture of her baby's twenty-week scan back from her mother.

'Don't talk about your beloved child like that. Can you not see how beautiful he or she is? And I'm telling you it has the Slattery forehead.'

Grace sighed. Her mum had been examining the scan for hours now. Every few minutes she'd announce how she thought it was definitely a boy, only to then uncover some new bit of evidence that would make her change her prediction to a girl.

'A girl would be so cute,' said Patsy as she poured Grace some more tea. 'Imagine a little girl all dressed in pink running around! It would be like the old days, when all you wanted were your Barbie dolls, a Wendy house and some peace and quiet from your rowdy brothers.'

All Grace still wanted was some peace and quiet from them. For the last two months Colm and Aidan had been teasing Grace and Ethan about their unborn child. Of course they were happy that their sister was pregnant, but that didn't stop the jokes about the possibility of the baby having red hair.

'Ginger Miller has a nice ring to it,' said Aidan.

'It will be known as "Redster" in school,' agreed Colm.

'What about Carrot Top Miller? CTM for short?' asked Aidan.

Poor Ethan couldn't handle the teasing. Grace was well used to the boys' digs about her red hair. She took after her mum, while the boys had both inherited her dad's dark brown hair. Ethan couldn't see the problem, though. In America he had thought the Irish red hair and green eyes look was kinda exotic. He hadn't realized the problems it caused in Ireland.

The last two months had been hard for Grace. It had taken weeks for herself and Ethan to get their heads around being pregnant. It was hard enough for Ethan to be in a new country, with new people and a new job, without having to deal with the idea of becoming a parent soon, too. She knew he missed not having his own brothers, Randy and Matt, to chat to. They both had kids, and she wondered if visiting them would have helped him see the good in having children. Another problem had been their dog.

'What about Coco? He's not good around children. He's not going to be happy,' worried Ethan.

At first Grace had worried about Coco, too. She had watched him online via Matt and Cindy's webcam, but then recently she had spent more time on pregnancy websites than the usual dog ones. Coco was like a child to her, too, and for years all she had worried about was him. But she had almost forgotten about his wellbeing since the baby news. She felt guilty, but she had more important things to fret about. After Christmas, they had finally moved from the hotel to a house in affluent Foxrock. It was a modest place, yet had a large garden, and was well protected from the road by large iron gates and a good security system. But even after the move Grace and Ethan had had many things to work out. Yes, Grace would have the baby in Dublin, but how soon after would they travel back to San Diego? If Patsy had her way Grace would be chained to Ireland and not allowed to leave the country. Patsy wanted her grandchildren to grow up knowing how to speak Irish, knowing where Europe was on a map, and most of all knowing her.

'How can this grandchild know me if you live thousands of miles away? It would break my heart to hear them speak in a foreign accent.'

'A foreign accent? Mum, I'm married to an American, you know,' said Grace, annoyed.

'Oh, I know, and Ethan is lovely, but Grace, there's no place like home, and your home is Ireland. All those shopping malls, swimming pools and sunshine might be fun, but surely you want your children to know how to play GAA, not baseball?'

'Children?' asked Grace. 'God, Mum, one child will be enough. Our world has been shaken enough by the news of this one baby. No, we will be a family of three, that's it.'

'You want your baby to be an only child? A poor little lonely child?' said Patsy.

'Oh Christ, Mum. Don't push me. One child is all we are having. My God, you're so into this whole thing, it's a pity you can't carry him or her yourself for the next few months.'

'Trust me I would if I could. Being pregnant is a blessing.'

Grace knew she was losing the battle, and so changed the conversation. But it was hard not to keep coming back to the same questions: would they stay in Ireland a little longer, what should they do about Coco, and what would Grace do about work? No one would want to hire a pregnant woman who was only planning to stay in Ireland for less than a year. There was a lot to do, but Grace was just so tired and wrecked the whole time that all she wanted was to lie down and sleep.

Ethan had taken a back seat in the pregnancy until the day of the big scan. They had gone nervously into the maternity hospital. As they watched people rub their bumps and smile, or kiss newborns, they had felt left out and awkward. They had felt like impostors. While everyone else had revelled in their baby being on the way, Grace and Ethan had been nervous at the thought of this unplanned arrival. Grace had sat with the cold gel on her stomach, while Ethan had held her hand. As the nurse had explained what was shown on the screen, Ethan had suddenly squeezed Grace's fingers.

'My God, that's the heart beating,' he'd exclaimed.

'Yes,' smiled the nurse. 'And if I move the camera down you can see the leg kicking.'

'A leg. A real little leg!' Ethan's hand had squeezed Grace's again.

'Wow, it's unreal. That's our little one. Right there!'

Grace had seen the look in his eyes change. The last few months Ethan had been in shock, knowing there was going to be change in his life, and even though he wasn't over the moon he had been willing to cope with it. He had helped Grace choose which hospital to book in to, and made sure she was feeling OK and eating well, but it was like he was just doing what he knew was his duty. He was just getting on with it. But as he had leant forward to look at the monitor screen and watch his child roll around, Grace had already sensed a difference in him. There had been something about seeing the images on the screen that had made Ethan finally realize his child was alive and kicking.

As they left the hospital Ethan's enthusiasm had soared.

'I know Randy said I would feel different once I held the baby for the first time, but I can feel the difference already. Just seeing him.'

'Or her,' Grace interrupted.

'OK, seeing him or her move, and the heartbeat, it just makes it real. Wow.'

Grace was happy for Ethan. He had always been an enthusiastic person, a real go-getter, but the last few weeks he had seemed confused and unsure of himself. The unplanned pregnancy had flung him into something he hadn't bargained for, and Ethan always liked to be prepared.

The days after the scan were the best time Grace and Ethan had enjoyed since they came to Ireland.

Ethan was getting very excited, and in-between buying Grace a ton of baby books and dragging her to the shops every weekend so they could look at cots, bouncers and car seats, he was finally beginning to enjoy the pregnancy. Grace was still tired, but as Ethan was eager to enjoy the city nightlife and see as much as possible before the baby was born, they spent most evenings eating out in the top Dublin restaurants. From the Unicorn to Chapter One, they spent meal after meal discussing baby names, baby toys and how they wanted to raise their child.

Grace was delighted that Ethan was happy, she knew with his energy and passion he would be a great dad, but even in the enthusiastic weeks after the scan she still had a niggling sense that she wasn't feeling how she was supposed to. She saw other mums as they walked around Dublin, with their hands proudly rubbing their bumps, and watched them tell anyone and everyone they met their due date. She sat in the doctor's waiting room listening to other soon-to-be mums as they told her how happy they were, and how they couldn't wait until the time came for their baby to be born. She listened as her mum recounted stories of her own pregnancies, all of them tales of joy, hope and expectation.

But Grace had a secret that she didn't want to admit to anyone: she still didn't wake up each morning and think about her baby, she didn't dream about its future, she didn't cry every time she felt it kick. Seeing the scans had made it a bit more exciting, but mainly Grace kept thinking about how different her year in Ireland would have been without unplanned parenthood looming ahead of her.

Grace had hinted at her reluctance to be thrown into motherhood to her oldest friend Sharon. The girls had met in primary school and become close friends. They'd done everything together, although once they finished college Grace had wanted to get out of Dublin, while Sharon had just wanted to make money and be successful. And she certainly had been. While Grace had set up home with Ethan, Sharon had gotten a great job in an Irish bank, met a man, and before long got married herself.

At first Sharon had visited Grace in San Diego at least twice a year to catch up and enjoy the sunshine, but before long she had said she just couldn't do it any more what with work, married life and saving to buy an even bigger house. Grace had missed seeing her, but they had kept in touch. And then, almost two years ago, Grace had been surprised when Sharon had announced she was pregnant. Grace had never seen her friend as the maternal type, but of course she had been happy for her, and had sent baby Chloe the cutest, most expensive clothes that the West Coast had to offer. Grace had been dying to hang out with Sharon once she'd moved back to Ireland, but it had been harder than she'd thought. They had met a few times to begin with, but then Sharon and her husband Mike had had to move into their new house in Co. Wicklow and had been up to their eyeballs. But once Sharon had heard that Grace had the pictures from her twenty-week scan she had longed to see what the baby looked like.

'You just have to visit next week! I still have Chloe's little scan photos. They are so precious.'

Grace wouldn't exactly call the scan photos precious; cute maybe, but they were so hard to interpret. And she just couldn't believe that the black-and-white grainy blob was actually her child. But even so, she set a date to visit Sharon and baby Chloe.

And now, as she drove past Greystones, she wondered when Sharon would return to work. She had taken extended maternity leave because of the baby and the house move, but Grace presumed that with her love for work, her career and making money, she would be heading back soon. After all, Chloe was now fourteen months old.

'I'm not going back,' said Sharon, as she poured Grace a cup of tea.

Grace was very surprised.

'Sure, how could I leave all of this?' Sharon asked, as she waved her hands around the huge shaker-style oak kitchen. With its expensive furniture and massive glass windows overlooking the extremely large country-style garden, Grace could see how Sharon would find it hard to go to work each day and leave it behind. It really was a beautiful home.

'I suppose it would be hard! I know I miss our house back in the US, too. We're lucky we both have such lovely big homes!' Grace joked as she tucked into another biscuit.

'No! I don't care about the house! It's Chloe I'd miss. It's all this I couldn't live without,' Sharon said, as once again she waved around the room. This time Grace noticed the other things. The large photos of Chloe, the frame that held a pair of bronzed first shoes, the yellow highchair, and the *Winnie The Pooh* DVD that was playing from the small TV in the corner. And then she looked at Chloe, who was sitting amidst a big pile of toys. She had a buttered cracker in one hand and was flicking the pages of a Dora the Explorer picture book in the other.

'How could I ever leave her?' Sharon asked again.

Grace looked on as Sharon picked up her daughter and gave her a big hug and kiss. Chloe squealed with delight. As she kissed her mum back Grace could see how happy both of them were. Chloe was beautiful and as bright as a button, but still Grace couldn't believe that the workaholic Sharon was about to throw in her career.

'Once you have a child nothing else matters. Yes, we worked hard to get this house, and it really is everything we dreamt of, but a house, a car, travel, clothes, make-up – they all come a distant second to a child, your own child.'

Grace said nothing.

'It took us a long long time to get pregnant. There were very tough times, but when we were finally blessed with our little angel I just knew nothing else could ever make me as happy again. She was worth all the hardship.'

When Sharon had announced she was expecting she had admitted to Grace that it had taken her a little while to get pregnant, but what her friend was saying now made Grace realize it had been much harder than she had let on.

'I couldn't get pregnant for a long time. We tried everything. Finally we had IVF.'

Grace put down her mug. She was so surprised. Sharon had never told her that. She hadn't even known Sharon had wanted kids that much.

'Nobody ever wants to admit that they can't get pregnant. I never told anyone apart from my mum and sisters. But that didn't make it any easier. At first we just kept trying by ourselves, but eventually we had to get help. Nowadays a lot of women are the same: I suppose our generation has left having children too late. I always thought I could just have kids whenever I wanted. If it hadn't been for Mike's interest in having children early then I might not have tried for a few more years, and then maybe I would never have had Chloe at all. God, I can't bear thinking about that, though. I was so selfish before.'

Grace didn't like her friend thinking badly of herself. Sharon was fun, kind, hard-working and a great friend.

'Don't say that,' said Grace, taking her hand. 'Look at you now, in your fancy Dan house, with a beautiful child, and the knowledge that you don't have to get up for work in the mornings. You're lucky!'

'So are you,' replied Sharon, as she swept the blonde hair out from Chloe's forehead. Chloe smiled and then made a beeline for the new kitchen presses, which had locks to prevent her from opening and breaking everything inside them. 'It's just such good news that soon you'll have a baby, too. Our children can be friends, just like us!'

'Oh yeah,' said Grace, once again reminded of how soon she would have her own child.

Sharon took in Grace's demeanour.

'I know this has been a big surprise, and you feel you were caught out, but we're not seventeen years old. Getting pregnant isn't something to be worried about. Yes, you got pregnant while on the pill, it happens to so many people. You might see it as an accident, but trust me, once you hold your baby you will realize it was a true blessing.'

Grace felt she was talking to a stranger. Sharon sounded like the perfect mother from a Disney movie. Grace had come here not only to visit her friend and her gorgeous baby, but finally to be able to admit to someone that she was nervous. Nervous that her maternal instincts and feeling hadn't kicked in, that she still didn't know if she wanted a child. But as she heard Sharon say once again how having children was a blessing she didn't think she would be sympathetic.

Even so, Grace admitted her fears, but rather than comfort her, Sharon got very defensive.

'Do you know how many women would die to get pregnant and have a child of their own? You should realize how lucky you are!'

'It's not that I hate children or anything. When I see Chloe I know how great children can be, but just because some women find it difficult to get pregnant doesn't automatically make me feel over the moon because I didn't.'

'Find it difficult? Grace, it's more than just finding it difficult to get pregnant that causes the pressure. I never told you, but my inability to have children almost broke me and Mike up.'

Grace looked at Sharon. She had never heard her speak so openly and truthfully.

'You don't know the pressure a couple can be under when all they want is children yet they just can't make them. At first it wasn't a big deal, but as the months wore on our whole lives revolved around my cycle and periods, around trying to eat healthily, trying to relax – yet not being able to – and, of course, the underlying unspoken thought that it might be all the other person's fault. If we hadn't fallen pregnant when we did, I honestly think we might have split up. We were under such pressure, and we were just so consumed with it all that we lost track of ourselves. When you want a child there is nothing else to talk or care about, but when Chloe was finally born we became a family, and the joy and happiness brought us back together again. We're so lucky to have Chloe, but so many people will never get pregnant, so you should be grateful. Try to be happy. More positive.'

After hearing how hard Sharon and Mike had struggled to have Chloe, and how it had pushed their marriage to breaking point, Grace could see how Sharon wouldn't understand how she was feeling. So she switched to another topic of conversation, and Sharon gave her a guided tour of their new home before they sat down to lunch.

Grace was helping Chloe put on her pink shoes when Sharon opened the dishwasher to get some clean cutlery out for lunch. Suddenly Chloe pushed Grace aside, flung the shoe on the floor and made a dash for the open dishwasher. Grace was amazed at her speed.

'She just loves all the kitchen appliances. She could stare at the washing machine all day,' said Sharon. 'And she adores helping me unpack the dishwasher. You're a great help, aren't you?' she said to Chloe.

As Sharon started slicing the bread for lunch Chloe went hell for leather trying to grab the clean plates. Grace watched in horror as the scene played out like a Greek wedding. Chloe systematically picked up every plate from the dishwasher rack and flung them on to the ground. The first two just rolled on to the floor, but the third smashed. Grace ran to grab the fourth out of her hand but she wasn't quick enough. Chloe held it high, and then smashed it on to the brand-new wood floor. Grace looked at Sharon, expecting her to give out to Chloe, but instead Sharon just smiled.

'She's a lively baby, isn't she? Always wanting to be into everything!'

Grace didn't know what to do. As she sat among broken china she wondered whether she should reprimand Chloe herself. Chloe needed to learn rules. But eventually Sharon picked Chloe up and asked her to not break mummy's plates again. Although she hugged Chloe as she said it, which Grace thought made it less likely that Chloe would learn that she'd done something wrong.

As the two friends caught up over the rest of the afternoon, Grace began to realize how much work a baby was: with mixing bottles, feeding, nappy changing and playing it was all go. Chloe was a cutie, but at the same time Grace was surprised how lenient Sharon was. The toddler chewed books, ripped up the newspaper, broke a cup and spilt water everywhere. Grace knew she didn't mean any of it, but still, she remembered Sharon as a tough-talking hard-working career woman, and couldn't get used to seeing her so soft and easy to walk over. Finally Grace knew she should go. She had enjoyed catching up with her oldest friend, but the conversation kept becoming one in which Sharon tried to make Grace understand how lucky she was, and to tell her how much she would love being a mum. Chloe and Sharon walked Grace to the door.

'You know, it took us three rounds of IVF to get pregnant with Chloe. It was awful. And as much as we'd love to have more kids, we couldn't go through it all again – the stress, worry, cost, medication and pressure. No, Chloe will be our only child.'

Grace didn't know what to say. After seeing how Sharon idolized Chloe she could imagine how unbearable she must find it, not being able to have another baby.

'I know I'm too soft on Chloe, but she's a great child, and she is the only person who is ever going to call me Mama. And that is worth more to me than any amount of china plates.'

Grace looked at Sharon, who had her arms wrapped tightly around the baby. Chloe had been her one chance at having a family. Grace leant forward and hugged both Sharon and Chloe at the same time. She wasn't converted, but as she watched little Chloe wave goodbye, she thought she felt her heart start to melt. Just a little.

29

'OK, hold your hand steady. It won't work if you don't stop moving.'

'What is it, Mary? I can't see properly without my glasses. What will it be?' asked Patsy Slattery excitedly.

Grace groaned, but at the same time watched with interest, as her Aunt Mary held a needle and thread over her right hand.

'It's a circle,' cried Grace's other aunt, Joan. 'A circle!'

'Oh my God, that means a girl. A little girl. I knew it!' exclaimed Patsy, as she hugged Grace.

'Mum, holding a bit of thread over my hand isn't hard science! It's an old wives' tale, so let's not start painting the nursery pink just yet.'

'Grace Slattery, how dare you!' said Patsy.

'It's Grace Miller, Mum.'

'OK, Grace Miller. Your Aunt Mary has been holding this "bit of thread" over women's hands for years. She has predicted every child in this road correctly for as long as I can remember. She kindly offered to let us know what Baby Miller will be, and I'm telling you now: if she says it's a girl then it is.'

Grace looked at her aunt.

'It's true. The needle doesn't lie!'

'Congratulations, pet,' said Joan. 'We've all been dying for a girl! Girls are just great! I mean, of course, I love my boys, but God what I wouldn't do for a bit of pink in the house. Every wash is black, grey or blue. And I swear if I have to watch any more football I'll explode! To have a little girl in the family would just be perfect. Imagine the clothes!'

Grace pretended she wasn't totally buying into her aunt's old-fashioned way of predicting the sex of the baby, but as her mum and aunts chatted about baby clothes she did start to imagine a little girl. She would have Ethan's fair hair and her own pale skin. She would be so cute.

As Grace allowed herself to fantasize about having an all-pink gorgeous daughter, Patsy was on the phone to Colm.

'OK, if you want to come home for dinner that's no problem. We'd love to see you! Sure I'm cooking Grace's favourite food tonight, don't I have to keep this baby healthy? What? Oh yes, Colm, the washing machine is free to use after dinner,' Patsy said, her voice changing. 'God, is that the only reason you ever come to visit me? To have your dirty T-shirts washed? Well, I'm telling you enjoy it while it lasts, because once this baby girl arrives it will be every man for himself. No, I'll be too busy with Grace and the baby to be washing your clothes. Anyway, we will see you tonight.'

Grace was staying with her mum for a few days while Ethan was away. He was on holiday with his parents in Italy. Sally and Bill Miller were lovely. Like Ethan they were healthy, full of energy and kind. They lived in San Jose, which wasn't too far from San Diego, so it had been easy for Ethan to visit them. Bill had retired last year, and once they'd heard about Grace and Ethan's trip to Ireland they'd decided it would be a great time for them to do the big holiday to Europe that they had always dreamt of. They started in Dublin, and after two weeks in 'Eire' they planned to head to France, Spain, Italy, Greece, Croatia and Poland. Their trip had been mapped out well in advance of Grace's pregnancy news, but they'd been delighted to get a chance to see the bump, their future grandchild, while in Dublin.

Patsy had been very nervous about their visit. She had met them at the wedding, of course, and seen photos of their big house in America, and knew they enjoyed a superb lifestyle. And she wanted to impress them. Bill and Sally had stayed in Foxrock with Grace and Ethan, but when they had arrived two weeks ago Patsy had decided to cook a big meal for them all, to celebrate Grace's pregnancy. Patsy, and Grace's two aunts, had spent all week cleaning, decorating, fixing the small garden and cooking – and Patsy had even got her hair done. Unfortunately the meal had gotten off to a bad start once Bill had arrived.

'So this must be your city house,' he had said as he'd walked up the short driveway. 'Yes, we keep a small place in the city, too. In San Fran it just makes more sense to keep the city home small. Like yourself, it's easier to keep.'

'Oh, what a cute townhouse!' Sally had said as she walked into the modest hallway.

Oh crap, had thought Grace. She had turned to see her mum's face flush with anger.

'Our "city house"? Our "townhouse"?' Patsy had said quietly to Grace. She'd been furious. 'This is our family house, where we raised three children. Teddy worked hard for this house and family home. My God, if he could hear them now!' Grace tried to persuade Patsy that Bill and Sally hadn't meant to be unkind. They came from very fortunate backgrounds, and they just weren't used to such small family houses. Eventually Patsy had calmed down and started cooking the dinner.

The small kitchen had been crowded as they'd

all sat down to one of Patsy's famous home-cooked meals: a chicken and broccoli bake with white wine and cream.

'Oh, Patsy, I'm lactose intolerant,' Sally had said, as she'd eyed up the plates dripping with cream.

Grace had panicked; this wasn't America, they didn't have a healthy alternative. Patsy's face had shown annoyance and distress, too. Suddenly Aunt Mary had come to the rescue by offering to make Sally a chicken salad instead. Grace had sat down, and hadn't been at all surprised to see the size of her plate. Ever since Patsy had heard that Grace was pregnant with her grandchild, she had taken it upon herself to make sure that Grace ate for two, although it actually felt like three. She was being force-fed all day long.

'You just have to eat well. We want to make sure this baby is healthy and happy.'

'Happy or fat?' Aidan had asked, on more than one occasion.

While making sure Grace ate plenty, Patsy had also done novenas for her grandchild. Half the road had been forced to join Patsy on her quest for the safest ever delivery of a child.

As Grace tucked into her food, Bill and Sally had told everyone about their trip. From Rome to Berlin, they wanted to see it all.

'God, sure, I haven't been to most of those places

myself,' Patsy had said, as she'd poured everyone, apart from Grace, some wine.

'Well, Patsy, we've been all around the world, from Africa to Australia, but really we've been meaning to do this big European trip for years, and now that Ethan and Grace are in Ireland it felt like the right time. But we would really love for the kids to join us, even for a part of it.'

Grace had looked at Bill, and then at Ethan. Bill and Sally had been asking Grace and Ethan to join them on their trip for months. Initially Ethan had said he couldn't ask for time off work, and then once Grace got pregnant he had told his parents he just wanted to stay with her, but Grace had realized they would love to have their son and daughter-in-law with them.

'Mom, you know I can't take that long off work,' Ethan had replied.

'We're not expecting you to come for the whole trip, but you've always wanted to see Rome and Pompeii, could you not even join us for a few days?'

Grace had seen Ethan weaken. He'd always longed to see where the Roman emperors had ruled, and where pizza originated, and marvel at the once-buried city of Pompeii. But Grace had been adamant that she didn't want to go away. She didn't feel that well, her back and legs hurt, and even though she was five months' pregnant she was still suffering from morning sickness. She was just too tired to spend hours walking around the streets of Rome and Pompeii. As she'd watched Bill explain the trip in detail she'd seen Ethan's eyes light up; he would love to go. All Americans dream of one day visiting Europe, and her husband had been no exception.

'Listen,' she'd said to Ethan, 'why don't you join your parents on the Italian leg of their holiday? I'm sure work could survive without you for a week.'

'How can I leave you and the baby?' he'd replied.

'I've a few months left until this baby pops out! So there's no fear of you missing the birth. Just go on the trip and me and our bump will still be here when you return.'

Ethan hadn't needed any more convincing, and before long he'd been talking itineraries, hotels and sightseeing with his dad. Patsy had also seen this as a golden opportunity.

'And Grace can stay with me,' she'd said proudly. 'In my townhouse,' she'd added. Colm and Aidan had sniggered.

'Mum, I've my own house now.'

'I know, but what would you be staying on your own in that fancy house in Foxrock for, when you could stay with me? I'll look after you.'

Grace hadn't felt like committing to staying with her mum immediately, but as the whole table had gazed at them, she'd realized her mum only meant well, and she hadn't wanted to embarrass her in front of their guests.

'I'd love to stay with you, Mum,' she had said quickly, much to the amusement of her brothers.

'Oh, that will be lovely for you,' Sally had said to Patsy as she'd passed around the water. 'I've no daughters, but I can only imagine what a wonderful relationship it is, especially when they are as nice as Grace. You'll miss her when they go back home. Especially with the baby. But you'll just have to visit us all in California more!'

'Oh yes,' said Bill. 'We can't wait to have Baby Miller visiting us at the weekends. He or she will just love our pool. I'll teach him how to swim!'

Neither Grace, Ethan or Patsy had responded. The issue of what they would do after the baby was born had been a sore subject for them all. Naturally Ethan wanted to return to San Diego, while Patsy was adamant her grandchild would be raised in Ireland, under her close eye. Grace didn't know what to do or say, she was still trying to get her head around the thought of being a mum, without worrying about what continent she'd be on.

'Oh well, we'll just have to see about that,' Patsy had said. Despite her best efforts she had spent the night being insulted or upset at every turn.

Luckily Bill and Sally had been tired from their long transatlantic flight, and everyone had decided to

258

head off early. Grace had known Patsy was ruffled, but she had seemed to mellow when Bill and Sally had insisted on taking photos 'of this gem of a house', that was so close to the city, to show their friends back home. Sally had also brought some beautiful crystal as a gift, and soon Patsy had been insisting they visit again.

For the next fortnight Ethan's parents had used Grace and Ethan's place as a base as they travelled around from West Cork to Blarney. Grace had known Ethan loved having them there, and their kindness had been never-ending: from meals out to gifts from all their trips, they had never stopped showing Grace how much they cared. But she hadn't been able to face another awful touristy Irish souvenir. All the gift shops had to have been sold out of their baby wear. From Babygros with leprechauns on them, to little hats covered in shamrocks, Grace had been amazed at how tacky and embarrassing the gifts were. She'd known Ethan's parents meant well, but there was no way her baby could hold its head high wearing a Blarney Castle snowsuit. Maybe in America, but not here. Also, after two weeks of explaining about the famine and other injustices, and marking on a map where Irish heroes like Michael Collins had died, she had been a little worn down. Their endless energy had made her realize she was right not to go to Italy with them. They might be double her age, but Grace and her ever-growing bump hadn't been able to keep up with them. Finally Ethan had packed his bag, and after hugging Grace and their bump tight, he had headed off to live out his Italian dream. Grace was a little worried he might be expecting Rome to look exactly like in the film *Gladiator*; she didn't have the heart to tell him it had probably been modernized since then.

And so Grace now found herself back home in St Joseph's Road, having an afternoon nap. She was wrecked after two weeks of entertaining her in-laws, and was actually looking forward to a week of pampering from her mum. She hadn't been sleeping well, but got up so she could talk to her brother Colm. Her mum cooked a huge lasagne, and Grace demolished her potion, but she still felt so tired. She just hadn't felt right all day. As Colm began using Patsy's washing machine to clean mountains of dirty clothes, Grace sprawled out on the couch watching TV. As she lay there she rubbed her hand over her belly; the baby had been quiet the last few hours. Usually the evening was when it kicked the most. But she presumed it was just asleep, and continued watching TV. Patsy had spent the whole afternoon talking about 'the beautiful baby girl'. Grace was sick of trying to persuade her that there was no way a needle and thread could predict the sex of her child, and so had just rolled with the conversation and listened as Patsy agonized over which school would be best for her little granddaughter. Grace was glad when Colm decided he would stay the night, too, as it meant she could go to bed early and leave him to keep her mum company. It was obvious that her mum still missed her dad; they used to stay up late watching TV and chatting. She knew it must still be hard for Patsy, adjusting to life alone. After kissing her mum goodnight, Grace climbed up the stairs and crawled into her old bed, and before long the sound of their loud old washing machine tumbling coaxed her into a deep slumber.

At 3 a.m. Grace woke, frightened. Something felt wrong. She turned on her light and sat up. She didn't know what it was. As she strolled to the bathroom, she caught a look of herself in the mirror. Looking at the reflection of her swollen belly in the dim light of the bathroom, she suddenly knew what was wrong. She hadn't felt the baby move in hours. She stood still. She could hear the sound of the old grandfather clock tick, and the light murmur of her brother snoring. She could feel the cold bathroom tiles against her bare feet, but she couldn't sense any movement inside her. She went back into her bedroom and lay down on the bed, and she pressed her hands against her belly, expecting to feel some kind of response. But nothing happened. She grabbed the glass of water from beside her bed, and downed it in one. Sometimes cold water helped the baby move. Again she waited, but nothing happened. She walked around the room, and even did some big yoga stretches, but with no result. And then she started to worry. She knew a baby could just stop moving at any day, any hour. Miscarriages could happen to anyone. Suddenly Grace thought back to the moment when her aunt had decided she was carrying a baby girl. Grace didn't want her little baby to be dead. She tried to remember what the baby book had said about movements: she knew she was supposed to feel a certain amount of kicks in a twenty-four hour period, but she couldn't remember how many. Ethan had read the books more intently than she had. She cursed her mother for not having the internet, as she could have gone online now and got the information at once. Grace sat for another twenty minutes in her bedroom before deciding she needed help. She crossed the landing and knocked on her mother's bedroom door.

Patsy was out cold when Grace walked into her room. She was lying with her hair curlers in, and a good lathering of face cream all over her face. Grace hated disturbing her from her slumber but she was beginning to panic.

'Oh my God, what's wrong?' Patsy said as she shot up out of the bed and flung on her old pink dressing gown.

Grace told her.

'Maybe I'm overreacting.'

'Well, was the baby kicking much all day?' Patsy asked.

Suddenly Grace realized she couldn't think of one time when the baby had felt active all day. She had just been so tired herself, that after dropping Ethan to the airport she had been glad to relax. She hadn't thought about the baby and its movements.

'You didn't feel any movements all day? Why didn't you say something earlier? Did you not notice? Were you not concerned?' said Patsy.

Grace felt like the worst mother in the world. She felt helpless. Patsy looked at her daughter, who had gone white as a ghost with worry, and knew exactly what to do.

'Let's go to the hospital.'

'It's the middle of the night.'

'Well, this can't wait until the morning. Now do you feel fit to drive?'

To be honest Grace didn't. She felt too anxious.

'Well, don't worry. I'll get you there, pet.'

'You can't drive,' said Grace.

'No, but Colm can.'

And before Grace knew it, Patsy had Colm out of his bed and changing into his tracksuit.

'I only came home to wash my clothes, I didn't sign up for delivering babies.'

'She's not in labour,' shouted Patsy. 'Just get into that car.'

Grace followed her mum and brother down the driveway. She shivered in the jumper she'd hurriedly pulled on.

'Get out of that car,' shouted Patsy to her son.

'What? You just told me to get in,' said Colm, confused with all the middle-of-the-night shouting.

'Can you not see your poor sister isn't feeling well? Help her into your car. And then drive as fast as you can, we need to get to the maternity hospital asap.'

Colm was only too delighted to use this as an excuse to speed through the dark Dublin city streets. But as he drove and Patsy prayed out loud, Grace felt numb. She tried to think back to every little thing she had done that day. While she'd been washing her hair, had her baby stopped moving? While she'd read a stupid gossip magazine had her baby held its breath for too long? While she'd painted her nails had her baby died?

How will I tell Ethan, she thought? How will he cope? How will he feel when he hears I didn't notice there was no movement, that I was too wrapped up in myself to worry about our baby? I should have gone to the doctor earlier.

'The baby is probably fine. Don't you worry,' said Patsy, as she rubbed Grace's hand. But Grace could see that in Patsy's other hand she had her rosary beads clenched tight. She was worried, too.

How will Mum cope? thought Grace. Of them all Patsy seemed to be the most excited about the baby. Grace didn't want to break her heart.

Before she knew it, Grace was being seen by a young-looking doctor.

'Now, can you tell me the last time you felt any movement?' he asked as he passed his hands over her belly.

'Some time yesterday, I think,' admitted Grace.

'OK,' he replied solemnly. 'And have you had any bleeding or abdominal pain?'

'No,' Grace said. 'But I'm just so tired. I'm tired the whole time. I wasn't thinking straight, I forgot to count the movements.'

The doctor nodded, but she could see in his eyes that he probably wondered what kind of person she was not to notice when her child was in trouble.

'OK, we need to do a scan on you. The nurse will bring you up to the fetal assessment unit department straight away.'

As Grace sat in a wheelchair, Patsy walked beside her.

'Good luck,' said the doctor.

Grace felt sick. He must think the baby is dead, she thought.

She began to cry. The nurse stopped pushing the chair.

'Are you OK?'

Grace couldn't see her through the tears flooding her eyes.

'Mum,' Grace said as Patsy grabbed her hand. 'Mum, what if the baby is dead?'

Patsy said nothing, but took hold of the wheelchair.

'My grandchild will be fine,' she said, but Grace could hear her voice crack. 'Now, let's hurry up and get this scan done.'

As Grace stared at the white ceiling she heard the nurse talk reassuringly as she poured the cold gel on her stomach, turned on the scanning machine and placed the camera on her stomach. Grace was too worried to listen to the nurse's words. She held her breath. Patsy said nothing. She suddenly looked so frail and old. Grace realized she shouldn't have brought her into the room. It wasn't fair that she would be shown the black and white images of her first grandchild, only to be told it was dead.

As the nurse silently pushed the camera from side to side and ran it up and down Grace's abdomen, Grace thought back to when she had first found out she was pregnant, and to all the times she had wished she wasn't. She thought of all the days she'd craved to be back in San Diego with nothing more to worry about than where to eat after a day's work. I've brought this on myself, she thought. I've caused this awful thing to happen. I was so sure I didn't want this child, but now I know better. I want my baby, she thought. All I want is my baby.

Apart from the sound of the machine the room was silent. Time seemed to stand still. Finally the nurse spoke.

'OK, I think I can hear something. Let's turn the sound up.'

Grace bit her lip. Patsy squeezed her hand so tight that she thought her bones would break.

'Yes, that's a heartbeat.'

A tear rolled down Grace's check. Patsy let out a cry.

'Oh, thank God,' she cried. 'Oh, Teddy, I knew you would help us. You answered my prayers.'

The nurse smiled.

'Your baby is breathing. It's very still, though. It must just have been having a big sleep.'

As the nurse rolled the camera over and over Grace's stomach, Grace arched her neck to look at the screen. It was all a little fuzzy, but she could make out the head and an arm stretched out.

She and Patsy were so happy.

Five minutes later an older, grey-haired doctor entered the room. He introduced himself to Grace.

'How do you feel now, Mrs Miller?'

'I'm OK,' she replied, 'but worried about my baby.'

'You don't need to be. Your baby is moving and breathing fine. I know you must have gotten a fright. The baby might just have been tired or sleepy today. And sometimes they get themselves caught in a position and just can't move. But either way it is OK.'

'Well, that's great,' said Grace, sitting up.

'Yes it is, but we'd like you to keep a movement chart, and note down your baby's kicks every day. At the baby's active time you should be getting at least ten kicks in a two-hour period. And if you don't, then do not hesitate to come to us. Never take a chance and wait, or worry you might be wasting our time. Nine times out of ten the baby will move, and then we can send you home, but always come in to get checked out. Some women leave it too late, and then there is nothing we can do.'

The thought of finding out her baby had died and she hadn't noticed appalled Grace. She promised to be more vigilant from now on.

'OK. Well, Nurse Lynch will bring you back down to the day ward to get a few other things checked out, and then you'll be free to go home. But take it easy tomorrow. Rest.'

And with that the doctor was gone.

The nurse took Grace and Patsy back down to the ward.

'You can relax now. You'll be fine. But I'd just like to check your blood pressure, and take some blood tests. You're very pale.'

Grace rolled up her jumper sleeve, and while the nurse took out a needle Patsy chewed the ear off her.

'Grace just won't relax, no wonder she's pale. Sure wasn't she doing a flipping bus tour of Dublin with her in-laws yesterday? And she was at the cinema the night before.'

The nurse smiled, she was used to protective mothers.

'Your blood pressure is quite low, and I would hazard a guess that your iron levels are, too. That's probably why you've been feeling so tired.'

'But I still should have noticed my baby's movements, or lack of them,' replied Grace.

'Listen, when you feel wrecked, it's hard to remember what to do. We should have these blood tests back tomorrow, and we can advise you then on what to take to help you feel better. But until that happens just rest and try to sleep.'

Grace promised.

'Don't you worry, nurse, I'll look after her,' said Patsy, holding Grace's hand.

The nurse smiled, winking at Grace.

As Grace and Patsy walked out of the large wooden doors of the maternity hospital and into the car that Colm had been banished to wait in, Grace couldn't help feeling dismayed. She could have lost her baby. She rubbed her hand over her belly. Inside was her precious little child, and she hadn't been paying attention to it. As she watched woman after woman enter the hospital she vowed to become more like them, more like a mother.

30

'I'm going to be sick,' yelled Colm Slattery.

Grace was laughing hysterically.

'Christ, Gracie, cover your belly up, will you? It's like there's an alien inside you. About to scrape its way out,' said Aidan, agreeing that their sister's moving stomach was disturbing.

'It's scary,' declared Colm.

Grace and her two brothers were sitting on the old family couch watching TV when Baby Miller started to make its presence known.

'Do you feel invaded? Does it hurt when the baby moves like that? Are you scared?' Colm asked his big sister.

Grace protectively ran her hand over her ever-expanding belly.

'No, is the answer to your three questions. I love it when it moves.'

Colm nodded. It had only been a week since Grace's trip to hospital, and more than anyone Colm had gotten a huge fright that night, seeing his sister so upset and worried that she might lose her child.

Grace had spent the week being pampered by her mum. In-between her novenas Patsy had found the time to stuff Grace to the gills with food, in particular iron-rich food. Grace's blood count had been low, and so Patsy had decided the whole house should be full of red meat, spinach and eggs.

'I swear to God, if we have to eat liver one more time this week I'll kill you,' Colm said, as they all headed into the kitchen for dinner.

'Can I remind both of you that you don't actually have to eat here? It's not like you live in this house any more!'

'You don't either,' replied Aidan, 'but you're always here. And anyway we want to keep you company.'

'And Mum has the house so full of food,' Colm said, 'that it's tempting to eat here every night. There's never anything to eat in my flat.'

'That's because you don't ever go shopping,' said Grace, scolding her younger brother, but really she was glad of Colm and Aidan's company. The last week had been hard for her. The minute Ethan had heard of her 'scare' he had wanted to abandon Rome and fly straight home, but Grace had insisted he didn't. She wasn't sick, the baby was fine. All she needed was to catch up on some sleep, take more iron, and – most importantly – start listening to her baby. In the last seven days Grace's whole attitude towards the little person growing inside her had changed. The old saying, that you don't know what you've got until it's gone, was certainly right for her. It wasn't until she realized she could have lost her baby, that she'd suddenly known she wanted him or her so much. She was actually glad to have had some time to herself this week. Ethan had been great, ringing her every few hours, but it had been good for Grace to have time alone to come to terms with her feelings, to let go of the worry, upset and disappointment she had felt when she had found out she was pregnant, and instead start thinking of the baby as a blessing. It was still going to take some time to get used to, but then having her mum around helped; Patsy's excitement about the baby was infectious.

'Now, I hope you don't mind, but I just couldn't face liver again tonight, pet.'

Colm and Aidan cheered.

'We only had sausages in the fridge, so I made your old granny's favourite – sausage sandwiches.'

Grace's mouth began to water. Granny Slattery had lived close by when Grace and her brothers were growing up, and as she'd lived alone, one of them often stayed with her at the weekends. They'd always fought over whose turn it was, as it was such a treat. First they'd be given a huge dinner, and chocolate éclairs for desert, followed by an evening of being allowed to watch anything they wanted on TV. Then they'd sleep in the spare room, where Granny would have used her old electric blanket to warm the bed. But it was the breakfasts Grace had liked best: sausage sandwiches and grapefruit juice, all served on a tray in bed! Grace used to think that that breakfast must be what millionaires ate in the South of France. To sit in your bed drinking grapefruit juice and eating sausages in bread was just so exciting!

Of course, when she grew up, she'd realized it probably wasn't that exotic, but still, no matter how many countries she'd visited, or fancy hotels she'd stayed in, she'd never come across a breakfast as wonderful as Granny Slattery's. The longer Grace stayed in Ireland, the more she remembered all the good things about the place, her family and what they had. She had wanted to get out of Dublin, travel the world, experience a different and better life, but now she saw that what she had here was as good as it gets. And that was mainly due to her loving family.

Grace dug in to her mum's big pile of sausage sandwiches and potato mash, while Patsy told her she was going to play bridge over in her neighbour's house later.

'I'd better bring a cake or some sweets to thank them all.'

Over the last week all of Patsy's friends had been calling in to check up on Grace. Even though she had kept explaining that she wasn't sick, they'd still insisted on making her lie down while they came to see how she was, and brought box after box of chocolates. Grace hadn't realized before how kind and caring her mum's friends and neighbours were. She'd also never known how loved and cared-for Patsy was by everyone that knew her.

'Anyway, are you sure you don't want to name the baby after a saint?' Patsy asked for the tenth time that week. 'It would just make the baby safer.'

'Mum!' all three kids replied.

'But what's wrong with Ada or Agnes for a girl? Or maybe Alphonsus for a boy?'

'Nothing, they're lovely,' said Grace, lying. 'But they are kind of old-fashioned. I'm not sure Ethan would go for them.' She didn't say any more. She was enjoying being in the lap of luxury at home, and didn't want to rock the boat.

'Hmm, yes, Ethan will probably want to call the baby Britney or some other weird American name. My only grandchild will probably be named after a pop star or movie actor.'

'Mum! He's not that bad. Anyway, as tonight is my last night here before Ethan comes back tomorrow, who feels like walking down to Boland's for some ice cream?'

'I'm in,' said Aidan.

'Me, too,' said Colm, as he stuffed the last sandwich into his mouth. 'I just need to put a clothes wash on first, though.'

Patsy looked at him disapprovingly, but Grace knew she didn't mind. Patsy had done nothing all week but look after the mum-to-be. She did drive Grace mad sometimes, but everything she did was for her children. She loved them all so much. Grace realized how lucky she was to have her.

As dinner was over and she had some spare time, Grace took this time to call her friend Rachel in San Diego. Grace had worked with Rachel, and couldn't believe it when she'd found out that she was also pregnant. Both their babies were due around the same time.

'I'm just home from my baby shower,' exclaimed Rachel down the phone, after greeting Grace with a scream of delight. She called Grace 'my pregnancy twin'. It made Grace cringe.

'So how did the shower go?' asked Grace, who was fascinated by these American baby parties. It was just so different from anything that took place in Ireland. Irish women were too superstitious to throw a party for it weeks or months in advance.

'Well, I had registered all my gifts in advance, but

even I was surprised at how cute some of them were. A baby Moses basket made entirely from diapers! An adorable baby yoga mat and DVD – because, really, babies can never start learning too young about exercise and keeping fit. A great baby sling, for when me and Brad go hiking with the little one. A beautiful cashmere Babygro . . .'

The list of mad items was endless. Grace knew Rachel's friends meant well, and Grace herself had to admit that she had bought a diaper stork for a neighbour once, but as she heard Rachel list the gifts, the baby plans, the list of pre-schools that she was hoping her little son would get into, Grace felt uneasy. She didn't know if it was because she was now in Ireland, or because she, too, was pregnant, but it all felt a little over the top. Although, as Rachel described the baby clothes she had bought, it did remind Grace just how much choice there was in America. Close to where she had lived there'd been some beautiful baby and gift shops. Not that Grace had had any interest in them at the time, but one had been beside the dog shop where she'd bought most of Coco's dog clothes, beds, and collars, so she'd often passed by its windows and looked in at its miniature designer clothes. After half an hour of baby talk with Rachel, Grace knew she had to go – not only would the phone call cost her a fortune, but her brothers were waiting impatiently for their ice cream.

'Are you sure you're well enough to walk to Boland's?' Patsy asked Grace worriedly.

Grace hadn't gone further than the garden all week, due to Patsy's fears she would do damage to the baby.

'Mum, I'm not sick, I'm fine. We will see you in a while.'

As Grace walked out the front door she saw her two brothers kicking a football on the road with some of the local kids. It was like the old days. The three Slattery kids walked down to the nearby shops and got into the queue of people all wanting a famous Boland ice-cream cone. After Grace had paid for the three 99s they walked back to St Joseph's Road and sat down on the garden wall. Grace felt like she was ten years old again. As she listened to her brothers bicker, she watched the kids play rounders; they were shouting, cheering and running as fast as they could. Grace remembered all the summers she and her brothers had spent out on the road doing the exact same thing. The local children would join teams and play for hours. They would play until it was too dark to see the ball. And only then would they sadly part until the next day, when they could begin another game, race or adventure. Grace thought about Rachel's plans for her baby in San Diego, herself and Ethan's fancy house in Foxrock, and their own secluded home back in California. She had strived for electric gates, pools, prestigious addresses, fancy bathrooms, private gardens. But as she saw the happiness and ease of the kids – walking out of their houses, joining forces and playing – it made her think. She also appreciated how she wouldn't have survived the week if it hadn't been for her mum, brothers and kind neighbours. They had all helped, and she was gradually realizing how important they were.

'I don't think I want to move back to America,' she said out loud.

'Are you serious?' asked Aidan, almost dropping his ice cream. 'I thought you couldn't wait to get back to your cool house.'

'I couldn't, but it's different now.' Grace watched a kid leave his bike out on the road, knowing it would be there the next day, ready for action.

'I want a place where our child can safely walk out the door and play. Somewhere where there are tons of kids. I don't want him or her to be raised behind a big gate, they'd be lonely. I want what we had.'

Colm and Aidan both looked a little surprised.

'OK, well, maybe a slightly bigger house than we had!'

They agreed.

'And also I want you guys and Mum nearby. I don't

have a clue about babies, I'll need her every step of the way.'

'But what about Ethan?' asked Colm. 'I thought he wanted to go home after the baby was born?'

Grace was stumped. It was the most obvious question but she didn't know how to answer it. It was going to be a problem. A huge problem.

31

Beth Prendergast stood in a long queue in Marks & Spencer's. She dipped one hand into the small plastic bag and pulled out a piece of the warm *pain au chocolat*. She rammed it into her mouth. The taste was so good it was unreal. She ate some more. She had become addicted to chocolate croissants. She'd heard of pregnancy cravings, but thought they were just an excuse people used when trying to justify why they ate mounds of chocolate and other fatty foods. But Beth realized now that these urges really did exist. All she wanted was *pains au chocolat*, and they had to be Marks & Spencer's, as they were the nicest. Luckily, as Beth worked on St Stephen's Green, she hadn't far to walk when popping down to Grafton Street to get her daily fix. But she felt it was getting a little out of hand. This morning, on her way to work, she had vowed to be strong and not buy one until lunchtime, when she would have time to stroll down and pick it up. But Beth had barely made it through her first board meeting this morning before needing to get her chocolate fix asap. It hadn't even been 10 a.m. when she had run out of the building, shouting to her assistant that she had to pop into the chemist. She hadn't wanted to admit she had to dash down to Marks again.

Finally Beth was at the head of the queue. She handed over the little clear plastic bag. The shop assistant looked at her blankly.

'What was in it?' he asked accusingly.

Beth was mortified when she realized she had eaten the whole thing while standing in the queue.

'Do you want to keep the bag?' the young assistant asked smartly.

She declined, quickly paid for the item, and tried to walk as fast as she could back to work.

She'd just got into the office when her friend Susan walked by. The girls stopped to talk.

'Just had another *pain au chocolat*?' teased Susan.

Beth smiled as she pulled out the small mirror she kept in her handbag, and checked her face for chocolate. Twice she had been caught with chocolate smeared all over her mouth by Tom, and they hadn't been pretty conversations. She certainly didn't want to be accused of looking unprofessional again.

Beth was so glad she had Susan around. If it hadn't been for her, being pregnant at work would have been a nightmare. Beth had decided not to tell anyone in Burlington Stockbrokers until she was forced to. She'd thought she might get away with it for a few months. But one day after a long lunch in Café en Seine, Susan had come right out and asked her if she was pregnant.

'If you're not pregnant, then you are sick, and I'm worried about you. You are tired and washed-out-looking and so quiet,' Susan had said, with a concerned look on her face.

Beth had known then that she could trust her only friend in Burlington, and so, against her own better judgement, she had been totally honest and admitted that she was sixteen weeks' pregnant.

'Wow, you've hidden it well,' said Susan, after congratulating her friend.

'Well, why do you think I've been wearing all these long shirts? They conceal everything! And really, I only started showing a few weeks ago,' admitted Beth. She had been so nervous about telling anyone from work, knowing they would ask who the father was. But Susan had been so kind, and so Beth had sworn her to secrecy, and told her it was Tom. Susan had spluttered out her coffee all over the table.

'Tom Maloney? The head honcho? You are joking?' she'd finally said, after recovering from her shock.

283

Beth had shaken her head and told Susan all about their romance and break-up.

'What a shit,' said Susan. 'So he just dumped you when he heard the news? What a creep.'

Beth was mortified, as that was exactly how it had happened. After that disastrous night in his house, Tom had persuaded Beth to go to one more dinner in a fancy restaurant, in the hope of luring her back to him – without the baby, of course. But Beth had stood her ground, and so they had spent the meal discussing how the pregnancy would work. Tom said he would pay for all she needed, but he didn't want anything to do with the baby. He wouldn't be accompanying her on hospital visits, and certainly there would be no afternoons spent wandering around Mothercare picking out cots. But Beth had felt relief when the meal was over, because at least she had now known exactly where she stood. She and Tom had agreed that to make their working life easier she wouldn't tell anyone who the father was. There were times when she had wanted to shout it from the rooftops, so he could own up to his responsibilities; but admitting she had been sleeping with her boss would do her no favours, and so she had kept quiet until she'd spoken to Susan.

At eighteen weeks she had told everyone in work that she was pregnant, but it had been so hard to do.

Beth was surrounded by men there, and while some were a little curious as to whom the father was, most weren't that bothered, and like any males preferred talking about work and the financial markets than babies and pregnancy. And that suited Beth; but it was the girls who had made things difficult. Beth knew she hadn't tried hard enough over the years to get on with most of the other women in the company, who mainly worked in the marketing, IT or human resources departments. And now they were having their revenge.

'Oh well, thank God you are pregnant! I thought all those muffins and croissants you'd been sneaking into your office were simply making you fat,' said the office bitch, Caroline, who was Tom's personal assistant.

Beth had tried to ignore her, and the constant questions about the mysterious father, and just concentrate on work, but at times it was lonely not to have anyone interested in her ever-growing bump and baby. Often she could go for days without anyone acknowledging that she was soon to become a mum. She hadn't expected people to fall at her feet, but a little enthusiasm and interest would have been nice.

At least Susan knew the truth. It had been four weeks now since Beth had told her, and it was the only thing

285

that kept her sane at work. Susan sat down at Beth's desk, which was covered by files, financial papers and a large calculator. Beth's whole life had been about numbers and figures – from excelling at maths in school, and coming top of her class in accounting in college, to reading share values. But now she found the only calculations that interested her were to do with pregnancy: how many weeks had passed, and how many weeks she had left until Baby Prendergast arrived.

'Oh, I sneaked this can of 7 Up out of our finance meeting this morning for you,' said Susan, pulling a can of the drink from her handbag. Beth noticed the others in her work pod smile. At this stage they were getting used to the pile-up of cans of fizzy drink on their colleague's desk.

Beth smiled, too: along with croissants, she was craving sugary drinks. And Susan was great at keeping her supplied with her favourite things.

'So how are you feeling?' she asked.

'I'm fine,' replied Beth, as she gulped back the cold drink. 'My flipping car is in for a service this week, though, so unfortunately I've had to get the bus, which is so annoying. Not only is it packed with pushy teenagers, but I end up having to stand the whole journey, and my legs just can't take it any more.'

'You've to stand? Surely people offer you seats?'

exclaimed Susan. 'I always give up my seat for an old person, or a pregnant woman.'

'Well, I think it's a difficult situation for them to judge. Yes, my belly is big, but it's not that big. I guess people are nervous of offering me a seat in case I'm just overweight. They don't want to insult me.'

Susan began laughing.

'So to help them confirm that I'm pregnant I begin rubbing my belly, and smiling,' Beth said. 'That seems to be the international sign for, "I'm pregnant, and just so happy." It also confirms I'm not just fat, because I guess most people wouldn't rub their overweight bellies in public! So after that I sometimes get a seat, but honestly I can't wait to get my car back, and just sit down when driving into work!'

'Yes, you deserve a rest. Anyway, how did the scan go?' asked Susan excitedly.

Beth ignored the glances from the three guys on her team as she pulled out her handbag and handed Susan an envelope. Inside was a printout of three grainy black-and-white photos of what looked like a big blob. Susan didn't know which way up was the right one.

'What am I supposed to be looking at, exactly?' she asked, confused. 'Is this your baby printout, or never-seen-before photos of aliens?'

Beth laughed. Yesterday she had had her twenty-week scan, and it had been amazing. The doctor had shown her the baby's limbs, heart and head. Her bump was still small, so it had been hard to believe all the magic that was happening inside of her. They had given her a printout of three views of the baby, and Beth hadn't been able to stop looking at it.

'OK, Susan, that is the head, and that's an arm. Can you see it?'

'Yes,' said Susan, unconvincingly.

'Well what about this one? Surely you can make out a foot? Although it looks huge, which is a complete disaster! I don't want the baby to be big-footed and too tall like me,' said Beth, putting the pictures back into her bag.

'You are a brilliant height,' said Susan encouragingly. 'I wish I was as tall as you. You can carry the bump so well, and you haven't put on a pound in weight. I bet whenever I get pregnant I'll balloon up and have to drag my swollen ankles and legs around!'

Beth giggled as they continued chatting, but she had already started finding it hard to get long-enough pregnancy trousers, and the pressure was on. The other day Tom had called her into his office, and said that he'd noticed she had worn the same suit three days in a row. Beth had explained that she was struggling to find any nice fitted pregnancy suits that were long enough. Tom had some sympathy, seeing as he was tall himself and couldn't just buy a suit off the hanger, but he said that he wanted to draw Beth's attention to it now, before others noticed. Beth knew looking smart was a high priority in Burlington. They paid people good salaries, and expected them to spend some of it on high-quality suits. They wanted their staff to look like employees of one of Ireland's most successful companies. Beth had seen many a young man, fresh out of college with only one or two suits, being called into management's offices and told to smarten up or find a job elsewhere. But she had never expected to be told off herself. She was annoyed with Tom, but knew he had only been trying to help her save face and give her time to get some new clothes. And so Beth planned to go shopping after work.

The day passed quickly enough, and soon Beth found herself in one of Dublin's most popular clothes stores trying on jeans. She knew she needed to get some work clothes, but she was also tired of wearing the one pair of loose jeans she had every weekend, and now that the weather was getting better she could do with some summer clothes too. She'd heard they had a good maternity range here, so she had high hopes. There were so many outfits, from frilly dresses to huge T-shirts. Beth couldn't ever imagine being big enough to fit into one of those. For now all she wanted was jeans, though. So she grabbed a few from the rack and headed to the changing room. They looked funny: some had stretchy waistbands, while others had large black elastic inserts that grew with your bump. Beth preferred the more subtle ones that were low rides, yet had waistbands that expanded. She tried on the first pair, and looked in the mirror. She laughed out loud. The legs were so short that she resembled Tom Sawyer. Beth hurried to get them off her. She picked up a pair of nice-looking black jeans and pulled them on. She laughed again. They, too, sat above her ankle. This is ridiculous, she thought, as she put on her own long trousers and headed out to find an assistant. She explained her problem.

'I thought you did a "tall" range,' she said.

'Oh, we do, we carry plenty of long trousers, jeans and clothes,' said the young girl enthusiastically. 'But not in maternity clothes, unfortunately.'

'So you are saying I can either buy maternity jeans or long jeans, but not both together?' Beth asked, annoyed.

'Yeah, I guess so,' said the girl, now trying to distance herself.

Beth went and looked at the maternity jeans again. They were exactly what she needed, but they were so short. She decided to head out to some of Dublin's leading maternity shops, presuming they would have what she wanted. But she was sorely disappointed. It seemed the fashion world assumed only imps got pregnant, as nowhere had long enough trousers. Beth had never felt comfortable wearing skirts or dresses in her very male-oriented office, so finding some kind of trousers was imperative. There was one shop that kept slightly longer ones, but even they weren't lengthy enough to cover Beth's feet.

'You see,' said Beth, as she looked in the mirror, 'when you're tall you need long trousers not just to cover your long legs, but your feet, too. The taller you are the bigger your feet, and as no one carries nice large women's shoes, I need long trousers to cover my rotten big feet and shoes!'

The owner of the maternity boutique sympathized, but couldn't help. 'Maybe you should try looking online?' she suggested.

Beth promised she would, but not before deciding that she didn't want the whole shopping trip to be a waste. She picked up a few shirts for work and a bump band. She had never heard of these before, but learnt that the band went under her shirts or tops to cover the gap that her ever-rising bump caused. She didn't need people at work seeing her belly, so was glad she had found it.

As Beth drove home she worried about what she was supposed to do about finding long-enough trousers. Surely there were millions of tall women getting pregnant every year? What did they wear for nine months, she wondered? Or was it only elves who procreated? She laughed as she put the key in the door of her apartment, and decided she would need to go online, and find help. She might be man-free having this baby, but still she wanted to look her best.

32

'What about the oak?' asked William Prendergast.

Beth looked at the thick oak cot. Her dad preferred more traditional-style cots, while she liked white painted ones.

'I'm not sure if the oak will go with my apartment,' she said, as she looked at the bed, wondering how she was going to fit all this baby stuff into her small place.

Beth and her dad had been in Mothercare for over an hour. She had been spending more and more time with him recently. She didn't know how she would have gotten through some of the weekends without him. Her girlfriends were supportive and excited for her, but once it came to Friday or Saturday night they went out drinking, and Beth couldn't handle another night of being stone cold sober and sipping water while they got drunk, repeated the same boozy stories to her, and then tried to meet men. No, she was getting sick of it, and with no boyfriend in her life she had started staying over at her dad's once a week. As the only man in Beth's life, William was taking the whole pregnancy thing very seriously, and once Beth came through the door of the family house she wasn't allowed to raise a finger. He cooked her big hearty meals, kept her bedroom spotless and warm, and had even said he would come on her hospital visits with her if she wanted. But Beth had had to draw the line somewhere; she was too old to be bringing her dad to the doctor with her, even if he was dying to see the baby scans.

Beth had been nervous going for her first visit to Dr O'Connor. Back then, she hadn't told anyone in work, so she had pretended she had an urgent dentist's appointment, when really she'd been sneaking out to Holles Street. She had literally run through the doors of the maternity hospital: she hadn't wanted anyone to spot her going in there, as it would have ruined her secret.

The midwife had met her before the visit and Beth had filled out the forms and medical questionnaires, but had found herself stuck once the nurse enquired about family history and allergies.

'I don't know about those,' she had admitted.

Yes, she had known most of her own family's medical history, but nothing of Tom's. She had cursed him for putting her in this situation. But the nurse had been very kind, and quickly moved on to the next part of the forms, and Beth had suspected she was used to mothers coming in on their own. It was hard, but Beth was realizing she wasn't alone in this situation. She had had so many questions for the nurse, and as her bloods had been taken she had asked her if she really had to avoid shellfish? And if it was true all first-time mums went overdue? The nurse had patiently answered everything.

'You know, one of the best people to ask advice from is your mum,' she had said, handing Beth some leaflets about labour. 'A lot of women end up having a similar pregnancy and labour to their mothers, so she's a good person to turn to.'

Beth had felt her mouth go dry. This pregnancy had constantly reminded her how much she missed her mum, and having someone female to turn to for comfort, advice and reassurance. She wished she could ask her mum about the labour, and about the food she'd craved, and how she'd known she was picking the right name for her child. If only Beth could have had her back for even one day!

'My mum's dead. She died a long time ago,' she'd said to the nurse.

'Oh, I'm sorry, pet,' the nurse had said, looking straight at her. Beth had realized what she was thinking: here she was, raised by only one parent, and now she was going to repeat history.

'Anyway Dr O'Connor will see you now, and he will answer any more questions you have. He's very kind, you'll like him.'

Beth had thanked the nurse, and had discovered she was right, Dr O'Connor was very likeable. He never asked her where the father of the child was. He had only been interested in Beth: asking her how she was feeling, and checking the baby's development. She'd got very emotional the first time he'd shown her the baby move on the screen. Her happiness had only been slightly marred by the fact that she'd had no one to share it with.

'I'll print out copies of some of the stills for you. So you can pore over them at home!' Dr O'Connor had said, helping Beth up from the table and passing her a tissue to clean the sticky gel off her stomach.

Those scan pictures were now proudly displayed on the fridge in William's kitchen. Every time Beth went to get a drink, or some food, she said hello to her child. She was still amazed at how well her father was taking her impending single motherhood, but Beth suspected it wasn't just the baby William was happy about, it was her new, closer relationship with him, too. And so now, many hospital visits and scans later, Beth and William stood in a packed Mothercare, amidst screaming babies, lively children, heavily pregnant women and exhausted looking dads.

'There is so much to get,' said Beth, exhausted. 'It's overwhelming.'

William put down a dirty-nappy disposal-unit, and looked at his only daughter.

'If you were able to work out how to get all As in your Leaving Cert, get a First in Commerce, and handle millions of euros' worth of client money in work, I think you'll be equal to deciding which car seat, Moses basket and cot to buy.'

Beth went a little red; she had been put in her place. And her dad was right, it wasn't rocket science, even if baby apparatus was alien to her. She looked at the rack of Babygros and realized she should try to enjoy choosing her baby's bed and clothes.

'OK,' she said, more enthusiastically. 'Let's have a look at the buggies. It's a little early to buy one yet, but I hear they take weeks to order in, anyway.'

Just as Beth was trying to practise folding a very complicated-looking buggy, she felt a tap on her shoulder.

'So this is where you spend all your hard-earned cash.'

Beth looked up. It was Eoin McSweeney, one of the traders in Burlington. Beth couldn't stand him. He was the kind of guy who gave stockbrokers a bad name. He spent his evenings in the various bars in

Dawson Street boasting about how much profit he had made, and how important he was to all the big-named clients he had. He blew money on expensive champagne and overpriced fast cars. Last year he had hit the jackpot by marrying the daughter of one of Ireland's wealthiest property developers. He never stopped talking about his trophy wife, her pad in Marbella and how much she liked to party. Although Beth suspected Eoin's party days were going to be curtailed, now that his wife, Astrid, was pregnant and due in two months' time.

Beth studied Astrid. Even though she had a large bump, she didn't seem to have gained a pound. Beth was instantly jealous: some people made pregnancy look so easy.

'You're not going to buy that buggy, are you?' she asked Beth accusingly.

Beth stared at the navy buggy. It looked the same as all the other ones. How could Astrid even tell the difference?

'I'm not sure, yet,' she said, placing it back on the stand.

'Well, everyone knows that brand is too basic. What you need is what we got, the Bugster. It's the most expensive, of course, but only the best for our baby!'

Beth gazed at Eoin, who was smiling at her smugly. Suddenly William reappeared at Beth's side.

'The assistant said she could show us the car seats now, if we want to go over and look. There's a lot to choose from, and we will need two, of course. One for your car and one for mine.'

Eoin looked at William and smiled. Suddenly Astrid's phone rang.

'We need to go,' she said to Eoin as she began to walk off.

'I'll see you in the office on Monday,' Eoin said to Beth, casting another glance at William. Beth's dad was too busy feeling the weight of the buggies to be interested in Eoin.

Beth said goodbye to her work colleague, and made her way over to the car seats.

On Monday morning Beth arrived in work early and knuckled down to a report she needed to finish for a 9 a.m. meeting with an important client. Just before the meeting she headed into Tom's office; as he was her boss, she had reports she needed to give him. He needed to make sure all his SPMs were meeting their targets. As she approached his door Caroline, Tom's personal assistant, greeted Beth with her usual cross face. Beth ignored her, and was just making her way into Tom's huge office when she caught Caroline eyeing her ever-growing bump.

'Well, I hear the father is an older man. A much older man.'

Beth stopped dead in her tracks. Had Tom told someone? She couldn't believe he would have done that without talking to her first. She was lost for words.

'I suppose we shouldn't be surprised. You always were a little too serious for the young guys in here. It must have been hard being the only female SPM in the office. But at least now you've got your older man. Good for you,' said Caroline smugly, as she walked off, clipping her expensive shoes along the ground. She was one of those girls who loved the sound of her own high heels. You would think she was CEO of the company, and not just some assistant. She was a complete cow. Beth felt like hitting her over the head with her stupid travel cappuccino cup.

Instead she took a deep breath and stormed into Tom's office, determined to get to the bottom of this. Just as she was about to berate him, she saw they were not alone and that two of the senior partners were also sitting in on the briefing. Beth fumed. How could Tom tell the office about their relationship and impending parenthood without talking to her first? Yes, she'd hated everyone gossiping and wondering who the father was, but she had felt it was better than them all knowing the truth. That news could hurt her career, and she had spent too long building it up for someone like Caroline to go and ruin it all with rumour and innuendo.

Beth found it almost impossible to sit through her two-hour client meeting. The minute it was over she tried to find Tom, but was told he had gone to another conference across town in the Central Bank. Beth then tried to make her way back to her office as quickly as possible, as she felt paranoid about everyone talking about her and Tom. And her fears were confirmed when three different people stopped to enquire about her older man. People are so nosy, she thought, as she texted Tom saying she needed to talk to him urgently.

She tried not to leave the sanctuary of her work station all day. She hid behind her large computer screen, but even within that shelter people kept plaguing her. She actually had an email from one of the desperate single girls who worked in marketing, asking if Beth had always been attracted to older men or whether she'd done it out of desperation? The girl's email was lengthy, and went on to explain that she had dated practically every single thirty-year-old in Dublin, and now felt the more mature man might be able to provide her with what she wanted, which, like Beth, was a child. Beth ignored the email and tried to focus on work. She wished her friend Susan had been in, so she could have found out exactly what everyone was saying, but Susan had taken the day off to go to the final dress-fitting for her wedding, and to meet her caterers and florist. Beth was happy for her friend, but wished desperately that she'd been there to help.

Beth texted Tom again, asking him to call her when he was free. She got no response, and so tried to get back to work. At one stage she ran down to the canteen to get some tea, only to be stared at by the big group of mean girls who worked in HR. She could tell they were delighted to have some gossip about her. Beth decided to get her tea to go and walked as quickly as she could back to her floor.

Just as she reached the top of the stairs she bumped into Graham O'Reilly, a fellow SPM. Beth found him to be one of the nicest men on her floor. He was slightly older than her, and had two kids. Unlike the majority of the young men, who were eager to prove themselves to everyone who worked in Burlington, Graham knew his work was less important than being a father and working to pay for his house and holiday home, and so, while some might think he was a steady Eddy, Beth thought he was more down to earth than the rest. She found him sweet, and enjoyed his company any time they had to travel together.

'What time is our flight on Friday? I was hoping we would have time to make it into the office before check-in. I have so much work to do, it would be great to get it finished before we have to go away.'

Beth looked at Graham, a little confused. 'What flight? To where?'

'To Cheltenham, of course. For another three days of wining, dining and getting money out of our wealthy clients!'

Graham saw Beth still looked perplexed.

'Tom said to me a few weeks ago that he'd got the go-ahead for a few of us to invite special clients to the races, and that the company had arranged flights, hotels and restaurants. I just presumed you were coming too, seeing as how you came last time.'

Beth was furious; she knew she should be going on this trip. Part of her job was to entertain her clients. She'd helped fly some of Ireland's wealthiest businessmen in helicopters down to the annual summer races in Galway, and to English football games, and even to rugby matches across Europe. She was well used to showing her clients that Burlington appreciated their business, and that the company were willing to spend money giving them a good time. She should have been invited to Cheltenham, but she didn't want Graham to see her disappointment.

'Well, I haven't talked to Tom about it, but it suits me fine,' she said cheerfully. 'I'm so busy myself at the moment.'

'Of course, of course,' said Graham, trying to hide his surprise at Beth's non-involvement with the trip.

'Anyway,' he said, slowly smiling, 'I hear you're the talk of the office.'

Beth groaned. She was sick of hearing about her older man.

'I'm sure you're sick of all the baby chat, but fair play to you for braving Mothercare on a Saturday afternoon! If there's one thing I've learnt it's to avoid baby shops at the weekends, they are a nightmare. Late night Thursdays are better, or online shopping!'

Beth wasn't listening to his tips, she wanted to find out how he knew she'd been in Mothercare on Saturday.

'How do you know about my cot-hunting trip?' she asked.

'Oh, well it was Eoin who was telling us about meeting you and your partner there on Saturday. He's such a gossip, he's worse than the women who work here.'

Finally all the gossiping made sense, it wasn't that they knew about Tom. No, they all thought her dad was the father! Suddenly Beth started laughing. Her poor father had only been trying to help her shop, and now he was the talk of the office.

Graham looked at Beth. 'What's so funny?'

'Graham, that wasn't my "partner" Eoin met on Saturday. That was my father!' she laughed again.

Graham was a little surprised, but promised her he would set all the wagging tongues straight.

Beth was so relieved to hear no one knew about Tom, although she was still annoyed that he had ignored her all day.

Once it hit 7 p.m. the office emptied, but Beth stayed on; she had a mountain of work to get through. She was heading back from the bathroom for what seemed like the twentieth time that day – she still couldn't get over how much pressure the bump put on her bladder – when she ran into Tom.

'Oh, you're still here?' he asked.

'Yes, well I've got a lot to get through tonight. I've been trying to contact you all day,' she said.

'Oh yeah, sorry. I've been busy,' he said, not sounding that sorry at all. 'But let's talk now.' He ushered them both into his office.

Beth sat down opposite Tom. He felt like such a stranger to her, now. It was over three months since she had told him her news, but she still hadn't forgiven him for how he had reacted and treated her. At first she'd thought she wouldn't be able to work in the same building as him, but then she'd realized she had to, and so had decided that when they were at work she would try to forget about their personal situation and view him as her boss and colleague. But today she had needed him, so they could talk about the office rumour, and he had let her down.

'I left messages for you all day,' she said.

'I've been busy,' he repeated.

'Busy or not, you can still have the decency to answer my calls. I'm not asking a lot from you. I'm the one doing everything for this baby, our baby, and when I do need you to spare a few minutes so we can talk you ignore me. That's not fair, Tom.'

He didn't say anything. Neither did Beth. She was so annoyed. She didn't deserve to be treated like this.

'OK, I'm sorry. What was it you needed to talk about?'

Beth explained the mix-up about everyone thinking her dad was the father of the baby. She knew it was slightly funny, but Tom didn't even smile.

'Do you honestly think I would suddenly tell everyone now? After all these months? I'm not that stupid.'

Beth looked at him, and once again wondered how she ever could have fallen for such a heartless man.

'Anyway,' she said, trying to keep her cool, 'Graham O'Reilly said he's off to the UK for some client entertaining. I should be going on that trip, too, you know that. What's going on?'

Beth could see Tom becoming uncomfortable.

'It's a little awkward. I didn't know if you would be up for all of that, what with your condition. So I thought it better to let Graham and a few others go on their own. But don't worry, I didn't tell him why I didn't ask you to go.'

'My condition?' said Beth, her blood pressure rising. 'I'm pregnant, not terminally ill.'

Tom could see how annoyed she was.

'Well, you might not have been up for the flight, and all that entertaining and socializing,' he said meekly.

'How dare you?' said Beth. 'This is my career, it's my choice whether I'm "up" for it or not. You made it quite clear you wanted nothing to do with this baby, and if that's your decision then stick with it. Either you're involved with all aspects of this pregnancy, baby and my health, or you aren't. You can't pick and choose.'

'I'm sorry, it won't happen again. It was a lack of judgement on my behalf,' Tom said, looking at his watch. 'I know you'd like to talk more, but I'm afraid I've got to be somewhere in a few minutes. I'm already running late, so maybe we could leave this to another time?'

Beth was about to agree, when, for the first time all day, she noticed how smart Tom looked. He was wearing his favourite suit – his hand-made Armani – and seemed to have gotten a haircut. He always looked well, but even for him he was unusually well dressed for an average Monday in the office.

'Where are you rushing to?' she asked, suddenly guessing what he might say, but hoping she wasn't right.

Tom flinched.

'It's nothing serious. Just dinner.'

'You shit. I'm pregnant with your child and you're seeing someone? What kind of man are you?'

'Calm down. It's just dinner with someone I met last week.'

'I don't care what it is. Who is she?' Beth demanded.

'No one you know,' he admitted.

Beth stared at him, waiting for a more substantial answer.

'She's my age, a friend of a friend. She's like me, enjoys work, and her kids are grown up.'

'Wow, could you make it any clearer to me? She doesn't want kids, like you. While I'm the "broody ex-girlfriend". Well, wake up! Whether you like it or not you do have a child on the way. Does she know that?'

'Christ! We've only met twice, of course she doesn't know. I told you I wanted to be with you, but you made the decision to leave.'

'Only because you gave me an ultimatum of you or the baby! I had no choice. But I didn't realize it meant you would rush head first back into the dating scene. How could you do this?'

Tom looked down. 'I'm sorry how it has all worked out.'

'Not as sorry as I am,' she replied.

Neither said anything for what seemed like ages. Finally Beth stood up.

'I'd better go, I've got lots of work to do,' she said, trying to sound calm, but her voice was shaking. She was so upset.

'I don't want to leave you like this. I didn't mean to hurt you.'

'You already have. Anyway, enjoy your night,' Beth replied, as she walked out the door.

The minute Beth sat down at her desk she started crying. She tried to concentrate on her emails, but she couldn't read them through the tears running down her face. It had never crossed her mind that Tom would start seeing someone so soon. There was a tiny bit of her that had thought that once the baby was born he might come to his senses and want to be involved, but she could see now she'd been deluding herself. He didn't care at all. Tom dating someone new was adding insult to injury, and she just couldn't take it.

Beth looked at the pile of folders on her desk; she had so much to do, but she knew she was too upset to work. It had been such an awful day: first everyone gossiping about her older man, then being left out of an important work trip, and now finding out that Tom was seeing someone new. She felt devastated.

She picked up her phone and tried to ring her dad, but then remembered he was playing golf in the K Club that day and spending the night with friends. And it wasn't fair to burden her friend Susan tonight with Tom's news, she could tell her tomorrow in work. Beth looked out of her big office window and watched the world pass by. She had never felt so alone.

Suddenly she felt a popping sensation. She gazed down at her stomach. It popped again. She lifted up her shirt and placed her hand on her bare stomach. It was only faint, but she felt something. Oh my God, she thought. It was a kick. Her baby's first kick! It was like popcorn popping, or a butterfly fluttering. It was weird, but amazing. Beth felt it again.

She realized she wasn't alone at all. All this time she had had someone close by. A little someone: her baby. She felt the popping again. She started crying once more, but this time it wasn't tears of sadness, but tears of pure joy.

33

'Were there any phone calls while I was out?' Erin asked Paula as she walked into their office. Her voice was full of hope.

'No, no phone calls,' replied Paula, blissfully unaware of Erin's broken heart.

It had been six weeks since John had moved out. Erin went through the motions of going to work, making dinner each evening and tidying the house, but it didn't feel real. She still couldn't believe that John wouldn't be at home, waiting for her. But he never was.

They had talked on the phone, and by email, but it had been like communicating with a stranger. His voice had been dead, distant. Erin didn't know if she had lost him for ever, but as the weeks passed it began to feel like that.

John had called in soon after leaving to pick up

some clothes. Erin had tried to reason with him, tried to explain how she had rung Ruth to apologize for her outburst that night.

'It isn't just about that night. If you can't see that, I can't help you.'

'Well, what's going to happen to us?' Erin had said. She'd barely been able to bring herself to ask the question, she'd been so terrified of his answer.

'I don't know,' he'd said quietly. 'I've some things I need to work out on my own. I've a lot to think about.'

John had then walked out the door, but not before making sure the house was all secured properly. 'Make sure you lock up every night, you need to be careful when you're here alone.'

Erin had almost cried. Even in his anger he had still been the most caring man she knew. She'd tried to hug him, but his body had gone rigid.

'Not now,' was all he had said, before turning away and leaving her alone again.

Erin hadn't told her family or friends, she hadn't been able to bring herself to admit that her seemingly perfect marriage was in bits. When she'd gone to Amy's wedding alone she'd lied and said John was ill with the flu. She desperately wanted to tell her sisters, she felt so alone and wanted someone to talk to, but she was worried that by doing so it would make the break-up real, and so she pretended to the world that life was good. She was busy at work, and so flung herself into that, but it was all meaningless now that she had no one to share her life with, no one to come home to in the evenings.

Erin was on her way home from yoga when she found a tape down the side of her car door. At first she didn't recognize it, but then remembered that Ula, the fortune-teller, had given each of the girls a tape-recording of their fortune.

'So many people get overwhelmed when they come in that they forget what I've told them, so I find it easier to make a recording that they can listen to later.'

Erin put the tape on. As she drove through Donnybrook and Stillorgan she heard Ula's calm voice telling her to appreciate what she already had. Ula was asking her to care for the important things in her life. Erin had thought Ula meant she needed to focus on the baby more, but this time, as she heard Ula tell her about her loving partner, a man with a good heart, she started to realize that Ula had meant she needed to care for John, give him more attention. Ula had tried to tell her what a good man John was, but Erin had been too blindsided to listen to anything but what she thought was information on a future baby.

I've been such a fool, she thought as she pulled the

car over. She felt her heart race as she listened to Ula telling her that she needed to let people know how she felt.

'You need to appreciate what you already have, before anything new can come into your life. And what is meant for you will then come your way,' Ula said.

Erin felt sick. She had disregarded Ula's advice, considering it useless, but Ula had seen what was going to happen.

'What have I done?' she asked out loud. As cars whizzed past her she thought back over the months before the break-up. Erin hadn't been to any of John's races, she had been too busy with yoga, or the gym, or researching pregnancy rumours. She couldn't remember the last time she had felt relaxed around the house, had just sat down with John by her side and laughed, just been happy to have him there.

Ula had told her not to let her wish of becoming a mum come true at the expense of her heart. I think it's all too late, Erin thought. I've been so obsessed and focused, on everything from the gym to healthy eating and green tea, that I forgot what was the most precious thing I had. The thing I had all along, the thing I needed the most – John.

Erin hadn't slept for two days. Ever since listening to Ula's tape she hadn't been able to concentrate.

Memories kept flashing back to her of the times she had flown off the handle at John for the slightest things, like buying her the wrong pregnancy tests, or sneaking the odd cigarette. She left countless voice-messages on John's phone, saying she longed to see him, and eventually she got one brief text back to say he would call the following day so they could chat.

Erin had to leave work early, she felt so tired and exhausted. Her stomach churned at the thought of what John might tell her the next day. It had never occurred to her before that her marriage could be in trouble. Now she saw that while she had been worrying about babies, or work, her husband had been suffering and she had been too selfish to notice. And as the thought entered her head that John might ask for a divorce she almost couldn't breathe.

Just before she got home Erin pulled into the local pharmacy. Her head was thumping, and she needed some paracetamol. As she joined a long queue to pay for the small pack of pain relief she looked around the shop. She had been inside it many times to buy ovulation and pregnancy tests, and almost laughed at that thought now. It was those tests that had wrecked her marriage. She turned her back on the pregnancy test shelf, but as she did so, something inside her raised an alarm bell. Suddenly she realized she hadn't had a period for ages. The last few weeks had been so emotional that she just hadn't noticed. It's probably because I'm stressed, she thought. But that alarm call niggled at her. She was tempted to buy a test, but pushed the idea aside. No, those tests are the reason I became so unhinged, she thought. Instead she paid for the paracetamol and went home to her empty, lonely house.

By 2 a.m. Erin couldn't stick wondering if she was pregnant any more. She ran into the bathroom, but couldn't find her box of pregnancy tests anywhere. The day after John had left she had hidden the box. She hadn't been able to face looking at those little pieces of plastic that had ruined everything. 'But I need one now,' she cried, as she took apart her bedroom and then the bathroom. Suddenly she found one. Erin ripped open the box and did the test.

She sat and waited, before finally allowing herself to look.

The test result was positive. She was pregnant.

Erin walked out of the bathroom with the test in her hand. She had imagined this day for years, but as she went into the now very messy bedroom, it was an anticlimax. Yes, she had the result she wanted, but without John there to hug and kiss her it felt wrong. It felt pointless.

'What is meant for you will come your way,' the fortune-teller had said. But as the news that she was pregnant started to sink in, Erin knew she had gotten what she always wanted, but not in the way she needed. She didn't want to do this alone. She had to have John.

Erin started crying. She had never felt so sad in all her life.

34

'Hi,' John said, solemnly, as he walked into their house.

Erin's stomach was churning. Over the last few hours she had experienced every emotion under the sun. She had swung between being overwhelmed with joy and pure excitement at being pregnant, to feeling sick at the thought of having lost John. Today should have been the happiest day of her life – she was finally pregnant – yet it had really been the worst. Erin could finally legitimately walk into a baby shop and ask about the products, or go to pregnancy websites and not feel like an imposter, but she hadn't bothered. Without John it didn't feel right. What have I done? she asked herself over and over. I've ruined my marriage, my life, all because I was scared I'd never get pregnant, and now finally I've got the test result I want, but no one to share it with.

Erin knew she had to tell John the news, but as she watched him walk into their living room and sit down on the couch opposite her it occurred to her that she shouldn't force him to stay with her just because she was expecting, that wouldn't be fair. No, she would let him say what it was he had come to tell her, and then she would tell him.

'How are you?' John asked awkwardly, as he looked around the spotless room. He felt like a stranger in the house.

'I'm fine,' replied Erin politely. She was uncomfortable, too.

'Would you like some coffee or tea?' she asked, looking for an excuse to do something, rather than just sit and stare at him. He might be her husband, but right now she felt like she was on some kind of bad first date.

'Yeah, I'd love a coffee,' said John. 'Let me help you,' he added, as they both headed for the kitchen.

While she boiled the kettle John politely asked about her work, but Erin couldn't stand the chit-chat any more.

'Work has been impossible, I can't concentrate, I can't eat, I can't sleep. I've been so worried and upset. John, I miss you. I love you. I've made some huge mistakes, and I'm so sorry. I know I can't change the past, but I really am sorry. Please give me a second chance.'

Erin's hand was shaking as she poured the milk into John's cup. She couldn't bring herself to look him in the eye. She dreaded what he would say. She knew he might tell her he wanted a divorce, that he never wanted to see her again.

John sat quietly for a few minutes, and as he did Erin dropped two sugars into his coffee and handed him the cup. Their hands briefly touched. Erin walked back to the kitchen counter and poured herself a cold glass of water.

'I've really missed you, too,' John finally said.

Erin held her breath.

'I've just been feeling so hurt and upset. I didn't know what else to do but to take some time alone. I needed space to think. I didn't mean to upset and worry you.'

'I know,' said Erin, remembering how kind he'd always been, and how he'd never meant to upset her. She was the one who had done all the upsetting; she had been cruel to him, and hadn't cared. She only hoped he would give her a chance to prove how much she had changed.

John looked around the kitchen, he seemed to be taking it all in.

'I've really missed living here, with you. Can I come back?'

Erin felt like a huge weight had been lifted off her shoulders.

'Oh my God! Yes, of course you can,' she said, smiling.

John looked so relieved. His face had been so pale and worried when he'd arrived, but now Erin could immediately see some colour come back to it.

She knew they still had a lot of things to sort out and talk about, but she just couldn't hold her news in any longer.

'I'm pregnant.'

John dropped his coffee cup on to the ground. The china shattered, the coffee spilt all over the tiles. For a moment neither he nor Erin spoke.

'What did you say?' he finally spluttered out.

Erin began laughing, all the day's worries and tension now transformed into extreme happiness.

'I'm pregnant. We're having a baby. That's if you still want one?'

'Want one? I want twenty! Oh my God, this is amazing,' and with that John stepped over the coffee disaster and wrapped his arms tightly around his wife.

'I love you. I hated fighting, let's not do that again,' he whispered.

Erin started crying, she was so overcome. Suddenly John pulled away.

'But how can you be pregnant? I thought we had missed the right time that weekend you were sick.'

'I thought we had, too, but it must have happened the night of Amy's hen.'

'That night?' he asked, surprised. He began laughing. 'All those months of cutting back on alcohol, and then we go and conceive our first child on the night you were literally on the floor drunk!'

'Don't tell anyone that!' Erin said, playfully hitting him on the arm. 'The poor child could be damaged for life!'

John placed his hand on Erin's flat belly.

'My child is fine, no, he's better than fine. He's a miracle,' and with that they both sat down and began talking about the best thing that had ever happened to them.

Erin knew they both had problems to work out, and that she had narrowly missed losing her husband and marriage, but for tonight there was just one thing on her mind, the baby. And for the first time in two months the house was full of energy, noise and life. As they discussed hospitals, doctors and baby names Erin felt her whole body relax. Right here in the room she had everything she needed – her husband and her baby. She had never felt so lucky in all her life.

35

'But I want to stay close to my family,' said Grace Miller, as she sat on the edge of the bed, attempting to put her second shoe on. Her massive belly made it almost impossible to bend over. The runner lay on the ground. It would be a miracle if it made it on to her feet.

'We're our own family,' replied Ethan. 'And soon there will be three of us.'

'OK, I know, but I just want to be close to my mum, and the boys.'

'Your mum drives you mad! I think she's sweet, but you're the one always glad to wave her off at the airport after a visit.'

Grace felt hurt. What Ethan was saying wasn't entirely true: her mum could be a bit overwhelming and tiring, but Grace did love and care for her. And the last few months in Ireland had changed their relationship. Yes, Patsy could still interfere a little too much, but Grace couldn't imagine life without her.

'Listen, I know you want to have your mum around after the baby arrives, and that's fine. I'm so busy with work that it's good that you'll have some extra support for the first few months, but, Grace, my job and our home are back in San Diego. And we do need to go back. That was always the plan.'

'Well, we didn't plan on getting pregnant. Plans change.'

Now Ethan didn't know what to say. Instead he walked over to his wife, bent down on one knee, and, like Prince Charming, put her shoe on her foot. He leant in and kissed Grace.

'I love you, and I want you to be happy, but we can't just suddenly change our plans on a whim. I know you're nervous about coping after the baby arrives, but we'll be fine. We have a good life back home, and once my work here is finished we can head back, baby in tow. It will be great. And your mum can visit as much as she wants.'

Grace said nothing.

'OK, well, I've got to go to work. I can pick you up later and we can go and get the cot. I know the superstitious Irish in you would rather wait until the baby is born, but I can't stand not being organized! We have a lot to buy, and we need to get cracking.

You should go back to bed, relax,' he added, as he walked out the door.

Grace wished Ethan goodbye, but didn't want to go back to bed. She was bored of lying down. Her bump was increasing daily, and she just couldn't sleep with it. Of course it was reassuring to feel Baby Miller, but his nightly dance routines were keeping her awake. While he (or she) partied, Grace sat wide awake. Her mind was constantly racing with the decisions she and Ethan had to make. Over the last few weeks she had tried broaching the subject of staying in Ireland permanently, but he just hadn't taken her seriously. He thought she was simply anxious about the baby; he didn't know that as every day passed she became more and more certain she wanted to stay at home in Ireland. She wanted Dublin to be her baby's home.

I should have married an Irish guy, she thought, as she walked into the kitchen, sat down with a bowl of cornflakes and turned on her laptop. Grace was bored. She knew she was lucky that with Ethan's salary she didn't have to work, but there was only so much maternity wear she could buy, or so many friends she could meet for coffee, and so many times she could discuss baby names with her mum. Grace opened her inbox, and checked her emails. There was one from her brother-in-law. He had sent her some new photos of Coco playing in his back garden. Coco looked so happy, but his collar was a little frayed. Grace decided to send him a present of a new one. She went online to her favourite dog store, chose a cute pirate-themed collar and ordered it to be sent to Matt's house.

She looked at the huge choice and variety of doggy apparel, gifts and toys, and thought how no one in Ireland offered anything like it. It was the same with baby gifts; compared to Ireland, America had every colour, size and style imaginable. There just wasn't the same range of stuff over here, and most of her favourite US shops didn't even ship to Ireland. Suddenly Grace had an idea. I should set up my own website, one that will sell the coolest and best baby and dog gifts, she thought. I can buy the supplies from all the shops I love in San Diego, get them sent to me here, and then I can sell and post them on to Irish customers. My God, it would be such fun! she thought. And I could do it from home, sitting in my maternity pyjamas! People could have the baby pumpkin outfit, or the dog tutu they had always dreamed of. She sat up in her chair, she felt so excited. I could do this, she thought.

Grace spent the rest of the day on the internet or on the phone. She looked up how to set up a website, the cheapest way to import goods, how much it would all cost. With her marketing background she had many ideas on how to promote and publicize a website. By 5 p.m. she was sure this was what she wanted to do.

It had been her most productive day in a long time. She actually looked forward to the work. But Grace didn't know how to tell Ethan. Setting up this Irish website would confirm that she wanted to stay in Ireland, and that was something she knew he hadn't bought into yet. I won't tell him at once, she thought. I'll do some more work on it and see how it all pans out before letting him know.

36

For the next few days Grace looked forward to getting up each morning and sitting down to look at stock she could order, from puppy raincoats to baby Ugg boots. Everything was so different and cute.

On Saturday she met a group of friends for lunch and decided to let them in on her secret idea.

'I think it sounds great,' said her old neighbour, Cathy.

'The fact that you're so excited about baby clothes is good enough for me,' said Sharon, who was delighted by Grace's new-found obsession with all things baby.

'Well, I don't think I would want my dog to be dressed like Superman, or anything!' said Aisling. 'But the doggy toys and beds look really great. I think you should go for it.'

'And it'll mean you can work from home,' added

Sharon, who as a mum herself was being very practical about the whole situation.

'OK,' said Grace. 'I'm going to do it!'

The girls all cheered.

'Now you'll all have to promise to buy things from the website!' Grace warned.

They promised, and before long they were discussing names for the website. Everyone seemed to have very different opinions. The only time I'm not thinking up a name for my baby I'm fretting over naming something else! thought Grace, laughing.

Grace felt like she was going to an interview. As she watched the clock tick, she sat nervously in her kitchen. Suddenly she heard the sound of the large wooden security gates to their rented house open, and saw Ethan's BMW drive in. As he drove over the gravel Grace once again checked the kitchen table. It was covered in printouts, catalogues and website designs. She had spent the last couple of weeks perfecting her idea for her baby and doggy website. She was sure that it was going to be a hit with parents and dog-owners alike. She hadn't said anything to Ethan until she knew she was going to go ahead with it, and that staying in Ireland was what she wanted. And she was now certain about both.

Ethan walked in the front door and took off his suit jacket. Through his Ralph Lauren blue shirt she could see his toned body. He ran his fingers through his blond hair. Grace still found him as attractive as the first day she'd met him.

'Hi, how are you feeling?' he asked as he kissed her.

'I'm fine. The baby seems to be trying out for the Olympics, though, there's been non-stop kicking, turning, rolling and elbow-nudging all day!'

Ethan laughed as he fetched a beer from the fridge. He worked long hours and still went to the gym on the way home, but he did like to indulge himself sometimes with an after-work beer, especially on a warm evening like tonight.

'What's all this?' he asked, sitting at the large oak table.

'It's my new idea. My plan. My new career,' she said all at once. She didn't know why she felt so nervous.

'What?' he asked. And so Grace sat down and began to explain her ideas.

Ethan was impressed.

'This would be easy to set up, and good fun, too. And you're right, America is the land of choice and variety! And people would love to get easy access to some of that stuff over here.'

Grace smiled.

'You should do it,' he said enthusiastically. 'And I can help you,' he added.

Grace hugged him.

'And the great thing about it being a website, and not a shop, is that when we move back to San Diego in a few months you can still operate from there. That's the advantage of the worldwide web!'

Grace's heart sank.

'Well, that's the thing. I want to work at it from here.'

Ethan put down the baby clothes catalogue, and said nothing.

'I don't want to move back. I want us to live here. To bring up our baby here.'

'Grace, I thought we had been through this?'

'No, we haven't,' she replied, trying to keep the tone of her voice steady. 'You kept saying you wanted to go back, but I'm saying I don't.'

Ethan loosened his shirt and stared right at Grace. His blue eyes seemed to bore through her.

'You knew this trip was only for a year,' he said. 'The Dublin office needs me until they get off the ground. But my real job and career is back home. Are you asking me to give that up?'

'No, of course not,' she replied. 'But maybe you could continue running the Dublin office?'

'It's not that easy,' he said. 'And it's not just about work. My family and friends are back home. My life is there. You're asking me to give it all up to live here for ever?'

'I did it for you many years ago,' she said, the tone in her voice changing.

'That was different. You were dying to get out of Ireland, away from Dublin. I've enjoyed my time here, but my heart is back home.'

'I thought your heart was with me?' she asked.

Neither of them said anything.

'That's not what I meant, you know that,' he replied eventually. 'You know I would do anything for you, and for our child. But you're asking so much from me.'

As she looked at Ethan's face, so full of worry and woe, she felt bad. She knew his home was California, not Dublin, but what else could she do? She was really sure she had to stay in Ireland.

Ethan poured himself another beer. Grace looked enviously at the alcohol.

'Do you want a sip?' he offered. She declined. She only had another few weeks to wait.

'I thought you liked our life back home? Weren't you happy?'

'What? No, that's not it. You know how happy I was. Having our wonderful house, our good friends, being able to walk to the beach, having every kind of shop, restaurant and service at our doorstep was perfect. I wouldn't alter one second of it. But our life is changing. We won't be a carefree couple any more, and much as I'd like to think the baby won't change

332

our life, I know it will. San Diego represents our life before all of this, and it was amazing. But I think our future should be here in Dublin.'

'And does my opinion count?' he asked, raising his voice.

'Of course, we need to work out what's best for us all. But I do desperately want to stay in Ireland. We can visit your family, and our friends, as much as possible. The baby will be half-American so it's entitled to see as much of its other home as it can. It will be a little traveller! But I want us to be based here.'

Ethan stood up.

'You're asking me to change my whole life for ever,' he said. And with that he walked out of the door.

Grace sat there as she heard the front door slam. He was gone.

Ethan was normally a very calm person. He was enthusiastic and energetic, but he rarely lost his head. Grace was worried.

At 3 a.m. Grace heard the sound of keys in the front door. She heard Ethan walk up the stairs. She held her breath. But he never came into their bedroom. She heard him walk across the landing, and the door to their spare room creak open. She stayed awake for hours waiting and hoping he might come to her. But he never did. Eventually she fell into a deep sleep.

By the time she woke up it was 10 a.m. and Ethan was long gone to work. Grace tried his mobile, but it was turned off. She left some messages, the last saying she would be in her mum's house later if he was looking for her. Grace had promised her mum she would call over later as it was Patsy's last afternoon of minding the children from across the road.

'I had to tell Brona and Angie that as much as I love those children, I just can't commit to minding other people's little angels when soon we will have our own to look after.'

'Mum, it's not like I will be asking you to mind our baby the whole time!'

'No, I just can't do it. I'll be up to my eyeballs helping you, and sure there's a lovely new lady who has just moved in down the road, and is looking for work. She's only too happy to help out with the kids. No, Grace, I have my priorities. And as much as I love those children, my own grandchild will come first.'

Grace was secretly delighted that Patsy was so eager to lend a helping hand with the new baby.

Grace spent the afternoon helping the children paint, giving them their lunch and watching them play in the garden. She was just showing Tara how to make daisy chains when she heard the front gate creak open.

'So this is where you want to live?'

It was Ethan. He looked tired and washed-out. He didn't look himself at all. He held his hand out and helped Grace up from where she was sitting on the grass. Standing up was getting harder and harder nowadays.

'Well, not exactly this house,' she replied. 'But yes, somewhere full of kids and gardens and near good schools. Of course I'd like a bigger place, a little bit like our own place back home. Without the pool, though!'

Ethan said nothing. Grace couldn't read him. She didn't know what he was thinking or going to say.

'I don't know if I want to live my whole life in Ireland. I'd always be the outsider, the foreigner, but if you think it would be best for our baby, and it will make you feel happy, then I'm willing to give it a go. I'll try it.'

Grace flung her arms around him. She knew how difficult this was for him, but she knew how kind and caring he was, too.

'I promise you'll like it. We just need to find the right house, a proper family home.'

'Well, I need to talk to Alex and the others at work first. I may have to take a pay cut. I probably won't be on the salary I was back home, you know.'

'That's OK,' she said, realizing that she couldn't expect to have the lavish lifestyle they had had before.

'And I'll want to go home as much as I can, to see my mum and dad. They will need time with the baby, too, to build up a relationship with him or her.'

'Of course,' she replied. 'I'm game to go back for holidays any time. It was my home, too, and of course I'll miss it. But I just feel that at this moment in our lives it's better for us to live here.'

'OK,' he replied. He looked exhausted. Grace knew how much he was sacrificing for her.

'You know I love you. You're going to make a great father.'

'I hope so,' he said.

'You will,' she said, as she wrapped her arms around him. A few months ago she couldn't have guessed how much her life would change. Or that being in her old front garden with Ethan, after deciding they were going to live here for ever, would be one of the happiest days of her life.

37

Erin Delany could feel her heart beat wildly in her chest. Her palms were sweaty and her throat was dry.

'Are you OK?' asked John, as they drove to Dublin's National Maternity Hospital.

Today they were going to meet their consultant, Dr Kennedy, and have their first baby scan. Erin was a nervous wreck.

'I just keep worrying that he'll say there is nothing there, that it's all in my head.'

'That's ridiculous,' replied John, slowing down and trying to find a place to park on Merrion Square.

'It's not. All my life I've wanted a baby, wanted to be pregnant, but it's taken so long that now I'm worried I've dreamt it all up. That I've imagined the positive test result, morning sickness and pregnancy cravings. Until I see that scan with a little baby in it

I just won't believe it's true. And that's why I haven't told anyone else. I know you're bursting to let your family know, but until we have that scan in our hands I won't believe the baby exists myself.'

John parked the car, turned off the engine and looked at his wife.

'I don't need a scan to tell me you're pregnant. Our baby is coming, I just know it.'

Erin liked the way he was so positive, but as they walked through the doors of the busy hospital she still felt sick with nerves. She watched expectant women rushing to doctor appointments, she smiled as mothers and their newborns passed her by, she noticed grandparents eagerly greeting their new grandchildren. The hospital was full of excitement, hope and happiness, but Erin couldn't relax until she knew she was really pregnant.

'Twins?' Erin Delany said with disbelief. 'Are you sure?' she asked.

'Yes, I'm sure,' replied Dr Kennedy, smiling. 'There are two heartbeats,' he added, looking at the blurry images on the screen. 'Congratulations,' he said.

John Delany suddenly felt light-headed. He sat down on the edge of the bed.

'Are you OK?' Erin asked her husband, who was looking very pale.

'Twins?' was all he said.

'I know it's a bit of a surprise,' said Dr Kennedy, who had clearly seen other overwhelmed fathers react badly to the news that more than one child was on the way. 'But we have some great support groups attached to the hospital who can give you advice, and I will write down the name of books and websites that will answer some of your questions.'

Erin was in shock herself. For the last few weeks all she had done was debate whether she was carrying a girl or a boy, and spend hours discussing baby names, but it had never crossed her mind that there could be two babies in there. She now had two babies' names to pick, two babies to care, love and look after. It was a lot to take in.

Erin and John asked the doctor as many questions as they could think of. Finally he managed to get them out of the door with the promise that they would be fine, adding that people gave birth to twins every day without any problems.

'Yeah, until you get them home,' said John under his breath. Erin gave him a dagger look, she didn't want the doctor thinking they didn't want the babies.

John was over the moon that Erin was finally pregnant, but his cousin had had twins and John knew how much hard work, chaos and lack of sleep they entailed.

'God, it will be tough,' he said, as they walked out of the Holles Street hospital and across the road into the park. Erin sat down on the first bench they passed. As people walked by, it occurred to her that they didn't know she was really three people. Suddenly she began laughing. John frowned at her.

'It's not funny,' he said. 'Of course we want kids, but not all at the same time.'

Erin took his hand and pulled him on to the bench. She wrapped her hand around his. Ever since they had been reconciled she had enjoyed the little things even more; holding hands, a kiss, or even a small hug were all pleasures she didn't want to lose again.

'Can't you see what good news this is? All we've ever wanted is children, and for some reason it has taken us a lot longer to get pregnant than we thought, and maybe we won't be so lucky next time. So this could be our only chance.'

John said nothing.

'I know it's going to be a lot more work, and we'll have to forgo that spare room as an extra playroom now! But maybe God is helping us make up for lost time by giving us two children instead of one. We're lucky.'

John gazed at his wife. She was glowing.

'I don't mean to sound ungrateful,' he said. 'It's just that twins will be a lot of work.'

'It will be fun,' Erin said automatically. 'Think of how cute it will be dressing them up in matching outfits! And they will be such good company for each other. They will have an instant best friend!'

'I suppose you're right. And it will be great for boys to have another guy to kick a ball around with!'

'They might be girls,' added Erin, smiling.

'You mean I'd have three girls in the house?'

'Yes,' laughed Erin. 'It will be pink city! And we'll be in charge of the TV, no more sports and blow-'em-up movies!'

John raised his eyes to heaven, but she could tell he was getting excited. Being pregnant had helped bring John and Erin back together, and she only hoped that their new deeper understanding of one another would be a sign that they could withstand anything, even twins!

'Well, can we finally tell everyone tonight?' asked John excitedly.

Erin and John might have being getting on well recently, but the only thing that they couldn't agree on was when to tell their families and friends. Of course, Erin was bursting to tell everyone that she was pregnant, but she was nervous. She had read up on the statistics of miscarriage in the first trimester, and, having watched her eldest sister experience one years before, she just didn't think it was fair to tell their families in case anything happened. John thought it was madness, but she had made him promise to keep quiet until she was twelve weeks.

'I'm only eleven weeks,' said Erin, pleading with him not to spill the beans.

'But tonight is the perfect opportunity,' said John. 'Both our parents will be there, and my brother. Come on, they'll be so excited and happy.'

Tonight was his thirty-fifth birthday, and months ago his parents had booked to bring Erin, John, John's brother Paul, and Erin's parents for dinner to Bentley's. John also had plans to celebrate his mid-thirties milestone with his friends, but that would be at the weekend, and would involve less food and more solid drinking.

John made a good case for telling their parents to-night, but Erin was trying to stick to her plan.

'No, John, I want to wait one more week. Please.'

He reluctantly agreed.

'He's an absolute disgrace,' said Maurice Delany. 'I know it's his birthday, but it's only half past nine and already he's so drunk.'

John's mum, Breda, had to agree. 'Paddy and Mary, we must apologize. We brought you here to help us celebrate John's birthday, not to watch him slur his words and spill his pint before we've even had our main meal.'

Erin watched and listened as John's parents ripped into her husband. John's birthday dinner in Bentley's

Oyster Bar and Grill on St Stephen's Green was not going according to plan.

'He's become a lightweight when it comes to drinking,' added John's younger brother Paul, smiling. 'We've both had the same amount of beer, yet he's off his head. I suppose being middle-aged does that to you!'

'We're not middle-aged,' replied Erin, but she had more important things to clear up.

John was drunk because of her. Unfortunately in Ireland, if you are of childbearing years and are known to want kids, the minute you go out and don't drink people assume you are pregnant. Erin didn't want her family guessing why she wasn't drinking, and so at the start of the night she had sat opposite John, and every time a glass of wine was poured for her, John would quickly down his drink and then swap the empty glass for hers, giving the illusion that she was drinking. But the consequence was that John was now drinking for two, and so while everyone else was still sober, he was completely hammered. The bottle of champagne sent to the table by an old friend John had bumped into on the way in had finished him off. John had had to knock back two glasses of champagne, along with Erin's white wine and his beer. It was at this point that he had excused himself to get some fresh air. While he wasn't at the table his parents voiced their disgust.

'I thought he'd enjoy a fancy meal out with us all,' said his mum. 'I know he's entitled to a few birthday drinks, but surely he can wait until the weekend and his night out with the lads to become so drunk? He just ate my starter instead of the one he'd ordered. I don't even like pâté, but I suppose I'll have to eat it now.'

Erin felt so guilty. John was getting this ear-bashing all because of her. Suddenly she saw him walking across the restaurant. He looked slightly unbalanced, and as he bumped into a waiter she could see he was lucky not to have knocked a whole tray of food over. John returned to his seat, but the look on his face as he saw the two full drinks in front of him made Erin sit up and realize enough was enough.

'Breda, Maurice, Mum, Dad and Paul. It's not John's fault he's so drunk, it's mine.'

They all looked at her strangely.

'He's just trying to cover up for me. I'm actually not drinking tonight. I haven't in weeks. You see, I'm pregnant.'

Erin just had time to see the look of relief and happiness spread over John's face, before she was swamped with hugs and kisses.

'I'm so happy for you.'

'Oh, pet, we're so proud.'

'It's wonderful news.'

'When are you due?'

'I'm locked,' added John. Erin laughed, it was great to finally share their big news with their parents. Erin's mum moved places to sit beside her. She couldn't stop hugging and kissing her daughter.

'I should have told you weeks ago,' said Erin, realizing how much she loved having her mum here to ask for advice and information. She knew that over the past year she had pushed her parents away – she had felt that by not getting pregnant and producing grandchildren she was a failure. But now, as her mum kept saying how proud she was of her, she saw that all Paddy and Mary had wanted was for her to be happy and well. They loved her no matter how many or few kids she had.

'It doesn't matter that you didn't tell me sooner. You and the baby are well, that is the main thing,' added her mum, who had her arms protectively around her. Mary Walsh had been the perfect stay-at-home mum to Erin and her two sisters, and it was because of her that Erin had had such a craving to become a mother, too. She might have let that craving become an obsession, and destroy her life, but now, as she listened to her mum's kind words and advice, she was reminded of what being a mother was all about: love and support.

Erin thought now might be a good time to tell them the next bit of news.

'I should also let you know that John and I are expecting more than one baby. You grandparents will have your work cut out for you, because we're having twins!'

The table erupted. The whole restaurant turned to look at them, but Erin didn't care. She had realized that being pregnant wasn't just about herself and John, it was about adding to both their families, and all the happiness that brought. She rang her sisters, and as they screamed with joy down the phone Erin felt herself get giddy with excitement.

For the rest of the night John kept to water, and even though Erin wasn't drinking either she felt drunk with emotion. Her head was spinning trying to answer all the questions, and as her mum tried to force her to eat more vegetables she looked around the table and thought how next year there would be an extra two people sitting at it. Two little people that she couldn't wait to meet.

38

'So, how are you feeling? Are the twins kicking like mad?'

Erin Delany sat down to relieve her tired legs as she chatted to her best friend, Amy, on the phone. Being thousands of miles away in Australia meant Amy couldn't be there in person for her friend, but she had rung every few days looking for updates on the pregnancy.

It had been three months since Erin and John had told their families and friends about the pregnancy and twins, and Amy had been so supportive to Erin since then. She had even sent her some pretty maternity clothes from Australia. Erin knew she was lucky to have such a good friend.

'Honestly, I've three months to go but I look like a dinosaur, I'm huge!'

'I'm sure you look great,' said Amy encouragingly.

'No, I don't. I can no longer see my feet, and I think the babies must enjoy swinging from my ribs, because they feel like they are right up there.'

'Two little monkeys!'

'Yes, I suppose they are,' replied Erin, as she pushed off her shoes and lay down. She was knackered after a day at work, and had been dreaming of the couch since 9 a.m. this morning.

'And how is John?' asked Amy.

'Oh, he's been so good. Making me breakfast in bed, rubbing my poor swollen rotten feet after a long day of work, making sure we have plenty of magazines in the house.'

'What about all your healthy eating? Are you still going to yoga?'

Erin laughed.

'Yoga, are you mad? I've enough exercise walking up and down the stairs these days. No, I have to admit I had a lot of unrealistic ideas about what I'd be doing while pregnant. I might have been a bit too high and mighty in my remarks about other pregnant mums, too. The other night I even had one beer. Honestly, a few months ago I would've been disgusted if someone had told me that I'd have a drink when pregnant, but now I've realized it's not about yoga, being healthy and playing classical music to your unborn. No, it's about being in your tracksuit, relaxing, and eating as much as you can before the madness begins!'

'I knew you'd come to your senses,' said Amy. She had known how much Erin had wanted a baby, and was so happy that now she'd got her wish, even if she'd got two wishes at once!

'But, honestly, John has been fab, although he seems to have convinced himself that the twins are boys. He keeps going on about getting football posts for the back garden, and wondering if he should apply for season tickets for Anfield for the boys now, as apparently they've such a long waiting list!'

'Oh God, isn't it bad enough he thinks they're boys, without making them Liverpool supporters too?' added Amy.

'Yes! I think it'll be girls, but then I also thought it was only one baby for the first eleven weeks, so I guess I could be wrong!'

'And how is work?' asked Amy.

'Work is good. I'm busy, which is great. Although I can see a worried expression come over new clients when they see me at their door for the first time. You can tell they're concerned I won't last long enough to see the work through. I look like I'm about to pop, even though I've got ages to go! Twins make me resemble a walking volcano about to explode! We've had to hire someone part-time to help us out, though, because I know soon I won't be in work, and Paula can't survive on her own.'

'Can you afford that?'

'Well, not really,' admitted Erin. 'But we need another pair of hands in the office. Of course the company can't afford to give me six months' full maternity pay along with the other two salaries, so John and myself will just have to survive on his salary and our savings. But we'll muddle through. We'll have to!'

The girls chatted for another half an hour. Erin wished Amy lived closer, but knew her heart and new husband were both settled in Oz for ever.

'Now, don't forget, Amy is a great name!'

Erin laughed, she had all her friends and family pushing names at her left, right and centre.

'OK, I'd better go. I can't believe the next time I'm home you will have two children in tow!'

'I know, it's all a bit mad, but we've been so blessed. A few months ago I'd started to think we'd never have children, and now we're having two. We bought our double buggy the other day and I keep staring at it. I just can't believe that soon it will be full. And I had to pinch myself last week when we ordered the two matching cots, it's unbelievable.'

'It's not unbelievable, it's amazing,' said Amy, who was full of admiration for her friend. 'You'll be the best mum ever,' she added, and with that they wrapped up their conversation, and Erin went back to her much-deserved nap on the couch.

★　　★　　★

An hour later she woke to see John flicking through her pregnancy and baby book. To her it was the Holy Grail, to John it was the book that kept his wife awake all night, and he usually had to rip it out of her hands, so she was surprised to see him reading it.

'What are you doing?' she asked.

John looked up, surprised she was awake.

'Well, you see, I was looking through the Mothercare catalogue and I noticed you can buy these baby carriers. They're amazing. You don't need to bring the flipping big double buggy, you just pop the baby into the carrier, strap it on to your chest and away you go!'

'And what about the other twin?' asked Erin.

'Oh, well, I'm only going to bring one twin at a time down to the yacht club for a little Saturday afternoon outing.'

'The yacht club?' repeated Erin, trying not to smile.

'Yeah, the twins can take it in turns to come with me, and these baby carriers will be perfect. None of this lugging buggies and big bags around. No, all I'll need is the baby and the carrier!'

'And what about the nappies, wipes, bottles, formula, and spare clothes?'

It was obvious John hadn't thought the idea through.

'Well, I can just leave that stuff in the car. Anyway,

351

it's just occurred to me – what if we have a girl and I'm in the yacht club? Where will I change her? Do I bring her into the Men's with me, or am I allowed into the female bathrooms now I'm with child? I thought there might be some info on toilet etiquette in your baby books, but they don't seem to cover that.'

'Well, first of all, you are not "with child", John, and no amount of baby equipment will gain you access to the Ladies. And anyway, those bathrooms are pretty rotten. You'll just have to change the baby somewhere else in the club house.'

'What? No, I'll talk to the club president about this, see what he can do.'

Erin tried not to laugh. They hadn't painted the nurseries, or bought any baby clothes or car seats, and yet all John was worried about was how the baby would get on in the yacht club.

'Anyway, I got you something,' said John, reaching into an Eason paper bag. He pulled out a *Marie Claire* magazine, a *Hello!* and a copy of the *Irish Times*.

Erin grabbed the *Marie Claire* and opened it wide. She pulled the pages full of high fashion, beauty products and hair styles close to her face.

'Oh, that's good,' she said, sniffing in the new print smell. 'That's really good.'

'You're such a weirdo,' said John, handing her the latest issue of *Hello!*

Erin opened the middle-page-spread interview with Tom Cruise and inhaled the smell there, too. For months she had been craving the smell of fresh print. From new magazines to unopened newspapers, she had to get that aroma. Other women might crave chocolate or tuna, but for her one whiff of *Heat* magazine was all she needed to feel good.

After thoroughly sniffing her way through interviews with Brad Pitt, Kate Winslet and the royal family of Monaco, Erin tossed *Hello!* on to a pile of magazines as big as the European food mountain.

'Did you already have that *Hello!*?' asked John, thinking he could spot the cover under a TV guide catalogue.

'Yeah, I've bought it twice already this week, but once opened the smell goes, so it's useless.'

'You could at least read them,' said John, settling into an armchair beside her and wondering why she couldn't have got addicted to something cheap like crushed ice, rather than expensive magazines that were rendered useless after a few sniffs.

'Don't worry, I'll drop them into Alison, she loves magazines,' said Erin, reaching into her handbag. 'Anyway, I got you something today, too,' she added, handing John three small black-and-white printouts of her latest baby ultrasounds.

'I'm sorry I couldn't make it, but there are just so many doctor's appointments. I can't ask for time off work for them all.'

'I know, don't worry,' reassured Erin. 'The babies are getting big, aren't they?'

'Wow, you can see two legs and a foot in that one. But this one is amazing, it's got a total side profile of one of them.'

'I know,' said Erin, getting up and perching on the arm of John's chair. 'The doctor asked me if I wanted to know the sex of the babies today; apparently he could tell by the way they were positioned. I was so tempted!'

John looked at her with his mouth wide open. 'And?'

'And I didn't, I want it to be a surprise.'

'Well, I think I know from looking at this picture,' he said.

'Oh really?' said Erin, unconvinced.

'Yes,' he said excitedly. 'This side profile of the baby looks so like me as a child. I'm telling you, this one is a boy!'

'That looks like you as a kid?' asked Erin, pointing at the small blurry mesh of black, white and grey blobs.

'Yeah, the chin, nose and forehead are exactly the way I looked.'

Erin burst out laughing. 'Well, unless your parents

took X-ray photos, I can't see how you can think that's like you.'

'Mark my words. That is a boy,' said John, gazing at the picture proudly.

'We can discuss this more in the car, we're late for Stephen and Ruth's.'

'OK, but bring the printout. I want to show them. Stephen knew me as a kid, I bet he'll think the baby looks like me, too!'

Erin shook her head in disbelief but stuffed the printouts into her handbag nonetheless.

Ten weeks ago their friends Ruth and Stephen had had their second child, Daniel. Their daughter Jessica was now twenty months old.

'Are you sure you want to babysit?' Ruth had asked Erin on the phone earlier that day.

'Yes, we need the practice, and I'm sure you could do with some time alone.'

'Well, we could, but we're not going far, just to that new burger place for some food. We never have time to cook any more, so anything other than tea and toast will be a real treat!'

Erin and John arrived just as Stephen was putting Jessica to bed upstairs.

'Don't worry, once she's down she usually stays asleep all night,' Ruth said. 'It's Daniel who will keep you busy! I'll feed him now, and we'll be back before his next feed, but if you're stuck I'll leave a bottle of expressed milk in the fridge.'

Erin saw John blush.

'But don't worry, we'll be back within two hours!'

Erin was listening to Ruth, but noticed John surveying the house, which looked like an atomic bomb had gone off in it. Jessica had her toys spread out everywhere, and in-between a Dora the Explorer kitchen and a farm set was Daniel's bouncer, his soft toy and a funny looking cradle.

'It's a newborn soother,' said Ruth, seeing them eye up the cream cradle that sat in the middle of the floor. 'It's like a motorized Moses basket. It has three different soothing motions. Daniel falls asleep the minute we turn it on. I wish we'd had one when Jessica was that age. When I think of all the miles we walked every night in an attempt to get her to sleep! That's how I shed the baby weight, it was all that exercise!'

'How is Daniel doing?' asked Erin, as Ruth began breastfeeding, and John awkwardly turned to look the other way.

'It's amazing how different girls and boys are,' said Ruth. 'Jessica was so alert, and even at a young age wanted to see what was going on, while Daniel is a real boy, and, just like any man, all he wants is food, sleep, and to be near a woman's breast! And like all the men I know he hates changing clothes or being asked to do anything he doesn't feel like! I swear he already protests at having to smile at strangers or say hello to visitors! Anyway, you're so good to take him tonight. We'll be back by ten, and since he's just been fed he will probably nod off, and you'll be able to sit down, relax and watch some TV.'

'Great,' said Erin, thinking that apart from the mess, looking after two children seemed pretty easy so far.

'OK, Jessica is asleep. We had better go, before you guys change your minds,' joked Stephen, as he came back into the room. Erin could see he had no interest in small chat, and just wanted to get out of the house.

'Ring us if there's a problem, and don't forget to use the newborn soother, it'll get Daniel to sleep in minutes!' said Ruth, as she flung on her coat, headed to the front door and didn't look back.

'Shall I put Daniel in the soother basket thing now?' asked John.

'No,' said Erin. 'We don't need all that electric motion. A baby should learn to fall asleep on its own. We won't be buying some quick-fix sleeping soother solution. And if needs be a little walking with the child won't hurt us. As Ruth said, it's good exercise!'

★   ★   ★

Forty-five minutes later there were tears rolling down Erin's face.

'My God, just turn the flipping soother on! What's wrong with you?' she shouted at John over Daniel's cries. His wails were reaching ear-piercing levels. Tears, sweat and snot were running down his face.

'It's so complicated. I can't get it to work,' said John, whose T-shirt was stuck to his back. The heat of the room and the sweat from walking with Daniel for the past thirty minutes was getting to him. The second Ruth and Stephen had walked out the door everything had gone wrong. Daniel had gotten really upset and refused to calm down, and his yells had woken Jessica, who was now sitting in her pyjamas in front of the TV shouting that she wanted Cheerios, and crying for her mum.

Suddenly a strange noise came from Daniel's nappy. Erin felt a damp wetness soak through his Babygro.

'Oh my God,' said John, peering at the baby in Erin's arms. 'At least we now know what was wrong with him: he needed to go to the toilet. But look at his back! He's got poo seeping through the Babygro.'

Erin almost vomited. This night had been a bad idea.

'OK, well, let's change him. You get the water, I'll carry him upstairs. And don't forget to bring Jessica, she can't be left alone.'

Erin walked up the stairs and placed Daniel down

on the nappy changer. John appeared with a bowl of water and Jessica, who was chewing on a rice cake. Erin started to remove Daniel's Babygro.

'Christ, he's up to his neck in poo. Forget the cotton wool, this is a baby-wipe situation.'

'I read that water is best. You see the water . . .'

'I don't care what is best,' John interrupted. 'This baby has poo under his armpits. Pass me the wipes.'

John opened the nappy, but at the same time Daniel kicked his foot and it ended up right in the middle of the explosion. His poo-covered foot was now waving in mid-air. Erin went to clean it, when suddenly Daniel spit up. And before Erin could do anything, he had moved his head sideways and stuck his face into the vomit. He now had sick in his eyes and poo on his foot, and his back was still glued to his Babygro.

'Bap,' said Jessica, whose latest word was bap, which apparently meant 'dirty nappy'.

'Bap, indeed,' said John, who was now opening a second bag of wipes. 'This is worse than cleaning out the toilet on a boat,' he said, gulping back the urge to vomit.

Finally they got Daniel cleaned up. Erin had the baby in her arms, and was just about to dress him in fresh clothes, when he was sick again. This time Daniel managed to miss himself, and the vomit went straight down Erin's expensive shirt. The sick collected in her rather large maternity bra. For a moment no one said anything. But then John started laughing, followed by Jessica, who'd laugh at anything that a grown up thought was funny.

'OK, I'll wash him. You change your top,' said John.

'I don't have any spare clothes,' whined Erin, who could feel the sick swishing as she moved her chest.

'Just fling on one of Ruth's jumpers, but hurry back. I can't do this alone.'

Erin filled a plastic bag with her shirt and bra. She found an oversized hoody of Stephen's and flung it on. Back in the bedroom John had gotten things a little more under control, and Daniel was at least clean now, and had stopped crying.

'OK, let me get him some new clothes,' said Erin, opening a large chest of drawers. In the top drawer she found plenty of worn-out baby-blue all-in-one vests and Babygros. She was surprised to see the expensive French designer yellow sleepsuit she'd bought Daniel in the drawer unworn, and with its tags still on.

'Well, you can wear this now,' said Erin, as she began unbuttoning the sleepsuit.

'Are you sure that's the right way round?' asked John. 'Don't the buttons usually go down the front?'

'No. In the shop all the gorgeous French clothes had the buttons at the back. I suppose it means the front looks nicer.'

John didn't seem convinced. 'How are we supposed to get him into it?'

Erin looked at the sleepsuit. She tried to lower Daniel into it, but realized in order to fasten all the buttons she would need to lay him down.

'But I can't lay him face down just so I can fasten the buttons, he'd suffocate,' said Erin, starting to realize there might be a reason the suit was unworn.

'Forget fastening the buttons, we'd have to break his arm just to get him into it, it's so small and tight,' said John, who now had the baby's arm wedged between the collar and the sleeve. Daniel's face started going red and he began bawling.

'My God, who invented these clothes?' asked Erin with disbelief, as she debated cutting the baby out of the useless outfit.

John managed to get Daniel out and decided to put him in a pair of pyjamas instead.

'His feet will be cold in them,' complained Erin.

'Fine, I'll get him some socks,' replied John, opening a drawer that was full of tiny accessories. His large hands fiddled with the baby socks, bibs and hats.

Erin turned to check on Jessica, and only then realized she wasn't in the room. Erin ran through the house in a panic, only to find her standing in the middle of Ruth and Stephen's bedroom. Jessica was painting the bedroom walls with an old dirty toilet brush. Erin ran and grabbed the toilet brush off her, only to notice Jessica's face and hair were covered in Sudocrem. Erin had misplaced the Sudocrem while changing Daniel, but had been too busy to fret about it, but now as Jessica's fair hair stood up stiff and white with the cream she knew she should have left it on a higher shelf. Erin found the half-empty jar of Sudocrem floating in the toilet bowl. She took a deep breath. Ruth and Stephen had only been gone an hour but already their house and children were in bits.

Twenty minutes later John was stuffing Daniel with the expressed bottle of milk.

'I don't want to know what's in this,' he'd said as he'd heated it up.

Erin had cleaned Jessica, and was now trying to pull her down from the coffee table. Jessica was full of energy, and seemed to like climbing, shouting at the baby and pulling the fake coal from the fire the best. It was while trying to piece the gas fire and its coal back together that Erin noticed Daniel's feet as John walked with him.

'What have you got on his feet?' she asked.

'Socks, like you told me,' replied her husband.

Erin took a closer look.

'They're not socks. They're mittens!'

Erin and then Jessica began laughing. Jessica took this opportunity and moment's distraction to turn over the kitchen bin. Erin watched as the poo-filled nappy, vomited stained clothes and toilet-water-flooded Sudocrem jar all rolled out on to the kitchen floor.

'We have to get these kids to bed,' she said, exhausted.

Finally, John put Daniel into the baby soother crib, which he had set rocking on full blast. As the crib rumbled away, John managed to persuade Jessica to return to bed by giving her Cheerios and juice.

'It's probably too late for her to have juice,' said Erin.

'I think tooth decay is the least of our worries,' said John, as he wearily carried Jessica out of the room, leaving Erin to finally sit down.

Erin surveyed the room, and already she didn't care about the mess. She was just glad it was quiet again. Who cared if it was untidy or dirty? It was just such a relief it didn't contain a screaming baby or Sudocremed toddler.

A little later Ruth and Stephen returned home.

'So, how were they?' asked Ruth, who looked better for her two hours out of the house.

John looked at Erin, and with his eyes told her to lie.

'They've been as good as gold,' said Erin. 'We had a few little hiccups, but nothing we couldn't handle!'

'Oh, that's such a relief. You two are such good friends.'

'Cheers, mate,' Stephen said to John. 'Why don't you both stay for a beer?'

Erin could tell from the look on John's face that the last thing he wanted to do was stay another five minutes. They were both exhausted.

'Thanks, Stephen, but I'll have to drag John home. My own two little bumps are kicking like mad. I need to lie down, but thanks for the offer.'

Erin had barely said goodbye before John had his coat on and was walking out to the car.

Neither spoke for the first ten minutes of the journey home.

'I never realized how much work it entailed,' said John, wrapped in his memories of the last two hours.

'I never knew a small baby could puke or poo that much,' added Erin.

'What have we got ourselves into?' asked John.

Erin didn't reply. Finally John started giggling, and then he broke into full, hearty laughter. 'If you had seen the look on your face when Daniel puked into your bra. It was hilarious!'

Erin couldn't help but laugh herself. The bag of dirty clothes lay in the boot of the car, a memento of their ill-fated babysitting episode.

'I didn't have the heart to tell Ruth that Jessica ate most of her Jo Malone body lotion.'

John laughed again, but they were both thinking that the fact they were expecting twins soon was suddenly very real and scary.

'Don't worry, Erin, our kids will be different, and it's probably much easier when you're minding your own children.'

'Yes, of course,' said Erin, but she didn't sound too convinced.

'But one thing I have decided is that tomorrow I'm going out and buying, not one, but two baby soothers for our children!'

'They're miracle machines,' whispered Erin, as she leant back into the seat and nodded off. For once she didn't dream about babies; she'd had enough of them for one night.

39

'And now let's have everyone on to the dance floor for "Rock the Boat"!' the DJ shouted to the crowd.

Beth Prendergast gazed at the sweaty DJ sitting behind his decks. Was he joking? 'Rock the Boat'? The corniest song ever, especially for a wedding. But obviously other people didn't feel the same way, as Beth was almost knocked to the ground by them pushing to get to the dance floor. Beth watched as they sat down in a line on the ground and began swaying from side to side. Christ, I can't do that, I'd go into labour, she thought. She looked for an escape route.

'You're not going anywhere,' said Simon. 'Pregnant or not, you will rock that boat!'

Beth laughed. Today was her friend Susan's wedding. Beth had listened to her plans for her big day for months. She'd been so excited for her, but as the date had got closer she'd begun to dread being sober and almost seven months' pregnant at an Irish wedding. And her misgivings were justified: the day had been fabulous, and Susan had looked beautiful in her Vera Wang dress and Jimmy Choo shoes, but now, as the night wore on and everyone else drank far too much of the free champagne, it was brought home to Beth how hard it was to go to boozy events pregnant and on your own.

The venue was beautiful, and Wineport Lodge was all Susan had said it would be. It was the perfect place for a summer wedding. Beth had booked a single bedroom months in advance, and had been lucky to get a beautiful one overlooking the lake and the boat jetty. Susan and her new husband Paul had both spoken so well at the service, and Beth had welled up as she'd heard Paul talk about the first time he'd met Susan, and how he'd known at once she was the woman of his dreams. Beth had been fortunate, too, to sit at a table that wasn't just full of Burlington employees. She liked most of the guys she worked with, but some of the people on Susan's team were hard work, and enjoyed grilling Beth on her pregnancy and attempting to work out who the father was. Beth had been placed beside one of Susan's cousins, a guy called Simon from Cork. He was a lot of fun, and seemed to be the only one delighted to hear that Beth was off drink.

'It just means there's more free wine for us,' he said to the table, all of whom had previously eyed Beth up and dismissed her as a party pooper.

Simon had three sisters and knew everything there was to know about pregnancy and babies.

'Trust me, I didn't want to become an expert on waters breaking, breastfeeding and expressed milk, but having a house full of girls means all this unwanted information has gone into me by osmosis. I'm telling you, Beth, if you have any questions on teething or weaning, I'm your man!'

Simon was very funny, and Beth was delighted to have him beside her at the table.

'I usually get stuck with one of my younger cousins at these weddings, so it's great that I've finally been put beside such a beauty. I always thought stockbrokers were slimy over-ambitious young guys! It's a shock to find out they can be lovely women, too.'

Beth laughed, but had to admit she was flattered by his compliments. It had been a long time since a man had given her any. She couldn't quite believe it was happening, considering she was wedged into the faithful black maternity dress that she had worn to every function since she'd been four months' pregnant.

The meal had been lovely, and unlike all the rest of the women at the table, Beth had asked for seconds. Her appetite was increasing, and she couldn't seem to resist potatoes. That was one great benefit to being pregnant, you could eat as much as you liked, and no one thought badly of you. And even though her doctor had reminded her that she was not in fact 'eating for two' during her pregnancy, Beth liked to imagine she was. She hadn't put on a lot of weight; she was just enjoying good food more than ever.

'You can have one glass of wine, you know. All my sisters did,' said Simon, as he poured Beth out a small amount of white wine. She was tempted, but resisted.

'No, I won't, thanks. It's not good for the baby. And anyway, the last thing I need is people in work thinking I get drunk while pregnant! No I'll get myself another 7 Up when the waiter comes back.'

Simon shrugged, and Beth did feel a bit like a wet fish, but she only had two months to go, and then she would be able to drink any time she wanted. And even though she was tempted to have the odd glass of wine now and then, on the whole she didn't miss alcohol.

Simon was just filling Beth in on his new job as a website designer when suddenly Matt, one of the guys in Beth's work pod, shouted over.

'OK, so what names have you got for us this week?'

Beth laughed. Every day she changed her mind about the best names for her unborn child. The guys on her team had some kind of internal bet going on about it.

'I still think it will be Jones, after the Dow Jones. One of Beth's favourite things!' Graham O'Reilly called out. 'Or maybe even Nikkei?' The whole table laughed.

'No, it's got to be Peter, after Peter Pan. You know because of all those *pains au chocolat!*' said Matt, cheekily. Beth pretended to be annoyed, and playfully hit him, but knew he was only messing. His wife had been obsessed by the smell of coal all through her last pregnancy, so he knew about funny cravings.

'Well,' said Beth. 'For a boy I still like Christopher or Robin, after my favourite book, *Winnie The Pooh.*'

Matt groaned and tried to tell Beth both were gay names. Beth ignored him.

'And for a girl I like Amy, Katie, Ellie and Kelly.'

'So, all names ending in y,' said Simon.

Beth was stunned, she had never thought of it like that. She would need to rethink her method of choosing names.

'I also like the name Harry for a boy.'

'Harry?' asked a snotty woman near her. 'God, that's so English. And old-fashioned. No, you can't call a baby that. And as for Robin, well, as your friend said, it's pretty dire.'

Beth stared at the woman in surprise. This

complete stranger was criticizing her name choices in front of a large table of people. It was OK for the guys from work to playfully tease her, but not some stranger.

'And what are your children called?' Beth asked her.

'Oh, well, I don't have any,' the woman replied. 'I'm not with anyone at the moment.'

'Hmm,' said Beth. 'I thought as much.' It was always the people furthest from something that liked to knock it as much as they could. This was obviously some single, jealous cow. Well, she might be envious of the baby, but that didn't allow her to take it out on Beth's choice of name.

'If you finally meet someone, and after a few years get engaged, and then married, and then years later have a baby, you can call it whatever you like. But, in the meantime, if I want to name my baby Harry, I will.' The lady looked embarrassed and dismayed. Beth had put her in her place.

'Well done,' said Simon to Beth. 'I once made the mistake of questioning my sister Jill's choice in calling her new son Elliot. I thought it was a bit too E.T. But trust me, after getting attacked by an over-protective first-time mum, I would never question a woman's baby-name decision again!'

'It's just so hard to pick a nice one. It's a lot of power to have. I mean, what you decide affects your child for ever. They'll be stuck with that name their whole life.'

'Well, what does your husband like?' asked Simon.

'I'm not married,' she replied. 'It's just me picking the names.'

'Oh,' he said. Beth thought she saw a little smile creep on to his face.

The rest of the meal went very well – that is, until the music started. The newlyweds were up swinging each other around to ABBA's 'Dancing Queen'.

'You have to dance,' said Simon, as he tried to usher Beth on to the packed dance floor.

'No way,' said Beth strongly. 'I think seeing a heavily pregnant woman try to swing her bump to the sound of ABBA, or any band, is disturbing. Like the unwritten rule of no white after Labour Day, pregnant women should not attempt to boogie. It's just wrong.'

Simon started laughing.

'I'm serious. Pregnancy takes away your balance, grace and mobility. Add all of that to a packed dance floor and some corny music and you have a recipe for disaster! Trust me, nobody wants to see me dance.'

'I do,' replied Simon.

After that Beth might have been able to resist 'Rock the Boat', but she had to have at least one small dance with Simon, especially once the DJ started playing Beyoncé. Beth ignored the stares from her colleagues, as they all tried to work out if Simon could be her baby's father. If only they knew the truth, she thought.

Once it hit midnight Beth decided that was an acceptable hour for a pregnant woman to leave a very drunken wedding. She said goodbye to Susan, who still looked beautiful, even if her dress was soaking up all the spilt beer. The minute Beth walked into the hotel corridor she bent down and took off her stilettos. Her legs and back were so sore. Pregnancy and high heels did not go well together. She had been tempted to wear her very comfortable flat shoes, but knew that was only one step away from being a complete granny.

'Were you not going to say goodbye?'

Beth looked up to see Simon walking towards her.

'God, if I hadn't needed to go outside for a smoke I wouldn't have seen you trying to sneak out of the wedding!'

Beth blushed. She knew she should have said goodbye to him, he'd been such good company all day, but she'd felt a little awkward. What was there to say? They wouldn't see each other again, and he was hardly going to ask her out when she was carrying another man's baby.

'Let me at least walk you to your room?' Simon asked, as he picked up Beth's shoes.

They were at her door in no time.

'Well, it was lovely to meet you. Susan has some gorgeous friends that she's been hiding away in Dublin!'

Beth smiled.

'Best of luck with your new job,' she said, as she searched her handbag for her room key.

'Thanks, and best of luck with the baby. Your whole life will change!'

Beth shrugged. She was sick of people telling her that. Her life had already changed quite enough in the last few months.

'But don't worry, I know you'll be able to handle it,' said Simon, sensing her mood. 'Christopher Robin or Amy will be a very lucky child.'

Beth was secretly chuffed that he had remembered her baby names.

'Anyway, I had better get back to the dance floor, there is a rumour that there's a Michael Jackson medley coming up, and I do a mean moonwalk!' said Simon, handing Beth back her silver shoes.

Just as Beth went to shake his hand, he leant in and gave her a kiss on the cheek, and then another brief one on her lips.

'Take care. And I pity the guy who's left you coming to weddings alone, and picking baby names all by yourself. He doesn't know what he's missing, the fool.'

And with that Simon turned around and headed back to the function room.

Stunned, Beth walked into her hotel room, and sat down on the plush bed. For the first time in months she felt attractive and wanted. Some guy she barely knew had liked her. It meant nothing, and wouldn't be going anywhere, but it felt so nice to know that even if Tom didn't want her, other guys did.

Beth's feet might be killing her, she was wrecked from all the dancing and tired from the long day, but it had all been worth it. Because today her confidence in herself was the highest it had been in a long time.

40

Beth watched the couple across from her. The woman, whose hair was in dreadlocks, was engrossed in a leaflet on breastfeeding, while the man – who had long dark hair tied in a ponytail – was actually on one knee, speaking to her swollen belly. Beth felt her mouth drop open. Is this guy for real? she thought. Suddenly he caught her eye.

'Speaking to the foetus is very important at this stage, so that they will recognize their parents' voices. I also play him classical music, it's supposed to increase his I.Q.,' he informed Beth in an American accent.

She looked at him in disbelief. What a nut! she thought. She turned away from him, and studied a leaflet on Vitamin K injections for newborns. As she pretended to read, Beth cast glances round the room. She couldn't believe the class she had got stuck with. Today was her first day of the ante-natal classes that took place in Holles Street. She hadn't realized you had to book them early to get the time, day and class you wanted, and so she'd been left with no choice: just the Friday afternoon Couples Class. What a nightmare! Beth had been dreading it – yes, she was dying to learn about the birth, labour pains and pain relief, but she didn't want to have to sit beside twenty happy couples each week and be reminded of her single status.

As people took their seats Beth was amazed by how old some of them were. She knew the average age of a woman's first baby had risen to thirty-one, but it was still funny to think that years ago women had finished having kids in their mid-thirties, and now it was when they started. Some women looked old enough to be grannies, not first-time mums. But regardless of their ages, at least they had partners, she thought, once again cursing Tom – which she did about twenty times a day!

She looked at all the bumps next. It amazed her how different everyone's were: some round, flat, huge, or very wide. Such different children lay inside them all. The mothers all looked so different, too. A few, like Beth, had obviously come straight from work, and were dressed very smartly, while others seemed to be wrecked from the pregnancy, and looked as if they had just rolled out of bed, flung on a tracksuit and forced themselves to come into the hospital for today's class. They all might be different but Beth did feel a slight connection with them: the whole class were going through exactly the same thing at exactly the same time, and would all have kids of the same age. It was amazing, really.

Suddenly a girl with bright red hair and a neat bump stood in front of her. She seemed nervous.

'Is this seat taken?' she asked. Beth smiled, the girl was alone. Finally someone who is in my boat, she thought, as she cleared her bag off the seat next to her so the girl could use it.

'I'm Grace, by the way,' said the girl, who had a slight American accent.

'Are you American?' asked Beth.

'No, but I lived there for years. I've just moved home from California. I didn't know this class would be so packed,' Grace said, taking out a notepad and pen. Beth suddenly noticed that almost all the women had notepads. God, she thought, I never know the right thing to do with this baby. She grabbed her handbag, and – amidst *pain au chocolat* wrappers, an empty bottle of Lucozade, her work BlackBerry, and some Rennies for the odd bit of heartburn she seemed to have developed – she found a blank piece of paper and a pencil.

'So, when are you due?' asked Beth.

'The twenty-fifth of July,' said Grace, placing her hand protectively on her small bump. Beth smiled, she always did the same these days, when talking about her future bambino.

'And you?' asked the girl.

'The twenty-ninth of July. It seems so far away in one way,' said Beth. 'But then, at other times I think it's coming too soon, and I won't have everything organized!'

The girl laughed. 'My husband feels the same way. He keeps worrying because we haven't got the cot or car seat yet, but when I suggest we spend a day baby shopping he says we have all the time in the world, and puts it off for another weekend! He can't be here today, but he'll come next week. You can meet him then.'

Beth smiled, but felt a little dismayed that the girl had a partner, too. Beth was definitely the only single lady in the group. Suddenly a nurse came in, shut the door and walked into the middle of the room. Everyone went silent. Here was the woman who knew the answers to all their questions, all their worries. They didn't want to miss a word she said.

'Hello, everyone! My name is Nurse Mary Egan, and I'll be taking you every Friday for the next eight weeks, to prepare you for the birth of your children. Now, before we begin I'd like everyone to introduce themselves and their partners, and tell us when you are due. You should try to remember the names because the woman sitting next to you could be sharing a hospital room with you in two months' time! And, guys, these men could be pacing the corridors with you, and when you feel like a hard-earned smoke or moan these will be your comrades!'

Everyone laughed. The couple at the far end of the room stood up and began introducing themselves. Beth listened to couple after couple reel off their due dates and names. She was dreading having to stand up on her own and say she was unmarried and single. It had been hard enough admitting it to friends and family, let alone complete strangers. Beth was just listening to the annoying hippy couple, who were telling everyone about their plan for a natural birth. 'No pain, no gain,' they were saying in chorus, when suddenly she heard the door open. Everyone stared. Beth almost collapsed: her father was there. William spotted his daughter, and as quickly as he could made a beeline for her. The young girl beside her moved up.

'Dad, what are you doing here?' Beth whispered.

William took his seat and removed his blazer.

'Well, I knew you were dreading coming here alone, and I was out in the garden doing the weeding when it occurred to me you shouldn't. I'm here for you.'

She smiled at him. It was a little weird to have him here, but she did immediately feel more confident in front of all the happy couples.

Suddenly it was her turn to stand up.

'I'm Beth. And this is my dad, William.' Beth stressed the word dad, she didn't want anyone mistaking him for her partner again! 'I'm due at the end of July, and I'm looking forward to learning all about the labour pain relief!' Everyone laughed, but Beth was being truthful. She wanted the epidural. Being tall had given her a bad back, and although it hadn't affected her too badly throughout the pregnancy she was told it could act up once she went into labour, so she intended to order her epidural as soon as she got into hospital.

On the other side of Beth was a nice-looking couple who introduced themselves as Erin and John. Erin's bump was enormous.

'Well, I'm not due until the end of September,' said Erin, who was a pretty girl with long brown hair.

Beth was shocked, she looked huge. How could she possibly last until September? she wondered. But, as if she read Beth's mind, the girl explained her gigantic bump.

'You see, I'm big because we're expecting twins! And as twins can be born premature I'm doing this early ante-natal class in case they end up coming early.' Erin smiled and sat back down.

Beth gazed at her. She'd thought her own bump was getting big, and she only had eight weeks to go.

This poor girl had much longer, yet looked like the *Titanic*.

'Congratulations! Wow! Twins. You're brave!' said Beth to Erin.

'Oh thanks! Yes, it was such a surprise, but it's been a real blessing,' said Erin, looking at her husband and taking his hand. He beamed back at her, and as he passed her a glass of water Beth could see they were deeply in love. It looked as if the twins would have great parents.

Once the introductions were over the class began. The midwife explained how each week they would be learning about the different aspects of childbirth: keeping well and active before the birth, how the labour ward worked, pain relief, and what to expect once the baby was born. Beth was fascinated. She cringed a bit when the nurse started reminding the women that they should be doing their pelvic-floor exercises. It wasn't something she wanted her dad to hear about, but William didn't seem fazed at all.

'God, it's all coming back to me now,' he said. 'I'll never forget how many holy medals your mother wore when we arrived here to have you. She didn't care about her clothes, make-up or the pain, all she wanted was to make sure you arrived safe and sound. I swear a newborn baby has never been blessed with more holy water then you! Your new Babygro was soaked! I'll tell you the full story when the class is over.'

Beth choked up. Her dad had never told her that. All these years she had always felt awkward asking him about her mum, because she hadn't wanted to upset him. Now she wondered if he had been longing to tell these stories to her.

The rest of the class passed quickly enough, and Beth was surprised how much she learnt. The nurse was an excellent teacher – she made light of many worries or concerns, but at the same time never failed to remind them how the baby was their main priority. Their birth plans would be overruled if the baby's health and well-being required it. She seemed to direct this remark at the overbearing American couple, who were insistent that their plan would be adhered to, no matter what.

'We don't want any drugs administered, and under no circumstances is my wife having a Caesarean. We believe in a natural birth.'

'We all believe in a natural birth,' interrupted the nurse. 'But if that baby gets into distress then it's the surgical ward for you, I'm afraid.' The couple looked very put out, but still couldn't resist confiding the rest of their crazy plans.

'And we're going to have a CD player in our room so we can play our special CD for him. Our baby will be born into the sound of dawn in the rainforest. It will teach him about the earth, and how we are all part of the circle of life.'

Grace started laughing. 'Are they for real?' she asked Beth.

Beth prayed she wouldn't go into labour on the same day as them, she could see they were going to be trouble.

'Listen,' said Nurse Egan, looking frustrated and just plain annoyed, 'this is a maternity hospital. We want to deliver healthy babies, and if your plan can work around a healthy birth, then that's great, but I must remind you, in this hospital the babies come first. Now we have run over time, so I will let you all go, but don't forget to eat well, practise your exercises, relax and get lots of rest. In a matter of weeks you won't know what sleep is, so stock up on it now! Take care, and I'll see you all next Friday.'

Beth and William walked out of the classroom, past the ward of expectant mums – who were all pacing the corridors, trying to go into labour – and through reception, which was filled with flower bouquet deliveries and exhausted-looking fathers trying to get five minutes' peace.

'Thanks so much for coming,' Beth said to her dad. 'I'd better head back to work now, but you're so

good to have come all this way just to be at my side.'
She kissed him.

'Back to work? Sure, it's half past four on a Friday, why would you be doing that? Let's go for dinner. It could become our Friday traditional – the ante-natal class followed by dinner.'

Beth didn't know what to do. She never took time off work unless it was an emergency or for her doctor's appointments. She was about to turn down the dinner offer, but then she thought of what the nurse had said about taking plenty of rest now. She also knew Tom couldn't complain if she decided to take the rest of the day off; after all, it was his baby she was going to the classes for.

'OK, let's do it!' said Beth impulsively. 'Where do you want to go?'

'Roly's,' said her dad. And so they headed off to one of Dublin's most famous restaurants, all the while laughing about the hippy couple's forest-themed baby music!

41

'For God's sake! I thought you said this was the best car seat on the market?' Grace Miller shouted at her husband, as she attempted for the fourth time to fit a baby seat into her car. Ethan was also struggling to get an identical one into his vehicle.

'We should never have bought two copies of the same thing without testing it out first,' Grace said, as she looked at hers. It was jammed half-way up the back of her front passenger seat.

'Well, all the women in work said this make was the best, and we needed one each. Let's look at the instructions again,' said Ethan.

'Thank God we decided to fit them before the baby came!' Grace laughed. 'It's like rocket science. I know they say you can remove them easily so you can take your child anywhere in its seat, but I swear if I manage to get this in it's staying there for ever!'

'Yeah, sure!' said Ethan, his head deep in the car-seat booklet. 'I bet in a few weeks' time you'll be one of those women with a latte in one hand, and a baby in its car seat in the other as you walk around Dundrum shopping centre.'

Grace laughed, but even as he spoke she still couldn't visualize herself with a baby. Grace was overdue, but even so found it hard to believe that the baby and motherhood could arrive at any moment.

'OK, I think I see what we've been doing wrong,' announced Ethan, as he took both the car seats out and placed them on the ground. 'Let's start again.'

Grace smiled as she sat down on their porch and watched her husband, who was intent on getting everything right. From assembling the cot to painting the nursery, Ethan was already a real hands-on father. Grace knew how hard it had been for him in the last few weeks, coming to terms with the fact that he was now going to be living in Ireland for the foreseeable future. But he was taking it well, and being positive about raising his child in a foreign country. All this only furthered Grace's belief that she really was so lucky to be married to him.

Ethan's company had been delighted to hear he was staying on in Ireland. His friend Alex would run the main office in San Diego, while Ethan would look after Dublin, and any further European offices. But having a job still didn't make the transition easy: it was a lot of change for Ethan. He also really missed Coco, and wanted him to come over as soon as possible. Grace had been nervous about how their dog would settle in Ireland, and how he would react to having a baby in the house, so they had decided to defer having him sent over for a few more months, until well after the baby was born. That way Grace could put her worries about Coco and Ireland on the long finger.

Ethan and Grace had also been looking for a new home. Now that they planned to live here, they both wanted to buy somewhere nice, yet near enough to Grace's brothers and Patsy. Grace had also found the last few weeks hard. Herself and Ethan had never fought, but the decision to stay in Ireland had rocked their life, and then they had both had different views about where in Dublin to live and what kind of house their baby should grow up in. Although, now, the biggest bone of contention was the baby name. Ethan still couldn't understand why Grace refused to find out what sex the baby was.

'But everyone in America does it,' he had argued on more than one occasion.

'I know, but it's different over here,' she had replied each time.

'But how can we make a shortlist of baby names when we don't even know the sex? It's madness! And such a waste of time when we could easily find out.'

But Grace held strong and refused to find out. Of course the suspense was killing her, and she had different theories every day as to the sex.

'The baby was kicking like mad last night when we were watching the *Transformers* DVD,' Grace had told their doctor the week before. 'I mean that's such a guys' film, surely it has to be a boy?'

'That's not a very scientific way of uncovering your baby's sex,' the doctor had replied, trying not to laugh.

But his refusal to confirm whether it was a boy or girl hadn't deterred Grace. She was convinced she could guess by its behaviour.

'Oh, I almost forgot to tell you, the baby was making a real racket yesterday when I was watching *Oprah*,' she told Ethan, as he finally got the hang of the car seats. 'So it must be a girl,' Grace continued.

'Or it could be a boy, and he was protesting at having to watch that girly crap,' Ethan replied, leaving Grace lost for words.

Maybe it is a boy, she thought.

'Anyway, if it is a little boy, how about Zac?' Ethan said.

'As in Zac from *Saved by the Bell*?' replied Grace, smiling.

'No!' he shouted. 'Zac's a strong name, a cool name.'

'It's too American,' she replied automatically.

'What?' he said, staring at his wife. 'I'm American, you know? And this baby will be, too.'

'That's not what I meant. Well it is, but not in a bad way. It's just not the kind of name that could blend in in Ireland.'

'OK, well if it's a girl then Cailin would be perfect. It's totally Irish,' said Ethan, proud of himself.

'Oh no,' she said, putting her foot down. 'That's too Irish.'

Ethan huffed. 'Well, what names do you like to-day? I know it changes on an hourly basis.'

'Yes, I'm finding it hard to make a decision, but it's a big responsibility. I mean you name that child Egbert or Mercedes and they are doomed for life. Anyway, I like Molly.'

'Molly Miller?' Ethan laughed. 'No.'

'OK, what about Sophie?'

'I had a cousin called Sophie and she was horrible. No, not Sophie.'

'Oh, for God's sake! We're never going to agree,' said Grace, deflated.

'Listen, let's just get these seats into the cars fast, then we'll have time to get dinner ready.'

It was a hot July day, and since it was such nice weather Grace and Ethan had invited Patsy, Colm and Aidan to a barbecue in their house that evening. Grace had been so busy all week setting up her new website and getting her first orders that she hadn't had time to see her family. Her business was already getting off the ground, and it was so exciting, but she knew her mum was dying to see her, and Ethan was looking forward to chatting to the boys, who were helping him get settled into Irish male life.

'There'll be no more talking about your Irish roots, or wearing your jumpers hanging over your shoulders. It just makes you look like a tourist,' Colm had said frankly the week before. 'You're living here properly now, so we'll need to get you used to pints, rugby and chipper chips.'

Ethan had realized that he had a lot to learn.

Grace had intended to get the house all tidy, clean and organized before the barbecue, but her massive bump just got in the way of everything. Instead she went in, lay down on the couch and decided to let Ethan worry about preparing the food. She ran her hand over her belly, and once again wondered when the baby was going to appear.

'You should drink some castor oil,' announced Patsy, as Grace and her huge bump opened the door to her mum and two brothers. They were all laden down with boxes of food.

'Mum, this baby will come when it's ready. And

why do you have all this food? We have steaks, burgers and salad for everyone.'

'This food isn't for tonight. It's for the next few days, to help you keep up your strength before the baby arrives.'

'Strength? Mum, with this amount of food in it, the baby will come out looking like a sumo wrestler.'

Colm laughed, but stopped when Patsy hit him over the head with a frozen garlic bread.

'Anyway, come on in,' said Grace. 'This could be the last meal we have together before the baby arrives!'

'Please God,' said Aidan. 'I swear if we have to spend any more meals discussing baby names, baby books, or baby equipment I will pass out with boredom.'

'Aidan Slattery, that's your niece or nephew you are talking about! How dare you?' said Patsy, annoyed.

'Don't worry,' whispered Grace to her brother. 'I promise there'll be no more baby-name discussions. We can't decide, so I suspect we'll just have to let the baby choose when it gets old enough!'

The barbecue went well, and while the boys tried to persuade Ethan what rugby club he should now pledge allegiance too, Patsy indulged in a little too much wine, and told Grace how amazing the night of her birth had been.

'Don't let your brothers know, but there's nothing quite like the birth of your first child. It's always a little bit special, a little more exciting.'

'I heard that,' said Colm, as he poured himself some more wine.

Ethan would have loved a glass of white wine himself, but Grace had had him under strict instructions not to have any alcohol for the last two weeks. 'In case I go into labour and need you to be sober enough to drive,' she kept saying.

'Oh, it's all so exciting. I just wish your father was here to see his first grandchild.'

Grace held her mum's hand.

'Dad would be so proud of you, Mum. I know how hard it's been without him, but you've been so strong and so active. You haven't let grief get the better of you.'

'That's because I have all of you, Grace. When you are a mother you don't have time to indulge in your own problems, you have to keep going for the family. For better or worse you need to push your own worries aside and be strong for your children. Without you all I would have curled up and died, but thank God I have my three children. That's why I've always put a little too much pressure on you to have kids. Yes, when you have them your life isn't your own any more! But it's better, fuller, and gives you strength you never knew you had. You'll learn about all this soon, Grace. Very soon!'

Grace smiled. She had never credited her mum with being so insightful. She realized you were never too old to learn something new about your mother.

Two hours later, and they'd decided to move indoors as the sun had gone in and there was a slight chill in the air. As her family drank the end of the wine, Grace had her own craving.

'God, I'd love a Frosty cappuccino now,' she announced.

'A what?' asked her mum.

'Oh it's a type of coffee with ice cream. We had the best coffee house beside us in San Diego. I couldn't start a morning without one of their treats. Starbucks actually do a version similar to the Frosty. I'd really love one now. I might go and get one,' said Grace.

'Good luck finding a coffee shop open at this time of night in Ireland,' said Colm sarcastically.

Grace looked at the clock and knew her brother was right. Ireland just didn't have the round-the-clock services that the States did. It was another thing Grace missed.

'That's so annoying. I would love one now,' whined Grace.

Suddenly Aidan sat up. 'Well, have you got ice cream in your fridge?' he asked.

'Yeah,' confirmed Ethan.

'And what about Coca-Cola, or 7 Up?' Aidan asked.

'Yeah, we have lots of fizzy drinks,' said Ethan. He disapproved of them, but Grace had been craving them lately so he had turned a blind eye to the fridge being stocked high with them.

'Well, I don't know how to make a Frosty cappuccino, but would you like Dad's special treat? An ice-cream float?'

'Oh my God, yes!' screamed Grace. She had forgotten all about her dad's speciality. On a Sunday evening when they'd finished their roast and vegetables, Teddy would take out five large glasses and fill them up with a mix of ice cream and whatever fizzy drink they had in stock. Sometimes it was Club Orange, some days it was Coke. Grace hadn't thought about those treats in a long time.

'Dad was great at making them,' she said.

Colm smiled. 'You'll have to pass on the family tradition to your baby. The Slattery ice-cream floats will be tasted by a new generation.'

Grace vowed to make them for her little one.

Ten minutes later they were all sipping on the frothy drinks.

'Yum,' said Grace and Colm at the same time.

'Oh, that's cold,' said Patsy, but she was smiling. She felt like her Teddy was right there with them.

Soon Grace's legs and back were aching, and she had to go to bed.

'We'll head home, pet,' said her mum as she hugged her. 'Now, sleep well, and I'll see you tomorrow.'

Grace kissed her mum and brothers and was just heading up the stairs when Patsy came running up them.

'I almost forgot to bless you and the baby,' she said as she pulled a small bottle of holy water from her handbag. She doused Grace and her belly in the liquid.

'God bless you and keep you both safe,' Patsy said, before going back down the stairs and leaving the house.

Grace smiled, she felt a little more protected already.

Two hours later Grace sat on the bathroom floor crying.

'Curse Aidan and those ice-cream floats, my stomach is in bits. I think I got a chill into it from the ice cream. I don't feel well,' she wailed, as Ethan rubbed her back.

Ethan resisted the urge to say 'I told you so' to his wife. He'd never thought the cold and fizzy drinks sounded like a good idea for someone who was about to pop. Instead he passed her a glass of water and listened to her rant.

Half an hour later and Grace still didn't feel well.

'Oh my God, you couldn't have cooked those burgers properly,' she shouted at Ethan. 'I told you I wanted mine well done.'

'Grace, if that burger had been any more well done it would have been a piece of coal. It was all but burnt to pieces.'

Grace nodded her head. 'My stomach is upset, and considering that burger is the only bit of meat I've eaten all day it must be the reason I feel so bad. You've given me food poisoning.'

'I thought it was the ice-cream float that had caused your stomach to be sore.'

'How dare you suggest my dead father's speciality could have caused this!' she shouted.

Ethan could sense he was losing this battle. He decided to be quiet while Grace sat on the toilet crying. Suddenly a shiver ran up his back.

'Are you sure you're not in labour?'

Grace glared at him.

'No, it's just an upset stomach. My waters haven't broken. I don't have contractions.'

'But you said your stomach is sore. Are you sure that's not cramps? Labour cramps?'

Suddenly Grace felt light-headed.

'Oh my God, maybe I am in labour. What do we do?'

Ethan stood up. 'You stay there. I'll ring the hospital.'

Ten minutes later Grace was sitting in the front of Ethan's car watching him lock up their house. The hospital had suggested she come in and be seen. As they sped through the city Grace rolled down the window and took deep breaths. The night air was crisp but fresh. The city was dark and peaceful, but inside the car she was beginning to panic.

'I don't think I'm ready,' she said, gripping Ethan's hand.

'You are, Grace. We've read all the books, talked about it for weeks. You'll be great.'

Grace dismissed his response – talking and reading about labour was bound to be completely different from experiencing it.

42

By the time Grace had been admitted to the maternity hospital and brought up to the labour ward she had decided she didn't want to give birth. The pain was bad enough already.

'Listen,' she said to the midwife, 'I don't want to be in this situation. I want to go home.'

The nurse just smiled and continued taking her blood pressure.

'Don't worry, the doctor will be here in a few minutes to assess you,' she said.

'OK, I don't think you've understood. I don't want to be here. I've changed my mind. I saw those women in the corridors as we were going by. I heard them screaming. I know I could be like them, waiting hours or days until I finally dilate and go into labour. They're walking around this hospital crying and in pain. No, I want out.'

'You're stronger than those women,' said Ethan, placing his arms protectively around his wife. 'You'll be fine. Trust me.'

Grace pushed him away. She gazed at the door; she was thinking of bolting out of it when a very handsome young doctor walked in.

'Hello. My name is Doctor O'Sullivan, and I believe you might be in labour? How are you feeling?'

Grace wanted to shout and scream. She felt sick, sore and anxious. But the doctor was so calm and attractive that instead she mumbled something about feeling unwell and let Ethan explain the situation. She held her tongue and considered the potential of the window as an escape route.

'OK Mrs Miller, you'll be glad to hear you are one centimetre dilated. Congratulations, you're in labour.'

'Can I have an epidural?' said Grace, asking before he had barely finished speaking. Yes, she was relieved to be in labour, but the pain in her stomach and back was getting worse and she wanted it to stop.

Dr O'Sullivan laughed.

'Wow, you know what you want! But first Nurse Kenny will explain to you about the gas and air option, and then . . .'

Grace interrupted. 'Listen, I know all about gas, air, breathing and the flipping yoga ball. But I've found the last half-hour excruciating, so I can only

400

imagine what is to come. Can you please order the epidural?'

The doctor looked at Grace's hand. She was squeezing Ethan's fingers so hard that they had gone blue.

'OK, it's your decision. I'll get the anaesthetist up to you straight away.'

And with that Grace Miller was in labour and beginning the countdown to her baby's arrival.

Ethan was about to voice his opinion, and remind Grace how they had hoped to be drug free for as long as possible in the labour room, but when he looked at her angry expression he knew it was best to keep quiet.

The nurse tied back Grace's long red hair, and handed her a cold facecloth.

'I can't let you have any food or drink, but this should cool you down.'

Grace thanked her, but all she really wanted was the epidural.

Soon she was changed into a hospital gown, and Ethan was sitting beside her, rooting through her hospital bag.

'I swear to God,' Grace said irritably, 'if you've brought that flipping camcorder in here I will kill you. This is not America, no one wants to see me pushing a baby out.'

Ethan placed the camcorder back into the rucksack.

He pretended he had just been looking for Grace's warm woolly socks instead.

'No, I just wanted to take these out for you. Everyone says your feet will get cold.'

Grace relaxed. 'Oh yes, thanks.'

Ethan looked at the nurse, who had seen it all before. She winked at him.

Forty minutes later Grace was in agony, but lay very still on her side as the anaesthetist carefully inserted a needle into her lower back. Grace sucked hard on the gas and air as she waited for the proper pain relief to kick in. She sucked and sucked.

'Try not to suck in that much,' said the nurse, but it was too late. Grace was tripping. She could hear the anaesthetist talk, but everything he said was repeated three times. She could hear the sound of music on the little bedside radio but the same song was repeated again and again. She looked at Ethan, he smiled back. It all felt so dreamlike.

'I love you,' he whispered. It repeated inside her head over and over. It was lovely. Love, love, love she thought, as the doctor told her she would start to feel the effect of the epidural soon. She began to let go and relax.

The next two hours passed quickly. Grace felt much better, the epidural made the whole process so much easier. Yes, she couldn't stand up or go to the toilet, but she didn't feel like her back was cracking, either.

Ethan never let go of her hand. He was a rock.

'You're doing great,' he said encouragingly.

Grace looked out of the window, it was still night. While people slept she was giving birth, while people lay in their beds she was here, waiting for her child to be born.

There was a small radio playing in the room.

'You can turn that off if you want,' said the nurse, but Grace liked the distraction. As one hit song after another played quietly she became calmer, knowing the end was in sight.

'OK,' said the doctor, who had just come in to check on her. 'You're ten centimetres now, which means in a few moments we are going to ask you to push. Now, don't push unless I ask you to, no matter how it feels. OK?'

Grace nodded. Oh my God, this is it, she thought. The room filled up with nurses and doctors. They were all talking, but Grace wasn't listening. She had total trust in them, she knew she would be fine. Instead she listened to the radio. As the sound of Coldplay, The Script and then Bell X1 all poured out into the room Grace wondered which song would be playing when her child was born.

'I hope it's Coldplay,' she said to Ethan.

'Grace! Just focus on the doctor and the pushing!' he insisted.

Grace turned to the doctor, who was now telling her to push. Grace could feel her baby getting closer and closer to entering the world.

Nine minutes passed, but it felt like seconds. Suddenly Grace gave one big push, knowing this was the one. As she felt the pressure of the baby's head she couldn't hear or see anything. It was like an out-of-body experience. Suddenly she heard a baby wailing, the doctor calling to the nurse, and Ethan crying.

'Oh my God, Grace. It's a girl. A little girl, and she's perfect!'

Grace looked down. The doctor was holding a tiny baby. That's my daughter, she thought.

'Can you hear the song playing?' exclaimed Ethan. 'Listen to the song!'

Grace didn't take her eyes off her baby, but started to become aware of the music.

Pouring out of the radio was a song so appropriate, so apt, that Grace couldn't believe it. If she had read about it in a book she would have thought it was made up. As she looked at her daughter the song played loud and clear. It was the Prince hit, 'The Most Beautiful Girl in the World'. Grace's little girl had been born into the world with that song playing.

The nurse wrapped the baby in a warm blanket, placed a little hat on her head and handed her to Grace.

She was perfect, she was amazing, and, as the song said, she was the most beautiful girl in the world. Grace's life could now be divided into two. Her life before and after meeting the most precious thing in the world – her daughter. She took one look into the big blue eyes of her child and knew it was love.

Two hours later the night attendant at Ireland's National Maternity Hospital opened the large wooden entrance doors to a woman frantically knocking.

'I'm looking for my grandchild,' she announced.

He looked down at the woman's slippers, it was then that he noticed she was also in her nightie.

Patsy Slattery pulled her coat tightly around her. She still had one curler hanging down from the back of her head.

'I'm here to meet my little angel, my first grand-child. I'm here to see Ava Miller.'

The attendant was about to explain their visiting hours, rules and policies to her, but as he saw the determination in her eyes, and watched her clasp a large bottle of holy water in her hands, he knew not to mess with this woman.

'I'll let them know you are on your way up,' he said as he watched her run up the stairs. He knew better than to stand between a woman and her first grandchild.

43

'So when will you return to work?' asked Tom Maloney, as he tried not to stare at Beth's ever-growing belly.

Maybe never, thought Beth, as she sat opposite him.

She looked around his huge office, with its superb view of sunny St Stephen's Green, expensive furniture and paintings.

'God, I think you can actually see the ducks from here,' she said, as she stood up slowly to look out of the large glass window.

'Ducks? We're talking about work here. Sit down,' said Tom.

Beth would have liked to ignore his command, but with only three weeks until her due date, she wanted to sit and take the weight off her feet as much as she could.

'I don't know the exact date of my return. But I'm taking the full paid maternity leave, and to be honest I plan on taking the unpaid, too,' she replied.

'Even the unpaid? I didn't think you would do that,' said Tom, who sounded shocked. 'Of course, legally you are entitled to, but what with your job being so sought after, I didn't think you'd want to leave your position for very long.'

'Are you implying my job could be taken away from me because I'm on maternity leave? You know you can't do that,' Beth replied calmly, staring into his eyes.

'Of course I'm not.' Tom was flustered. 'I'm just surprised. You love work.'

'Not as much as I plan to love my baby,' she replied.

There was silence.

Suddenly Tom's shoulders slumped. 'OK, let's talk about this properly. If you want to take the unpaid leave from work, then I can personally help you out.'

'It's not about your money. I don't need it or want it. All I needed was you.'

'We've been over this a million times. I'm sorry, but I don't want any more children.'

'I'm not expecting you to become the father of the year, but you have sat in your office, metres from me, every day for the last few months, and rarely asked how I'm feeling. Or how the baby is. What kind of man are you?'

Tom looked ashamed. 'I'm sorry, I didn't know how to handle it.'

'And I do?' shouted Beth. 'I've never been pregnant before. Never been dumped, then had to face working with my ex-boyfriend day in, day out. God, get over yourself. I don't know what I'm doing, either.'

'I'm sorry,' he said again.

Beth stood up. She'd had enough of his expensive, yet icy, office. And mainly she'd had enough of him. He might look the part, but underneath he was a cold-hearted empty man. She walked out of his office knowing it might be the last time she ever saw it. Beth was beginning to lose interest in her work. The numbers and figures were becoming boring. She was sick of spending her day making wealthy clients even richer. There had to be more than that to life. She had made some bad life choices, but now she was determined not to make the same mistakes again. She was taking ten months' maternity leave off work, and while that was happening she was going to make some big decisions – one of them about her future at Burlington. But, for now, she was just going to get through her last day in the office.

'This is from all of us, Beth. Best of luck,' said Susan, as she stood at the top of the office canteen.

'We're really gonna miss you,' added Graham O'Reilly, as he put a protective arm around her and gave her a kiss on the cheek.

Beth stood forward, accepted the envelope from her friend, and thanked all her co-workers. She couldn't believe how fast the last few months had gone, and that in another few weeks she was due. She'd insisted on working right up until the end, as she wanted to have as much time as possible afterwards with the baby, but she had to admit that in the last few weeks it had been hard to get out of bed early, and she had dreaded fighting her way through the packed Dublin streets every day. She had also found it hard to fit into the maternity work suits that she'd had custom-made by a dressmaker. Even though they'd been specially cut to fit her, they had had their limits when it came to a very large bump. She was looking forward to lie-ins and her tracksuit for the next few weeks. Nothing else seemed to matter when you had a little person kicking inside you, or when you were wrecked from a bad night's sleep. Work had always been so important to her, but over the last few months she had seen how she had focused way too much on it, to the detriment of her relationships with family and friends. But today her colleagues had been kind enough to buy her a gift and were all wishing her well.

Beth opened her present. Inside was a card and

two vouchers. One for Mothercare, and another for a health spa.

'So, one gift for the baby and one for you!' said Susan, giving her a hug. Beth would have been lost without her the last few months. Susan was still the only one of her co-workers who knew it was Tom's baby. Tom had been working in America a lot recently, and so Beth had been spared having to see him every day. But it had still been the hardest few months of her life. Beth had always done well at everything she had put her mind to: from school work and college exams to getting a great job and working her way to the top. But her relationship with Tom had been a failure. All she had ever wanted was a good strong man by her side, and instead she had chosen a selfish coward. She was still upset at how things had turned out, but after months of hating him, she knew she had to try to let things wash over her, and instead just focus on keeping well, and being prepared for the baby.

She had a lot to do the next few weeks, between preparing the nursery in her apartment and looking for a nice crèche. Secretly she was hoping not to go back to work, but in case she had to she didn't want to be caught out, the way she had been with her choice of doctor and ante-natal class. This time, she was going to be one of those ultra-organized women, and book her unborn child into the best crèche she

411

could find. She might even book him or her into a good school right this moment!

Beth took one last look around the busy office, thinking of all the work it had taken to get there. She was proud of what she had achieved. But when she looked at the window she was very glad that it was now her turn to be on the other side of the glass: one of those people taking a child by the hand and bringing them to see the ducks. Afternoons in the park would be her plan now. It was a far cry from the stock exchange, but she didn't care. Motherhood, here she came!

44

Beth was sitting watching the newest George Clooney film when she started to feel unwell. It was so hot in the cinema that there was sweat pouring down her face. She gulped down her large Coke.

'Are you OK?' asked her friend Laura.

'I'm fine, just a little hot, and these seats were never built for a six-foot, extremely pregnant woman.'

Laura laughed, and then turned back to the large screen.

Beth was now two days overdue, and had decided not to sit at home waiting for the baby, but to enjoy her last few days of freedom. Ever since she'd finished work she'd been meeting friends, shopping, going out for dinner and cinema trips, and taking long walks down the pier. Today she had finished organizing the baby room, gotten her hair blow-dried, had lunch with her dad, and was now mid-way through a cinema date with two of her school friends, Laura and Michelle. But she wondered if maybe she had pushed herself and her extremely large belly too far.

'I think I'm gonna have to leave,' she said to Laura. 'Even the sight of the divine George Clooney can't stop me feeling that I'm about to burst out of this seat. I need to stretch my legs.'

Both Laura and Michelle looked at her, alarmed.

'No,' Beth said. 'Before you ask, I'm not in labour. I just feel the need to stretch and get out of this roasting hot over-packed cinema. Listen, I'm going home. Enjoy the rest of the film. I'll talk to you tomorrow.'

The girls protested, but Beth assured them she was fine, and then left the dark cinema.

She drove home, and had never been so glad to see her bed. She climbed in, fully dressed. Too tired to remove her stretchy pants and large T-shirt, she lay down, enjoying the relief of letting the bed carry the weight of her unborn child. Suddenly her phone beeped. It was a text from her dad. She felt guilty. Her dad had made her sleep in his house the last week, in case she went into labour during the night. He had her hospital bag in his car, and was all ready to go in case of a middle-of-the-night emergency. He hadn't drunk alcohol in weeks in case he had to drive her into Holles Street. But tonight was his best friend's sixtieth, and so Beth had insisted he take a night off from baby watch and enjoy the party, and, more importantly, a few drinks. She had promised she would get one of her friends to stay the night with her after the cinema, but she'd lied. She didn't want or need someone else staying with her, she was fine. And to be honest, she was glad to be alone. Her dad and friends were all being so kind and helpful, but she hadn't had five minutes to herself in weeks. She replied to her dad's text, telling him she was fine.

Beth got herself a large glass of water and tried to relax. But she couldn't, she still felt so uncomfortable. Eventually she got up and turned on the TV. She watched a couple of old episodes of *Friends*, but she couldn't concentrate even on that light-hearted comedy. Instead she felt a sudden urge to make sure the baby's room was organized. She walked in and began folding and refolding Babygros, blankets and cardigans. She dusted down the bookshelves and was just about to remake the cot bedclothes when she felt a wave of nausea come over her. She felt so sick that she ran to the bathroom. She couldn't keep anything down. Finally she crawled into bed. She lay back, pushed aside all her pregnancy books, and tried to sleep. Eventually she managed to doze for a few hours. But even her sleep was interrupted by indigestion.

★　　★　　★

At 3 a.m. she got up. She was wrecked, really not feeling well. Could I be in labour? she wondered, as she tried to flick through the labour check-list that the hospital had given her. Her waters hadn't broken, and she didn't think she had labour cramps, although her stomach didn't feel right. She didn't know what to do. She needed to ask someone who knew, someone who could tell her if what she was feeling was labour, or just the usual pregnancy pains and aches. It was at times like these that she wished she could have had even one day with her mum. Her mum would have known what to say and do. Instead Beth tried to walk off the pain. She began pacing around her apartment, but hadn't gotten as far as the kitchen when she suddenly doubled up. She had a really bad period pain. Then it was gone, and she felt fine, but it came back again almost at once. She just about managed to reach her bed. Oh God, I'm in labour, she groaned as she lay down. It was now 4 a.m. She couldn't ring her dad, who would be fast asleep after a night of wining and dining with his friends, and there was no way he could drive, either. But Beth knew she needed to get to hospital. I should have made my friends stay over, she cried. She began panicking. She had no one to help her.

There was no other option, she picked up the phone and began dialling.

★   ★   ★

Ten minutes later there was a loud bang at her door. It was a struggle for Beth to get to it, but eventually she undid the locks.

'Are you the lady in labour?' asked an oldish man, looking hot from running up the stairs. He was the taxi driver. 'I'm Joe.' He went on: 'Christ. I was just about to knock off work when they rang saying I had to collect you first. We had better get you to Holles Street as fast as lightning. Are you all right?'

Beth thanked God her local taxi company had sent someone kind. She certainly had not planned to be driven to hospital by a complete stranger, but Joe would have to do. Once she knew what was happening she could ring her dad, but in case it was a false alarm there was no point in waking him at this ungodly hour. And she remembered the midwife telling the ante-natal class that most people thought they were in labour before they actually were.

'OK, well, I promise I'll get you into the hospital as fast as I can. Now, where are your bags?'

Beth's heart sank, she had forgotten her bags were in her dad's car.

'I don't have them,' she almost cried.

Joe looked a little shocked, but he knew it was important not to let her get upset.

'It doesn't matter. The hospital will give you anything you need, and the baby won't care what you, or it, is wearing. Don't worry.'

Beth went into the bedroom to get her handbag and shoes. She saw on the locker her mother's Immaculate Medal on its old silver chain. Her dad had given it to her to protect her while she was pregnant. It meant a lot to her. She put it around her neck, and said a quick prayer that everything would go OK. Then she slowly staggered down the stairs and into the taxi. They headed into town. Joe was very kind and tried to help her by playing Lyric FM and rolling down all the windows. As Mozart blared out, Beth tried not to scream every time she felt a contraction. She prayed she wouldn't give birth in the back of the taxi. Finally they were in Holles Street. The door man ran out to her with a wheelchair. He helped Beth into it, and said he would bring her straight up to admissions.

Beth opened her handbag and tried to find money to pay Joe.

'As if I'd take money off you! You've enough to worry about,' he said. Beth thanked him for his generosity and kindness.

'I just hope it all goes well for you. Take care.' And with that Joe was gone.

Beth was whisked up to admissions, and as she gave the lady her details confessed she didn't have her bags.

'That's OK. We can give you a gown and anything else you need later. I'll bring you up to a room now, and one of the doctors will be with you straight away.'

Soon she was hooked up to the ultrasound machine. The nurse was very kind and kept reassuring her.

'I know on your first it's hard not to panic, but you'll be fine. We deliver thousands of babies a year. You just relax, let us do the worrying.'

Before long the doctor came in and explained to Beth what was going on.

'Now, we can see on the screen that the baby is very far down and his heartbeat is good. But you're not dilated just yet, so technically you're not in labour.'

'I'm not?' said Beth, shocked.

'I know it feels like you are, but you're not quite. But I would say once those contractions get a little stronger you will be, and we'll transfer you to the labour ward. You just might have another couple of hours to go before that.'

Beth couldn't believe it, she'd thought she was very far along.

'The nurse will bring you one of the yoga balls, they are great to help with movement, and plenty of walking the corridors is good, too.'

'Can I get some pain relief?' she asked.

'Only paracetamol for now.'

'My back is so sore,' Beth said, almost crying. 'When can I get the epidural?'

'Not until you're dilated. But I promise the minute you are you can have it.' And with that the doctor's pager beeped, and he was off to help someone else.

Beth was being transferred to a ward, and as she waited with a nurse for the old-fashioned lift to arrive she felt nervous. As mothers in their dressing gowns passed by with their newborns she began to feel panicky. They all looked so calm and relaxed, but Beth didn't think she could do this, she wasn't ready. Just then she heard her name being called. She turned around to see Grace Miller, one of the girls she'd met at her ante-natal classes. Grace looked great in denim cut-offs and a pink top. She was being followed by her husband Ethan, who was carrying a car seat. Inside the seat, peeping out from under a primrose-yellow blanket, was the most beautiful baby she had ever seen.

'This is Ava!' exclaimed Grace proudly. 'She's only three days old.'

Beth looked at the tiny curled-up little girl. Ava had fair hair and big blue eyes, and was gorgeous.

'We're heading home now,' said Grace. 'The last few days here have flown by. I still can't believe I'm a mum!'

'I've just been admitted,' said Beth, who could suddenly feel her back and stomach tighten.

'We'd better let you go,' said Ethan, sensing they should leave her alone.

Grace gave Beth a quick hug.

'You'll be fine,' she said. 'If I can do it, anyone can!' she added.

'Best of luck,' wished Ethan, and with that he and his new family walked down the stairs.

Beth felt so happy for them, but seeing Grace with her husband by her side made her feel very alone. The nurse reassured her that everything would be OK, but she wasn't listening as the pain in her back was strengthening. She couldn't wait for this to be over.

Once she got to the ward, Beth tried to rest but she couldn't, due to the strong contractions. There were three other girls in the room, all at the same stage as Beth. But the big difference was that they had husbands to rub their backs and get them water. Beth looked at her watch, it was now 6 a.m. She had waited long enough. She rang her dad.

'What?' he screamed. 'Jesus Christ, this is really happening. Why didn't you ring me earlier?'

Beth almost laughed, it was so unusual to hear her dad curse.

'OK, I'm getting into the car this second. Don't you worry, pet, I'll be there as fast as I can. You hang on.'

Beth put down the phone and swallowed some more paracetamol. She tried to sit on the ball, but her back was just so sore. She kept checking her watch to see what time it was, and wondered when her dad would be in. She had never needed or wanted him so badly.

Half an hour later, she heard the sound of her dad's shoes.

'Beth? Beth?' he called out.

She pulled back the blue curtains. There stood William Prendergast with his hair sticking up, his face unshaven, and his clothes looking crushed. He had her hospital bags in his hands.

'I don't think I even locked the house,' he said, aware that she'd noticed how dishevelled he was. 'But don't you worry, pet. I'm here for you now.'

He bent down and gave her a big hug. Beth dissolved into tears. She had never needed one more.

'You'll be fine,' he said, as he passed her a bottle of cold water and began to rub her back, the way he had been told to in the ante-natal class. Beth felt herself relax, she wasn't alone. She had the best man imaginable by her side, her dad.

45

The next few hours were very tough. Beth paced the corridors, bounced on the yoga ball and prayed as hard as she could – anything to help her get things moving. She was in immense pain, but finally she was transferred to the labour ward.

'This is it,' said a young nurse. 'You can change into this gown now, as things will get a little messy.'

Beth thought she would have been embarrassed sitting in a small gown in front of her dad, but once her waters broke, there was nothing left to be embarrassed about.

'I've seen it all before,' was all William needed to say, to remind Beth that this might be her first time, but it wasn't his.

Once Beth knew the end was in sight she calmed down, until she heard it was too late to get the epidural.

'I'm sorry, Ms Prendergast, but you've progressed so quickly that it's too late for that now. But you can still use the gas and air.'

Beth started crying; she had crippling back pain. But, encouraged by her dad, she tried to soldier on. And really, labour was not as dramatic as films made it out, there was no shouting, roaring or fighting.

'Childbirth is a natural thing,' said the nurse reassuringly.

Her dad held her hand as the nurse and doctor explained what was happening. Beth trusted the experienced staff and knew they had her baby's best interests at heart, although that still didn't ease the intense pain she was in. At times she couldn't help but cry out. She often felt like she wouldn't be able to continue – the pain was too much. But with the encouragement and support of her dad she found the strength to carry on. And at this point she just couldn't wait to see her little child, and find out if it was a boy or girl.

'OK, Beth, you're doing really well, but soon we are going to need you to push. Wait until I tell you, and then push very hard.'

Beth held her dad with one hand and had the other firmly grasped on the holy medal around her neck.

*   *   *

For a few minutes the room seemed to spin, she was pushing and pushing and listening to the doctor, but it all felt like an out-of-body experience.

'Well done!' shouted the nurse.

'It's all over,' said another.

'That was quick for a first-time mum,' said the doctor. 'You've done great. Congratulations.'

Beth tried to look down but couldn't see properly. She gazed at her dad. There were tears rolling down his face.

'It's a boy. A beautiful little boy,' he said, as the nurse placed the little bundle into his arms. Beth felt as if she had just won a hundred million euros. She was the luckiest person in the world. The nurse checked the baby and wiped him clean, and though Beth tried to listen as the doctor explained what was happening, she couldn't concentrate. All she wanted was to hold her son. Finally her dad walked over to her.

'He's amazing. I'm so proud of you, Beth. And I know your mum is, too.'

William placed the little baby into Beth's arms. Beth felt the world grind to a halt as she looked into his eyes for the first time. She was in love. He was beautiful. He held her gaze. Beth suddenly felt complete. All these years she had been lonely, without a mother, siblings or a real man in her life, but now that was over. She had her family right here. And when her dad put his arms around them both she knew her son was safe. He would be protected by them both for ever. Herself and her dad would do everything to love, care and provide for him.

Beth snuggled her son into her. She could feel his heartbeat. She touched his soft skin. She was amazed that this thing of pure beauty and perfection had come out of her.

'I've been dying to meet you,' she said to him. 'I'm going to mind, protect and love you for ever.'

The baby snuggled deeper into her chest. Suddenly he moved his hand and it brushed against the medal hanging from her neck. Beth was sure it was a sign from her mum. Tears of joy rolled down her face.

'Welcome to the world, William,' she said. Her dad looked at her, surprised.

'Yes, Dad. I want to name him after you. I love you,' she said. 'Thank you for the last few months, I couldn't have survived without you.'

William stood looking at his only child and his grandchild. He felt he would burst with emotion. 'I'm your dad, what else could I have done? I adore you. And now we have this little man to love. We're very lucky.'

Beth knew he was right. Her situation with Tom had not worked out, and bringing up a baby alone was not ideal, but as she looked at her son she knew she wouldn't change a thing. He was all she needed and wanted.

Beth was wheeled down to her own room. As the nurse helped her into the bed, her dad was whisked off by an older midwife to help clean, wash and dress the baby.

'The men have to get used to helping out from the start,' insisted the nurse, as she pushed William and the baby into the nursery.

Beth sat up in bed, still amazed at how much her life had changed in the last months – and again in the last few minutes. It wasn't long before her dad returned, talking to little William.

'Now I'll teach you all about rugby, football and golf. You're going to be great at sport, and I can tell by your eyes that you'll be clever, too. I'm so proud of you,' he said, hugging the baby tight.

Beth suddenly saw that little William could be the son her dad had always wanted, someone to talk to about sport, someone to kick a ball around with. Her dad had made mistakes when Beth was growing up, but she could tell now that he would be a better grandfather than father, and that her son would be so lucky to have him around.

Later on, when her dad had gone home for a well-earned sleep, Beth sat in her bed staring at her new son. He was curled up, dozing in her arms. He was like all the Prendergasts, and had her fair hair, but it was the shape of his eyes that surprised her. They were Tom's. It seemed to her that there was the faintest hint of green to them. Beth knew she would need to ring Tom, to let him know he had a son, but that phone call could wait. Little William might have driven Tom and Beth apart, but he had also helped cement the bond between Beth and her own dad. And for now the only man in her life that she wanted to talk to was him.

Beth smiled at William Prendergast Junior. She knew he hadn't been born into the most idyllic family set-up, and that rearing him alone would be hard work. But as she looked at his little nose, eyes and mouth she knew she couldn't possibly love anything in the world more. She squeezed him tight. He was all hers. He was her little boy. She couldn't ask for anything else, she had it all right here.

46

'I owe you an apology, Ciara.'

Erin Delany stood on the doorstep of her former client's house. Through the open door she could see the kitchen extension that she'd helped design. But a lot had happened since she'd last been here.

'I should have been more available to meet and work together with you on the job I started. I'm sorry,' said Erin. Ever since Ciara Ryan had announced her pregnancy and decided she needed help decorating a playroom and designing a nursery, Erin had been avoiding her. She always found excuses not to call in with fabric or flooring samples, instead sending them by post or with her partner, Paula. And she tried to do most of their communicating by phone even when she knew Ciara would prefer to see her in person. Erin had let her jealousy cloud her judgement and professionalism.

'It's OK, I understand you were so busy with other work. We were very happy with how the house turned out, and the way it was done just in time, before baby Jake and all the madness came upon us,' said Ciara, who, rather than looking her usual immaculate self, appeared a little frazzled in her tracksuit. Her hair was tied back and her face pale.

'Yes, I heard the good news. He must be a month old now?'

'Yeah, he is. He's gorgeous, and I adore him more than anything in the world, but as you can see I'm wrecked. I thought my job as a teacher was hard work. But it's a walk in the park compared to changing nappies all day, and being awake feeding all night!'

'I brought a small gift for Jake,' Erin said, as she handed Ciara a little package. 'I know I shouldn't have arrived unexpectedly but I was passing your way.'

'Oh, come in, but excuse the mess.'

Erin walked through into Ciara's new kitchen and living space. She didn't notice the stone floor she'd helped pick, or the kitchen units she'd advised on. She didn't detect the milk stains on the expensive new couch or the clutter of tea cups overflowing on the handmade island unit; all she saw was the perfect little baby boy lying asleep in a beautiful Moses basket. Erin saw he had Ciara's eyes, and her fair hair.

'Oh, Ciara, he's gorgeous,' said Erin, melting at the sight of such a beautiful baby.

'Thank you,' said Ciara. 'I heard you were expecting, too, but I didn't know it was so soon!' She stared at Erin's enormous belly.

'I'm expecting twins, that's why my belly is as big as a car. I'm actually not due for another eight weeks!'

'Well, congratulations, and you don't look that big for twins. You carry it well. My tiny frame exploded like a hot air balloon on my last few weeks with Jake!' said Ciara, as she began opening Erin's gift. She unwrapped the dinosaur-print paper to reveal a soft blue blanket with Jake's name sewn into the corner of it. There was also a matching hat.

'I love it. You're so kind and thoughtful. Honestly, there was no need.'

Erin knew it might seem odd to be buying her client a gift, but she felt she owed Ciara more than just an apology for leaving her house project mid-way.

'Ciara, I should explain why I left your job. You see, I've always wanted children . . .' and with that, Erin was honest and told Ciara everything.

And later, when Jake woke from his nap, Erin was delighted to hold him tight, and when he needed changing she was only too happy to carry him into the nursery she had helped create. She had been there when the nursery had only been an old box room, and when Ciara had just found out she was pregnant, and now Jake had arrived, and the room had become his little home – it was the perfect end to any project.

47

'Can you please buy me a can of 7 Up and two *Cosmopolitan* magazines?' Erin Delany asked her husband. 'Now, John, do not buy the magazines from the front of the stands, but reach to the back and buy them from there. People are always opening the flipping magazines to sneak an unpaid peak at the latest celebrity news, and that renders those magazines useless for me. I need a 100 per cent pure unopened fresh print smell, OK?'

'OK, bossy boots, but when our children start sniffing glue at thirteen don't blame me or society, blame your own inhaling addiction. People will say the poor buggers never stood a chance, when they remember the afternoons you spent hanging around newsagents sniffing all the new magazines, or the nights I was forced to print crap off the internet just so you could smell the fresh wet ink on the page.'

'I can't help my cravings. Honestly, I just need those magazines, and that 7 Up – it's so hot today. Anyway, what time will you be home? I was thinking we could finally assemble the cots and the cot changer, what do you think?'

'I was hoping to meet Paul for one pint. Just one, after all he is the godfather-to-be, and maybe I can rope him into helping us assemble the cots.'

'OK, but just so you know, I'm in my tracksuit again. I can't get dressed up for your brother. I have decided I'm never wearing maternity jeans or trousers again. I'm just too big, swollen and unattractive to care at this stage, so it's full steam ahead with tracksuits and pyjamas for the next eight weeks.'

'That's fine with me, as long as you know I plan to watch football for the next eight weeks solid, and sail as much as possible, all in preparation for when our lives get turned upside down and I never get to watch TV or go out on a boat again.'

Erin laughed, said goodbye and hung up the phone, while John walked into the local newsagent to buy *Cosmopolitan* for the third time that week.

Erin sat on the floor of Baby One's bedroom. After months of discussion they'd decided that each baby should have its own room. While it might have been easier, in some ways, to let the babies share one nursery, Erin and John hoped that if they had their own rooms they might sleep better.

'I don't think any baby sleeps,' John had said the night before, as they'd watched a documentary on childbirth. 'It's just an urban myth. The birth of your child signifies the end of sleep for you, or at least that's what all my mates say.'

'Well, at least we will be getting all the bad years of sleepless nights over in one go,' said Erin, trying to remain optimistic.

She was getting sick of the look that parents gave her when they heard she had twins on the way. But even though she realized that her organized and tidy life would soon be gone, she still couldn't wait. She wanted finally to meet her babies, her children. To see what they looked liked, to hold them. She'd waited thirty-three years to become a mum, and now it was within touching distance. They had been told to be prepared for early labour, but even so, Erin had superstitiously delayed decorating the nurseries, or buying any clothes. But as she would be thirty-two weeks this weekend she'd decided she could throw caution to the wind, and once John got home she wanted to crack open all the flat-packed boxes and begin setting up their babies' bedrooms.

Erin was trying to decide which room should get the ivory changing-table when she felt a burst of liquid run down her legs and into a large puddle on the floor of Baby Two's room. For a minute she just looked at the new beige carpet that was now spoiled, and couldn't work out what had happened. It'll take me ages to clean that, she thought, when suddenly, like a wake-up call, she realized what it meant. Her waters had broken! She stood in the room that lay un-decorated and empty, apart from the large box which held the cot. Erin had printed out notes on what to do when your waters broke. She had sellotaped them to her bathroom mirror and inside the front door; there was even a printout in her car. Her pregnancy and birth guidebook lay right beside her bed, ready for easy access, but she stood perfectly still. She was in shock, and for the first time in a long time was clueless as to what to do. Finally, she stumbled to her bed and lay down. She grabbed the phone and tried to ring John. His phone rang out again and again. Just as she was about to ring an ambulance John rang her back.

'Sorry, I'm in the pub. I just had a Coke instead of a pint. I decided I might need my wits about me for the cot installations so I'm alcohol-free! I'll be home soon.'

'Forget the cots, you need to come home right now.'

'What's wrong?' John asked, running out to his parked car.

435

'I think I'm in labour,' she replied, her lips trembling.

'Labour? But you're only thirty-two weeks. It's—'

'It's too early?' Erin interrupted. 'I know that. That's why I'm so scared. Please come home now.'

Erin hung up the phone and tried to remember all the things she needed to bring to hospital. Her bags and hospital chart were ready and waiting by the door, but she needed to get her handbag, wallet and phone. Erin could feel her heart race. It's too early to have these babies, she thought. They will be too small, they won't be able to survive. She began to get frantic with worry. She picked up her pregnancy book and flicked through the tattered pages, trying to read about early labour, but she couldn't see anything because her eyes were filling up with tears. She was worried, nervous, excited and scared all at the same time.

Fifteen minutes later John burst through the bedroom door.

'I just went through three red lights, and mounted a kerb in order to avoid another one. I'm pretty sure I forgot to tell Paul I had to leave the pub, too. He probably still thinks I'm in the bathroom.'

Erin smiled – even in the middle of all this worry and madness John could still make her smile.

'Let's go,' she said as he helped her up. 'I'm fine,' she added, knowing she could walk. She just felt a bit wobbly.

As they walked through the hallway Erin took one last look at the babies' bedrooms. The next time she saw them, God willing, she'd have some little people to put in there. Silently she said a prayer that it would all go OK, that they'd be born healthy and well. She wouldn't be able to face coming home if anything bad happened. As if reading her thoughts, John put his arms around her.

'Trust me, they'll be fine, and the next time we see those bedrooms they'll be covered in Babygros, nappies, poo and nappy wipes!'

'But the rooms aren't ready, the cots aren't made up. I have all these prints I want to put up, some new curtains to hang. And the car seats are still in the shed.'

'I'll take care of it all,' said John, as they walked out the front door of their house. 'You just take care of yourself and our precious cargo. I'll worry about the cots, curtains and car seats later.'

John got Erin settled into the car and then packed up her bags. As he sped them through the streets of Dublin Erin held his hand tight, feeling as if she was on a rollercoaster ride. The ride was just about to start, and she couldn't wait to see the sights from the top, or experience the rush and excitement, but even so, just as the seat belts were being fastened and the carts checked, she suddenly felt nervous and unsure as to whether she wanted to go ahead.

'Don't worry. It will be a thousand times better than we imagined,' John said, squeezing her hand, and with that Erin was ready. She knew she wanted the ride to start at once.

48

'But I don't want a Caesarean,' Erin said to Dr Kennedy. 'It's not my birth plan.'

'I know, Erin, but we talked about this extensively, and you knew there was always a much higher likelihood that you'd need one because of the twins.'

'I know, I know, but can we not try to deliver the babies normally first?'

Dr Kennedy sat down on the edge of the hospital bed. His kind eyes looked steadily at Erin.

'I know you're nervous about this, but we have to go with a C-section. The first twin isn't head down, so that means we need to move quickly and get you into theatre.'

'But I read that babies born by Caesarean have a greater risk of developing diabetes, and I also read that—'

'Forget what you've read, you've been overdoing

it,' John said, interrupting her. 'Dr Kennedy has just told us what is best for the babies. I know you only want what is best for them, too, so let's just go with this, OK?'

He took her hand and squeezed it tight. Erin knew the doctor and nurses only wanted to do what was best for the babies, but she still felt very nervous about it.

'It's not what I wanted or expected,' she said, feeling dismayed.

'I know, but you can't plan everything, and Dr Kennedy is the best there is. He's only doing all he can for the babies, our babies.'

Dr Kennedy smiled.

'OK, we're going to get you ready for theatre. An IV infusion will be started to provide you with fluids, a urinary catheter will be inserted into your bladder, and we will get the anaesthetist down to start you with an epidural. I'll see you again in a few minutes. But in the meanwhile, don't worry, it will all be OK.'

Erin tried to subdue her rising sense of panic as she was prepped for her transfer to theatre. John was very calm and held her hand as she was wheeled along the busy corridors. She watched the doctors and nurses rush to the labour wards, to help deliver countless new babies into the world. New life all around her, she silently prayed for her two babies. Just then she spotted a girl from her ante-natal class. Beth Prendergast was standing in the corridor outside the nursery talking to a midwife, and in her arms was a tiny but long-legged brand-new baby. From the small blue hat on the baby's head she guessed Beth had a new son. Erin felt a rush of emotion at seeing someone she'd sat beside every week now becoming a mum. Very soon it would be her turn.

Once in theatre John asked the nurses if he could bring in the camera, while Erin came to terms with the fact that her perfect birth plan, along with the classical CD she'd brought, was now gone to the wayside.

While Erin received the epidural John squeezed her hand.

'I'm so proud of you,' he whispered.

'I haven't done anything yet,' she said.

'Yes, you have,' he replied. 'You've carried and looked after our babies. You've experienced the back pains, the leg pains, the nausea, the tiredness, the heartburn, the crazy cravings! You've done so well. We've just got the last hurdle to go now, and we'll be home and dry. In a few minutes the Delany family will double in size!'

Erin felt her spirits rise. John always knew the right thing to say.

'OK, how are you doing?' Dr Kennedy asked Erin from behind the screen at the top of her abdomen.

Erin couldn't see what was being done to her stomach, and didn't want to. The whole thing felt surreal. In all these years that she'd dreamt of becoming a mum, she'd actually looked forward to the rush that childbirth must bring, the excitement, the wondering when it would happen, but now as she lay still on the operating table it felt wrong. The stomach behind the screen could have belonged to anyone, she couldn't see or feel it. Suddenly she remembered something she'd seen on the internet.

'Dr Kennedy, I read something on the internet.'

John tried to silence her. 'Leave the doctor alone, he's trying to deliver our babies,' he said.

Erin ignored him.

'Dr Kennedy, I read that some women who have not seen their babies come out feel disconnected from them. Could you drop the drape after the incision, so I could see them being born? It would help me so much.'

John looked hopefully at the doctor.

'All right,' Dr Kennedy said. 'I'm about to make the incision, and once that's done I will drop the drape.'

Erin was delighted. Having a C-section was certainly not something she'd planned or wanted, but if she could at least see her children coming into this world that would help take away the feeling of uselessness.

★   ★   ★

Less than five minutes later Erin's whole life changed.

'OK, here we go,' said Dr Kennedy. He dropped the drape, and as the machines beeped and the nurses passed orders to each other Erin saw a little head of hair emerge.

She held her breath. Suddenly there wasn't a sound in the room. She couldn't focus on anything as she waited to hear a breath, waited and prayed for her baby to breathe.

A nurse sucked the fluid from the baby's nose and mouth, and suddenly the room was filled with the sound of crying. It was the sweetest sound Erin had ever heard.

'It's a boy!' shouted John. Erin began to shake. All she wanted to do was jump up and touch her son. Instead the nurse took the baby aside. He looked so small and fragile, his little body hadn't planned to be born into the world just yet.

'One down, one to go,' Dr Kennedy said enthusiastically.

Erin looked back at her stomach, and before she had time to think another tiny baby had appeared. Like a miracle her family had arrived.

'A little girl,' smiled the nurse.

Erin began crying. She had it all, a girl and a boy.

John was hysterical as he stumbled between the two tables, touching each of his children as they cried and made their presence known to the world.

It felt like for ever before John walked over to his wife and handed her their daughter. Then he picked up their son and wrapped him tightly in his arms.

'They're perfect,' he whispered.

Erin looked into her daughter's eyes. They had a wise expression. All at once Erin felt calm. She forgot all her worries.

'Welcome to the world,' she said, as she held her little daughter tight. She rubbed her daughter's nose, and stroked her soft skin. Both babies were so small, so delicate, but it made Erin love them even more: all she wanted to do was protect and care for them.

Erin didn't notice what happened for the next half an hour in the operating room. She only had ears and eyes for her two babies.

As she watched her son curled against his daddy's chest she felt a new respect and love for John. He was a father now, and he wore it well. His eyes never drifted from his children, he kept them close and protected them from the outside world.

The twins were like two little animals, as they lay snuggled into their parents. Like little bunnies, they were almost too cute to be real.

'Ben Delany?' asked John, as he kissed his son's forehead.

Erin nodded in agreement, it was a name they'd both liked.

'Ben, come and meet your sister Molly,' said Erin.

John laughed, they'd both picked their favourite names.

'Ben and Molly,' said John, scarcely believing that they and their names were real.

'The twins,' she said.

'Our kids,' he added.

Erin smiled, it felt good.

'I can take that picture for you now, if you want,' offered one of the nurses.

Erin wouldn't be moving for another few hours, so John and Ben came and lay down beside her and Molly, who with her long legs was already shaping up to look like her mother. As the babies huddled beside Erin she felt like her heart would burst. She was so happy, proud and relieved. They were two beautiful, healthy, albeit still very small babies – she knew she couldn't have asked for anything more.

As the nurse took their first family photo Erin knew the years of longing for children were over. She had it all now, right here, and she was never going to let it go.

Acknowledgements

Thank you to Jessica Broughton, Kate Tolley, Aislinn Casey and all the team at Transworld in the UK, for their hard work, help and advice.

A big thanks to Eoin McHugh and Lauren Hadden in the Transworld Ireland office for their support and kindness.

To all in Gill Hess Ltd, Dublin, in particular Gill and Simon Hess, Declan Heaney and Helen Gleed O'Connor.

With immense gratitude to Francesca Liversidge for all her guidance, help and support.

To my husband Mick – thank you for all your help; from taking Holly to the park so I could write to giving me a man's perspective on pregnancy, but most of all thanks for being you. I love you.

To my beautiful daughter Holly – I love you so much. You are so loving, sweet, funny and kind

– you are my little pet, and I adore you. You were the inspiration for this book.

To my Mum, Marita, the best Mum in the world, thanks for all your love, friendship, encouragement and belief in all of us.

To my Dad, James, who can always point us in the right direction.

To my two sisters, Laura and Fiona, and my brother James, you are all so caring, kind, thoughtful and fun. I'm so glad we get to see each other every day!

Thanks to Tom and Breda Hearty – my wonderful in-laws.

To Louise Malone, a great doctor, but an even better friend, thanks not just for all your help with this book, but for answering all my own medical and baby questions! Any medical errors in the book are my own fault.

Thanks to Geoff McEvoy for his insight into stock-broking.

Thank you to Amy Shortall and Denise O'Connor for all their help with my research.

Thanks to all my friends for their encouragement and support.